"HE SENT ME HERE TO *TEST* ME."

Reg plucked a pine needle from the pile he sat on and launched it toward the fire. It burned in a flash of brightness, then crumbled to ash. "He expects me to fail at this as I have everything else." He looked past the fire, at the looming darkness outside the cave. "It appears I'm already on my way."

"How can you say that? It's hardly your fault we had a late spring storm. You can't control the weather," Abbie countered quietly.

"A more experienced man would have known to move the cattle earlier." He turned to her. "You knew."

"A person isn't born with that kind of experience," she said. "It has to be learned. You learned today."

He clenched both hands into fists. "I haven't got time to learn every lesson through trial and error."

She leaned toward him, wanting desperately to break through the gloom he had wrapped around himself like a cloak. "That's why you've got me. Remember? I'll teach you."

His eyes locked with hers, dark and challenging, the eyes of a wounded animal. She fought the urge to reach for him. Would he accept any gesture of comfort, or lash out in pain and fear?

And if she dared to touch him, would she be content to know only the feel of his hand in hers, or would she pursue greater intimacies? She had never thought to have this curiosity about a man. What would it feel like to touch him? To kiss him, even . . . ?

Dear Romance Reader,

In July, we launched the Ballad line with four new series, and each month we'll present both new and continuing stories set everywhere from medieval England to the American West—the kind of passionate, romantic stories you love best, written by the most gifted authors. At the back of each book, we'll tell you when you can find subsequent books in the series that has captured your heart.

Beloved author Jo Ann Ferguson continues her *Shadow of the Bastille* series with **A Brother's Honor,** as a French privateer and the spirited daughter of an American ship captain brave Napoleon's blockade and discover the legacy that will shape their passionate destiny. Next, rising star Cynthia Sterling invites us back to the dusty Texas Panhandle as the second of her *Titled Texans* learns the ropes of ranching from an independent—and irresistibly attractive—woman who wants to become a lady in **Last Chance Ranch.**

Beginning this month is newcomer Tammy Hilz's breathtaking *Jewels of the Sea* series, a trilogy of three sisters who take their futures in their own hands—as pirates! In the first installment, a stubborn earl wonders if the fearless woman who was **Once A Pirate** will decide to become his bride. Finally, fresh talent Kelly McClymer introduces the unconquerably romantic Fenster family in her *Once Upon A Wedding* series, starting with a woman whose faith in happy endings is challenged as a man who refuses to believe in love asks her to become **The Fairy Tale Bride.** Enjoy!

Kate Duffy
Editorial Director

Titled Texans

LAST CHANCE RANCH

Cynthia Sterling

ZEBRA BOOKS
KENSINGTON PUBLISHING CORP.
http://www.zebrabooks.com

To my agent, Pam Hopkins
Thanks for your enthusiasm and support

Chapter One

Texas Panhandle, March 1882

You seem to have a peculiar talent for snatching failure out of the jaws of success.

His father's words echoed in his head as Reginald Thomas Worthington surveyed the ocean of grass spread out before him in all directions. This time of year, his native England would still be dormant in the dregs of winter, but Texas had already rushed into spring, like a headstrong colt leaving the gate before the starter's gun had fired.

Reg felt time running away from him, like that colt. One week in this country, and already he felt behind, his father's words goading him. He had one year to turn a profit on the Ace of Clubs Ranch. One week of that precious time had already passed, and he was no closer to seeing his way to success than he had been when he stepped off the train at the Fairweather station.

"I won't fail this time!"

His horse, a raw-boned gray with the ignoble name of Mouse, flicked its ears at this exclamation. There was no one else to hear him on this lonely stretch of prairie. Not for the first time, he wished his older brother, Charles, had remained in Texas. Charming, likeable Charles had always known the right thing to say and do. He had deftly managed the earl's first ranch, the Double Crown, with nary a problem, and made himself one of the most popular men in town in the process. Reg didn't have Charles's talent for fitting in, and had counted on his older brother to help smooth the way.

As eldest and heir, Charles had been called back to England to help care for their ailing father. When Reg had watched Charles's buggy pull out of the drive, he had felt a sinking feeling in the pit of his stomach, like a shipwrecked sailor cast ashore on a deserted island. It might well be months before Charles was free to return to Texas. In the meantime, Reg had to muddle through on his own.

He wiped the back of his neck with the red bandanna the storekeeper in Fairweather had insisted he would need. The man had also sold him the stiff canvas trousers, heavy cotton shirt and high-heeled boots he now wore. The new clothes were ill-fitting and uncomfortable, and the boots hurt his feet. Thinking of the perfectly tailored linen suit he had left hanging in his room and the butter-soft English leather riding boots in his wardrobe, he shook his head and nudged the horse forward. With the sun high overhead, he had no idea in which direction they were traveling, and at this point he didn't particularly care. He was in the mood to ride and mope about the poor hand he had been dealt this time around.

He squinted into the glaring sunlight, searching for some familiar landmark. A stunted grove of trees broke the straight line of the horizon off to his right. Trees in this arid land meant water, and shade. He would ride there and water the horse and himself, then debate his next move.

As he neared the trees, he saw a cowboy working to pull a cow out of a mud bog along the creek bank. A black-and-white dog danced around the perimeter of the mud hole, barking. The skinny cowhand had roped the cow around the neck and tied the rope to his saddle horn. At his command, the horse began backing up the slope away from the mud hole, but the cow didn't budge.

Reg waited to cross the creek, not wanting to interrupt the man's work. Horse and heifer both bore the markings of the Rocking W ranch, his neighbor to the west. At least now he knew in which direction his own land lay.

He admired the efficient way the cowboy and the horse worked together. He himself was a good rider, but he couldn't claim to have that kind of command over these half-wild Texas mounts.

"Are you going to sit there gawking all day, or are you going to help?" The cowboy's high-pitched voice startled Reg. He looked closer at the small-framed figure on the horse, at the delicate curve of cheek showing beneath the shading brim of the hat. The cowboy looked up, and Reg found himself staring into a pair of emerald eyes fringed with thick brown lashes.

The cowboy he had been admiring wasn't a boy at all, but a decidedly attractive young woman!

Abbie glared at the stranger who had ridden up just as she was roping the cow. He hadn't bothered to say a word, just sat there staring, as if he'd never seen anyone try to work a heifer out of a mud bog.

He was riding an Ace of Clubs horse; she recognized

the brand on the gelding's hip. But she'd never laid eyes
on the man before, and she generally knew all the hands
on the neighboring spreads.

He didn't really look like your average cowboy, she
decided. For one thing, he wasn't wearing a hat. The wind
ruffled his thick dark hair, which was cut short, just above
his collar. His face was close-shaven, with a neatly trimmed
moustache above a full mouth. He didn't slouch in the
saddle, but sat erect, broad shoulders squared in an almost
military bearing. He was altogether too neat and too well
groomed to be a cowboy.

So what was the stranger doing way out here on the
Rocking W?

Her dog, Banjo, grew bored with harrying the stuck
heifer and turned his attention to the stranger. He rushed
forward, barking, and the gray gelding danced nervously
sideways.

"Calm down, old boy," the stranger said in a deep voice
full of both comfort and command.

To Abbie's amazement, Banjo obediently quieted and
wagged his tail at the stranger.

The bogged heifer let out a distressed moan. Abbie
glanced at the cow. This time of year the cattle tried to get
away from nagging heel flies by standing in any available
puddle of water. The weaker ones ended up stuck, and
Abbie and the Rocking W *vaqueros* stayed busy pulling them
out. This poor old thing wouldn't last the night if Abbie
didn't free her soon.

Exasperated, she turned to the stranger again. "Are you
going to help me or not?" she asked.

He gave an elegant formal bow. "Madam, I would be
happy to assist you in whatever way I may."

The cultured British accent and formal manner were as
out of place here on the prairie as his clean-shaven chin
and uncovered head. She stared, at a loss for words, until

another moan from the heifer reminded her of her duty. "Fine, then. Just drop a loop around her neck. If we both pull, we'll be able to haul her out."

The stranger frowned. "Drop a loop?"

She sighed. "Lasso? You know—rope her?"

The stranger looked around him, then cleared his throat. "I'm afraid I don't appear to have a rope with me."

"If you did have a rope, could you get a loop around her neck?"

His scowl deepened, and he squared his shoulders. "There is not much call for that sort of thing in the Devonshire Hunt Club."

The man was next to useless! "Then, you're about the poorest excuse for a cowboy I've come across yet," she snapped.

His face flushed, and his eyes flashed with an anger that made her shrink back. Looking into those eyes was like staring down an enraged bull. She bit her tongue, cursing herself for once again letting it get her into trouble. She ought to know better than to rile a stranger out here in the middle of nowhere. As unobtrusively as possible, she slid one hand toward the pistol at her side.

The man's gaze flickered to the gun. "First you insult me. Do you intend to shoot me also?"

He nudged the horse toward her. Abbie pulled the gun from its holster and leveled it at the man, though it took both hands for her to hold it steady. "Don't come any closer," she said. "Put your hands up."

"I heard Texans were trigger-happy, but this is absurd." He ignored her order to raise his hands, but did stop closing the distance between them. "I also heard the women here were rather outspoken, but I never expected they would have taken to wearing men's clothing as well." A half smile curved beneath the moustache as his eyes swept over her. "Though I must say, those trousers do a rather nice job of *emphasizing* the feminine form."

The heat of his gaze lingered in the blush that engulfed Abbie. She steadied the heavy pistol against her saddle horn and studied the man more closely, looking for clues as to his intentions. He was dressed like a typical cowboy, in denim pants and heavy cotton shirt like her own, except that his clothes were so new the creases still showed. And he lacked one essential component of cowboy garb. "Why aren't you wearing a hat?" she asked.

He looked up, as if gazing at an imaginary hat. "I enjoy the feel of the wind in my hair."

A cowboy would as soon be caught out without a gun than to ride around minus his hat. "Who are you?" she asked.

He made another of his formal bows. "Reginald Thomas Worthington, at your service."

She blinked. "People actually call you that?"

His moustache twitched as if in amusement. "Among other things. My friends usually address me as Reg."

"Any relation to Charlie Worthington?"

More amusement. "Charles Worthington is my brother. And you are?"

"I'm Abbie." No need to tell him her last name. The less he knew about her, the better, as far as she was concerned. "What are you doing on Rocking W land?"

The stranger shifted in the saddle and cleared his throat. "I was out for a ride, and it appears I may have become slightly disoriented and—"

"You're lost." At his look of discomfort, Abbie had to smile. Texas men as a whole, and ranchers and cowboys in particular, were a peacock-proud lot, but this fellow won the prize for being full of himself.

He raised his chin and regarded her with a disdainful look. "I momentarily lost my bearings. However, I have no doubt now that I have only to ride east to be on Ace of Clubs land once again.''

She wagged the pistol at him, unable to resist another jab at his haughtiness. "You know what the penalty around here is for trespassing, don't you?"

He glowered at her, a look that sent a tremble through her. "No." The single word was spoken in a commanding tone of voice that no doubt made lesser men cower.

She cleared her throat. She'd only intended to have a little fun, but Lord Loftiness here obviously didn't have much of a sense of humor. She struggled to keep her tone light when she spoke again. "In the mildest cases, it's just a fine. Though folks who make a habit of straying onto other folks' property, especially if they wander home with a cow or two, usually end up swinging from a rope, or with a few extra holes in their heads."

"Well, Miss Abbie, do you intend to hold that gun on me all afternoon, or will you shoot me now and be done with it?" To her shock, the hint of a smile tugged at the corners of his mouth. "Or would you consider my having endured your onslaught of insults as just punishment for my infraction of the rules?"

Abbie wasn't sure if all his fancy talk was genuine, or a show for her benefit. For all his attempts at good humor, she couldn't forget the anger she'd glimpsed in his eyes only moments before. She wouldn't breathe easy until he was out of her sight. But out of the corner of her eye, she could see the heifer's head drooping lower by the minute. "Reg" here might be her only chance of freeing the animal.

She took stock of his broad shoulders once more. He looked strong enough. Maybe he *could* help her. "How about if you help me get this heifer out of the mud and we'll call it even?"

He nodded slowly. "That would seem a fair bargain. A

small enough price to pay to be away from here. I assure you I won't make the mistake of traveling this way again."

She shoved the pistol back in its holster. "All right. I'll lasso her around the neck again." Still keeping one eye on him, she half turned in the saddle and untied a coil of rope from behind her. "Then I'll throw the end to you, and you dally it on your saddle horn. With both our horses pulling, maybe we can free her."

He swept his gaze over the length of rope that stretched between her saddle and the stuck heifer, then nodded. Abbie suppressed a smile. Of course; he hadn't understood the term "dally" but he'd figured it out. "I'm ready when you are," he said.

The cow was too weak to put up much of a fight, so it was a simple enough matter for Abbie to drop the second loop around her neck. She tossed the rest of the rope coil toward Reg. He caught it with one hand and wrapped the end around his saddle horn.

"All right now, head that nag of yours uphill," she said. She clucked to her horse, Toby, and he began to pull also.

The heifer bellowed in protest as the ropes tightened around her neck. Abbie urged her horse on and heard Reg do the same. Banjo ran around the edge of the mud bog, barking furiously. The cactus-fiber braid stretched taut as a guitar string, and still the heifer didn't budge. "Let up!" she yelled, letting her horse fall back until the rope sagged.

"What now?" Reg asked.

Abbie studied the heifer. It stood, head drooping until its nose was almost in the mud. "We need a running start," she said after a minute. She maneuvered Toby until he was facing away from the bog, then looked at Reg. "At the count of three, I want you to dig in your heels and send your horse running up the creek bank."

He stared at her. "You're insane. You'll break the cow's neck. Or the horses'. Or mine."

"I'm not crazy enough to let a perfectly good heifer die if I can help it." She didn't wait for his agreement, merely braced herself in the saddle. "One, two, three—*now!*" She dug in her spurs, and Toby shot up the bank. He strained forward, hooves scrabbling in the dirt as he came to the end of the rope. Glancing to her left, Abbie saw Reg urge the gray up the slope.

The heifer let out a strangled bellow, and Banjo's barking reached a fever pitch. But underneath all this, Abbie heard the noise she'd been listening for: the wet, sucking sound of a cow being pulled from the mud.

Toby stumbled forward as the heifer slithered free of the bog, and Abbie dropped the reins and slid from his back even before the horse had come to a complete stop. She ran to the heifer, who lay on her side, eyes bulging, panting for breath.

Reg reached the cow before she did and was already pulling the rope from around the animal's neck when Abbie stopped beside him. She knelt and wrestled with the second rope. By the time she was freed, the heifer had risen to her knees and was blinking at them. "Go on, girl," Abbie slapped the animal's flank. "Get on up!"

Banjo barked and nipped at the heifer's heels until she struggled to her feet. Black mud dripping from her red and white hide, she ambled forward a few yards, then put her head down to crop the fresh spring grass.

Abbie sat back on her heels, relief washing over her. Success didn't come often enough out here to dull its sweetness. Already this morning she'd found one heifer dead; she'd fought hard not to lose this one as well.

"May I help you up, madam?" She looked up and found Reg standing beside her. He could no longer claim to be cleaner than the average cowboy; mud streaked the front

of his new trousers and shirt and clung in clumps to his
boots. Still, he managed to retain his dapper manner. He
offered his hand.

She hesitated a moment, then clasped his palm, realizing
too late that while Reg had removed his mud-caked glove,
she'd failed to do so. He stared at the sticky mud smeared
across his palm and compressed his lips into a thin line as
he wiped his hands on his trouser legs.

"I'm sorry," Abbie said. "And I'm sorry I insulted you,
too." She stared at the toes of Reg's boots. "I have an
awful habit of saying whatever comes to mind, without
stopping to think first. My daddy tried to break me of it,
but he didn't have any luck."

"I pity the man who would try to teach you anything,"
he murmured. But when she raised her eyes to meet his,
she found his anger had faded, replaced by a look she
imagined might be amusement.

She stripped off one muddy glove and extended her
hand. "Truce?"

He stared at her hand a moment before taking it gently
in his own. His thick, masculine fingers made hers look
tiny and delicate. She gasped as he brought the back of
her hand up to meet his lips. The silken sweep of his
moustache brushed across her skin, and the warm whisper
of his breath blazed a heated trail as his mouth caressed her
skin. She closed her eyes, rocked by a tremor of unfamiliar
emotions.

Then, as quickly as he had kissed her, he released her.
She opened her eyes and took a step back, afraid of showing how shaken she was. A moment ago, she had feared
this man. Now she craved his touch. How could a mere
brush of the lips kindle such a fire of feelings?

But of course, Reg would feel none of this, she reminded
herself. In England men probably went around kissing
women's hands with no more thought than a cowboy would

give to tipping his hat to the schoolmarm. Reg was merely treating her as he would any other lady.

She looked away, embarrassed at the trail her thoughts were taking. She was about as far from a lady as anyone could get. It was just that she felt all dainty and feminine in this Englishman's presence.

She wasn't sure she liked the idea. She knew how to handle herself like a cowhand. Being a lady was out of her league entirely. "Thank you," she mumbled, and hurriedly backed away. She busied herself bundling the rope into two neat coils. But she couldn't keep from watching Reg from underneath the brim of her hat. He brushed what mud he could from his clothes, leaned down to pet Banjo, then mounted the gray once more. "Would you be needing anything else?" he asked, riding up beside her.

"What? Oh, no. Thank you. You've done enough already." She scrambled to her feet and looped the rope coils over her saddle horn, then swung up into the saddle. That was better. She was more comfortable facing him here, on horseback. She'd practically grown up in the saddle, after all.

He nodded. "I'll take your leave, then. I would say it has been a pleasure, but I make it a point to never lie. So I will say it has been *interesting*." He bowed low, then turned the horse away and set off toward the east, and the Ace of Clubs.

Abbie watched him until he was a dim figure on the horizon. More than once she thought he looked back in her direction, but perhaps that was just a trick of the light, like a mirage shimmering on the prairie. She shook her head and turned Toby to continue her ride along the creek. Until heel fly season ended, she and Banjo and Toby would take their turn on patrol here, and spend more than a few nights camped under the stars.

It wasn't the kind of life most women would have

enjoyed, but it suited Abbie fine. At least most of the time it did. Then something would happen, like Reg Worthington kissing her hand today, to remind her of the things most women had that had passed her by.

Things like a husband and a nice home, and children. For the past few years, children had been on Abbie's mind a lot. She couldn't pass a child on her infrequent trips to town, or even ride by a passel of calves, without feeling a funny tightness in her belly and a longing for a baby of her own.

She'd always meant to marry up and raise a family, the way other women did. But after her father had died and left the ranch for her to run, time had gotten away from her. Now here she was, twenty-six years old and well on her way to permanent spinsterhood if she didn't get busy.

Still, overseeing five thousand head of cattle didn't leave much time for polishing up her flirting skills or keeping up with the latest fashions. And despite the fact that men outnumbered women at least ten to one up here in the Texas Panhandle, most of those fellows weren't exactly what you would call prime husband material. Most cowboys would as soon have rocks tied around their ankles and be thrown in a stock tank as be lassoed into holy matrimony.

The other ranchers gave Abbie their grudging respect, but she'd earned that by being as *unlike* the women they knew as possible. Her father had taught her early on that the only way to do business in this man's world was to act like a man. That attitude had kept her safe and made her successful, but lately that success was a pretty lonely pill to swallow. She had nothing in common with the women who lived in the area, and she didn't fit in with the men, either.

The only men she really counted as friends were her neighbors on the A7, Alan Mitchell and his father Brice. She sighed as she thought of Alan. The blond, blue-eyed rancher had a smile that would set any woman's heart to racing. Abbie had fancied herself half in love with him since the time he'd reprimanded a cowboy for cussing in the presence of a lady. When the cowboy had denied seeing any ladies around, Alan had fired him on the spot, and won Abbie's heart.

If only she could take the friendship she and Alan shared and turn it into something more. She was sure they'd make a good match. They were both skilled ranchers, and they loved the half-wild Texas Panhandle. Together, they could build up a fortune and a family. She smiled, imagining the blue-eyed, blond-haired children they'd raise. Twenty-six wasn't too late to start a family. All she had to do was find a way to make Alan see her the way she really was inside—as a warm-hearted woman, ready for love.

Chapter Two

Two days after his encounter with the cowgirl on the prairie, Reg stood among the wagons parked around the A7 Ranch headquarters, surveying his first taste of the rustic entertainment Texans called a barbecue. The outdoor celebration was a sharp contrast to the overly formal and consequently excruciatingly dull garden parties he had endured as a young man in England. The Texans stood in big, noisy groups, laughing and talking loudly while consuming large plates of smoked meat and drinking tankards of beer and lemonade. No doubt the earl would laugh to see Reg reduced to dining on underdone beef on a tin plate, amid a crowd dressed in denim work clothes. He would be shocked to learn that his second son was actually enjoying himself.

Reg tried to look more relaxed than he felt, and nodded affably to anyone who passed by. Few bothered to conceal their open interest in the newcomer in their midst. He felt like a raw midshipman standing for inspection his first day aboard ship. Judging from the disdainful looks some of his neighboring ranchers sent his way, he wasn't passing muster.

"So you're another of those Britishers who thinks he can make a quick killing in the ranching business, are you?" A man who introduced himself as Joe Dillon, owner of the Triple D, challenged him.

Dillon had the short, squat build of a Hereford bull, and Reg amused himself by imagining the man with a ring in his nose. The image allowed him to smile and reply pleasantly. "I would certainly hope to profit as a rancher. Sooner is better than later, wouldn't you agree?" Of course, if he didn't show some profits fairly quickly, his father would likely disown him, and he would be back in England struggling to live on a junior clerk's wages.

"Hmmmph!" Dillon snorted. "The country's crawling with foreigners as it is."

Reg gave the man a cold look and directed his attention elsewhere. His hosts, Alan and Brice Mitchell, came out of the house they used as ranch headquarters and stood on the veranda that stretched across the front. A stranger could have pegged the pair as father and son. They shared the same deep tans and silver-blond hair, though Brice's was more silver than blond these days. Twenty years in the Texas Panhandle had carved permanent lines in their bronzed faces, like gullies worn into sandstone. They stood side by side in identical poses, thumbs hooked in their belts, right hips cocked.

Several of the other guests immediately hailed the pair. Alan and Brice returned the greetings and stepped off the porch, moving through the crowd with an ease born of years of working together, each man anticipating the move the other would make.

Reg watched them stroll toward him and felt a stab of envy. He and his father had never enjoyed so much as an hour of the kind of closeness the Mitchells seemed to live and breathe. All his life Reg and the earl had been separated by the invisible specter of the "perfect" son his father was always trying to shape him into.

"Tell me, Worthington, what's your syndicate going to do about these big outfits fencing off the best watering holes for themselves?" Dillon nudged Reg's shoulder with one pudgy finger. "Answer me that, why don't you?"

Reg kept his expression calm, though his mind raced. He hadn't the slightest idea what Dillon was babbling about. Was it something important, or merely a made-up issue to test the newcomer? "I'd be interested in hearing your opinion of the matter, Mr. Dillon," he said after a moment.

"Mr. Worthington, I hope you're settling in all right, meeting everyone." Alan Mitchell smiled warmly as he and his father paused in front of Reg, cutting off whatever answer Dillon had been about to make.

"Yes, I'm acquainting myself with all my neighbors." He returned the smile, some of his tension easing in the presence of his congenial hosts. "Please, call me Reg."

"Then, it's Alan and Brice. Hello, Joe." Mitchell Senior nodded to Dillon, then surveyed the crowd around them. "We've had a pretty good turnout this year, if I say so myself." He turned back to Reg. "I always like to start the season off with one of these shindigs, let everybody catch up on the gossip, help newcomers like yourself get to know the folks they'll be working with come roundup."

"As if we needed any more green hands on the roundup," Dillon muttered.

Reg ignored the remark. "I believe I've met everyone but my neighbor to the west, A. B. Waters," he said.

"You haven't met A. B.?" Alan's grin broadened. "Well, then you're in for a treat."

Brice added his deep-throated chuckle to his son's easy

laughter. Reg wondered what the joke was that he had missed. Apparently the owner of the Rocking W was quite a character. He had his doubts about a man who would employ a woman to work his cattle. Especially a woman as stubborn and sharp-tongued as the cowgirl, Abbie. He didn't know what had stunned him more—the fact that she had leveled that man-sized pistol at him, or the knowledge that she had been fully prepared to use it.

She was definitely a far cry from the women he had known in England and the daughters of English landowners he had occasionally called upon during his days in India. He had feared for a moment that all women in Texas would be so outspoken and unfeminine, but a brief survey of the females in attendance at today's barbecue had reassured him this was not the case. Already more than one lovely coquette had cast her eyes his way, inviting flirtation. The fact that their fathers and brothers all wore revolvers at their sides limited his chances at all but the most casual acquaintance, however.

He wasn't here for amusement, he reminded himself. He was here to make a profit as quickly as possible, so that he could go home. Once back in England, he would have plenty of time to acquire the suitable bride his father was always going on about. Right now, his business wasn't women, but cattle.

He turned to Brice, who had one booted foot propped on the wagon wheel Reg leaned against. "What does the market for cattle look like this year?" he asked.

Brice gave a half smile. "So far it looks good. Especially if we get some rain this spring to green up the grass. But you'll learn soon enough that out here, anything can happen. A late spring snowstorm, a fire or a drought, and the whole herd's wiped out." He shrugged. "I don't know of any place on earth where the weather moves back and forth between such extremes as the Texas Panhandle. You have to be prepared for anything. I've never been to England, but I imagine things are different there."

Reg nodded. He recognized a warning when he heard one. Be prepared for anything. Already he had begun to see how unprepared he might be for this particular venture. His stomach tightened as he contemplated the prospect of failing yet again.

He looked over Brice's shoulder, past the milling crowd to the empty prairie that stretched to the horizon. Despite his misgivings about the ranch, the sight of all that open space held a certain fascination, in the same way the endless expanse of rolling waves had captivated him as a young seaman.

"Texas is different, all right." Alan spoke up, following Reg's gaze toward the horizon. "It's something you can't rightly explain to someone until they've been here. But there's—I don't know—a *feeling* about the land that sorta reaches out and grabs you, makes you want to sink deep roots."

Reg thought about his own roots. He would have said they were in England, though he had spent precious little time in his homeland these last few years.

"Well, will you look who finally made it? I was beginning to think she'd forgotten about my invitation."

Reg followed Alan Mitchell's gaze and spotted a woman walking toward them through the crowd.

Though she moved with the ease of a girl, her wide skirts and full-sleeved bodice reminded Reg of the fashions he had seen in paintings of his mother in her coming-out years. The outdated design was made worse by an unflattering shade of russet orange that stood out among the cool blues and greens and purples of the other women in the crowd. The broad-brimmed straw hat, with its sweep of ostrich feather, effectively hid the woman's face from view. A Soho charwoman would have dressed more stylishly for a party. Who was this eccentric female, and why was Alan greeting her so enthusiastically?

"Glad to see you made it," Alan said, pumping her hand as if she were a man.

"I had to mend the buggy wheel before I could hitch it up," the woman said in a voice Reg found strangely familiar. "I guess I could have ridden Toby instead, but I wanted to wear my new dress." She smoothed her hands awkwardly down the front of her skirt.

"I hardly recognized you in that getup," Dillon said, looking the woman up and down.

"You didn't have to go to all that trouble," Alan said. "We're all neighbors here, after all." He took her arm and led her to Reg. "Allow me to introduce you to your newest neighbor. Reg Worthington has taken over the Ace of Clubs on behalf of one of those British syndicates. He'll be overseeing things for a while."

The woman raised her head, and Reg found himself staring into a pair of brilliant emerald eyes—the same eyes that had mesmerized him on the prairie yesterday.

"Reg, this is Abigail Waters, your neighbor to the west." Brice chuckled. "Otherwise known as A. B. Waters."

"Abbie." Reg spoke the name over the sound of Dillon's laughter. "Why didn't you tell me you owned the ranch?"

The woman raised her chin higher, a glint of amusement in her eyes. "I didn't think it was particularly important at the time."

"Do you two know each other?" Alan asked, looking puzzled.

Abbie ducked her head and busied herself straightening the row of black braid down her bodice. "Mr. Worthington and I met briefly yesterday. He helped me pull a heifer out of the mud."

"If I know our Abbie, she didn't really need much help,"

Alan said. He clapped his hand on her shoulder. "She's a better rancher than most of the men I know."

A blush washed her cheeks pink, and she fussed more with the braid. Her hands, freed of the heavy work gloves, looked slender and delicate in their covering of brown cotton. Reg found himself watching them, remembering the way her fingers had trembled as he had brushed them with his lips yesterday. She had appeared so tough and capable out there in the wilderness; the trembling had startled him.

"Abbie's kept the Rocking W going since her father died," Brice Mitchell said. "Not many women, or men either for that matter, could have done what she has. You can count yourself lucky to have her as a neighbor."

"Oh, Brice, go on," Abbie protested. She tried to push the drooping ostrich feather out of her eyes to give him a mock glare, but as soon as she lowered her hand, the feather drifted back into place, spoiling the effect.

"You should have just worn your Stetson," Alan said, laughing.

"You're not going to show up at roundup in all that feminine froufrou, are you?" Dillon asked.

Reg saw the hurt that flashed through Abbie's eyes before she glanced away. He had the urge to stomp smartly on Joe Dillon's foot.

But the Mitchells seemed oblivious to any *faux pas* on their guest's part. Rather than dissolve in tears, Abbie rallied with a jab of her own. "Even if I did, I'd probably manage to outrope you," she said. She blew out a breath, sending the ostrich feather waving. "Not to mention this feather keeps the flies out of my face."

Alan chuckled and clapped her on the back once again. "That's what I like about you, Abbie," he said. "Not only are you modest, you're quick, too." He nodded toward Reg. "I'd better go see to some of the other guests."

"I'll go with you," Dillon said. "I want your opinion on some stock I'm thinking of buying."

"You make yourself at home, you hear?" Brice Mitchell called over his shoulder as the three men departed.

Reg watched the Mitchells make their way through the crowd, stopping often to shake hands or exchange greetings, jokes, or insults with other ranchers. "I must say, I find the Texas sense of humor takes some getting used to," he said.

"They don't mean anything by it," Abbie said. "I ought to be flattered they treat me as an equal—like one of the guys."

Reg studied the look of raw longing on her face as she watched the Mitchells move away from them. So that was the lay of the land, was it? Abbie Waters was wearing her heart on her sleeve for Alan Mitchell, and the Texan treated her as "one of the guys."

He shifted his gaze to Alan. If Abbie treated Alan anything like she had treated him on their first meeting, it was no wonder the rancher didn't exactly see her as a fainting feminine flower in need of a gallant man to come to her rescue. In fact, Reg couldn't imagine anyone *less* likely to need assistance than the quick-tongued cowgirl who had leveled a gun at him.

He studied Abbie again. She wasn't a bad-looking woman. In fact, she was quite attractive. She was totally lacking in feminine manners, of course, but a man like Alan might overlook that in light of her obvious skill as a rancher.

He would wager a handsome sum she would have known the answer to Dillon's question about water rights. Even sour-faced Dillon hadn't discounted Alan's praise of Abbie's ranching ability.

Maybe all she needed was a little coaching on how to dress and how to behave. He winced as she reached up to brush the ostrich feather from her eyes yet again. All right, she would need *a lot* of coaching. Still, he had experienced his share of relationships with women. Surely he could teach Abbie Waters a thing or two to help her win the man she had set her cap for. In turn, she could repay him by giving him a few tips to help him make the Ace of Clubs a success. Given time, he could learn what he needed to know on his own, but he didn't have time. He needed results quickly. He could take advantage of Abbie Waters' expertise, post a hefty profit and book passage on the next ship home. He smiled to himself as he shaped the plan in his mind. With any luck, he would be Christmasing in Devonshire, raising a toast to A. B. Waters.

Abbie forced her gaze away from Alan and busied herself straightening her skirt. When she'd first put on the outfit this morning, she'd been very proud of herself for digging it out of her mother's things. It was the first dress she'd worn in years, and she'd hardly slept last night, thinking how pretty it was, and how pretty she felt wearing it.

But now that she was here, she could see the dress was all wrong. The style wasn't anything like the slim-skirted gowns with bustles that the other women wore. And the deep russet color, which she'd loved because it reminded her of the velvety coat of a newborn calf, was anything but flattering to her skin.

Alan is right, she thought bitterly. *I should give up even trying to be feminine. I don't have the knack for it.* She sighed, and pushed the annoying ostrich feather out of her eyes for the umpteenth time.

"Why don't you take it off?"

She started when the Englishman spoke. He'd been so quiet she'd forgotten she wasn't alone. "What did you say?" she asked.

"If the hat bothers you so, why don't you take it off?" His moustache twitched as if he were keeping back a smile.

She looked around, at the other women with their neat straw or cloth bonnets. Her spirits sank further as she realized the hat, too, was hopelessly out of style. Suddenly, she couldn't wait to get rid of the cursed thing. She reached up, fumbling with the hat pins.

"Allow me." The Englishman deftly plucked the long steel pins from her hair, then gently lifted the hat from her head. He stepped back, smiling. "There. That's much better."

The gesture was innocent enough, but to Abbie it seemed intimate, as if this stranger had removed not only her hat, but her dress as well. Flustered, she took a step back. "If you'll excuse me, Mr. . . . ."

"Worthington. But I've noticed the custom here seems to be for the neighboring ranchers to address each other by their Christian names. Therefore, perhaps you should call me Reg."

She accepted the hat from him. "All right, Reg. It was nice meeting you again. But I really must go now." She intended to climb into her wagon and drive out of here as fast as she could. Then she would bury this dress and hat back in her mother's trunk and never make the mistake again of trying to be what she was not. Even as she formed the thought, a stab of sadness shot through her. If Alan Mitchell could never be made to see her as a woman, how would he ever come to think of her as a wife? Did she have no choice but to spend the rest of her days alone?

"I was hoping you would do me the favor of granting me one dance before you leave." Reg Worthington bowed low before her.

Abbie looked around, realizing for the first time that two fiddlers had set up on the Mitchells' front porch. They were playing a lively waltz, and couples were whirling on the wagon sheet someone had spread on the ground to serve as a dance floor. "I . . . I don't dance," she stammered. She looked back at Reg, feeling more awkward by the moment. "I always intended to learn, but what with running the ranch and all, there was never really time." She felt the heat rise in her face and silently cursed her ineptness. This fine English gentleman was probably biting his tongue off to keep from bursting out laughing. Surely he had never seen a more unladylike woman in his entire life.

But Reg merely smiled pleasantly and held out his hand. "You're obviously very graceful. I'm sure you could learn the steps in no time."

Caught off guard by this praise, Abbie let him take the hat from her. He draped it carefully over the side of the wagon, then took her hand and led her toward the dance floor.

As the fiddlers began a new song, Abbie and Reg faced each other. He clasped her right hand and put his other hand at her waist. She could feel the heat of his touch even through her clothes, and a blush swept over her as she realized Reg must know she wasn't wearing a corset.

She'd studied the pictures of the women's undergarments in the mail order catalog, but she couldn't see anything beneficial in being trussed up that way. She hadn't thought she would ever be in a situation where anyone would know the difference, but she realized her mistake as soon as Reg's palm touched her. She watched for his reaction, but he was apparently too much of a gentleman to show any.

"The first thing you must do is learn to relax and follow your partner," he said as the music began. He took a step forward, pushing her gently back.

She tried to relax, but found it impossible. The sensation of being held in a man's arms was too unfamiliar, and she was too aware of all the other couples around them watching. Her nervousness increased when they moved past Alan Mitchell, who was expertly twirling Miss Hattie Simms, the town banker's daughter, around the floor. Hattie wore a sky blue silk dress and a dainty little hat, and she floated in Alan's arms. Abbie felt weighted to the ground. As Reg pulled and pushed her around the dance floor, she moved in awkward, jerking movements, apologizing each time she trod on his toes. "I'm sorry. Oh, do forgive me. Oh, I'm making such a mess of things!"

Even Reg's pleasant smile faded in the face of this constant assault on his highly polished boots. He let out a muffled grunt as she came down firmly on his instep yet again. Mortified, Abbie heard laughter from the couples around them. She looked up and saw Alan and Hattie chuckling to each other. Angry tears stung her eyes.

"Perhaps we should take a break for some refreshment," Reg said, and led her from the dance floor.

Head down, Abbie followed him to a table where glasses of lemonade and plates of cakes and cookies were arrayed. "Thank you, but I really must be going," she said when he offered her lemonade.

"Take it." He pushed the glass into her hand. Droplets of condensation ran down to dampen her glove. Automatically, she took a sip of the pale liquid, which tasted of too much sugar and not enough lemon. "Let's go somewhere where we can talk," Reg said, taking her elbow.

They walked around the side of the house, to a spreading oak not far from the pit where two calves roasted for the evening's feast. The smell of mesquite and roasting meat hung heavy in the air. Except for the old cook tending the meat, the area was deserted.

Reg pulled out a chunk of wood and offered it to Abbie as if it were a throne. Then he took a seat on an old stump and absently rubbed his shin.

"I'm sorry I stepped all over you," she said.

"I should have known better than to try to teach you in a crowd like that."

She stared into her glass, the laughter of the other dancers still ringing in her ears. "I don't really have much call to know how to dance anyway," she said, as a tear rolled down her cheek.

"Now, Abbie, please don't cry." Reg's voice was soothing as a cool breeze on a scorching day. She raised her head and saw him watching her, eyes warm with concern. "I'd wager you've faced down worse than a little harmless laughter in your time," he said. "From what little I've seen, you're stronger than many a man I've known."

He meant to comfort her, she knew, but the kind words merely tore through the thin barrier of reserve she'd been clinging to all afternoon. Her tears flowed in a steady stream, and then a torrent. "I don't want to be a man!" she sobbed. "But I don't know how to be a woman!"

Reg pressed a handkerchief into her hand. She buried her face in the soft, sandalwood-scented linen, fighting a fresh wave of tears. "Now you probably think I'm insane, making a statement like that," she said.

"I'm waiting to hear the story behind it." He settled himself on the stump once more and looked her up and down. "You obviously are a woman. Only a blind man could fail to notice that."

She shook her head. "Of course I'm a woman. But I don't know how to behave like one—how to dress and talk and react like one." She sniffed and dabbed at her reddened eyes. "My mother died when I was a baby, and my father raised me like a boy. He taught me to ride and rope and help him work the cattle. He always dressed me like a boy, too. He thought I'd be safer that way."

Reg nodded. Encouraged, she continued her story. "Daddy said I didn't really need to know all that fancy stuff like how to dance or pour tea and such. He said making money ranching was a lot more important than knowing how to arrange flowers or walk in high heels, and when the time came I'd meet a man who'd understand that and marry me for myself and not a lot of outside trappings. I thought he was probably right, but then he died. . ."

"And you've managed the ranch alone ever since?"

She folded the damp handkerchief. "Yes. Most of the time I love the work. It's just lately . . ." She looked past him, back toward the front of the house, where the music of the fiddles still filled the air.

"Lately you think about finding a husband, having a family."

She jerked her gaze to him, startled. "How did you know?"

He smiled. "Those are the normal dreams of every young woman."

She bowed her head. "But they're just dreams, aren't they?"

"I noticed you watching Alan Mitchell this afternoon."

She felt as if her heart sank to her stomach. "Is it that obvious?" she said softly.

"He seems a nice man. There's no reason he shouldn't like you."

"I told you, Alan thinks of me as just another rancher—one of the guys."

"Perhaps because he's known you so long, he only sees one side of you." He leaned forward and gestured toward her. "He doesn't really see those enchanting emerald eyes, or the gold highlights in your thick brown hair, or the very feminine curves your masculine clothing does little to conceal."

Reg's voice was like velvet, purring out compliments Abbie might have thought meant for another woman. But when she raised her eyes, she found his gaze fixed on her. The heated look he gave her made her mouth go dry and her heart race.

Abruptly, he looked away, and rose from his seat on the stump. "I propose you and I enter into a business arrangement," he said brusquely.

She blinked, made dizzy by the sudden shift in the conversation. "A business arrangement? What for?"

"By all accounts, you're a good rancher. I must learn everything I can about ranching, as quickly as possible, if I'm to make a success of this job. The sooner I succeed, the sooner I can return to England." He stood in front of her, hands clasped behind his back, his expression grave. "If you'll agree to teach me what I need to know, I'll coach you on the proper behavior for a lady. I have no doubt once Alan Mitchell sees the more feminine side of you, he'll be swept off his feet."

Abbie stared up at him, breathless. What he was proposing was unbelievable, preposterous. Did he really think he could turn her into a lady? She thought of Lady Cecily Thorndale, the British beauty who had been Charlie Worthington's fiancée, and tried to imagine herself walking and talking and acting like Lady Cecily. She shook her head. "How could that ever work?"

"We would make it work." He held out his hand. "Do we have a deal?"

Her heart raced, though whether in anticipation of the bargain before her, or from the warmth she thought she'd glimpsed in the depths of Reg's brown eyes, she could not at that moment have said. Hesitantly, she slipped her hand into his. "It's a deal."

Chapter Three

In the pale light of early morning, Reg sat alone at the long dining table in the Ace of Clubs ranch headquarters, sipping tea and battling a familiar enemy, doubt. Mounted heads of deer and elk stared down from the corners of the room, their glass eyes solemn with mute accusation. What kind of man would have agreed to the bargain he had made last night? they seemed to ask. Who but a simpleton would trust a woman to teach him what he needed to know to succeed as a rancher?

And who but a fool would think he could turn a hoyden like Abbie Waters into a proper lady?

He frowned and studied his reflection in the heavy silver teapot the housekeeper, Mrs. Bridges, had set before him. The face that stared back at him might as well have been his father's, scowling in disapproval. People said that of the three boys, Reg looked most like the earl. But he didn't have his father's knack for always coming out on top. The earl could spin straw into gold, turn defeat into triumph.

He made success seem effortless and couldn't hide his disdain for losers.

The earl would laugh himself into an apoplectic fit if he knew of Reg's "bargain" with Abbie Waters. Reg shoved the teapot away and looked out the tall front windows. From here he could see the pens where the saddle horses stood. Two cowboys leaned against the board fence, smoking cigarettes. They would probably laugh, too, if they learned of the scheme.

Then, too, there was Reg's end of the bargain to consider. Could he really turn the awkward, inept creature he had seen last night into a woman that a man—most specifically Alan Mitchell—would rush to marry?

He winced as he remembered Alan's kindness toward him. Already he had begun to think of the rancher as a friend. It hardly seemed cricket to make him the prize in this highly unorthodox game.

He pushed these guilty thoughts from his mind and turned from the window, reaching for the silver bell on his breakfast tray. The delicate peal echoed through the silent house. In a few moments a short, stout woman waddled into the room. "Would you be needing anything else, Mr. Worthington?"

"The ranch books, Mrs. Bridges. Do you know where they're kept?"

She tipped her head to one side in thought, and the white cap she had pinned to her halo of slate-colored curls slipped toward her ear. "Why, that'd be in the study, I suppose."

He followed her into the small, dark chamber across the hall from the dining room. "Mr. Grady wasn't the most orderly gentleman I've ever met," Mrs. Bridges said as she opened the heavy drapes.

Dust motes swirled in the shaft of bright light that poured from the window. Reg walked over to the desk and shoved aside an Indian war bonnet, one of the many odd artifacts left behind by the ranch's previous owner, former sheriff John Grady. The memory flashed through his mind of Abbie Waters and her absurd feather-trimmed hat. He smiled in spite of himself, remembering the way her green eyes had flashed when she had returned Joe Dillon's insult with that flippant remark about keeping the flies from her face.

He couldn't deny Abbie intrigued him. Part of him wanted to unravel the mystery of the bold woman who wore men's clothing with such ease, yet looked like the ragman's daughter in a dress. She had challenged him with a gun on the prairie, but had dissolved into tears when confronted by something as innocent as a dance.

His father would not have approved, of course, but then, his father would never know. By the time Reg returned to England, having secured the family fortune in Texas, Abbie would be no more than an interesting memory of his time spent here. Right now, she was a means to accomplishing his goal.

"Is this what you're lookin' for, Mr. Worthington?" The housekeeper blew the dust from an oversized book bound in maroon leather.

"Thank you, Mrs. Bridges." Reg took the book from her. "Now, if you'd be so kind as to send for Mr. Jackson."

She squared her shoulders, like a pigeon fluffing her feathers, and scowled at him. "I hope you're not taking it into your head that I'm to be some kind of maid-of-all-work here. I was hired to cook, and I've got work to do in the kitchen. I can't be running here and there, fetching and carrying."

He bit back a long-suffering sigh. Charles, from whom Reg had appropriated the cook, had warned him of her "tetchy" nature. With effort, he fixed what he hoped was a charming smile on his lips. "Of course not, Mrs. Bridges.

I would not dream of taking advantage of your generous nature. Once you've let Mr. Jackson know I wish to speak with him, by all means, hurry back to your kitchen and the culinary delights I know await me at luncheon."

This decidedly overdone speech seemed to please her. Solemn-faced, she nodded, sending the cap dipping down over her brow. "All right. As long as you understand, then."

He turned away, hiding a smile, while she shuffled from the room. He cleared a space on the desktop, then settled into the chair and opened the ledger. Starting with the most recent entries, he worked his way back through the book. A picture quickly began to form in his mind of the ranch's financial situation. His spirits sank as he studied Grady's cramped script. Despite good calf crops and relatively high market prices, the ranch had been steadily losing money. He frowned, trying to make sense of this conflicting information.

The scrape of spurs on the hardwood floor disturbed his scrutiny of the ledgers. He looked up and saw his foreman, Tuff Jackson, striding toward him. Jackson was a compact, sinewy man, legs permanently bowed from years on horseback, the skin of his hands and face tanned to leather by long hours in the brutal sun. He regarded his new boss with a sour expression. "Got a lot of work to do to get ready for roundup," he said. "Can't waste time talking."

"It would be in your best interest to speak with me." Reg ignored the scowl Jackson directed at him and turned back a few pages in the ledger. "Can you explain this series of entries?" He pointed to a column of figures dated the previous fall.

Jackson sidled up to the desk and peered over Reg's shoulder. He squinted at the numbers, then turned and aimed a stream of tobacco juice at a spittoon, narrowly missing Reg's trouser leg. "Can't say as I ever concerned myself with numbers much. My job is to see to the cattle, not lollygag around with bookwork."

Reg bit off a sharp retort. From his insolent slouch to his barbed remarks, Jackson was doing his best to challenge his new boss. Reg refused to take the bait. "Your job is also to keep count of the stock, is it not?" he asked, his voice deceptively even.

Jackson shrugged. "What about it?"

"Then, it is time you concerned yourself with *these* numbers." He jabbed a finger at the ledger. "According to these entries, this ranch had a record increase last spring. Yet by the time of fall sales, only half the stock are accounted for."

"A lot can go wrong in half a year. Rustlers, lobos, rattlesnakes." He tipped his hat back, giving Reg a better look at his milky blue eyes. "Of course, you bein' green and a foreigner to boot, you wouldn't know that."

Reg slammed the ledger shut and rose from his chair to face Jackson. With a small feeling of satisfaction, he realized he was a good two inches taller than the foreman, though he had an idea Jackson hadn't earned the nickname "Tuff" by looks alone. "What I do know is that those kinds of losses show you aren't doing a very good job of 'seeing to the cattle.' I expect a better performance or I'll find someone who can do the job to my satisfaction."

Jackson's nostrils pinched as he sucked in a deep breath. "Are you threatening me?" he growled.

"I'll do whatever I have to in order to make this ranch successful."

Jackson's lip curled in a sneer. "Without me and my men you'll fall flat on your ass inside of a month." He pointed a tobacco-stained finger at Reg's chest. "You need me a hell of a lot more than I need you. Don't be forgetting that."

Reg's stomach clenched as he balled his hands into fists at his sides. He would like nothing better than to banish that sneer from Jackson's face with a good left jab. But underneath the sneer and the insolence lay enough truth to stay his hand. Until he had learned more about ranching, and this ranch in particular, he needed the foreman and the men he commanded.

Of course, he would never admit that out loud. He couldn't afford to show any weakness to these men. Untamed by society's niceties, they circled around him like wolves, ready to pounce if he faltered or fell behind.

He couldn't back down, and he couldn't lash out with his fists. He could, however, use a skill that had served him well in past skirmishes. He looked down his nose at Jackson with aristocratic disdain and spoke in his best upper-class Brit diction. "It is not my intention to argue with you. Your reputation as a top foreman is undisputed in this area. See that it stays that way." He gave a nod of dismissal, then turned back to the opened ledger.

Jackson hesitated, his mouth working as though ready to fire off a retort. But none came, and after a moment, he turned and hurried from the room, spurs jangling.

Reg sank into the chair and let out a heavy sigh. He felt like a man who had thrown down the gauntlet and now was waiting for his opponent to choose his weapon and name the date and time. *This isn't England,* he reminded himself, frowning at the war bonnet draped across the corner of the desk. Jackson would no doubt prefer a quick and dirty ambush over the *code duello*. From now until he boarded a ship for home, he would be wise to watch his back.

"Anybody home?"

Alan Mitchell's broad shoulders filled the doorway to the study. "I knocked, but nobody answered," he said.

"Come in, Alan, please." Reg rose and pulled up a chair

for his neighbor. "I hadn't expected to see you again so soon. What a pleasure."

"I just stopped by to talk for a few minutes." Alan pulled off his tan Stetson and smoothed back his blond hair. "I met Tuff Jackson on the way out. He looked madder'n a wet hen. What did you say to get him so riled?"

Reg frowned. "We had a *discussion* about what I felt were some discrepancies in the books." He tapped the ledger. "Mr. Jackson and I didn't exactly see eye to eye."

Alan nodded and rubbed his chin. "Don't suppose you'd care for a bit of advice?"

Reg leaned back and looked at his neighbor. This burly blond Texan was the least threatening man he had met in his life, like a tame bear. He was also one of the few people Reg felt he could trust in his new home. "I'd welcome anything you have to say."

"You want to walk easy around Tuff. Folks around here respect him and he's good with cattle."

"So I gather from talking with people at the barbecue."

Alan ran his thumb around the brim of his hat, as if testing it for sharpness. "He's not as book smart as some, and he can be ornery at times; but he's a good man if he's on your side."

Reg picked up a pencil and tapped it on the desk. "And if he's not on my side?"

Alan shrugged. "You might find yourself in trouble. I don't have to tell you, syndicates like the one you represent aren't very popular in these parts."

"My brother didn't report having any problems."

Alan grinned. "Yeah, well, would Charles ever have problems? He was one of those guys everybody seemed to like right off. Not that you're not—"

Reg shook his head. "You don't have to explain it to me. Charles never met a man he couldn't befriend. I tend to be more reserved. I take it I can't expect to be welcomed with open arms by everyone."

"It has more to do with business than where you're born." Alan gestured toward the ledger. "Most of the folks around here have close ties to the land. They live here, raise their families here, give up their own sweat and blood to succeed or fail. Whereas a syndicate is a group of people living somewhere else, far away, buying up land and using it as long as they turn a profit. They don't necessarily care if the land is preserved for the next generation, as long as the board of directors and stockholders get their money now."

Reg looked away from Mitchell, out the window to his right. An ocean of prairie stretched toward the horizon, silvery green grass undulating like waves rolling beneath the steady wind. He thought of his family's estate in Devonshire, land passed on through six generations of Worthingtons, deeded and entailed and shackled to the family name in an unbreakable bond.

Yet Reg could honestly say he had no more feeling for that parcel of land than he had had for the Indian tea plantation he had managed. Land was a means to an end, a source of income and position in society. Everything Alan Mitchell had said about what he was doing here was true, but Alan made it sound so wrong.

Reg felt the first uncomfortable stirring of guilt. He shifted in his chair and gave Alan a slight smile. "The syndicate sent me, rather than hiring a local manager, to demonstrate that they *are* personally concerned with what happens here," he said.

Alan grinned. "I'm glad to hear it."

Reg felt the warmth of that smile wash over him. He relaxed some and settled back in his chair. "If there's anything I can do to help you or my other neighbors, please let me know," he said.

"I stopped by to see if you'd be willing to supply a chuck wagon and cook for the roundup. I'd like to have a couple of the smaller outfits throw in with you. They'd pitch in to help with the work and expenses."

Reg nodded, careful not to show his ignorance. He made a mental note to ask Abbie what exactly supplying a chuck wagon entailed. "I'd be happy to help. Who do you have in mind to work with me?"

"I thought the Rocking W crew and maybe Fred Lazlo's Lazy L to the southwest. They're both pretty small outfits. Not more than three or four men each."

Reg raised one eyebrow. "I was under the impression the Rocking W was quite a large ranch."

"Large in territory. Small in manpower." Alan grinned. "Or maybe I should say 'womanpower.' It's just Abbie and two Mexicans who run the place, with the help of that herding dog of hers. She hires extra hands for some chores, but most of the time it's just them."

"I would have thought she could afford more."

Alan shook his head. "It's not a matter of being able to pay or not. Abbie's probably got more money in the bank than some of the rest of us. She's just conservative. And truth be told, it's probably hard to find men who'll work for a woman. She probably sees it as easier to do the work herself than put up with the grief some cowboys would give her."

"From what little I saw, she'd have no trouble 'giving them grief' in return." Reg chuckled, remembering the way she had sized him up on their first meeting. Her words had stung like the lash of a whip.

Alan gave him a considering look. "Say, what happened between you two?" he asked. "Did you really help her pull a heifer out of the mud?"

Reg nodded. "I'd heard American women were quite

liberated, but I'd hardly expected to meet one in trousers, lassoing cattle.''

"Well, our Abbie's not the usual female,'' Alan said. "But she holds her own with the other ranchers.'' He stood and replaced his hat on his head. "One thing you'll find out here. If you do your share of the work and mind your own business, nobody much cares how you choose to live your life. We tend to be a little rough around the edges, but we're sure of the things that really count.'' He extended his hand. "I'll see you at my place in two weeks.''

Reg shook Alan's hand, the firm grasp of two men who had taken the first steps toward friendship.

When Alan was gone, Reg resumed his study of the ledgers. But five minutes with the dry columns of numbers left him feeling as restless as a sailor who had been three months at sea. He pushed aside the stack of books and grabbed his new Stetson from the rack by the door. Two weeks would pass quickly enough, and he had plenty to do to get ready. The time had come for his first lesson with Abbie Waters.

Banjo's barking alerted Abbie to the presence of a visitor. Tossing aside the harness she'd been mending, she walked to the open doorway of the cabin and looked out. Her jaw dropped at the sight of Reg Worthington riding up on the gray. The Englishman was dressed in his ridiculous imitation-cowboy garb, made worse today by the addition of a black-and-white cowhide vest. She bit back a smile. Old Hiram Pickens had been trying to unload that vest for a year or more. He must have about fell over himself when Reg walked into the store.

At least the Englishman had the sense today to wear a hat. She had to admit the broad-brimmed Stetson made his dark hair and square jaw look even more masculine and handsome.

"Hello, Abbie," Reg said, swinging down from the gray and leading the horse to the watering trough. Banjo ran out to greet him, barking. "I thought it time we had our first lesson."

She put both hands on her hips and looked him up and down. "The first thing we have to do is get you out of those clothes."

"I beg your pardon?" He looked up from petting the dog. "Madam, I'm flattered at your interest, but I assure you, that is not what I had in mind."

Abbie's eyes widened, and her face grew hot with shame. "I didn't mean . . . I wanted . . . you don't really think . . ." There she went again, speaking rashly and getting herself into trouble. She put one hand to the porch post to steady herself and took a deep breath. "I only meant that the clothes you're wearing don't suit you at all. The newest hand could spot you as a greenhorn from half a mile across the prairie."

Reg glanced at his stiff denim trousers and starched plaid shirt. "This is the same sort of outfit every cowboy and rancher around here wears." He frowned at her, and she was conscious of his gaze sweeping over the pants she had stuffed in her boots. Her cheeks grew even hotter as he took in the oversized shirt she knew still failed to disguise her feminine form. "They're the same kind of clothes you're wearing," he said.

"Except that those cowboys, and me, too, for that matter, were practically born in these duds. They make you look exactly like what you are—a foreigner playing at being a cowboy." She stepped off the porch and walked around him, studying him with a critical eye.

Reg stiffened under her disapproving stare. "I fail to

see what my mode of dress has to do with my abilities as a rancher.''

She paused in her circuit around him. "You'll have better luck with the men who work for you if you present yourself as someone in authority.''

"Would you stop pacing around me like that? I'm beginning to feel like a cobra being stalked by a mongoose." He took her arm. "Why don't we go inside and discuss this?''

She shrugged out of his grasp and led the way up the single step to the porch, across the plank floor and into the house. She walked on into the kitchen, Banjo at her heels. When she looked back, she saw Reg stopped in the doorway, hat in hand. A frown creased his brow as his eyes swept the room. Suddenly the scrubbed wooden table, ladder-back chairs and open cupboard looked so plain and drab. Everything was clean and functional, but not so much as a crocheted doily or an embroidered cup towel lent the slightest femininity to the room. Reg Worthington was probably used to polished mahogany furniture and Turkish carpeting. She flushed and looked away, busying herself with stoking the fire in the cookstove. "I know it's not much," she said. "But it's just me here, and a lot of the time I'm out with the cows—''

"You live here by yourself?" he interrupted.

"Well, there's Banjo, of course." At the sound of his name, the dog thumped his tail against the wooden floorboards. "Jorge and Miguel live in a bunkhouse over by Buffalo Draw.''

He hung his hat on the rack by the door and stepped into the room. "Don't you have a maid? Or a companion?''

"Why would I need one of those?" She moved the coffeepot over one of the stove eyes.

He looked at her, eyebrows raised. "To keep your clothing in order. To arrange your hair. To act as a companion and chaperon.''

She fought back a smile. "I can't say my clothing needs much upkeep. I can brush and braid my hair myself. Banjo makes a good enough companion, and as for a chaperon, well, my daddy always said a revolver was the best chaperon any girl could want.''

He made a noise in his throat which she took for disapproval. "Holding a gun on a man in case he should decide to behave unseemly is not the best way of charming potential suitors,'' he said. "A maidservant would serve the purpose far better.''

She shook her head. "Over here in America, most of us don't have servants like you do in England.'' She filled two mugs with the reheated coffee and brought them to the table. "Now, about your clothes,'' she said, taking a seat and motioning for him to do the same.

"You seem eager to divest me of my garments,'' he said, sitting across from her.

Laughter sparkled in his eyes as he spoke, but she couldn't suppress the blush that heated her skin once again. "Charlie said something once about having a brother who'd been in the navy. Was that you?''

He nodded, looking wary.

"Well, on a ship, everybody knows the ship's captain, or the admiral or whoever, by the uniform they wear, don't they?''

"Of course.''

She nodded. "Well, you don't have the years of experience or the benefit of having grown up in these parts to establish who you are. So you need clothes—a uniform of sorts—that will let everybody know from the start that you're the boss.''

He leaned forward. "What do you suggest?''

"Nothing too flashy.'' She frowned at his spotted vest.

"Something you're comfortable in. What do you wear in England?"

He straightened and struck a dignified pose, hands clutching the front of his vest. "I wear suits from my personal tailor."

She bit back a smile. He sounded impossibly vain, but the dignified posture suited him. He reminded her of portraits she'd seen in books of European monarchs and war heroes. In fact, she decided, that regal air of his was the reason Reg Worthington looked so out of place in a common cowboy's clothes.

"Wear your suits here, too," she said. "You'll do better work if you're comfortable. But nothing too fancy. Remember, you're liable to get pretty dirty."

His moustache twitched in the beginnings of a grin. "Especially if I'm anywhere near you and a mud hole."

"I'm beginning to think you say things just to make me blush," she said as her cheeks once again grew uncomfortably warm.

"You do it so beautifully." He leaned forward, chin in hand, and fixed her with an intense gaze. "I find you such a contradiction, my dear. An independent woman who can rope and ride like a man but hasn't mastered the simplest dance steps. A woman who talks of using a gun as a chaperon, who blushes like the greenest girl."

"You're making fun of me," she protested, looking away.

"On the contrary. I find you . . . intriguing." He lowered his voice to a soft purr.

A not unpleasant shiver danced up her spine. She shifted in her chair. "You're changing the subject," she said. "We were talking about you, and your clothes." She nodded toward the boots on his feet. The fancy lizard-skin uppers were barely scuffed. "What about those boots? Are they comfortable?"

He grimaced. "They hurt my feet."

"What do you wear to ride in England?"

His expression relaxed. "English leather riding boots. The finest made."

"Of course." She rolled her eyes. Nothing but the best for Sir Galahad. "They'll do here as well, though you might want to talk to someone about fitting your stirrups with *tapaderos.*"

"*Tapaderos?*" He stumbled over the foreign word.

"Stirrup covers to keep your feet from slipping through and hanging up." She raised one foot to show him the worn heel of her boot. "The high heel keeps your foot from slipping through. If your horse throws you and you hang up, you could easily be dragged or trampled to death."

He nodded. "I'll keep that in mind."

"Now that leaves the hat."

He waved his hand toward the Stetson hanging on the rack by the door. "Now, that's one piece of western dress I rather admire."

"Then, keep it. It suits you." At his pleased look, she fought back another blush. "Let's see. What else? From what I've seen you're not a bad rider, and I'm assuming that revolver you're wearing is for more than show."

He raised his chin. "I can hit the bull's-eye nine times out of ten at fifty paces."

"That's great, but could you hit a running lobo, or a striking rattlesnake, or even a two-legged varmint up to no good?"

He stiffened, his expression fierce. "I am not the total incompetent you obviously believe me to be. Despite your inflated opinions of yourselves, you Texans are not the consummate experts in everything. The British were riding and shooting and hunting and tracking when your state was still overrun by savages."

"Speaking of inflated opinions of oneself—"

He flattened his hands on the table and shoved himself up out of the chair. "I do not have to submit to these continued insults."

Abbie shot up to face him. "The truth hurts, does it?"

"You are the most insufferable woman—"

"I'm the woman who's going to save your bacon—"

He strode to the door and plucked his Stetson from the rack. "I don't need any woman to save me, much less a sharp-tongued shrew like you."

"Then, why are you here?"

He froze in the act of putting on his hat. "I came because we agreed to a bargain and I am a man of my word," he said stiffly.

"This 'bargain' was your idea. Why did you propose it?"

He turned to face her, still looking as if he had a steel rod for a backbone. "It is my desire to make my first season at the ranch profitable. The sooner I do that, the sooner I may return home to my own affairs."

"But you don't know enough about ranching to do that on your own, do you?"

His jaw worked, as if it took great effort to dredge up words. "No," was his single, clipped answer.

"Then, you'd better leave your precious pride with your hat on that rack and come sit down. The sooner we get to work, the sooner we'll both have what we want."

They glared at each other for a long minute. The steady beat of the mantel clock sounded as loud as a blacksmith's hammer on iron in the silence. Her flood of anger ebbed as quickly as it had risen, replaced by a jittery anticipation. She found herself wishing for Reg to stay; despite his aggravating manner, she'd never met a man who intrigued her more.

Banjo trotted over to lean against her leg. She glanced

down at the dog, and when she looked up again, Reg had replaced his hat on the peg. "I suggest we begin," he said, and took his seat at the table.

Smiling to herself, Abbie went to sit across from him.

Chapter Four

Reg set out the next morning for the nearby town of
Fairweather, his head still reeling from the information
Abbie had rattled off to him. She had lectured on the
supplies he would need and terms he must know and had
him parrot the information back to her like some dull-
witted schoolboy. She seemed to enjoy seeing him brought
down to this level, her emerald eyes alight with glee as she
drilled him.

He had never met such a forward woman in all his life.
She said exactly what was on her mind, without the slightest
simpering or feminine hesitation. He was accustomed to
women who deferred to his judgment; Abbie contradicted
him at every turn and never hesitated to let him know
every time he was in the wrong.

In short, she spoke to him exactly as a man would. It
was damned unnerving at times, to gaze into that delicate
face and meet her unwavering stare. A proper woman
never looked at a man that way.

A proper woman never made his heart race the way his had when confronted with the ocean depths of Abbie's eyes. That moment of arousal had caught him completely off guard. He shook himself. He would be foolish to think such feelings were anything more than a reaction to the novelty of Abbie's beauty and brashness. Now that his head had had a chance to clear in the cool morning air, he could see Abbie was so far from his ideal of the proper woman as to make him laugh.

He studied the lengthy list she had made of the items he would need for the chuck wagon. Two hundred pounds of flour. Fifty pounds of beans, twenty pounds of raisins. She had written down enough food to feed a ship's crew for a month! Some of the items listed sounded strange to him. Two gallons of sorghum. One hundred pounds spuds. Twenty-five pounds Arbuckles. What the devil were Arbuckles? And why did he need so many of them?

Scowling, he shoved the list into his shirt pocket. He wouldn't put it past that little minx to write down a bunch of nonsense in order to play him for the fool. He remembered the way she had smiled at him when she had given him the list. "Be sure you get everything on here," she had said.

"Hmmmph. We'll see about that," he muttered as he turned the gray down the town's one main street. "I've got a few ideas of my own about what's needed from town." Abbie Waters wasn't the only one who would give orders in this "business arrangement" of theirs.

Despite its lofty name, Fairweather was a feeble excuse for a town. Most of the buildings were little more than hovels, constructed of scrap lumber covered with tar paper. Some of the more substantial structures were made of mud bricks, which the locals referred to as adobe. A few buildings, including the general store and the train station, were built of sawn lumber, though even this was left unpainted.

Pickens General Mercantile sat on one side of the street in the center of town, directly across from the Texas and Pacific depot. Reg tied Mouse to the rail in front of the mercantile and crossed the broad front porch. A trio of Texans by the door eyed him suspiciously as he passed. He was glad he had taken Abbie's advice and traded his cowboy clothing for his more usual mode of dress. The short cutaway jacket, fitted trousers and high boots made him stand out more, but at the same time, he felt more at ease. He nodded formally to the men by the door and stepped into the cool darkness of the only shopping emporium for twenty miles.

"Mr. Worthington, sir. So happy to see you back so soon." The proprietor, Hiram Pickens, a small man with a nervous manner who reminded Reg of a cairn terrier he had once known, rushed forward to shake hands. On their first meeting, the day after his arrival in town, Reg had let slip that his father was the Earl of Devonshire, and Pickens had almost fainted. One would have thought the little man was entertaining the Prince Consort the way he bowed and scraped whenever he and Reg crossed paths. "Come to buy some more clothing, or perhaps another hat?" He eyed the Stetson on Reg's head.

Selling two of his finest, and most expensive, hats in two days would no doubt send Pickens to new heights, or perhaps depths, of obsequiousness. "I'm in town to pick up a few supplies," he said, pulling the list from his pocket.

"Anything you need, Mr. Worthington, sir. You just say the word and I'll fix you right up."

As Pickens led the way through the store, Reg read from his list. Aware of the many interested ears straining his way, he left off the more questionable items. Even with the omissions, purchases piled up at an alarming rate. By the time Pickens and his assistant carried everything to the counter, the little man could hardly see over the stack. "Oh, I almost forgot." Pickens reached into a cubbyhole behind the counter and withdrew a slim envelope. "This came for you yesterday afternoon." He leaned forward and placed the letter carefully in Reg's hand. "I think it's from the earl," he said in a conspiratorial whisper.

Reg frowned at the familiar crest on the pale blue envelope. He recognized the copperplate script of Avery Endicott, his father's secretary. The old man felt it more efficient to dictate all his correspondence, thus Endicott was privy to every bit of scandal or petty gossip brewing in the Worthington household and its spheres.

Reg shoved the letter into his coat. He didn't have to read it to know what it would say: a formal greeting, followed by several pages detailing what he was doing wrong so far, and why his plans, whatever they might be, would never work. He had received many such letters in India. Before that, they had awaited him in every port of call, like land mines set to destroy whatever good feelings he might have mustered about himself in the intervals between communications.

"Are you sure there won't be anything else?" Pickens licked his pencil and began calculating his column of numbers.

"That will do for today, thank you." Reg laid a twenty-dollar gold piece on the counter. "Have your boy deliver it at your earliest convenience."

Pickens' eyes widened. He swallowed hard, his Adam's apple bobbing like a fishing float in his throat. Everyone in the room had gone silent. Reg stiffened. "Is something wrong?" he asked.

"Well, Mr. Worthington, sir, it's just that, uh, folks usually take what they buy with them." Pickens loosened his collar, then wiped his suddenly sweating forehead.

"He means he ain't got no 'boy' to do your beck and call," one of the men by the door called out. "Out here, we do our own haulin'."

The back of Reg's neck burned as the room erupted into laughter. He took a deep breath, struggling for calm. No sense in making things worse by losing his temper and shoving the oaf back there out the door.

"Just put the order in my wagon."

He turned at the sound of the familiar voice and saw Alan Mitchell striding toward him, hat tipped in a friendly greeting.

"I was headed out your way this afternoon, anyway," Alan said, shaking Reg's hand.

"Thank you, Alan. I'll accept your kind offer."

Alan clapped him on the back. "Come on, then. I'll help you load up." He hefted a fifty-pound sack of flour over one shoulder and tucked a can of lard under his arm, then led the way out of the building. Reg picked up another sack of flour and followed him, casting a scowl at the hangers-on by the door that sent them rushing back like chickens in the path of a charging horse.

Refusing Pickens' nervous assistance, the two men loaded the supplies in the back of Alan's wagon. As Reg shoved the last sack of sugar into place, Alan stepped back and surveyed the purchases. "Getting ready for roundup?" he asked.

Reg nodded. "I thought it best to get the chuck wagon stocked now."

Alan brushed flour off his hands. "Mind if I make a few suggestions?"

Reg smiled at his easygoing friend. "Considering how you helped me save face just now, it would be ill-mannered to object."

Alan nodded toward the load in the wagon. "If you show up at roundup without coffee, you're liable to have a mutiny on your hands in a hurry. You English may prefer tea, but out here, coffee's the fuel that keeps us going."

"Coffee. How could I forget?" He had already noted that he could not go anywhere without being offered a cup of the black, strong brew Texans drank by the gallons. Had Abbie purposely left it off the list?

"Ask for Arbuckles. Pickens'll know what you mean."

"Arbuckles?" Reg gave himself a mental kick.

"It's the most popular brand. Comes in a red sack." Alan walked around the side of the wagon and peered in. "While you're at it, don't forget the lick."

Reg swallowed, almost afraid to ask. This was an item definitely not on his list. "Lick?"

Alan looked at him and grinned. "Sorghum syrup. It's a kind of sweetener." He nodded. "Gotta have lick. Cowboys like a little something sweet after working all day."

Feeling slightly foolish, Reg turned on his heels and went back to purchase the rest of his supplies. He would know better than to question Abbie's judgment next time. Perhaps the gleam in her eye when she had given him the list was merely amusement over his reluctance to unbend enough to ask the meaning of the unfamiliar terms.

While he and Alan were loading the last of his purchases, the door of the depot across the street flew open and slammed back against the wall. A flame-haired woman ran out, struggling to free herself from the grasp of a disheveled, disgruntled man. "Take yer filthy hands from me at once!" she ordered, and bashed him on the head with an oversized carpetbag.

The man staggered, but kept his grip on her arm. "I paid six hundred dollars for you, woman!" he bellowed. "I don't intend to let go."

"You bought me passage, sir. You did not buy *me*." She readied her carpetbag for another swing, then stomped down on the man's booted foot. Howling like a kicked dog, the man sprang away.

The woman backed up against the train station, carpet-bag clutched in one hand. "You needn't be complainin' about yer money. I'll find me a job and repay every last copper."

"You said you'd come to Fairweather and be my wife." The man shook his finger at her.

"*You* said you was a handsome gentleman." She swept her gaze over his doughy face and dirty clothes. "You said you had a fine *ranch* and a home fit fer a queen." He flinched at the disdain in her voice. "You never said nothin' about a soddy shack on the edge of a prairie and a few sorry cattle the knacker wouldn't pay to take."

The man straightened and folded his arms across his chest. "You won't find work in these parts, and I know you don't have the train fare out of here. You might as well take me up on my offer. You'll starve if you try to fend for yourself."

"I'd rather be taking that chance than be spending me life shackled to the likes of you." Her face was stern, but Reg thought he detected a glint of tears in her eyes. She pinched her lips together, as if trying to keep them from trembling.

"Have you ever seen anything like it?" Alan said softly.

Reg shrugged. "Apparently one of those 'mail-order bride' schemes that didn't quite work out. She sounds a long way from home, though. Judging from the accent, I'd say Ireland."

"Her hair. Have you ever seen that shade of red on a woman?"

Startled, Reg looked over at his friend. Alan's gaze was locked on the woman, a hint of a smile lurking at the corners of his mouth. "It's almost the color of a Hereford calf," Alan murmured. "It looks as soft, too."

Reg looked back at the woman. She was pretty in a common sort of way. Her figure was well-rounded, plump even, and she wore a dusty black skirt and white shirtwaist. Her one striking feature was her hair, which had come loose and tumbled from beneath her crumpled porkpie hat. The trailing locks were the same russet shade as the dress Abbie Waters had worn to the barbecue. And like Abbie, this woman appeared capable of defending herself against all comers.

"Come on, we've got to help her." Alan started across the street.

"We've got to help her?" Reg asked as the woman's spurned suitor reached for her again and was rewarded with another crack on the head from the carpetbag. "My friend, it would seem the young woman has the situation under control."

But Alan was already halfway to the depot. Reluctantly, Reg followed. "Ma'am, could I be of any assistance?" Alan asked, pulling off his hat as he approached the woman.

She gave him a wary look. Reg imagined her taking stock of the clean, neat and no doubt well-to-do stranger before her. She glanced at her erstwhile groom, then back at Alan, and apparently decided in the handsome rancher's favor. "Mr. Farley here has asked for me hand in marriage, and I've refused his offer. But he must be hard of hearing because he won't take no for an answer."

Farley glared at Reg and Alan as if they were two rattlesnakes who had blocked his path. "I paid six hundred dollars to bring her here to be my wife," he grumbled. "A deal's a deal. She can't back out now."

"Haven't you heard a lady always has the option of changing her mind?" Alan asked.

"Lady my eye! Back home she was no better than a scrub maid at some rich fella's house." Farley shot her a wounded look. "I'd say marryin' me would be a step up in the world. At least she'd have her own house to see to."

"I was upstairs parlor maid!" the woman protested. "A few more years I'd have been promoted to ladies' maid. I'll have you know the estate where I lived was a far sight better than that . . . that *hovel* you showed me."

"Where do you think you'll go if you leave me?" Farley shot back. "There's only one way to make a living for the likes of you, and that's flat on your back. At least with me you'd only have one man to answer to, and not a half dozen a ni—" The last word ended in a strangled tone as Alan grabbed Farley by the shirt collar and hoisted him up against the depot wall. "That's no way to talk to a young woman you were recently engaged to marry," the rancher said in a low voice. "Now apologize and get out of here before I decide to teach you a lesson."

The man's eyes bulged as his face turned the color of raw beef. He managed to nod, and gasp, "All right."

Alan released his hold, and Farley slumped against the wall. "I'm sorry we ever laid eyes on each other," he croaked, rubbing his throat. He scowled at Alan. "What about my money?"

Alan reached in his pocket and pulled out a leather wallet. "I'll gladly pay it just to see you gone."

"Wait jest a minute, sir." The woman's hand on Alan's arm stayed him. She blushed as his eyes met hers, then took her hand away and stepped back. "I won't be having you makin' the same mistake as Mr. Farley here, thinkin' I'm to be bought and sold like a milch cow." She held her head up, eyes bright. "I'm a nice, proper lass, I am. I won't be beholdin' to no man. I'll find a job and repay Mr. Farley meself."

Alan hesitated. "I'm afraid there aren't many jobs in a town this size. Perhaps you would consider a loan?"

She worried her lower lip between her teeth, hesitating,

then shook her head. "It's bad enough bein' in debt to Mr. Farley. I won't be owin' you also."

Reg almost felt sorry for Alan as he watched him struggle between his chivalrous impulses and his desire to remain in the young woman's good graces. What was it about these modern women that made them so set on looking after themselves? Whatever happened to damsels in distress who welcomed the avenging knight? "Perhaps I could be of assistance," he said, stepping forward.

The others turned to look at him. "What did you have in mind?" Alan asked.

"The young woman has expressed an interest in finding work. I believe I know of a position for which she would be suited."

Alan frowned. "I hadn't heard of anyone who was hiring—"

"I understand Abbie Waters is looking for a ladies' maid."

"A ladies maid? Abbie?" Alan looked at Reg as if he had suddenly grown two heads.

"Well, more of a companion, really. Someone to keep her company, help look after her clothing, that sort of thing." He ignored Alan's astonished expression and turned to the woman. "Miss Waters' ranch house, while not luxurious, is quite comfortable, and the work would not be too strenuous."

"It sounds like just the thing." She glanced at Farley, who was slumped against the depot wall, rubbing his neck.

Alan grabbed Reg's arm and nodded to the woman. "If you'll excuse us, ma'am." He pulled Reg to the end of the depot's front veranda and spoke in a low whisper. "Are you sure about this?" he asked. "I mean, Abbie's always been the independent sort. If she was gonna hire another employee, seems like she'd want someone who could ride herd and mend fence."

"I'm quite aware of Miss Waters' desire for autonomy," Reg said. "Still, even in the United States, it's not considered proper, is it, for a young woman to live alone as she does? A female companion would be more socially acceptable."

Alan frowned. "Abbie's never really concerned herself with what's 'socially acceptable.' I'll admit her situation's a little unusual, but most of us don't think anything of it these days."

Reg raised one eyebrow. "You mean you don't think of Miss Waters as you would another young woman?"

Alan rubbed his chin. "I guess not. It's her daddy's fault, really. Ever since she was a little tyke, he raised her like a boy. I think sometimes he wished she *was* a boy." He shrugged. "At least he taught her to take care of herself. Nobody around here's ever worried about Abbie."

Then, perhaps it's time someone started, Reg thought. He turned back to the woman. "What is your name?"

She dropped the carpetbag and executed a prim curtsey. "Maura O'Donnell at your service, sir."

"Well, Miss O'Donnell, why don't you come with us right now."

"Wait a minute," Farley straightened. "What about my money?"

Alan tensed, his big hands knotted into fists. "I warned you, Farley—"

Reg reached into his coat and pulled out a money clip. He peeled off six one-hundred-dollar bills and pressed them into the man's hand. "I suggest you take this and make yourself scarce." He glanced at Alan's scowling face. "In fact, perhaps you should purchase a ticket out of town." He picked up Maura's carpetbag and led the way across the street.

"I promise to repay you, sir," Maura said, following close behind him.

Reg nodded. "Of course." They reached the wagon, and he stowed the bag behind the seat. He turned to offer Miss O'Donnell a hand up, but Alan beat him to the punch. The rancher assisted the young woman into the spring seat and settled in beside her.

Reg smiled to himself as he untied his horse and swung up into the saddle. He was still smiling as he followed the wagon out of town. He couldn't wait to see the expression on Abbie's face when she realized she was getting a dose of her own brand of interference.

Chapter Five

The loud knock on her door startled Abbie so much she snapped the lead off the end of her pencil. She'd been sitting at her kitchen table, making a tally of the month's expenses, when the knock shattered the afternoon silence. Banjo leapt up and began barking and running in circles around her. Who would come calling at this time of day? Abbie wondered as she shoved the excited dog out of the way and pulled open the door.

A plump, red-haired woman wearing a battered hat and a plaid shawl stood on the porch. Behind her Reg Worthington had one hand raised in the act of knocking. When he saw Abbie, he gave a slight bow. "Abbie Waters, may I present Miss Maura O'Donnell," he said in his most pretentious British accent.

Abbie stared at the woman. She had waist-length red hair that fell in curls like the illustration of a princess in a children's story book. Her dimpled, heart-shaped face was pale as milk, and her hazel eyes sparkled with flecks of gold. She had a feminine, curved body and delicate, long-fingered hands in black gloves. Beneath her full skirts, buttoned ankle boots encased her small feet. As Abbie gaped, the woman dropped into a curtsey and spoke in a voice like an Irish fairy's. "Pleased to meet you, ma'am. I hope you'll be happy with me services."

"Reg, what—"

"Miss O'Donnell has traveled a long way and is anxious to get started." Reg urged the redhead over the threshold and followed close behind her.

Abbie shot him a furious look. "Get started with what?" she asked, following the pair to the table.

"I was telling Miss O'Donnell about our conversation only yesterday, when we discussed your need for a companion and ladies' maid. She's perfectly suited for the position." Reg had the audacity to wink at her over the top of Miss O'Donnell's head.

Abbie ground her teeth together. Of all the nerve! She took a deep breath and gave the woman what she hoped was a sympathetic look. "I'm afraid Mr. Worthington may have misunderstood—"

"Oh, but he's explained to me that you're not looking for a ladies' maid like we'd have back home." Miss O'Donnell smiled brightly, revealing teeth like a row of matched pearls. "I understand I'd be the only female employee, and that I'd be expected to cook and clean as well as sew and help with your hair and such." Her gaze lingered on Abbie's head. "I'm sure I could help you a great deal."

Abbie put one hand up to the twist of hair at the back of her neck. It was held together with another pencil and was beginning to come undone. She looked down at the man's shirt she wore, streaked with what might have been blood from last week's butchering. She felt awkward, and ugly. Surely Reg and Miss O'Donnell must see her the same way.

She looked at Reg, expecting to find him laughing at her predicament. But he was carefully avoiding her gaze. "Miss O'Donnell worked as an upstairs parlor maid at home in Ireland," he said.

"But I was training to be a ladies' maid," she interjected.

"Yes, but then she decided to emigrate to the United States," Reg concluded.

"Mr. Worthington makes it sound so nice and simple, ma'am, but I'll not have you thinking better of me than I am." Miss O'Donnell hung her head. "I answered an advert from a man looking for a woman to come to Texas and be his wife. But when I arrived here yesterday, I discovered I'd been sorely misled." She glanced at Reg, eyes shining with admiration. "If it hadn't been for Mr. Worthington here, I don't know what I would have done, for I didn't have but a dollar to me name, and Mr. Farley—the man who brought me here—was demanding six hundred dollars for me fare."

Abbie looked at Reg again. "You paid the six hundred dollars?"

He coughed. "It was a loan. Miss O'Donnell can repay me out of her wages."

"We'll get along famously, we will," Miss O'Donnell said. "I'm a hard worker, and I'm not one to be overly particular."

"Why did you decide against marrying Mr. Farley?" Abbie asked.

The young woman looked indignant. "He lied to me—said he was young and handsome and had pots of money, when really he was middle-aged and homely and poor as the village tinker." Her expression grew wistful, and her voice softened. "I could have stood all that if it hadn't been for the way I felt whenever he looked at me." She shook her head. "No sparks at all. I knew there wasn't a chance of me ever falling in love with him. I'd rather die an old maid than be living the rest of me life without love."

Abbie swallowed a knot of tears that rose suddenly in her throat. Hadn't she felt the same way when she looked at her own life? What was this ranch and all her money worth without someone to share it with—in love? Yet such happiness had eluded even a beauty like Maura O'Donnell.

She shook off her melancholy and forced her mind to consider more practical concerns. It was all well and good to sympathize with Miss O'Donnell and her misfortune, but a ranch in the middle of the Texas plains was no place for someone so feminine and delicate. She would end up being a liability, not a help.

Her father had always said women had no business on a ranch, at least not if they were going to act like women. Their clothing was impractical; they couldn't ride or rope or handle a gun. They had the wrong focus in life, he had said.

He'd worked hard his whole life to make sure Abbie maintained the proper "focus" to be a successful rancher. George Waters' highest compliment to his daughter had been to tell her she was thinking like a man.

But as she watched Reg place his hand on Miss O'Donnell's shoulder and offer her a chair, Abbie recognized an unfamiliar, but highly feminine jealousy heating her blood. If Reg was going to insist on her hiring a maid, he could have at least had the decency to find some homely old woman.

She sank into the chair opposite Miss O'Donnell and scowled up at Reg. "I'll leave you two to get acquainted," he said, smiling and replacing the Stetson on his head. "I'll stop by again tomorrow afternoon."

"What for?" Abbie snapped. "Don't you think you've interfered enough?"

"On the contrary, I've hardly begun." He stopped and

looked over his shoulder at her. "Don't forget, we have a bargain. I fully intend to live up to my end of the deal." He was out the door before she could answer.

She gave an exasperated sigh. *Of all the dirty tricks—*

"You're so fortunate to have a friend like Mr. Worthington," Miss O'Donnell said.

"What makes you say that?" Abbie stared at her hands to avoid looking at the pretty young woman. She noticed her fingernails were dirty. She had no doubt Miss O'Donnell's nails were pink and white and spotless.

"He was telling me all the way over here how concerned he's been about you, living out here all alone. I know women who'd give their eyeteeth to be having a man like that take such an interest in them." She leaned across the table toward Abbie. "And he's easy on the eye like, ain't he now?"

Abbie tried to ignore the odd fluttering of her heart. Yes, Reg was handsome. Many a woman would be tickled pink to have him interested in her. Even Abbie would have been pleased if she'd believed it was true concern that had prompted Reg's actions. But no, he was merely trying to live up to his end of their bargain.

She stood and began gathering up the papers strewn across the table. That pact she'd made with Reg had to be one of the silliest ideas she had agreed to yet. Even this ultrafeminine ladies' maid wasn't going to be able to undo twenty-six years of her father's teachings and turn her into the kind of woman Alan Mitchell would want to marry.

"Here, ma'am. Let me do that." Miss O'Donnell took the papers from her. "That's my job now."

"Look, Miss O'Donnell—"

"Please, call me Maura."

"All right, Maura. I'm afraid there's been some mistake."

"Mistake?" The brightness faded from Maura's eyes,

replaced by an edgy look of panic. "You mean I won't do? I promise you, ma'am, I can sew a fine hand, and I'm neat and tidy. I can't cook fancy, mind, but we won't starve, neither. And I—"

"No, no, it's not you at all." Abbie took her by the hand and led her back to the table. "It's just that a ranch like this is no place for a woman like you. It's . . . well, it's dirty. It's isolated. And it's dangerous. There's snakes and wolves and cattle rustlers and—"

Maura smiled, a perfect dimple on either side of her mouth. "You're jest trying to scare me, ma'am. I'm not afeard of any of that." She slipped her thumb under a chain around her neck and pulled out a silver medallion. "I've got me St. Christopher for protection." She reached into the pocket of her skirt and withdrew a shriveled lump of fur. "And I've got me lucky rabbit's foot, too." She sat back in her chair. "Besides, you're a woman and Mr. Worthington told me you've lived here all your life."

"But I'm not like other women," Abbie said. "My father raised me knowing I'd run the ranch one day. He taught me to ride and to rope and to shoot, and other kinds of things I needed to know."

"Who says I can't be learning those things as well?"

Abbie fought back a smile. She didn't want to like this woman who had intruded on her life, but Maura's enthusiasm was contagious. "You said yourself you came here thinking to marry," she said, taking another tact. "But there aren't a great many young men in these parts—at least not any who would make good husbands."

Maura twirled one red curl around her finger. "I've had me fill of Texas men after Mr. Farley," she said. "I'll be happy just to work and pay back Mr. Worthington. After that—who knows?" She gave Abbie a considering look. "What about you, miss? Don't you get lonely, living out here all by yourself?"

"I'm used to it, I guess," Abbie said. "And I've got Banjo."

"And a dog's not the same as a living, breathing human being who can talk and laugh and share a cuppa tea with you." She leaned forward again and put her hand over Abbie's. "Just give me a try for a few weeks. You never can tell. We might be good friends."

Abbie looked down at Maura's delicate gloved hand atop her own work-worn fingers. She'd never had a female friend before. If she was going to learn to be more like other women, maybe the place to start was with someone like Maura. Anything was better than continuing to rely on the advice of that interfering, arrogant British boaster, Reginald Worthington!

The front door of the Ace of Clubs ranch house burst open, ushering in a bitter cold wind and a red-faced Tuff Jackson. Reg spread his arms wide to still the tumble of papers across the desk and looked up at his foreman. "Did you need something?" he asked.

Tuff shrugged out of a heavy coat that looked to Reg as if it had been made out of a grizzly bear hide. He tossed the coat onto the hall tree by the door and shuffled over to the desk, spurs jangling. "I been waitin' all morning for you to come to me, but then I figured it wasn't gonna happen." He propped one hip on the corner of the desk and pulled a twist of tobacco from his shirt pocket. "I want to know what you're gonna do about this weather."

Reg frowned at the letter he had spent the better part of an hour composing, now wrinkled like so much scrap paper beneath Jackson's hip. "What about the weather?"

The foreman bit off the end of the tobacco twist, then stuffed the rest back in his pocket. "Don't you ever look up from that bookwork?" He jerked his head in the direc-

tion of the front window. "There's a norther blowin' in.
The mercury's dropped thirty degrees in the last hour."

Intent on composing his first report to the syndicate,
Reg hadn't felt the change. He had only barely registered
the icy gust that had preceded Jackson into the room. Now
he turned his head to look out the window and raised one
eyebrow in surprise. The sky was the deep blue-black of a
bruise, and the stunted willows by the horse corral popped
like buggy whips in the wind. "I've heard of the vagaries
of Texas weather, but I don't see that a late spring cold
spell should concern us that much."

Jackson snorted. "I don't know about vagrants or whatever it is you're babblin', but this ain't no little cold spell.
This is a hell-freezin' norther." He spat, hitting the spittoon with a forceful *Zing!* "If it don't 'come a blizzard by
nightfall, I'll eat my boot."

Reg fought the urge to order Jackson to stand up straight
and look him in the eye and come to the point. The
foreman's every action seemed designed to set Reg's teeth
on edge. If he had any other choice, he would fire the
man, but right now the ranch was more important than
his personal feelings. As much as it pained him, he would
have to play Jackson's game, at least for the time being.
"All right, then," he said. "Obviously, we'll need to protect
the stock."

"You're the boss. You tell me what you want to do."
Jackson gave him a blank look.

Reg could feel a vein throbbing at his temple. He tried
to think back to his lesson with Abbie, but "northers" were
not a topic they had found time to discuss. He glanced at
Jackson. The foreman was studying the dirt under his nails.
He wore the superior expression of a schoolmaster who
knew the pupil before him had no idea of the correct
answer to the question just asked.

"We'll need to move the cows and calves to a more

sheltered area," Reg said, counting on common sense to get him through this standoff.

Jackson gave him a considering look. "Yeah, but where?"

Reg searched his memory for details of his ride around the ranch. The unfamiliar terrain blurred in his head like a sea chart he had seen only once. He looked away from Jackson's challenging gaze. Was it his imagination, or did the sky seem darker? The room, which had been comfortable only moments before, now felt chilled. As he stared out the window, an empty water barrel fell over onto its side and tumbled across the yard.

"Time's a wastin', chief," Jackson said. "Don't take long for those calves to freeze."

"You know where to move them—move them!" Reg's voice was raspy with anger as he faced the foreman once more. "You're wasting my time and yours with this 'twenty questions' routine."

Jackson had the audacity to smile. Reg gripped the edge of the desk to keep from lashing out at the man.

"We ought to move them to Oxcart Canyon," Jackson said. "But we'll need every man's help to make it in time. Should have been done this morning, really."

Reg ignored the goad and followed Jackson to the door. As the foreman shrugged into the bearskin, Reg reached for his lighter wool greatcoat.

"Goin' somewhere?" Jackson asked.

"You said you needed every man to help."

"I didn't mean you, chief. You'd best stay here warm and dry with your books."

"I can ride, dammit." Reg jerked open the door, the shoulder cape of his coat blown back by the fierce wind. "Don't waste any more time arguing about it."

The cold wind cut through Reg's clothing as if he were naked. Any other time, he would have gone back inside and dressed more warmly for the task. But he wouldn't give Jackson the satisfaction of riding off without him. He clenched his teeth and leaned into the wind, counting on the heat of his anger at the foreman to help warm him.

Mouse balked at being forced from his warm stall into the cold. He fought against the bridle and bowed his back when Reg threw the saddle on him. Reg elbowed him in the belly and tightened the girth, then leapt into the saddle and held on while the gelding bucked and tossed. *At least the exercise warmed us up,* Reg thought as he rode out of the corral at last, Jackson's figure already a dark blur in the distance.

Jackson must have assembled the cowboys before riding to the ranch house. They waited on the edge of the pasture closest to the house, a string of horses bunched behind them. With a few mumbled orders from Jackson, they rode toward the Plum Creek pasture, where most of the cows and calves had spent the winter.

Reg followed Jackson and watched the other men for a clue as to what he should do. The cattle were restless, and reluctant to get moving in the cold wind. The work of driving them consisted mainly of riding among them, shouting and waving, forcing them to bunch tightly together and move slowly toward the sheltered canyon.

Within minutes, Reg's hands and feet ached with the cold. Ice clung to his moustache, and he couldn't feel parts of his face anymore. But he forced himself to keep riding, to keep working. Jackson's comment about leaving him behind with the books still rankled. He would show the foreman he could work as hard as any man here.

Some time after they left Plum Creek, it began to sleet, the icy needles stabbing his face, melting and refreezing in his lashes and on his moustache. He clenched his jaw to keep his teeth from chattering, and thought with envy of Jackson's bearskin coat.

The sleet became snow, and the men's shouts took on

a new urgency. Reg saw a calf stumble. A skinny cowboy stopped his horse and scooped the calf into his arms, then rode off again with the animal cradled in front of him.

That cowboy had saved one calf from freezing to death. But what if more fell—too many to pick up and carry? This year's calves represented the ranch's future profit. If they died in this storm, Reg would have to sail home without a penny to show for his efforts, defeated before he had even gotten started.

Despair washed over him as he thought of having to face his father with the news that he had failed once again. He shut his eyes and let his head fall forward until his chin touched his chest. Anything would be preferable to seeing the scorn in his father's eyes. Even letting go of the reins and slipping from his horse right here, freezing on this foreign prairie. Even that would be better than knowing he would never live up to his father's dreams.

"Are you all right? Hey, Reg, wake up. Are you okay?"

Someone was shouting at him over the howling wind and driving snow. He looked up and saw the skinny cowboy who had picked up the calf. Except the cowboy wasn't a boy. It was Abbie, wearing a long shearling coat and wool mittens, a red wool scarf wrapped around her neck. Reg blinked and shook his head, trying to push back the fog that enveloped him. He remembered seeing her pick up the calf . . . yes, there it was, draped over her saddle, half-covered by her coat tails. Then he had dreamt about cattle freezing and his father's disapproving face. . . .

"Reg, answer me!" Abbie leaned over and grabbed his arm and shook him hard. "My God, you're nearly frozen! You've got to wake up."

His limbs felt like lead weights, and even breathing required a great effort as he fought an overpowering lethargy.

"Here, drink this." Abbie unhooked a canteen from

her saddle horn and started to hand it to him. She shook it, and he could hear the ice rattle. "Oh, blast it!" she cried, dropping the canteen and reaching back toward her saddlebag. Reg watched, dazed, as she fumbled with the buckles, then threw back the flap and pulled out a tin flask. She unscrewed the cap and thrust the flask into his hands, shaping his stiffened fingers around the container. "Drink it!" she commanded, forcing his hands toward his mouth.

He smelled the brandy before he tasted it, and felt the liquid sloshing down his chin and over his gloves. But he managed to swallow a good amount, the burning liquor reviving him somewhat even as he began coughing.

Abbie took the flask away and pounded him on the back. She leaned forward and peered into his face. "That's better," she said, nodding. "You don't look so gray anymore." She held out the flask. "Take another swig, then we'd better see about catching up with the others."

He took another swallow, feeling steadier now, and returned the flask to her. "What are you doing here?" he asked, when he could finally speak again. "Don't tell me I'm all the way over on your land."

She shook her head. "I came over to help you." She urged her horse forward, and Mouse fell into step beside her.

"What about your own cattle?" he asked.

"We moved them this morning, when I saw the weather turning bad. Most of them were already over by Apache Canyon anyway, so it didn't take long."

He winced. Abbie had known enough to move her cattle this morning. How much time had they lost through his ignorance?

They rode up behind the main herd and began driving them toward the canyon. The snow grew thicker, until Reg was able to see only a few feet in front of his face. Even when he couldn't see her, he was aware of Abbie working beside him. He could hear her higher-pitched voice above the bawling cattle and the shouts of the other men.

Reg knew the moment they entered the canyon. The wind calmed, and the cattle began to move faster. Tuff Jackson rode by, brushing drifts of snow from his shoulders. "All right, men. Let's head back to the house before the worst of it sets in!" he shouted.

Reg removed his hat and shook off a crusting of snow. If this wasn't already "the worst of it," he didn't want to linger to experience the rest. He looked out at the cattle. Some were drinking in parts of the creek not yet frozen over, while others settled with their calves in the thick underbrush. "Do you think they'll be all right here?" he asked Abbie as he watched her tuck the calf she had been carrying in beside its mother.

She pulled herself back up into the saddle and nodded. "They've got fresh water and shelter, and there's grass under that snow, even if it is frozen. They're in good shape." She looked at him. "I can't say the same for you. What are you doing riding out in this mess with no more of a coat than that? I'll bet you've got your regular suit on under it."

He shrugged off the question. What would Abbie understand about his need to prove himself to Jackson and the other men? "I've been through worse at sea," he said. "At least here the land doesn't pitch about beneath your feet."

"No, only the horses do that."

He glanced at her and saw she was smiling above the red scarf. He hadn't noticed what a nice smile she had before. The expression of good humor lit her eyes and brightened her whole face. Merely looking at her made him feel a little warmer.

"We'd better go," he said. "Too much longer and I'm not sure we could find our way back."

"I think it's probably already too late to try to make it back."

Reg looked around. Snow still fell steadily, piling up in tall drifts on the edges of the canyon. The cattle had spread out across the area, but not a single cowboy was in sight.

"They probably thought we were right behind them," Abbie said. She scanned the canyon walls. "We'll have to find somewhere around here and wait for the worst of the storm to pass."

Chapter Six

Abbie guided Toby along a narrow path next to the canyon wall. Reg fell in behind her. "We can't stay out here," he said. "We'll freeze."

"Should have thought of that before you ran out of the house in that thin coat," she called over her shoulder. Now that she'd had time to think about it, she was getting angry at the Englishman. When she'd first spotted him, nodding off in the saddle, his skin the color of old ashes, she'd felt as if someone had clamped a hand around her heart and squeezed. All she could think of was what if he died? What if he froze to death right in front of her?

Then, while she poured brandy down him and prayed he'd snap out of it, she'd started blaming herself. She *knew* how tricky the weather could be this time of year—why hadn't she thought to warn him about northers? What kind of a teacher was she anyway?

Still, she reasoned now as they picked their way around

snow-dusted boulders, who would have thought she'd have to tell a grown man to put on a decent coat?

"What are you doing?" Reg asked. She could hear his teeth chattering in the silence that followed.

"I'm looking for a cave." She tilted her head back and scanned the ledges along the canyon walls. It was snowing harder now; fat flakes melted on her cheeks. "There's lots of them around here. Cougars and bears use them as dens."

"I can't imagine they'd appreciate us dropping in unannounced," he said.

She started to hurl back a sarcastic reply, then looked over her shoulder and saw that he was smiling—a tight grimace formed by lips frozen blue, but a smile nonetheless. She turned around again, so he wouldn't see her answering grin. "I thought maybe I'd let you go in first and make sure nobody was home," she said. She spotted a shadowed depression in the canyon wall ahead of them. "I think I see a place."

The scooped-out area in the wall wasn't very deep; Reg wouldn't even be able to stretch out without exposing his feet to the elements. She dismounted and walked closer for a better look.

"Rather small, don't you think?" he asked, walking up beside her.

"Too small for a cougar or a bear." She crouched down and stuck her head inside. "Something was in here at one time; there's a pile of leaves and stuff, like a bed. But I don't think they've been here in a while."

Backing out, she bumped into Reg's legs and almost fell over. He reached down and helped her up. "Careful there," he said.

"Don't worry about me. What about you? How are you feeling?"

He flexed his fingers in the fine leather gloves. "I stopped feeling anything hours ago."

"Here." She pulled the saddlebags and canteen from Toby's back and shoved them into his arms. "Get inside and clear out a place for us. I'll gather some wood for a fire."

He started to protest. "Please?" she said. "This once, let's do something without a debate."

He stiffened, then gave a curt nod. "As you wish."

The gray pallor had returned to his skin. Alarmed, Abbie realized he'd stopped shaking, one sign that he might be freezing to death. "Hurry up and get out of this wind." She urged him toward the cave. "I'll be back in a jiffy."

It took longer than she'd thought it would to collect a load of deadfall limbs and broken branches. "You shouldn't have brought so much," Reg scolded, coming out to help her.

"I wanted enough to last all night." She knelt and began stacking twigs and branches to start a fire. "I'll go for more in a minute."

Reg grabbed her arm. "What do you mean, all night? I thought we only had to wait out the storm. Will it last that long?"

"It could." She searched through her saddlebags and found a tin of sulfur matches and struck one on the side. Sheltering the flame with her hands, she guided it to the nest of dried leaves and twigs at the base of the fire. "Even if it doesn't, it'll be dark soon. Better to stay put until morning." She watched the flame lick at a curl of peeled bark, then catch. "Don't let that go out," she said to Reg as she rose.

"Where are you going?"

"For more wood."

The snow was falling steadily now, and she had trouble finding wood in the drifts. She'd collected all the bigger pieces during her first search and had to settle this time for half-rotten logs and green limbs she tore from trees. When she staggered back to Reg once more, she was relieved to see the fire blazing brightly in the entrance to the cave. Reg crouched before it, warming his hands.

Her skin felt prickly and numb with cold, and the ends of her fingers ached. She wanted nothing more than to sink down beside Reg, but there was still work to do. She dumped her load of wood near the blaze, where it would act as a windbreak and be handy during the night. "I'm going to see to the horses," she called to Reg.

"I'll help." He started to his feet.

"No!" The last thing she needed was Reg wandering off in the storm and getting lost, or falling over frozen at her feet. "Why don't you make some coffee?" she suggested. "The pot's in my saddlebags."

By the time she'd hobbled the horses in a nearby grove, the snowstorm had escalated to a full-fledged blizzard. She squinted into the blinding whirl of flakes, feeling her way along the canyon wall until she came to the cave and its welcoming blaze. Squeezing in beside Reg, she stripped off her thick gloves and crouched down, holding her hands to the fire and inhaling deeply of the reviving scent of brewing coffee.

When the feeling had returned to her fingers and face, she looked over at Reg. He sat as far away from her as possible in the close confines of the cave, his back pressed against the rock wall, legs drawn up to his chest. He had stopped shivering, and his moustache had thawed, but he still looked cold, his arms hugging his body, lips compressed in a thin line.

"Are you all right?" She patted the space beside her. "Move here closer by the fire where you'll be warmer."

He shook his head.

"What is it?" she asked. "Is something wrong?"

He cast her a wary look. "I suppose I'm fortunate your father is not alive to come after me with a shotgun tomorrow," he said. "Unless, of course, you intend to do that yourself."

She frowned. Had the cold affected his thinking? She'd heard incoherence was a sign of someone freezing to death. Alarmed, she leaned toward him. "Reg, what are you talking about?"

He cleared his throat, avoiding her gaze. "You will, of course, be thoroughly compromised by spending the night alone with me."

She sat back on her heels, still staring at him. "Compromised?" The word wasn't one she had heard used much. Then its meaning struck her. "Oh!" She felt a blush heat her cheeks. "But we aren't *doing* anything!" she protested. "We're just trying to survive."

He glanced at her. "Then, you won't insist I marry you?"

"M . . . marry you?" She choked on the words.

He raised one eyebrow and gave her a long look. "More than one woman has been known to trap a man by such means."

"Well, I'm not like that. You can put that out of your head right now. Besides, I'm going to marry Alan Mitchell, remember?"

He nodded slowly, his shoulders relaxing a bit.

"Good. Then, there's no need for either of us to worry." She reached for her saddlebags, hoping to hide the trembling in her hands. Marry Reg? Just because they'd spent one night in a cave together? The idea was preposterous.

As she fumbled with the buckles of the bag, she was aware of him seated mere inches away. She could hear his breathing in the stillness of their shelter. The intimate sound sent a tingle up her spine. Surely it was just the aftereffects of the cold. She took a deep breath to steady her nerves, and inhaled the male scents of leather and fine men's cologne, along with the aroma of roasted coffee.

Ignoring the sudden racing of her heart, she pulled her tin cup from her saddlebags. "Do you want some coffee?" she asked. "There's only one cup, but we can share." She spotted the silver flask of brandy and pulled it out also. Maybe the liquor would ease this sudden jumpiness she felt.

"Yes, coffee sounds good."

She filled the cup, then added a generous dollop of brandy and handed it to Reg. She watched as he drank, for the first time noticing the prickle of beard dusting his chin and throat. At one time, she'd only thought of him as Reg, the caustic Englishman she'd agreed to help.

But he was also a man. A man with dark, curly hair that looked soft as silk. A man whose full, sensuous mouth had once placed a lingering kiss upon her hand. A man fully capable of "compromising" her out here in the wilderness. Had he said that because it was something he wanted, or something he feared?

"I was thirstier than I thought," he said, returning the cup.

She looked away and poured coffee for herself, adding the brandy with a free hand. "The cold's like that. Dries you out without your knowing about it." She took a warming sip from the cup and settled back against the wall.

They didn't speak for a while after that. The only sounds were the crackle of the fire and the moan of blowing snow. Abbie stared into the flames, savoring the pleasant lightheadedness from the brandy she had drunk.

"Why Alan Mitchell?" Reg asked after a while, pulling her from a doze.

"Huh?" She started and gave him a puzzled look. "What are you talking about?"

"Why are you so set on marrying Alan Mitchell?"

She straightened and stretched her stiffened limbs. "He's good, and kind," she said after a moment. "And he's a good rancher." She squirmed. She'd never had to put her feelings for Alan into words before.

"I notice you don't mention anything about love." Reg took the empty coffee cup from beside her and refilled it from the pot.

She looked up and found him watching her, his dark eyes mirroring the glow of the fire. "Well, of course I love him." But was the affection she felt for Alan anything more than friendship? "The best kind of love grows out of friendship," she said firmly.

"You talk like an expert on the subject," he said. "Or is that another of your father's teachings?"

"No, it's my own observation." She looked away from his challenging gaze, into the fire. Her father had never had much to say on the subject of love and romance. When, as a young girl, she had dared to ask him about his feelings for her mother, he had dismissed her question with an impatient shrug. "Don't waste time dwelling on the past," he'd said. "You must always look to the future."

"I wouldn't worry if I were you."

Reg's voice broke through her musings. She looked over at him.

"Many a marriage begins without love," he continued. "I suppose the fortunate few come around to that, but it isn't absolutely necessary." He jabbed at the fire with a stick.

"Have you ever been in love?" she asked.

He shook his head. "In lust, yes. Never in love."

Leaning back, he reached for the flask and poured a measure into the cup. Abbie noticed the way his shoulder muscles strained the fabric of his coat. A man didn't develop muscles like that sitting in the drawing room. What had Reg done that he was so fit?

Who had he been "in lust" with, and what was it like? The words spoke to her of unbridled passion and heady abandon, of a life lived outside the confines of society's rules.

"Who would have thought to bring brandy along for a few hours' work?" he asked, holding the flask to the light. His gaze shifted to Abbie. "Are you always so prepared?"

"My daddy taught me to never leave the house without rations for a couple of nights. You never know what you're going to come across out here."

His eyes seemed to burn into her. "Yes, isn't that true?"

She forced her gaze away from his and rummaged in the saddlebags again. "Are you hungry? There's biscuits and ham."

He took the biscuit she offered. "Looks good. Did you make it?"

She shook her head. "Maura did."

He smiled, and again she felt that uncomfortable stab of jealousy. Would a man ever smile at the mere mention of her name?

"And how is Miss O'Donnell working out?"

"That was a dirty trick to play on me, dumping her on my doorstep like that."

"You didn't answer my question."

She shrugged. "She's a sweet girl, a long way from home."

"Then, you're enjoying having a female companion after all."

She watched him out of the corner of her eye. He was regarding her with a satisfied look, a look that made her reluctant to admit he was right. "I never had a female friend before," she said after a moment. "I don't rightly know how to behave."

"I take it you've no sisters."

She shook her head. "Or brothers. My mama died when I was very young. I never really knew her."

He set the coffee mug between them, the tin ringing against the rock. "I lost my mother when I was seventeen," he said quietly. "I still miss her."

She missed the *idea* of a mother, but she had no memory of an actual person to miss. Her father had filled the role of both parents for her; his passing had left an emptiness too big to measure.

"I have two brothers, though," Reg said.

"That must be nice."

"Sometimes it is." He sighed. "I'm closer to my older brother, Charles. He's the sort of man it would be easy to despise. He's handsome and talented and, as heir to the earldom, quite wealthy besides. But he's also one of the nicest chaps you could ever hope to meet, very much a hale-fellow-well-met sort. Never a care in the world."

Abbie nodded. "I'd say that describes Charlie Worthington right down to a T."

"Of course, my younger brother, Cam, is much quieter, as I suppose is fitting a vicar."

A version of Reg as clergyman? She bit back a smile. No, that didn't work either. "And you're in the middle?" she asked.

He nodded. "Yes, I'm the middle son. The one no one knows what to do with. Certainly my father doesn't know how to take me."

The bleakness in his voice surprised her. "But he sent you here to represent him," she said.

"He sent me here to *test* me." He plucked a pine needle from the pile he sat on and launched it toward the fire. It burned in a flash of brightness, then crumbled to ash. "He expects me to fail at this as I have everything else." He looked past the fire, at the looming darkness outside the cave. "It appears I'm already well on my way."

"How can you say that? It's hardly your fault we had a late spring storm. You can't control the weather."

"A more experienced man would have known to move the cattle earlier." He turned to her. "You knew."

"A person isn't born with that kind of experience," she said. "It has to be learned. You learned today."

He clenched both hands into fists. "I haven't got time to learn every lesson through trial and error."

She leaned toward him, wanting desperately to break through the gloom he'd wrapped around himself like a cloak. "That's why you've got me. Remember? I'll teach you."

His eyes locked to hers, dark and challenging, the eyes of a wounded animal. She fought the urge to reach for him. Would he accept any gesture of comfort, or lash out in pain or fear?

And if she dared to touch him, would she be content to know only the feel of his hand in hers, or would she pursue greater intimacies? She had never thought to have this curiosity about a man. What would it feel like to touch him more intimately? To kiss him, even?

Her heart pounded at the thought. She'd never spent this much time so physically close to a man before. She couldn't recall wanting to touch a man this way, or wanting to be touched. But here, in the darkness, with the storm raging outside and the fire burning within, with the brandy warming her blood and awakening some primitive need deep inside her, she felt anything was possible.

She drew back, away from Reg as well as away from the direction her thoughts were turning. Forcing a laugh, she gave him what she hoped was a teasing look. "Well, don't forget, you've got your end of the bargain to keep up," she said.

He nodded, and gave her a long look. "Your hair," he said. "You're wearing it differently."

She put one hand to the elaborate twist of braids. "Maura arranged it for me."

He leaned closer. "And your face. There's something different around the eyes."

She blushed. "Maura, uh, she plucked my eyebrows." She'd also sewn lace trim on every single pair of Abbie's drawers and put more lace and ribbons on her plain cotton camisoles. But she wasn't about to tell that to Reg.

He smiled, his dark mood seemingly passed. "Perhaps, to pass the time, I should conduct a lesson now."

She regarded him warily. "What kind of lesson?"

"A lesson in the art of flirtation."

"Flirting is an art?"

"Done properly, it is." He crossed his legs in front of him, barely brushing her knee in passing. A jolt of feeling shot through her at the brief contact.

Reg raised one hand in a lecturer's pose. "Now, the first rule of flirtation is to remember it is a game. In order to get the most enjoyment from a game, both parties must participate. For every movement or gesture one party makes, there is a proper response. For instance, suppose I catch your eye from across the room and I do this." He lowered his right eyelid in a slow wink. "Now, how would you respond?"

She tried to ignore the rush of heat to her face. "I might think you had something in your eye," she teased.

"Would you really?" He leaned toward her. "Suppose I approached you and said, 'Miss Waters, I believe that is the most charming outfit I have ever seen.' How would you answer?"

She glanced down at her faded woolen trousers and grinned. "Then I'd say you really ought to get out more, Mr. Worthington."

He chuckled. "Perhaps that is how Texans flirt. But in the rest of the world it is understood that my compliment was directed not so much to the clothing itself as to the woman wearing it."

"Well, you tell me what I'm *supposed* to say."

"Let's try again." He took her hand, cradling it in the warmth of his palm. "Your hands, Miss Winters, I could never tire of watching them. I believe you can tell much about a person's character from their hands."

"You do?" she breathed, barely able to speak around the sudden tightness in her throat.

He nodded. "Your hands speak of honest work." He brushed the tips of his fingers across her knuckles, sending shivers of sensation up her arm. "And a high degree of skill in that work." He flattened his palm against her own. "A skill I admire, even as I envy it."

She felt dizzy and hot, mesmerized by his touch and the velvet sound of his words.

"Now you try," he said, releasing her hand. "Pretend I am Alan Mitchell. What would you say to me to hint at your true feelings?"

She swallowed, unable to even remember what Alan looked like. All she could see was Reg. She closed her eyes, and the memory of Alan's open, familiar face swam into view. "Why, Alan, I . . . I never knew anybody who could . . . who could cut a calf the way you do," she blurted.

Reg made a choking noise. She opened her eyes and found him staring at her, red-faced. "By 'cut a calf' may I assume you are referring to, uh—"

"Well, yes, castrate." She felt the heat of a blush engulf her own face as she said the word. "But it's true!" she protested. "Nobody's faster with a knife than Alan, and with roundup coming up I just thought of it and . . ."

Reg was laughing now, his whole body shaking as he collapsed against the cave wall. Abbie looked away, blinking back tears. How could she be so stupid? Of course that wasn't the kind of thing a real lady would say. A lady would probably go on about Alan's blue eyes or something. "I'm no good at this," she said.

"No one becomes an expert after a single lesson," he said. "As you have so rightly pointed out to me. Come now, let's try again. You're on the right track. Women appreciate an appeal to their vanity. Men like to be admired for their strength and skill. What's something else you could say to Alan at roundup?"

She took a deep breath. "I . . . I really admire that new mare you're riding," she said. "You always have had a good eye for horseflesh."

"Excellent. Now, next you should suggest consulting him about a horse you wish to purchase."

"But I don't want to buy a new horse."

He smiled. "You want Alan Mitchell to come to your house and spend some time alone with you, discussing the purchase of a horse. You want to give him the chance to get to know you better."

"Then, why don't I come right out and say so?" She crossed her arms over her chest. "I don't know as I see the purpose in all this talking in circles, anyway."

He took her hand again and gently drew it toward him. "People talk in circles when their feelings for each other are too deep, too heartfelt, to be exposed in public. If you rebuff my efforts at flirtation, I may be wounded, but the wound is not fatal. If I declare my affections more bluntly and you turn me away, I would be hurt, indeed."

She could feel her pulse throbbing against his fingers as he clasped her wrist. She stared at him, wide-eyed, hardly daring to breathe. When he looked up, she leaned toward him, drawn by an invisible longing to be even closer to him.

"Abbie," he whispered.

"Shhh." She closed her eyes and inhaled deeply of his

cologne and leather scent, losing herself in the wonderful flood of sensation as her lips met his.

The first touch was all softness: the feather brush of his moustache and the satin caress of his lips. She slipped her free hand about his neck and pulled him even closer. With a groan, he deepened the kiss, opening his mouth to cover her's fully. She tasted coffee and felt the hard slickness of his teeth, and then the hot sweep of his tongue drove away her last virginal fantasies of a chaste caress between friends. This was a kiss as she'd only imagined it, full of heat and need and raw longing.

She abandoned herself to a wildness she'd never felt before, unable to think in the face of such passion.

A sound like gunfire shook her, and she wondered if it was simply the thundering of her blood in her ears. The noise came again, echoing in the rock canyon. Reg pushed her away and staggered to his feet. "Sounds like a bloody cannon," he said, and headed for the door.

Chapter Seven

Reg stumbled out of the cave, shielding his eyes against the onslaught of swirling snow. His lips still burned with the memory of Abbie's mouth upon his, even as the icy wind cut through his thin coat. Her boldness in kissing him had surprised him, but not as much as his own powerful reaction to the kiss.

The thunder of gunfire shook the air once more. Looking toward the front of the canyon, he saw dark shapes moving through the curtain of falling snow. He blinked, and the shapes coalesced into riders on horses, thrashing through the drifts. As he watched, the lead rider paused and fired a shotgun straight into the air.

An answering shot sounded almost at Reg's side. He staggered back and gaped at Abbie, who stood in front of the cave entrance, smoking pistol in her hand. "Just letting them know we're here," she said as she holstered the weapon.

Reg turned away, afraid to look at her too long, fearful

of betraying the confused feelings that wrestled in his chest. His body still craved her woman's touch even as his mind told him what he was feeling was improbable—impossible.

The lead rider gave a shout and spurred his horse forward. Reg's first thought was that these others were stranded, too, like he and Abbie. Safety in numbers, he told himself, even as he savored the already fading rush of passion their interlude alone had produced.

No. He shook his head as the riders drew nearer. *Abbie Waters is nothing to me. Can be nothing to me.*

The lead rider brought his horse to a halt in front of them. One thick-gloved hand came up to pull down the bandanna that covered his mouth and nose. "Glad to see you two alive and well," Alan Mitchell said, grinning.

"Alan! What are you doing out in this storm?" Abbie hugged her arms around her body and rocked back and forth in the snow.

"When you didn't come back with Jorge and Miguel, Maura—I mean, Miss O'Donnell—rode over to my place and insisted I go out after you." He swung down off his horse as two other men rode up beside them, leading a pair of extra mounts. "I tried to tell her you had sense enough to hole up somewhere 'til the weather cleared, but she wouldn't hear of it."

"I can't believe you let her talk you into coming out in a storm like this," Abbie said. "And for nothing. Reg and I are fine."

Alan glanced around, at the blazing campfire and the cave. "Yep, looks like you folks are settled in real cozy." He chuckled, and Reg felt his face grow hot. Did Alan think that he and Abbie . . . ?

"And now I suppose we've got no choice but to ride back out in the snow with you." Abbie gave him a mock scowl. "Really, Alan, I thought you had better sense than that."

So much for the lesson on flirting, Reg thought. Nothing like a good scolding to endear a man to a woman.

"Just goes to show you aren't the only stubborn female around. Ain't that right, Reg?"

Reg shook his head. "This country is infested with obstinance."

"Yeah, well, you're one to talk. I heard tell you were so set on riding out with Jackson and the others you braved the elements in a cloth coat." Alan pulled a bundle from behind his saddle and tossed it at Reg. "We all believe Limey blood's about half-frozen anyway, but humor me and put that on."

Reg unrolled a blanket-lined shearling coat. The weight of it dragged at his shoulders when he slipped it on, but it succeeded in blocking the arctic wind. He would be able to ride back to the ranch without fear of freezing in the saddle.

Did anyone but Abbie know how close he had come to doing just that on their way to the canyon? he wondered as he followed her and Alan toward the sheltered nook where she had left their horses. He hadn't found a way yet to thank her for saving his life. If she hadn't come along when she had. . . .

He shook his head. Even if he had avoided freezing then, he would never have made it this long in the canyon alone. He had no doubt Tuff Jackson had been happy to leave him behind. If he had failed to return, then everyone, Alan included, would have shrugged off his disappearance. After all, here in Texas every man—and in Abbie's case, every woman—was responsible for looking after himself.

"I've got to hand it to that little Irish gal," Alan said as they rode the horses back toward the cave. "She rode in this storm all the way to my place, like it was a Sunday drive." He grinned. "Said she stopped every hundred yards or so and tied a piece of red flannel to a fence post so she'd be sure to find her way back. Who would have thought a city girl would come up with an idea like that?''

Who, indeed? Reg wondered. He couldn't say he would have been so wise himself. He hunched lower in his coat.

"Where is she now?" Abbie asked.

"Daddy insisted on seeing her back to your place. I told them to wait for us there.''

They stopped at the cave while Abbie went inside and retrieved her saddlebags. Alan kicked snow over the dwindling fire; then they remounted and headed out of the canyon.

They rode single file, horses nose to tail, taking turns breaking the trail through the heavy drifts. Though the wind kicked up swirls of flakes around them, new snow had stopped falling. In the frosty light of a half moon, the land looked soft, smothered in down. The snow muffled the sounds of the horses' shod hooves and swallowed up all noise but the huffing breath of the laboring animals and the creak of stiffened leather saddles.

Alan paused from time to time to study the sky. Reg realized he was using the stars to guide them home. He tilted his own head back. The bright star Isis winked back at him from the eye of Draco, the dragon tail of the constellation curved around the Little Dipper. How many nights had he stood on a ship's deck and watched this same pattern of stars in the sky overhead? Finding them here now was like seeing a friend's face in a crowd of strangers. When it came his turn to take the lead, he did so with confidence. He may not know all there was to know about surviving in this rugged land, but his years at sea had taught him to read the sky like a map. If necessary, he could have found his way home unaided.

Abbie's cabin glowed like a lit jewel box, golden light pouring from every window, spilling out onto the snow. As the line of riders rode into the yard in front of the cabin, Reg heard barking. The front door burst open, and Banjo raced out, followed by Maura. "I've been worried nigh to death," she said, over the dog's joyous cries. She held aloft a beaded rosary. "I've about worn the beads smooth with prayin'."

Brice Mitchell came to help Alan's men lead the horses toward the barn. Maura shooed Abbie and Reg and Alan inside. "I've a great roaring fire going, and a pot of stew that'll be warming your bones up right," she said.

The warmth of the house hit Reg like a blanket, draining his last reserves of strength. He managed to slip the heavy coat from his shoulders, then sank into the chair Maura offered him by the stove. Maura shoved a mug of brandy-laced coffee into his hand, and he drank it in one long, greedy draught.

Warm and sated, he listened, half-dozing, to the swirl of conversation around him. Brice and the others came in from the barn, like rowdy schoolboys followed by a swirl of snow. They laughed and slapped each other on the back, jostling for a place in front of the stove.

Maura fluttered among them, distributing bowls of stew, refilling cups. Her lilting Irish voice was a pleasant melody over the men's deeper tones.

Abbie left the room and returned a few moments later, dressed in trousers and a man's white flannel shirt, the tails left out, hanging almost to her knees. Wisps of hair escaped from the braids piled atop her head, framing her face like a bronze halo. Reg smiled at the sight of her. Maura might have the pink-and-white prettiness of a Botticelli cherub, but Abbie looked more like an angel to him. Who else but an angel would have saved him tonight?

His thoughts were rambling wildly, he knew, but he hadn't the energy to rein them in. He watched Abbie move among the men gathered around the stove and felt again that awareness of her he had experienced when they were alone in the cave. In that cramped, cold shelter he had counted every breath she drew, felt her every movement in his bones.

Even so, her kiss had caught him unawares. The wanton passion of her action had made his heart race and his blood heat to a fever pitch. Yet when he had looked at her again he had seen only innocence. She hadn't been brought up to think of what she was doing as wrong. Abbie had responded to him with a yearning as real and honest as breathing.

Abbie's father may have raised her as a boy, but he hadn't been able to smother the woman's heart within her. The glimpse she had given Reg today of that part of herself moved him, but at the same time it made him wary. He would have to make certain Abbie understood that nothing more would come of their brief indiscretion.

"Alan, I was wondering if you could stop by for a spell one evening next week. I need your advice on something." Abbie's voice pulled Reg from his musings. She was seated next to Alan on a long bench pulled up beside the stove. Cheeks flushed, lips slightly parted in anticipation of his answer, she leaned toward the rancher.

"Advice? Since when did you need my advice on anything?" Alan gave her a sleepy grin.

Abbie shifted on the bench and stared down at her folded hands. "I, um, I'm thinking of buying a new horse, and I want your opinion on some things."

"You don't need my advice," Alan said. "You know horses as good as any man I ever met."

"Come and you can stay for dinner." Abbie glanced at Maura, who was adding another stick of wood to the stove. "I'm sure Maura won't mind."

At the mention of the Irish maid, Alan raised one eyebrow slightly. "Well, now, it might be nice to sit and visit with you girls for a spell at that," he drawled.

Abbie sat back and sighed. She continued to smile at Alan, her face glowing. Reg's stomach tightened. How could Alan be so ignorant of Abbie's feelings for him?

"I've never seen a storm this fierce." Maura came and sat on the bench on the other side of Alan. "And it came on so sudden."

Alan nodded. "Still and all, I'm grateful for the moisture. It's been entirely too dry for my liking this year. Without more rain, the grass won't last through the summer."

"Then, we'll just have to burn pear," Abbie said.

"Won't matter if the tanks dry up," Alan said.

Reg struggled to make sense of this exchange. How could burning fruit help the grass grow? And what kind of tanks was Alan talking about? Water tanks? He didn't recall seeing any on his ranch.

He stared into his half-empty coffee cup, as if he might divine the answers to his questions in the cooling brown liquid. So much he needed to know, and so little time to learn. He couldn't afford many more mistakes like the one he had made today.

"You're right about the storm coming up fast, though." Alan turned toward Maura. "They say if you don't like Texas weather, wait a minute and it'll change. Daddy and I had just come in from seeing to our own herds when you rode up. I knew something had to be wrong to bring you out in that weather."

"It was sweet of you to worry, but it really wasn't necessary." Abbie leaned over and gave Maura's hand a squeeze. "Reg and I were fine."

"But I didn't know you were with Mr. Worthington at the time." Maura flashed Reg a grin. "If I had, I'm sure I wouldn't have worried so much."

"I don't know when I've met a braver young woman," Alan said, beaming at Maura.

Of course, Abbie had braved the blizzard first, to save

her own animals and then to help him, Reg thought. Or did Alan not think of Abbie as a young woman? He shifted his gaze from the rancher to Abbie. She was still smiling fondly at Alan despite his unwitting snub. Reg felt his heart sink. Abbie was as besotted as ever with his friend, but from what he could tell, Alan felt nothing in return. In fact, all indications pointed to a growing infatuation with Maura.

As if sensing his gaze upon her, Abbie turned toward him. Her lips curved in a sleepy smile—lips that had pressed against his own only a few hours ago. He knew he should look away, avoid encouraging any lingering attraction she might feel. Today in the cave, he had glimpsed the volatile emotions smoldering beneath her almost masculine practicality. Abbie was a banked fire; at the touch of the right man, she would blaze.

Reg knew he wasn't the man to warm himself at that fire. In a few months, he would return to his gentleman's life in England. Abbie belonged here in Texas, with a man who could share her love of ranching.

A man like Alan Mitchell.

He shifted his gaze to Alan, who was still deep in conversation with Maura. What would happen if all his efforts at turning Abbie into a "lady" did not help her win Alan's notice? Would she blame him for her unrequited love?

Would he have to add Abbie to his growing list of failures?

Reg awoke the next morning to an awareness of someone else in his bedroom. He opened his eyes and stared up at a short, rounded form looming over him. He blinked, and the image sharpened into that of his housekeeper. He sat upright. "Mrs. Bridges, what are you doing in my chambers?"

The elderly woman blushed to the shade of a ripe raspberry. "There's a man here to see you," she said. She turned even redder. "A colored man. He refuses to leave the parlor until I fetch you."

Reg leaned forward and plucked his dressing gown from the end of the bed. "What does he want to see me about?"

She shook her head. "He won't say. But he asked me half a hundred questions about my kitchen. Impertinent, he was."

"All right, then. Tell him I'll be down momentarily. And please bring a pot of tea into the dining room."

"*He* asked for coffee." She sniffed.

"Tea, Mrs. Bridges."

"Yes, sir." She sailed out of the room on a wave of offended dignity. Reg dressed, trying to shrug off the weariness that plagued him like a hangover. It couldn't have been much more than five hours since he had made the cold ride back to the Ace of Clubs from Abbie's house. The newly fallen snow made the Texas prairie look like a wedding cake, thick with frosting. He hoped the cows and calves had managed to survive the night in the canyon. As soon as he dispensed with the man in his parlor, he would ride out to check on them.

A man with a blacksmith's shoulders and skin the color of walnut shells stood when Reg entered the parlor. He held a flop-brimmed black felt hat in his hands. A faded feed sack bulging with unidentifiable objects rested at his feet. "Mr. Worthin'ton, suh," he said before Reg had a chance to speak. "Ah'm here for the cook's job."

Reg paused halfway across the room. Mrs. Bridges did an adequate job preparing his meals. What made this man think he wished to replace her? "I already have a cook," he said.

"Beggin' pardon, suh. I was made to understand the

position was still open." He squared his jaw and nodded. "Miss Abbie sent me; she was right certain about it."

Reg groaned and crossed to the wing chair by the window. Abbie again. Was there no escaping the woman? "I'm afraid Miss Waters was indeed mistaken," he said. "Mrs. Bridges cooks and keeps house for me."

As if on cue, the door flew open, and Mrs. Bridges marched in, bearing a loaded tea tray. She glared at the visitor and set the tray on a low table before Reg. "Will there be anything else, Mr. Worthington?" she asked.

Reg shook his head, then waited until Mrs. Bridges had stalked out of the room before pouring the tea. He carefully added two lumps of sugar and a dollop of cream to his cup. He was stirring this brew when he heard a loud chuckle from his visitor's direction. "What do you find so amusing?" he asked, giving the man a sharp look.

"That old hen ain't gonna cook for no crew of cowboys, that fo' sho'."

Reg frowned. "Of course not. The men do their own cooking."

"Not on roundup they don't." The man shook his head. "But maybe I misheard. I thought Miss Abbie said you was furnishin' a chuck wagon this year."

Understanding slowly dawned. Did furnishing the wagon and food mean he was also supposed to supply a cook to prepare the meals? "So you're a chuck wagon cook?" he asked.

"I cooked for Miss Abbie's pa." He took a step closer and peered down at Reg's teacup. "I kin brew up a batch of coffee that'd wake the dead."

"I would prefer the dead stay safely asleep." Reg sipped his tea, considering. If Abbie had sent this man, he knew better than to ignore her judgment. Still, he was the one who would pay if the man turned out to be incompetent. "What's your name?" he asked.

"Clarence Green. But most folks jus' call me Cooky."

"Well, Mr. Green, what other qualifications do you have for the job, besides the ability to brew strong coffee?"

"I can show you." Green walked over to the feed sack and hefted it to his shoulder. "I got my tools right here."

"Your tools?" Reg raised one eyebrow in question.

"My knives and fryin' pan, rollin' pin, and a few other things I use." He shook his head. "Don't trust other folks' tools. Half the time the knives are dull as spoons and the fryin' pans ain't seasoned proper." He threw out his chest, muscles straining the faded fabric of his shirt. "Jus' show me the kitchen and I'll fix you a breakfast better'n you ever had."

An hour later, Reg was enjoying a three-inch-high stack of what Green described as flapjacks, along with half a rasher of thick-sliced bacon and fluffy eggs cooked in butter. He had enjoyed his share of *cordon bleu* cuisine in his time, but none had satisfied as this plain fare did. He would be sure to thank Abbie for sending Green his way.

With Mrs. Bridges having accepted the rest of the day off in exchange for the use of her kitchen, there was no one to announce Tuff Jackson's arrival. The foreman stalked into the dining room with his usual bravado and helped himself to the pot of coffee that sat, untouched, on the sideboard.

Reg fought the urge to confront Tuff about abandoning him and Abbie in the canyon. He had his doubts that they had been left behind purely by accident. But he didn't see how he could accuse the foreman without admitting his own incompetence. "How are the cattle?" he asked instead.

Tuff turned one of the dining room chairs around and straddled it, then poured a measure of coffee into his saucer and blew on it. "They're all right." He took a sip of the cooled coffee. "Only lost half a dozen calves."

Reg frowned. Every calf lost was profit the ranch would never see. If they had gotten the cattle to the canyon sooner, would they have been able to save more? He laid aside his fork and shook his head. No good would come of brooding over past mistakes. "The Lazy L and the Rocking W will be working with us during the roundup," he said.

Tuff nodded. "There's some decent hands there, though I don't trust those Mexicans over at Waters' place as far as I could throw them." He drained the last of his coffee and set the saucer down with a thump. "I heard about Alan Mitchell riding out last night to rescue you."

Reg stiffened. He hadn't missed the derisive tone of Tuff's words. "Mr. Mitchell came at the insistence of Miss Waters' maid," he said. "There was no need. We were perfectly fine."

"That's right. Abbie Waters was with you, wasn't she? I heard you two was snuggled up in a cave, real cozy-like." He leered at Reg. "I always wondered about her. Acts like a man, but I reckon all women are the same once you get their clothes off, huh?"

China cups rolled to the floor and shattered as Reg shot up. He glared down at the foreman. What he would give to teach this oaf some manners. But a fight would give Jackson the perfect excuse to leave. *That's what he wants, isn't it?* Reg thought. *Why else would he be baiting me?*

"You'll show Miss Waters the respect due a lady or you'll answer to me," he said, his voice heavy with menace.

"Since when is Abbie Waters a lady?" Tuff shoved away from Reg and gave a harsh laugh. "You might as well try to turn some grizzled old cowpuncher into a Knight of the Round Table as make the likes of her into a lady."

Reg clenched and unclenched his fists. What made Tuff so sure Abbie was irredeemable? Couldn't he see the

tender woman beneath her rough exterior? Or did it take
a stranger to this land to recognize her potential?

He gave Tuff a withering look. "I would never have
mistaken you for a man who had had much association
with ladies," he said in his haughtiest voice.

An angry red color washed Tuff's face. "Why, I'll—"

"What the devil is goin' on in here?" The door swung
open, and Clarence Green stalked in, flour-covered rolling
pin raised in one hand. He surveyed the broken dishes on
the floor, then turned to the two men squared off in front
of him. "If you be wantin' more flapjacks, why don't you
jus' say so, 'stead of fightin' over 'em?"

Tuff's gaze swept over the cook, taking in the white
apron tied around his waist and the streak of flour across
his nose. "Who is he?" he demanded.

"Cooky to you, cowboy," Green answered. "That is, if
you 'spect to eat at my chuck wagon."

Tuff took a step back, then scowled at Reg. "I won't eat
anything cooked up by the likes of him."

Reg took a deep breath, struggling for calm. "Then, I
guess you won't eat," he said evenly. "I've hired him to
cook on this roundup."

"You can't do that," Tuff protested.

In the silence that followed, Reg could hear the steady
tick of the mantel clock over the fireplace and the whistle
of the wind around the corner of the house. "I can and
I will," he said after a moment.

"That's the foreman's job," Tuff said. He folded his
arms across his chest. "Mr. Grady left those decisions to
me."

Reg took two steps toward the foreman, until barely a
handspan separated them. "I am the boss here now. From
now on *I* have the final say on all decisions." He glared
at Tuff for a long moment, allowing that announcement
to sink in.

Tuff stared back at him, nostrils flaring with each enraged breath. But he held his tongue.

"You can choose your course," Reg continued. "You can choose the role of my adviser and prove yourself a valuable asset to this organization, or you can fight me all the way. But I warn you now. You will not win."

A shiver ran down Reg's spine as he stared into the foreman's hate-filled eyes. But he refused to back down.

"We'll see about that," Tuff growled. He turned on his heels and pushed past Green, out the door.

The cook watched him go. "Looks like a bad 'un there, boss," he said.

Reg nodded. Tuff was a bad one, all right. Had he made a mistake alienating the one man who might stand between him and success or failure? He shook his head and moved back to his seat at the table. He had to prove himself here on his own terms. He would take the blame for his own failures, but he wanted to savor the sweetness of victory as his alone as well.

Chapter Eight

"For certain, I'll be going on roundup with you." Maura looked up from the skirt she was pressing. "Whatever made you think I'd be wanting to stay home, missing all the fun?"

Abbie frowned. The Irish maid's view of things continued to startle her at every turn. "It's not fun, Maura. It's work. Hard, dirty work."

"Beggin' your pardon, miss. I'd be knowing all about hard work." She bore down on the iron, pressing perfect, straight pleats down the length of the wool skirt. "I started as scullery maid when I was ten. Up to me elbows in hot water and lye all day, lifting iron pots almost as big as meself, I was." She set the iron on the stove to reheat and picked up a second one. "When I moved upstairs, I thought life would be easier. But if you've never polished nine rooms of baseboards on your hands and knees, you don't know what a sore back is. Then, of course, I got to stretch me legs a bit whenever the master came home and felt like a game o' slap and tickle with whichever maid was unlucky enough to be in sight at the time." She looked at Abbie and winked. "Lucky for us the old man suffered from gout somethin' awful. Cook looked out for us girls, always temptin' him with rich foods and such."

Abbie listened to this recitation in awe. "I suppose there are different kinds of hard work," she said. "But I still don't think you'd enjoy a roundup."

"If your ownself be going, then I'll be going as well. After all, you can't very well go out there with all those men by yourself."

"Why not? I do it every year."

Maura's eyebrows rose in surprise. "Then, it's about time someone put a stop to it. It's not seemly for a young woman to be traveling alone with all those men."

Abbie sighed. "I've tried to explain to you that I'm not like other young women—"

"You've tried to explain to me, but begging your pardon again, miss. As far as I can see, the only difference between you and me and other women is what you've been taught—not what you are." She looked up from her ironing again and grinned. "How'd you like that lace I sewed on your drawers?"

Abbie blushed at the mention of her underwear. "Uh, it was very nice," she said. "Pretty."

"See there? You like pretty things same as the next lass." She set the iron aside and shook out the skirt. "Your hair looks nice that way, don't you think?"

Abbie put one hand to the intricate arrangement of braids. "Yes, it does."

"I'll wager Mr. Worthington noticed it, didn't he?"

Abbie's face grew hot as she remembered Reg's compliment, and the kiss that had followed soon after.

"I knew it!" Maura cried. She shook her head. "You aren't any different from other women, so don't be pretending you are." She held the skirt out to Abbie. "Now, try this on, miss, and I'll be checking the hem."

Abbie looked at the charcoal gray skirt in her hand. "What is it?"

"It's a riding skirt. So you don't have to ride in trousers all the time." Maura stepped up and caught the hem, then fanned it to reveal a split in the skirt.

Abbie frowned. "But I don't mind wearing trousers—"

"Lord Worthington gave me the money for the fabric. Said they were all the rage in Europe among ladies of quality such as yourself."

"Ladies of qual—" Abbie dropped into a chair and gaped at Maura. "Reg said that about me?"

Maura nodded. "He should know, shouldn't he, him being such a fine gentleman? Course, it really goes without saying, you being an heiress and all."

"An heiress! Maura, who has been filling your head with that kind of nonsense?"

"Alan, I mean Mr. Mitchell, told me you'd inherited this big ranch from your father. That makes you an heiress, don't it now?"

Abbie shook her head and stared at the skirt in her hand. "I'm a rancher's daughter, not an heiress," she said. "And I don't need a fancy skirt to ride in, thank you all the same."

"Mr. Worthington said he expected you'd say as much. So he told me to tell you this skirt is your new uniform."

Abbie frowned. "Uniform?"

Maura shrugged. "Can't say as it makes much sense to me. But he said you'd understand—something about a lady being recognized by her clothes."

Abbie groaned. Of course. She had preached at Reg about dressing like a person in authority if he expected to be accepted as an authority. Now he was turning the tables and telling her that in order to be treated like a lady, she had to dress like one. "All right." She stood and began unbuttoning her trousers. "I suppose I can try it on."

She pulled her skirt over her hips and dropped her jeans. Stepping out of the trousers, she kicked them away, then fastened the row of buttons up the side of the skirt. Maura clapped her hands together in delight. "Oh, miss, you do look wonderful!"

Abbie took an experimental few steps. The skirt was surprisingly unconfining. In fact, she felt almost naked without the familiar cloth clinging to her legs.

"Course, you'll want to wear some good stockings and garters," Maura said. "With those and your boots, a nice shirtwaist and maybe a waistcoat, you'll be all set."

Abbie frowned. "The other ranchers are liable to laugh me out of the roundup if I show up in a dress."

Maura's eyes widened. "Oh, no, miss, they wouldn't dare!"

"You don't know Texans very well yet, do you?"

"They'd have Mr. Worthington to answer to if they dared insult you," Maura said firmly.

"Goodness knows, we don't want to disappoint Mr. Worthington," Abbie said, holding back a smile. "I'll give the skirt a try. But if it interferes with my work, I'll go back to trousers."

"I'm so glad," Maura said. "I've already ordered the fabric for two more—and one for me own as well." She flushed. "Mr. Worthington said it was all right."

Abbie nodded. "Of course. But promise me, Maura, if you go on the roundup with us, you'll be extra careful."

"Oh, I will." She grinned. "Besides, you don't have to worry about anything happening to me. I've got me St. Christopher's, and a bottle of Holy Water for extra protection."

* * *

The first day of spring roundup held all the excitement of Christmas, Camp Meeting, and the beginning of school combined. Everyone was fresh from a winter's rest, horses groomed and newly shod, saddles oiled and polished. The chuck wagons were full, branding irons ready. Even the promise of hard work ahead couldn't dull the sharp anticipation that hung in the air like the smoke from mesquite cook fires.

Abbie inhaled deeply of the fragrant aroma of burning wood and boiling coffee as she and Maura approached the rendezvous on the edge of the Mitchells' land, Banjo trotting alongside. Jorge and Miguel had ridden ahead, driving their extra horses. "This is my favorite time of year," she said.

"Seems to take a great lot of people to do the roundin' up," Maura observed as they guided their horses past a wagon piled high with cowboys' bedrolls. "I didn't realize there were this many souls in the whole county."

"When I was a girl, there were even more," Abbie said. "There weren't so many fences then, and cattle roamed farther. We'd travel for weeks and ride hundreds of miles to collect what was ours and see the calves properly branded. Now it's just a matter of helping each other brand the stock within our little territory, and any that may have roamed over the winter."

Maura watched two cowboys toss armloads of wood into yet another wagon, then looked back at Abbie. "I can't imagine anyone bringing a wee child out in all this chaos."

Abbie smiled. "Daddy never left me out of any part of his life. He wanted me to learn everything he knew about ranching." She rubbed her thumb across her saddle horn. "I don't think he thought of me much as a child. I was more of . . . an apprentice, I guess."

"Mornin', Miss Abbie. Miss Maura." A cowboy with a big-toothed grin and a face dusted with freckles rode up to them. "My name's Tim O'Rourke," he said, tipping his hat. "You ladies need anything, you let me know."

"Now, you don't listen to him, ladies." A broad-shouldered man wearing a butter yellow shirt rode up. He, too, tipped his hat. "Donnie Best is the name. If you need anything, you remember to ask for the Best."

Abbie flushed. This unaccustomed attention from the young men was refreshing, but she was honest enough to know the lion's share of credit for it must go to Maura. The Irish maid stood out like a polished ruby among the cocklebur roughness of the cowboys. She'd swept her russet hair into a high bun and topped it with a wide-brimmed gaucho's hat. Dressed in white blouse, red fitted waistcoat and black riding skirt and boots, she made a fetching picture astride the little mare she'd chosen as her mount.

Abbie shifted in the saddle and looked down at her own gray wool skirt. The fabric was smooth against her stockinged legs, lightweight and unconfining. Maura had arranged her hair in a coil of braids, and she wore a simple shirtwaist with embroidery at the collar and cuffs. Studying herself in the mirror back home, she'd felt almost beautiful for the first time in her life.

Now, watching the men ride out of their way to smile and bow at Maura, she felt awkward and foolish. Her father would have laughed at her, arriving at roundup in such a getup. "There's work to be done!" he'd have said in a voice accustomed to issuing orders. "No time for all that feminine folderol."

"Good morning, Miss Waters. Aren't you a fetching sight." A new cowboy joined their group, his hearty British accent at odds with the scuffed boots and tall Stetson he wore. He pushed his hat back on his head and grinned.

"I take it you don't recognize me, miss. Can't say as I blame you. Last time we met I was togged out a bit different."

Abbie peered closer, then grinned. "Nick Bainbridge! Of course I remember you." She looked the cowboy up and down, remembering how he'd looked when she first met him, dressed in a black suit, low shoes and a bowler hat. He'd been footman to Cecily Thorndale, Reg's brother Charles's fiancée. A love of cowboying had soon infected him, and he'd elected to stay behind when Cecily and Charles returned to England. "You've turned into a regular waddie!"

"We've been working real hard on Nick and have about got all the polish worn off those fine manners of his." Tim O'Rourke gave the Englishman a playful shove.

"And how is Alice?" Abbie asked. "I heard you two got married."

Nick's grin broadened. "Aye. We tied the knot last month. Until we start our nursery, she's helping Miss Simms with the Academy."

"Please tell her I said hello, next time you see her."

"I'll do that, miss." The three men walked away, but before Abbie could urge her horse to follow, another voice hailed her.

"Why, if it ain't Miss Abbie. I hardly knew you, decked out so fancy like." Clarence Green raised a hand in greeting and walked toward them. A snowy apron covered most of his torso, and he carried an enormous ladle in one hand. "You two ladies are lookin' right pretty this mornin'," he said, flashing them a grin as dazzling as his apron.

"It's good to see you again, Mr. Green," Maura said.

"Now, we cain't have none of that 'Mister' nonsense," he said, shaking the ladle at her. "Out here, my name's Cooky." He puffed out his broad chest. "The army's got its generals and colonels and such, but out here on roundup, the straw boss is the only one who outranks Cooky."

Abbie smiled. Clarence had cooked for her father when she was a girl. Having him here reminded her of those happy times, when she'd been the pet of every cowboy on roundup, and her father's constant companion. "I'm glad you got the job," she said. "I can hardly wait to eat a plateful of your beans and biscuits."

"It's son-of-a-gun stew and corn pone for dinner today." His expression sobered. "I sure 'preciate you recommendin' me, Miss Abbie. Times been hard lately."

She nodded. "I'm sure Mr. Worthington was happy to find someone so capable."

"Yeah, well, he dug into my flapjacks quick enough." Cooky shook his head. "The man don't appreciate good coffee, though. Asked me to make him tea."

Abbie bit back a grin. Asking a chuck wagon cook for special favors violated an unwritten law of the plains. A cowboy who complained could expect burned beans and cold coffee for the duration of the roundup. "What did you tell him?" she asked.

"I got riled a little at first, but then I figured I had to make allowances, him bein' a foreigner and all." His grin broadened. "I told him I'd boil an extry pot of water, but he had to mess with his own tea leaves and such."

"I don't mind making Mr. Worthington's tea." Maura turned to Abbie. "I've made many a cup in me life. It's the least I can do to repay him for his kindness."

Abbie fidgeted, uncomfortable with the sudden tightness in her stomach. She didn't like the idea of pretty Maura waiting on Reg. Even though his highfalutin ways wore on her nerves sometimes, Reg Worthington was a good-looking man. And he was the only man who treated her as anything more than just another cowhand. It was bad enough that all the cowboys could hardly bear to take their eyes off the lovely redhead; once Reg was around Maura regular, he'd forget all about Abbie.

She shook her head and silently scolded herself. What did she care who Reg paid attention to? Maura had no doubt served hundreds of cups of tea to men like Reg and nothing had come of it. Besides, it might solve her problem of what to do with Maura while she was working.

"Cooky, do you have anybody lined up to help you?" she asked.

He shook his head and glanced at the dozens of men working around them. "These waddies would prob'ly be useless as tits on a boar hog when it comes to servin' up chuck."

"Would you mind if Maura helped you, then? She does all the cooking at my place."

Cooky cast a critical eye on the maid. "It's hot, dirty work," he said. "Peelin' spuds, gatherin' chips for the fire."

Maura looked him in the eye. "Aye, and I'd be wagering I've done worse work in me life."

He nodded. "All right, then. Hop down off that horse and we'll find you an apron. Time's a wastin'." He nodded to Abbie and set off toward the chuck wagon.

"You don't mind helping him, do you?" Abbie asked.

"Of course not." Maura dismounted and handed Abbie the reins to the mare. "I'd better go now, miss."

Abbie watched Maura walk across the gathering ground. Every few feet she was stopped by a cowboy who wanted to give his personal welcome to the beauty in their midst. Abbie hadn't seen so much bowing and scraping since a coach load of female dancers spent the night in town, on their way to California. The queen of England herself probably didn't receive such homage.

Thinking of England reminded her of Reg. She hadn't seen him since the night of the snowstorm, when he and

Alan and the others had left her cabin to return to their homes. To tell the truth, she'd been half afraid to face him again. What had she been thinking, kissing him that way? She'd told herself the brandy had addled her mind, but she knew she hadn't been drunk when she'd sought Reg's lips with her own. She'd merely wanted to satisfy her curiosity about what it would be like to touch a man that way. Being with Reg in that cave had presented the first opportunity she'd ever had to kiss a man, and she hadn't wanted to pass it by.

She'd never expected the simple meeting of lips could be so powerful. Indeed, the kiss she and Reg had shared had barely resembled the few chaste caresses she'd had the opportunity to witness. The moment she'd touched Reg, warmth raced through her, as if their lips formed a conduit for his body heat. Her heart pounded. Her skin tingled. If anyone else had related these symptoms to her, she might have thought them stricken with some dangerous fever.

If that were true, it was a fever she longed to experience again. She'd never felt more alive, more aware of her own body, than when she'd been in Reg's embrace. Was this what lust felt like? She feared it was, and hung her head in shame, even as she reveled in the memory of the moment.

"Are you going to sit up there gathering wool all day?"

She let out a small gasp and looked around to see Reg striding toward her. He was handsome as ever in his tailored suit and Stetson, English riding boots sheathing his well-muscled legs to the knees. She silently cursed the blush that heated her face at the sight of him. It was bad enough that she'd allowed herself to revel in her wanton behavior; now she would have to do her best to convince him the moment had meant nothing to her. After all, she was in love with Alan. She could never have any real feelings for this stuffy Englishman, could she?

"I . . . I was looking for Alan," she blurted when Reg stopped beside her. "I wanted to let him know we're here."

Reg nodded and looked away. Was she imagining things, or was that a flush coloring his cheeks? "He knows you're here. He saw Maura working with Green, and she told him."

"You'd better learn to call him Cooky or the cowboys will give you a hard time about it."

"As if their opinion of me makes a whit of difference." But his very stiffness as he spoke told her he valued the opinion of the men far more than he cared to admit.

She frowned at the top of his hat. She didn't like not being able to see his face, to read his emotions in his eyes. "You'll have a much easier time of it if you try harder to fit in," she said.

He shook his head. "The others would probably accept me soon enough. But Jackson relishes keeping the kettle boiling, so to speak."

She swung down out of the saddle to stand in front of him. But still he refused to meet her gaze. She fought the urge to put her hand on his shoulder in a gesture of comfort. Her body still trembled with the memory of the last time she touched him; she couldn't risk making contact again.

"Tuff will come around if you give him time," she said. "He's suspicious of outsiders."

He rolled his shoulders, as if shrugging off her advice. "Where will you be working this morning?"

"I'm not sure. Wherever I'm needed." She scanned the crowd around them and spotted Alan. "Hey, Alan, where do you want me to work?" she called, waving to him.

She noticed the way Reg winced at her unladylike behavior. Well, what did she care what he thought anyway? Alan was the man she wanted to impress.

Alan returned her wave and sauntered over to them.

She thought again how handsome he looked, dressed in a crisp white shirt, jeans, a calfskin vest and chaps. "Hello Abbie, Reg." He stopped a few feet in front of them and looked her up and down. "What's this outfit you're wearing?" he asked.

"It's a riding skirt." She gathered the skirt in one hand, enough to show him that it was divided. "Maura made it."

"Well, how about that?" He grinned. "You still going to be able to handle a lasso rope in a skirt?"

"Of course."

"Then, I want you with Fred Lazlo, roping calves." He turned to Reg. "Abbie always was top hand with a lariat."

Reg nodded. "Where do you want me to work?"

Alan rubbed his chin, considering. "I guess I figured you'd kinda take it easy and watch. Sort of an overseer's position."

"I didn't come here to 'take it easy,' " Reg said. "I came here to work, as everyone else is working."

Alan frowned. "I don't know. This is pretty tough work."

Abbie could see Reg bristle. He straightened like a porcupine readying its quills for an attack. "Just because I'm an Englishman and the son of a nobleman, doesn't mean I can't do my share of work. Some of these cattle are my cattle, and I intend to do everything I can to make the ranch a success."

Alan clapped him on the shoulder. "All right, then. You can help Jorge and his crew at the fires. I'll introduce you, and they'll show you what to do."

They nodded goodbye to Abbie and headed out through the crowd. She mounted once more and guided Toby toward the group of cowboys at the edge of the gathering. Some of these were men she had known most of her life. Others were new to the area. Young and old, veteran or new recruit, they all had one thing in common. They could make a rope obey their commands, sailing through the air to snag a fleeing calf's heels.

Usually the men paid little attention to her presence among them. When she'd dressed in men's clothes and tucked her hair under her hat, more than one newcomer had mistaken her for a boy. By the time they discovered the truth, she'd already proven herself as a capable hand.

Today, she noticed a difference in the men's behavior from the start. Men who had known her for years edged away from her, casting curious glances in her direction, but never meeting her gaze. Strangers eyed her with open suspicion.

"What's she doing here?" a dark-haired youth with a pock-scarred face asked.

"I've been assigned to help bring in the calves," she said, adjusting the fit of her leather gloves.

"Since when does a woman do a man's job?" the youth asked.

"Since she owns one of the ranches we're ropin' for." Moses Wilson spoke up. Moses was fifty years old if he was a day, and he'd taught Abbie much of what she knew about roping. He glanced at her with knowing eyes, then leaned over and spit tobacco juice on a dung beetle making its way across the ground. " 'Sides that, she's a dab hand with a rope."

"I never heard of such," the youth said.

Moses shrugged. "We ain't payin' you for your opinions," he said, and turned his horse toward the open prairie.

Alan stood on the back of a wagon and gave the orders to move out. Cheers shook the air as the various work crews raced across the prairie, headed in all four directions. They'd start with the calves closest to camp and work out, moving base over the next few days in order to cover as much territory as possible.

Abbie spotted her first calf. Making a mental note of the brand on the cow the calf ran beside, she sent her rope spinning. She leaned forward, Toby racing alongside the frightened calf. A flick of her wrist and the rope snaked out and caught the calf around the heels. Toby backed to tighten the rope, and they dragged the bawling animal to the branding fires. "This one's Lazy L," she called out to the men waiting to brand the calf to match its mother.

As the sun rose, Abbie settled into the rhythm of the work. Ride out, rope, return. The sun was warm on her back, the breeze cool on her face as she raced beside a fleeing calf. The air around the branding fires reeked of burnt hair and hide and the scent of burning chips—the dried dung that fueled the fires. This was the perfume of a roundup, an aroma steeped into her brain, lacing her memories.

After an hour of steady work, she took a break to rest and water Toby. She stood by the water barrel and watched the activity around the fires. Alan and Reg flipped a calf on its side. "Rocking W," the roper called, and Jorge reached for the glowing brand. The calf bawled and kicked as the hot iron pressed against its flank. While Jorge worked, Alan reached down between the animal's hind legs and neatly gelded the bull calf, while Reg cut a double notch in the right ear and tossed the severed slice of ear into a nearby bucket. The tally man noted the calf and its markings in his notebook. Later, he'd count the contents of the bucket and match it to the tally in his notebook.

The men stepped back, and the calf leapt to its feet and shook itself, then trotted over to its mother, waiting by a makeshift holding pen. Another roper arrived, dragging another calf, and the process began again.

Abbie admired Alan's smooth efficiency. He worked without wasted energy, quickly so as to produce the least trauma in the animal. A flick of his wrist and the job was done, while Reg still struggled to make the proper marks in the ear.

She shifted her gaze to the Englishman. He was holding his own, muscles straining as he pinned the calf's neck beneath his knee. He'd discarded his suit jacket, and his fine linen shirt was splattered with blood. More blood dripped from his expensive leather gloves and stained his trousers. He wore a grim expression, intent on the job at hand.

Abbie turned away, one hand over her stomach, trying to quell the sudden fluttering there. Where was the Reg she knew, the cocky Englishman with the impeccable manners? He'd been replaced by this fierce warrior, bloodied but not bowed. Her heart pounded as she watched him release the calf. The muscles in his thighs and buttocks tensed as he stood. She swallowed hard. This different Reg, stripped of fancy clothes and fancy manners, reduced to raw masculinity, drew her. He stirred emotions she didn't want to examine too closely. How could she be lusting after Reg when she meant to love Alan?

Chapter Nine

Reg could not find a part of his body that did not ache. Muscles burned from wrestling several hundred-pound calves to the ground. His fingers were crisscrossed with cuts from the knife that sliced him as often as it notched the calves' ears. His eyes stung from the constant assault of smoke from the branding fires, and his head throbbed from noise and heat and the sickening stench of burning hair and hide and the metallic odor of blood.

He dragged one arm across his brow, trying to keep the sweat from running into his eyes, and took a firmer grip on the ear of the calf that writhed beneath his knee. He would never think of these animals as cute babies again. Up close they were wide-eyed demons, all sharp, lashing hooves and butting heads. He wiped the knife on his pants leg and notched a V into the right ear. With practice, this was getting easier. He didn't slip as often, or take as long to make the cuts. He leapt up, standing clear of the thrashing animal. The calf righted itself, shook, then prodded by a cowboy, raced toward the gathered herd, to be reclaimed by its mother. Later, each ranch would "cut out"—separate from the herd—the cattle that bore that ranch's brand.

"How 'bout taking a break and grabbing a bite to eat?" Alan clapped a hand on his shoulder. "Come on, I'll show you where to wash up."

Reg looked down at his blood-spattered shirt and trousers and frowned. He doubted there was enough water in camp to get himself clean. This suit would be fit for nothing but the ragman after today.

He followed Alan to a wooden trough set up near the chuck wagon and took his place in a line of cowboys waiting to wash up. Aware of curious glances in his direction, he stood straighter. Here was his chance to prove himself to these men, by working among them and with them.

"Where's the calf you've been butchering?"

Reg snapped his head around at the sound of the familiar voice taunting him.

Tuff Jackson looked him up and down, then spat a stream of tobacco juice on the ground between his feet. "I ain't seen so much blood on any one person since I found old Andy Goebler scalped by Comanches."

Reg stared at the tobacco juice slowly sinking into the dirt at his feet. He clenched his jaw, commanding himself to rein in his temper. When he felt able to speak, he raised his head and gave Jackson a cool look. "As I recall, we are all here to work, not to engage in a fashion show." He narrowed his eyes. "Not that you would ever win a prize in either case."

Jackson blinked, the closest Reg had seen him come to flinching. Several of the men around them chuckled, and the foreman's expression grew darker. Reg sensed he had risen a few points in the estimation of some, though at the expense of Jackson's increasing animosity. He would have to deal with the foreman eventually; better to hold off until after the roundup. While he was here, he would scout for Jackson's replacement. He couldn't afford to be without a competent foreman for long.

After his turn at the wash trough, he took a tin plate from a stack at the end of the chuck wagon and walked to the fire, where Maura and Green—Cooky—were ladling out the contents of various iron pots.

Reg stared at his filled plate. Nothing looked familiar. Well, the dark brown stuff was some kind of beans. The other was apparently bread, though he was sure it wasn't made of wheat. The third dish was fried pieces of something. Liver, perhaps? He looked around for a place to sit. Of course, there were no tables or chairs. Everyone else was seated on the ground, holding his plate in one hand and shoveling food in with the other. So much for his tutor's lessons on table manners, he thought as he lowered himself to the ground.

He was taking his first bite of the fried substance when Abbie, accompanied by her dog, Banjo, settled down beside him. She hardly looked winded, though he knew she had been busy all morning roping calves. He wondered if her new skirts got in the way of her work. The brown wool puddled around her as she sat with her legs tucked under. The new wardrobe definitely lent her a softer, more feminine air, though he had to admit, part of him missed watching her walk or ride in the more form-fitting trousers.

"Tell me what this is I'm eating," he said. He paused to chew. Whatever it was, it was tough as hide, and had a peculiar flavor.

She leaned over a little to study his plate. "That's corn bread." She pointed to the chunk of bread. "Those are Cooky's famous beans. That stuff you just ate is calf fries."

"Calf fries?" He poked the curious food with his fork.

124   *Cynthia Sterling*

"Some people call them mountain oysters." She grinned, but a telltale flush swept up her neck.

"Uh, exactly what part of the calf is, uh, fried?" he asked.

The blush made its way to her cheeks. She looked away. "It's the, well, you know, the, um, the part Alan cuts off."

He clenched his teeth against the rising sour taste in his mouth. Good Lord, he had thought these Texans barbaric before; this proved it.

"You're looking a little green around the gills, chief. What's the matter? Don't you like the local specialty?" Jackson's jibe drew laughter from the crowd around them.

Reg stared down at the grayish lumps on his plate. He had given up the comforts of his class and society to come here, worked like the most menial slave in an attempt to gain these people's respect, and endured the scorn of Jackson and others without fighting back—but by God, there were some things he would not do. He offered one of the "calf fries" to Banjo. The dog gulped it down and wagged his tail for more. "To each his own," Reg said quietly.

"Why don't you admit what we already know?" Jackson snorted. "You're just another rich man playing at being a cowboy, thinkin' you're too good for the likes of us. You've never done an honest day's work in your whole damned life, and now it's about killing you."

Reg saw the unspoken agreement on the faces of the men gathered around him. Their expressions ranged from pity to open hostility, but to a man they looked on him as an outsider. Only Abbie's eyes spoke of understanding, and encouragement.

Jackson wiped his plate clean with a piece of corn bread. "I've seen men like you come and go out here. You stay for a season or so—long enough to ruin a ranch with your ignorance. Then you head back home and spend the rest of your life cadging free drinks from all your cronies, telling them what a lot of shit-kickers we are out here in Texas."

Reg heard Abbie's gasp. He tightened his grip on his plate. He didn't have to sit here and take this from Jackson. He didn't even have to *be* here. He could run things as well from his office at the ranch.

Only then he would be doing exactly what Jackson expected him to do. What Jackson *wanted* him to do.

If he backed down now, he would lose face before all these men. Before Abbie, too. So far, she and Alan were the only ones who seemed to have much faith in him; he was loath to let them down.

He raised his chin and addressed the foreman. "If you have something to say to me, Jackson, then say it," he said. "But I'll thank you to watch your language in the presence of a lady."

Jackson glanced at Abbie and let out a harsh laugh. "I say if she can't stand the heat, she oughta get out of the kitchen."

Reg shoved his plate aside and started to stand.

"Reg, no, it's all right." Abbie put a hand on his shoulder.

Reg glared at Jackson, silently daring him to say one more word, make one move toward him. He would show these Texans he could fight with more than words. The only thing that held him back now was the conviction that he ought to hold himself above the taunts of a man like Jackson.

The foreman's pale blue eyes stared back at Reg, unflinching. The air around them had gone dead quiet as everyone stared on the two would-be combatants.

"Time to get back to work, boys." Alan's command cut through the silence. He stepped up between Tuff and Reg and glanced at each man in turn. "Y'all know what to do. What are you waiting for?"

Reg grabbed up his plate and headed toward the chuck wagon. Abbie reached out to stop him, but he shrugged off her hand. His anger against Jackson hammered in his head; he didn't trust himself to talk to anyone at the moment.

But he couldn't avoid Alan. The rancher confronted him as he walked away from the washtub where he had left his plate. "I want you to work a spell helping to hold the herd," he said. He lowered his voice and studied Reg's face. "And for God's sake, stay clear of Tuff. He's like a wounded bull when he's riled. Give him a chance to cool off."

"He'd do well to stay clear of *me*," Reg grumbled. He shouldered past Alan, not waiting for a reply.

Working the herd gave Reg a chance to catch his breath. As he sat atop his horse, waiting for the next calf to head his way, he watched Jackson snatch a brand from the fire. With one booted foot planted on the calf to hold it steady, the foreman pressed the brand against the animal's flank, leaving a blackened mark in his wake.

The calf leapt up, still bawling, and a cowboy prodded it toward Reg, who stayed close by to ensure the calf and its mother did not try to break from the rest of the loosely bunched herd. He glanced at the brand as the calf galloped past. He didn't recall seeing the Circle 8 mark before.

"Whose brand is that?" he asked a cowboy riding by.

"Which one?"

"The Circle 8."

"Oh, that's Tuff Jackson's brand. He's got a little herd he runs mostly up around Spanish Creek."

Reg looked back at the calf. Recovered from its ordeal, it was now playfully butting heads with a calf marked with Alan's A7 brand. He frowned. Was it usual for a foreman to have his own herd? It seemed to him such a practice would encourage cheating.

"Hey, Worthington! Heads up. Got one headed your way." He snapped to attention in time to head off a calf intent on bolting across the prairie. With little need for direction from him, his horse blocked the fugitive's path and guided it back toward the herd.

Reg spent the rest of the afternoon watching Jackson. He seemed to have an awful lot of calves with his brand, while Abbie's man Jorge, who worked the other fire, hardly ever pulled that iron from the coals. After a while he began counting, and discovered that Tuff branded more calves overall than Jorge. Did speed and experience account for this rapid turnover? Everyone agreed Jackson was an excellent cow man.

Why, then, couldn't Reg shake the feeling that something was wrong?

Abbie stirred the remains of her son-of-a-gun stew and fought to avoid looking toward the chuck wagon. But a burst of laughter broke through her resolve and dragged her gaze in that direction. As she'd expected, Maura stood by the wagon, holding court with a line of cowboys. Donnie Best was there, along with his friend Tim O'Rourke. Even Banjo had forsaken Abbie in favor of the maid and her admirers. The dog sat at Maura's feet, gazing up at her with an expression of doggy adoration. A tin box lay open on the pull-out shelf by her side, and she had her head bent over Reg's hand, carefully daubing salve on his palm.

Reg's face looked grim. Abbie felt a stab of sympathy. The black draught salve burned as it sank into the cuts— a sure sign, her father had told her, that it was working.

But then, Reg's expression might have nothing to do with the salve or his cut palm. He'd been scowling all afternoon; was he still brooding over Tuff's insults at dinner, or was something else the matter?

Maura laughed again, and the cowboys joined in, their deep chuckles a counterpoint to her lighter sounds. The heat of the cook fire had tinged her cheeks a faint pink, and her hazel eyes danced with merriment. Abbie felt drab in comparison, and she was irritated at the maid for being in such a good humor after working all day. Really now, did she have to spend so much time rubbing that salve into Reg's hand?

"Never saw the men so anxious to be patched up before." Alan took a seat on the ground next to Abbie. He smiled and nodded toward the line at the chuck wagon. "Next thing you know, they'll be getting hurt on purpose, just for a chance to visit with the nurse."

Abbie smoothed her skirts over her knees. "Maura is very pretty."

"Yes, she is." He smiled. "You're looking right smart yourself these days. I guess Reg was right—having a little feminine influence is good for you."

She flushed. Surely Reg hadn't told Alan about their bargain. "When did he say that?"

"Oh, that day we met Maura, I mean, Miss O'Donnell. Reg offered her the job as your maid, said she was just what you'd been looking for."

She nodded, relieved. Then the thought hit her that Alan had actually sought her out, and complimented her to boot. Maybe Reg's plan was working already. Smiling, she looked up, only to find he was still watching Maura.

She searched for some topic to draw his attention back to her. Her eyes flickered to Reg as he moved away from the wagon. "Do you think Tuff will make more trouble about the argument he had with Reg at dinner?"

"I don't know. A lot depends on what Reg does next." He glanced at her. "The men are still trying to make up their minds about him. A lot of them think what Tuff said is true."

"Do you think it's true?"

He rubbed the back of his neck. "At one time I did, maybe. Not anymore. I never saw a man work harder to prove himself." He grinned. "If he stays here long enough, we might make a cowboy out of him yet."

"What do you mean, if he stays?" The idea had never crossed her mind that Reg would leave. Why would anyone come here and want to leave?

Alan shrugged. "I kind of got the impression that he meant to go home as soon as things were running smoothly here. After all, England's where his family is. I imagine he's got some property there, maybe even some sort of title, or responsibilities."

Abbie nodded. "Of course."

"Speaking of responsibilities, I've got a few of my own I'd better see to." He rose and brushed dirt from his pants, then ambled off across the campground.

Abbie traced a pattern in the dirt with her finger and thought about Reg. He was different from the rest of them—that was true. But she'd grown used to his odd ways—his formal dress and stilted manners. His differences didn't stand out now the way they had when she'd first met him. Now she thought about the things they had in common. They were both outsiders in the cowboy world. They had to try to fit in with a group that didn't readily accept foreigners or women. They had to learn to adapt. Well, she had learned. Reg was having a harder time with that lesson.

He'd asked her to teach him, hadn't he? If she failed to do a good job, he was liable to sail home that much sooner. Maybe before he'd finished teaching her all she needed to know about being a lady.

She stood and brushed the dirt from her skirts. No sense wasting any more time, she thought. She wasn't going to let Reg leave yet, not when they were just beginning to be friends.

Reg spread his bedroll on the edge of the fire, a little apart from the main group of men. Mouse was staked nearby; he could hear the horse cropping the short grass. Some of the men were already asleep, wrapped in their blankets, hats tilted over their faces.

Reg sat on his bed, staring toward the fire, too keyed up to sleep just yet. A shadow fell over him, and he looked up to see Abbie. "I came to say thanks," she said.

"Thanks for what?" He rose to face her in the flickering light. He caught a whiff of the lavender Maura must have added to Abbie's clothes trunk. The scent reminded him of the lavender that bloomed in kitchen gardens all over England. It was a soft, feminine aroma that seemed as out of place here on the Texas plains as he felt.

"Thanks for defending me earlier, with Tuff. Even though it wasn't necessary." Abbie tilted her head to look up at him, and the light fell soft across her cheeks. She had removed her hat, and her hair curled in wisps around her face.

She looked so young, and vulnerable. He fought the urge to reach out and brush back the delicate strands of hair. "I couldn't let him stand there and insult you like that."

She shook her head. "But he was right. I chose to be here. To do this work. I've been around cowboys all my life. They aren't going to change because of me. They shouldn't have to."

He tensed. What made her so convinced these Texans were in the right? "Are you telling me they're exempt from common courtesy?"

She sighed. "I don't want them to treat me any differently than they would any other rancher. I've worked hard to get to that point." She looked away, her eyes hidden in shadows. "Don't you see?" she said, her voice pleading. "It's the only way I can succeed in this business."

How far did one have to go before giving in to succeed was a failure in itself? How much did one give up before losing the best part of oneself? The questions nagged at Reg as he looked at Abbie. "So anyone different is doomed to fail, is that it?" he asked. "A woman or a foreigner is driven out."

"It's a hard life out here. It demands a lot of people. That's the way it is."

"I'm not sure if I can accept that. I'm used to living life on my own terms."

She raised her eyes to meet his once more, and this time her gaze held a challenge. "My father used to say, 'The nail that sticks up gets hammered down.' "

"What is that supposed to mean?"

"I think it means you can be too proud for your own good. It doesn't hurt to let the other man win the small battles, as long as you win the war."

He folded his arms across his chest. "Are you saying I should give in to Tuff?"

"Why ask for trouble?"

He shook his head. "I didn't ask for it, but now that it's here, I won't run away."

She was silent for a moment, and he thought she would leave. Then she raised her hand and lightly touched his wrist. "This is about more than what he said at dinner, isn't it?"

He hesitated. When all was said and done, Abbie was one of these people. How much could he trust her? "What is your opinion of Tuff Jackson?" he asked.

She shrugged. "Everyone says he's a good man with cattle. He's lived here a long time."

"Yes, but what do *you* think?"

"I don't really know him that well . . . but I guess I don't really like him that much."

"I don't trust him," he said. He glanced at the men nearby. They were sleeping or visiting in small groups. He bent his head close to Abbie, until he could feel the warmth of her skin, smell the clean scent of her hair. "What can you tell me about branding?"

She frowned. "What do you want to know?"

"Are there ways to brand a calf—but not really brand it?"

"Well, there's hair branding."

"What's that?"

"That's when the brander presses the iron against the calf just long enough to burn off the hair. It looks good from a distance, but after a few days or weeks, someone can come along and rebrand the calf with another mark."

"In other words, steal the calf?"

He heard the sharp intake of her breath. "You don't think Tuff's hair branding, do you?" she whispered.

"Certainly not every animal. But I watched him today, and he seemed awfully quick with some of them."

She shook her head. "I don't know. Tuff has lived here for a long time. Grady trusted him, and Mr. Preston, who owned the ranch before that. Why would he risk everything to steal a few calves?"

"I found out today he already has his own herd."

She nodded. "My father would never allow that sort of thing. But some folks think it's a way to keep a good man working for you."

"I don't like it, but I don't suppose I can do anything about it now. One thing I know—I'll be watching Jackson very closely from here on out. I don't intend for anyone to cheat me out of what is rightly mine."

Her eyes were huge in the darkness, deep pools drawing

him in. Her lips parted, and in an instant Reg was back in that cave, ready to lose himself in her kiss. His heart pounded, and he forced himself to step back, distancing himself from a danger as great as any Tuff Jackson presented.

"Be careful," she whispered.

The words lingered in his ears as he turned away. Of all the complications he might have expected to make his work here more difficult, he would have never thought a physical attraction to a fellow rancher would be one of them!

Nothing would come of these feelings; he would see to that. Not only were he and Abbie totally unsuited for each other, but he had already promised to help her win another man. A man he counted as one of his only friends.

He looked out across the campground, trying to sort out his muddled feelings. A familiar figure stepped out from the shadow of the hoodlum wagon, which held the cowboys' bedding. Tuff Jackson gave him a malevolent glare, then moved on into the darkness, like a highwayman lying in wait. Reg clenched his hands into fists. Jackson and the rest wouldn't get the better of him. He wouldn't go home a failure again.

Chapter Ten

Reg had never spent so much time out of doors in his
life as he did during the next few days. Even in his sailing
years he had had the solid feel of oak planks beneath his
feet and the confining walls of a ship's cabin to block out
the sky. Now he had no such refuge. The Texas plains
stretched around him, an endless sweep of wind-bent grass
beneath a pale banner of sky. How could one help but
feel insignificant in the face of such vastness? Perhaps the
Texans' brashness was only an attempt to keep from losing
themselves in the great expanse of land.

He found himself viewing the land as a challenge to be
met in the same way he fought to overcome the Texans'
prejudice. He vowed to learn to sleep on the hard ground
without complaining, to lean into the wind that constantly
buffeted him, and to ignore the swirling dust that found
its way into his shirt and his food and his blankets.

In spite of the hardships, he discovered things to admire
in the landscape. Wildflowers bloomed in profusion in

places, carpeting the prairie as if some painter had spilled his pallet. Deer, quail, prairie hens, and a host of other wildlife that he never tired of watching for lived here. At night, the stars shone so bright and clear, they looked like shards of diamond against a field of black velvet.

"Do the stars look like this in England?" Abbie rode her horse up beside his as he took his turn at watch one evening.

He glanced over at her. She wore a man's blanket coat against the night chill, and her hair was tucked under her hat. But the masculine garb did little to conceal her identity. Something about the slightness of her shoulders, or the tilt of her chin, telegraphed her femininity to one who knew what to look for. How could he ever have thought she was a boy that day they first met?

He reluctantly pulled his gaze from her and looked up at the sky once more. "They're never this bright in England. I don't think they're this bright anywhere else on earth."

She moved closer, until her leg practically touched his. "My father used to tell me every star was an angel's lantern, waiting to guide some soul home." She sighed. "I used to wonder which one belonged to my mother."

He couldn't keep from looking at her. She had her chin pointed skyward, her neck looking very white and smooth. "I'm trying to imagine you as a little girl," he said.

She laughed. "More like a little boy, really." She looked at him, smiling. "No petticoats and pinafores for me. I wore pants and boots and rode my own pony. When I was five, Daddy gave me my first little rope to twirl."

"But why? Why not dress you in pinafores and give you dolls to play with? Why make you something you're not?"

Her face took on a fond expression. "We were alone. Daddy had work to do. He needed a helper, someone who could ride and rope and take over the ranch one day when he was gone."

"He needed a son."

"He never once said he regretted having me instead." She leaned forward and stroked her horse's long mane. "I can't complain. Not many women my age have what I have—land and cattle and money in the bank." She raised her chin and gave him a defiant look. "That ought to count for something, don't you think? After all, you can't take fine manners and pretty dresses to the bank."

"Or tailored suits and a British accent either, I'm afraid." He stroked the lapel of his suit coat. In the darkness, the dirt and bloodstains didn't show. Not that they bothered him so much anymore. He was beginning to think of the stains as battle scars, proof that he had fought and lived to tell the tale. In the end, he hoped to count himself among the victors.

Abbie edged her horse out in front of him. "Ride with me while I make a circuit," she said.

His horse fell in step with hers as they circled the herd in a slow walk. "Teach me another lesson," she said after a moment.

He blinked. So despite her talk of liking her lot in life, Abbie hadn't given up on their scheme to win Alan. "What do you want to know?"

"When Alan comes to visit about the horse, what shall we talk about?"

"*Don't* ask him about business," he said.

"Why not? Didn't you tell me before to talk about what interests him?"

"Business is the one thing the two of you have always had in common. He won't think of you any differently if you remind him of that."

"Then, what should we talk about?"

"Ask him if he ever gets lonely."

"Why should he be lonely? He lives with his father, and they must have twenty cowboys working for them."

Reg smiled into the darkness. "A man can be surrounded by other men and still be lonely for the company of a woman."

"Oh."

He could sense the comprehension overtaking her. He wondered if she was blushing, but the darkness and the shadowing hat brim hid her face from view. "Don't you get lonely, Abbie?" he asked gently.

"Yes."

The word was filled with longing. He felt as if a hand clamped around his heart. He tried to imagine all the years Abbie had spent alone in that little cabin, waiting for the right man to come along and see beyond the cowboy clothes and mannish ways to the woman she truly was. Would Alan ever realize what a great prize she offered him? He swallowed. "It's all right to tell Alan that, if you want," he said.

"All right." She nodded. "What else?"

"By then we trust Alan will be carrying his end of the conversation, and things will move along nicely."

"But what if he doesn't?"

Reg frowned. *Then, he's blinder than I thought.* "You might mention how nice you imagine it would be to come home to someone every evening."

"Maybe I should tell him how much I like children."

The fist around Reg's heart squeezed tighter. A picture of Abbie cradling a golden-haired baby flashed through his mind. The image had a haunting appeal. He resolutely shoved the thought aside. "No, I wouldn't mention children just yet," he said. "He might think you're trying to trap him."

"But that's exactly what I'm trying to do, isn't it?" She sighed again, a heavy, sad sound. "I don't know, Reg. Why can't Alan love me just because I'm me?"

Yes, why can't he? Reg shifted in the saddle, wrestling with the question. "I suppose, knowing you all your life, he has formed a certain image of you in his mind, an image of you as just another rancher, a cowboy. It's similar to a horse wearing blinders—he sees only what is in front of him. We have to find a way to take those blinders off, to allow Alan to see all the things you are in addition to being a rancher. We have to show you to him as a woman."

"Is that why it's so easy for you to see me as a woman—because you haven't known me all my life?" She leaned toward him. "Or is it because you're different in other ways?"

"Because I'm English?" He shook his head. "I cannot say we have a reputation as being particular connoisseurs of women."

"It's more than that. You're . . . more thoughtful. You notice things."

"My father said I was the daydreamer in the family. A serious fault in his eyes."

"It's not a fault at all." She glanced around. "A person can be too practical, you know. There's more to life than cows and horses."

He raised one eyebrow. "Such blasphemy from a Texan?"

She laughed. "We're not that different, are we, Reg?" she asked. "My father made me into what he wanted so I could take over his business. It sounds to me as if your father tried to make you into *his* kind of businessman, and you refused to be poured into that mold. I'd say that was a kind of success in itself."

His stomach quivered. No one had ever, *ever* seen his defiance of his father as a success. He let out a deep breath and shook his head. "No, that's not success. Just stubborn foolishness. It never brought me anything but failure."

"But you won't fail this time, will you? Alan said as soon

as you have things running smoothly, you intend to return home."

He nodded. "I have to. I intend to prove to my father once and for all that I can succeed—on his terms."

She turned away from him and stared out across the still prairie. "I've never known anyone quite like you, Reg. I'm going to miss you when you go."

He tried to shrug off the sudden melancholy that blanketed him. "I'll be here for many months yet. By the time I leave, you may be glad to see me depart."

She turned to look back at him. He could feel the caress of her gaze, even though he couldn't see her eyes. "I don't think I'll ever be glad to see you go, Reg. I'd as soon you stayed forever." Then she turned her horse and rode away from him, fading into the shadows somewhere on the edge of the herd.

Reg stared after her. The words weren't idle sentiment; he knew she meant them. Worse still, he realized he would miss her. How strange to think he had wandered half the world, only to find his first real friend on the vast Texas plains.

Abbie gazed blindly out over the backs of the sleeping cattle, silently cursing her wayward tongue. Why had she told Reg she didn't want him to leave? A real lady would never come right out with her opinion like that, unasked.

She'd been trying to let him know she liked him—as a friend. He'd seemed so down and all about his father; she'd wanted to cheer him up. Instead, she'd managed to once again confirm what he already knew—that she was a hoyden who said, and did, the first thing that popped into her head.

She sighed and shifted in the saddle. At least she didn't have to worry about Reg getting the wrong idea about her feelings for him. He'd been nothing but a gentleman since they'd kissed in the cave, as if he realized the kiss had been prompted by curiosity, not passion.

So why did she feel this twinge of regret? After all, Alan was the man she wanted to attract, not Reg. Reg was a good friend, and her teacher.

He was also her pupil, though not the most cooperative student she'd ever come across. She didn't know when she'd met a man whose pride could be so easily offended. Every time he had to ask her for help, you'd have thought he was being forced to eat ground glass for supper. He could hardly get the words out.

A figure on horseback moved out from the group of horses. She glanced up at the moon, high in the sky. Time to change watch. As the rider headed toward her, she recognized Tuff Jackson's familiar form. Tuff had been cowboying in these parts ever since she could remember. He'd worked his way up from horse wrangler to top hand in just a few years. Folks said there wasn't a better cowboy in Texas than Tuff Jackson.

Too bad he and Reg got off on the wrong foot, she thought as Tuff rode up. The foreman could have taught Reg a lot.

"Evenin'," she said.

He grunted and reined his horse in beside her.

She watched as he pulled a twist of tobacco from his pocket and bit off a hunk. "It's quiet tonight," she said.

He nodded, jaw working. "Saw you talkin' to Little Lord Fauntleroy," he said after a moment.

She stiffened. "Reg isn't at all like you think."

Tuff leaned over and spat on the ground. "I had him pegged the day he walked in the door and took the first look down his long nose at me. His kind won't last long out here. Hard livin' wears them down fast."

"I think you're wrong."

He looked her up and down. "Yeah, well, it's easy enough to see those fine manners and smooth talking have taken you in." He shook his head. "I used to think better of you than that, Abbie. You've gone all soft on us, acting like some simpering schoolmarm, with your fancy hairdos and long skirts. Thought your pa raised you up to have more sense."

"He raised me to have the sense not to judge a man before he's had a chance to prove himself." She gripped the saddle horn, anger making the words almost stick in her throat. "And he taught me not to cheat a man—especially right under his nose."

Tuff stopped chewing and leaned toward her. "Who said anything about cheating?" He spoke softly, an edge of warning in his voice.

"Reg isn't stupid, you know. He's seen how many calves you've put your brand on."

Tuff spat. "He can't prove those calves aren't mine—which they are." He straightened in the saddle. "I've put in a lot of years, working for other people. Nobody that knows me is gonna begrudge me getting a little back now—especially not from some damned British syndicate."

"It's stealing whether you take from a British syndicate or from your own mother. It's still wrong."

He shrugged. "Who says I stole anything? Who are people around here going to believe—some tight-ass foreigner or a cow man they've known half their lives?"

She glared at him. How could she have ever thought this man was the image of what a cowboy should be? Her father would have knocked Tuff off his horse for saying half the things he'd said tonight. If she'd been a man, she would have done the same.

But she wouldn't let him ride away tonight thinking he was getting away with theft. "Reg was asking me about hair branding the other night," she said quietly.

He raised his head slightly, like a mustang, ready to bolt. "Planning to change a few of his neighbors' brands, is he? That's one way to get free passage home—in a pine box."

She leaned toward him, keeping her voice low. "Maybe I ought to suggest Alan check the brands on the calves you burned today," she said. "What would he find?"

He shot out a hand and grabbed her by the collar, almost dragging her from the saddle. "You'd better watch what you say, little girl," he growled. "You want to play rough, I'll show you how."

She was close enough to see his pale eyes, glittering in the shadows beneath his hat brim. Her heart hammered in her throat. Banjo began barking, jumping and growling as he raced around her horse.

"That damned dog's gonna stampede the herd."

"Then, you'd better let go of my coat."

He released her with a shove, so that she had to clamp her legs tight against the saddle to keep from falling. Tuff glared at her. "You'd best stay out of what's none of your business," he said. "Or you'll wish you had."

Shaken, but determined not to show it, she turned Toby away from him and walked him toward her waiting bedroll. Inside, she wanted to spur the horse to a gallop and ride fast and far away from Tuff's hate-filled stare. As her first panic subsided, she felt sick to her stomach. A man she had respected and trusted all her life had turned dishonest and mean right before her eyes. Or had that side of Tuff Jackson been there all along? Maybe she'd been too busy trying to fit in with the men to study them with a critical eye before. If she looked closer, would she see things to dislike in all of them?

She'd never thought the view from a woman's perspective would be so unsettling.

* * *

"I don't like the looks of those storm clouds." Alan crouched beside Reg as the two men finished their breakfast the next morning.

Reg followed his friend's gaze to the line of blue-black thunderclouds hovering low on the horizon. "Can we expect another norther?"

Alan shook his head. "More likely rain, coming from the east like that. Lots of lightning and thunder." He drained his coffee cup and set it on the ground beside him. "Stampede weather. I can almost guarantee it."

Reg frowned. He had heard talk around the campfire about stampedes—tales of cattle running out of control for miles across the plains. Right now, by his best estimate, more than a third of the Ace of Clubs stock was gathered in the roundup herd. The thought of having them scattered across the countryside once more made his stomach clench. "What do we do if there's a stampede?"

"Chase 'em down and try to get them into a mill." At Reg's puzzled look, he explained: "We try to turn the leaders and get them running into a circle. The rest of the herd will follow. They'll wear themselves out, running in a circle like that." He stood and straightened his hat on his head. "Maybe we'll get lucky and the storm will pass around us without doing much harm."

As Reg headed toward the branding fires, he felt the first raindrop strike his cheek. Fat drops splattered the dust at his feet, and thunder rumbled in the distance. The storm wasn't going to go around them. Indeed, it looked as if the brunt of it would pass directly over them.

The rain hissed and sizzled on the hot fire, sending up wisps of steam. Cowboys donned slickers and cursed the weather, but work did not visibly slow. Within a hour,

Reg was soaked to the skin and caked with mud. He had discarded his slicker after only ten minutes, when he discovered the long coat got in the way of wrestling calves to the ground and holding them long enough to brand and cut.

Reg's mood grew as dark as the weather. The constant moaning of the cattle set his teeth on edge, and he flinched at every crack of lightning. He held himself tensed, anticipating the sudden charge of the herd, the way a man with his head on the block might anticipate the fall of the executioner's ax.

"Heads up! Got a lively one for you!" Abbie skidded her horse to a halt beside the crew by the fire, showering them with a spray of mud. She laughed as the calf she dragged fought for footing on the slippery ground. "You all look like a bunch of half-drowned calves," she said cheerfully. "You gonna let a little rain get you down?"

"I don't notice you down here in the mud," Reg snapped. Despite water dripping off the brim of her hat and running in rivers down her slicker, Abbie appeared to be as energetic as ever. The dampness made tendrils of hair curl around her face in a soft cloud, and lent a dewy quality to her skin.

She grinned and shook her head. "You boys seem to be doing a fine job without me."

Reg tried to wipe the mud from his brow with the back of his hand, but only succeeded in smearing it in his hair. "We'd no doubt do even better if *some* people would take their duties more seriously," he growled. He grabbed the calf and forced it to the ground, then jerked her rope from around the animal's neck. "The cattle are nervous enough without your riding up here at a gallop like that."

Her smile vanished. "I don't need *you* telling me how to do my job." She whirled around, then spurred her horse, sending a new shower of mud over Reg and the calf.

Reg looked away and found Alan watching him. The rancher winked. "Women sure can be touchy, can't they?" he asked.

Reg grunted in agreement and set about notching the calf's ear. Already, he regretted his words to Abbie. But why did she have to be so bloody cheerful, when he felt as if another disaster hovered on the horizon?

He doubted if anyone could understand the dark foreboding that sank into his bones with the dampness. He didn't understand the feeling himself, but he recognized it from past failures. The weather had conspired against him before; he couldn't shake the belief that it was about to happen again.

The rain had slowed to a heavy mist by the time they broke for the noon meal—which the Texans always referred to as dinner. Reg took his place in line and accepted a plate of beans and bacon, though he hadn't much appetite.

Searching for a place to eat, he spotted Abbie seated next to Maura. He owed Abbie an apology, and now was as appropriate a time as any to offer it. Perhaps Maura's presence would soften any sharp retort Abbie might have prepared for him.

But before he could make his way to the two women, Alan stepped up. Their smiles and gestures made it obvious, even from a distance, that they were inviting him to join them.

Reg drew up short. He didn't mind making amends with Maura looking on, but he couldn't bring himself to admit his wrongdoing in front of Alan. He lowered himself to the ground and set his plate in his lap. He would wait here until Alan left and talk to Abbie then.

As he ate, his gaze continually strayed to the threesome. Abbie sat between Alan and Maura. She smiled often, and fluttered her lashes at Alan like a skilled coquette. She leaned toward him, and even reached up and touched his shoulder for a moment. Reg tensed. So much for Abbie's claims that she did not know how to flirt.

Their laughter drifted to him, and the low murmur of conversation. Alan bent his head toward Abbie, as if to better hear what she had to say. Maura leaned forward, too, to complete the cozy grouping, three heads together, oblivious to the chaos around them.

Reg shoved his plate aside, unable to force down the cold beans and corn bread any longer. What were they talking about that was so interesting?

Abbie looked toward him once, and for a brief moment their eyes met. Her expression clouded, and she quickly focused her attention on Alan once more.

Reg snatched up his plate and stood. He would talk to Abbie later—alone. Right now, he had work to do.

Most of the other men were still eating, so he decided to take Mouse and ride a circuit of the herd, to satisfy himself that all was in order. He was headed toward the spot where he had staked the big gray when he spotted Tuff Jackson adjusting the saddle on another horse. Now wasn't the time for another face-off with the surly foreman. He started to veer out of the way. But then something made him pull up short.

He took a closer look at the horse with Tuff and recognized Abbie's gelding, Toby. Why would Jackson have Abbie's horse?

As Reg started toward Jackson, the foreman turned and saw him. He stiffened, then slipped a long peg through a loop at the end of the stake rope. With his heel, he gouged a hole in the ground, dropped the pegged rope in and filled the hole in with dirt. As Abbie had explained to Reg, a horse on a long lead couldn't pull free, provided the hole was dug deep enough. "You want something from me, chief?" he asked, with the familiar scorn that set Reg's teeth on edge.

"What are you doing with Miss Waters' horse?"

"Came unstaked. Figured I'd better tie it down before it wandered off." He straightened and fixed Reg with a challenging glare. "What about it?"

Tuff's gaze shifted to Reg's shoulder, where a glob of mud rested like an epaulet. He studied the blood-smeared shirt and wet trousers, a glint of amusement coming into his eyes.

Reg was conscious of Tuff's own comparative neatness. His slicker and chaps bore signs of wear and rain, but they merely added to the man's aura of rough competence. Tuff looked like a man at home in the outdoors, ready to tame the wilderness rather than be tamed by it.

Reg thought the differences in the two of them went beyond appearances. Tuff was a man who had succeeded in everything he had ever tried. He had no place for, or patience with, failure in his life. Whenever they met, Reg felt as if he were confronting a shark that scented blood. As he stared into Jackson's cold blue eyes, the hair at the back of his neck rose up in warning.

He was opening his mouth to speak when the ground shook beneath them and a loud *Crack!* rent the air. Bark exploded from a tree near the horses as lightning blazed to the ground. A woman screamed, horses reared up on their stake ropes and men shouted curses. The crash of thunder from the skies was replaced by a more ominous rumble as cattle, bawling with fear, began to race across the prairie.

"Stampede!" Tuff shouted and ran for his horse.

Reg followed close behind the foreman, reaching the

area where he had staked Mouse in time to see the big gray bolt and race out across the prairie.

"Bloody hell!" Reg stared after the gray as men galloped past him in pursuit of the herd. He whirled, searching for another mount. The other horses in his string were in the herd, unsaddled. Reg was a competent rider, but he didn't think he was up to the challenge of riding the half-wild Texas broncs bareback.

Then he spotted Abbie's gelding, still staked where Jackson had left it. He ran to the horse and untied it. "Where's Abbie?" he asked a passing cowboy.

"Saw her over at the chuck wagon tending Maura. Looked like that Irish gal cut her head or somethin'."

She wouldn't be needing her horse if she was busy nursing Maura, Reg reasoned. He swung up into the saddle and spurred the animal into the race.

The gelding was fast, and soon caught up with the tail of the herd. Reg watched the other cowboys, observing how they worked to keep the cattle bunched together as they raced along, seemingly out of control. Presumably men at the front of the herd would be trying to turn the leaders—to get them into a mill, Alan had said.

Reg rode alongside the racing cattle. He was close enough to read the brands on their flanks, to see their nostrils flare with each panicked breath, their eyes rolled back with fear. The air was thick with the smell of churned earth and sweating livestock. The ground shook with the pounding of their hooves, and the sound was a deafening rumble, like a freight train bearing down upon him.

A cow with horns as wide as bedposts veered from the pack. Reg spotted her and tried to bring the gelding up to block her path. He thought he had succeeded, but as they came alongside, the cow swung her head, barely grazing the horse with the tips of her horns. The gelding jumped sideways, narrowly avoiding a collision. Reg struggled to keep his seat, but even as his legs clamped around the horse, he felt the saddle slipping. The gelding bucked again, and he felt himself falling, into the path of the stampeding herd.

Chapter Eleven

Abbie was slipping her dinner plate into the tub of soapy water Cooky kept by the chuck wagon when the sharp crack of lightning rent the air. A high-pitched scream cut through her, and she whirled to see Maura bent over, clutching the side of her face. As she took a step toward her friend, the ground began to vibrate, and she heard an ominous rumbling that didn't originate from the sky.

Heart pounding, she looked over her shoulder and saw a wave of cattle surging across the prairie, a rolling tide oblivious to anything in its path. Around her, men shouted and vaulted onto horses, spurring their mounts to a gallop in pursuit of the herd.

She started to join them, then remembered Maura. *I'll just make sure she's all right,* she told herself. *Then I'll catch up with the others.*

Abbie and Cooky reached the maid at the same time. Abbie gasped when she saw the blood running down the side of her friend's face. "Looks like a splinter from the tree done gashed her," Cooky said. He gently pulled Maura's hand away from the cut.

"I knew I shouldn't have been goin' out today without me rabbit's foot," Maura wailed. "I forseen bad luck in me tea leaves last night." She flinched as Cooky probed the deep cut just below her temple.

Abbie glanced over her shoulder at the stampeding herd and the pursuing cowboys. Already, they were a long way off. If she waited much longer, she'd never catch them.

"This is gonna need sewin'," Cooky announced.

She jerked her attention back to Maura. The gaping cut would definitely need a few stitches to help it heal and minimize scarring. Then she realized Maura and Cooky were both staring at her. "What are you looking at me for?" she asked, backing away. "You don't think *I'm* going to sew her up, do you?"

"It'll be jus' like stitching fancy needlework," Cooky said.

Abbie shook her head. "I don't do needlework." She turned to Maura, pleading. "Tell him I can't sew."

"I thought all womenfolk did that stuff," Cooky said.

"Miss Abbie's not like other women," Maura said gently. "She's not been taught women things."

Abbie flushed. Had she detected a note of pity in Maura's voice? Was she less of a woman because she didn't know how to bake and sew and arrange flowers?

"I reckon I could patch you up right enough if Miss Abbie will help me. Come on over here." Cooky led them to the fold-down table at the back of the chuck wagon. "You sit right up here. Miss Abbie, you get the medicine kit."

Abbie sighed. It was just as well the men were already out of reach. Maura needed her more right now. She retrieved the gray metal box from its nest amid the sacks of beans and flour and coffee. "What do you want me to do?" she asked, taking the kit to Cooky.

"Well, now, first I reckon you better fetch the jug of whiskey I keeps for snakebite. It's hid down behind the driver's seat."

She found the heavy crockery jug wrapped in a faded flour sack. She brought it to Cooky, and he pulled the stopper. "All right, Miss Maura, I want you to take a big swig o' this."

Maura stared at the jug, her blue eyes wide and frightened. "Oh, no, I couldn't be drinking that," she protested.

Cooky shook his head, his expression grave. "It's the only painkiller we got, miss. I couldn't conscience sewin' on you lessen I thought you'd had at least a little somethin' to take the edge off."

Maura worried her lower lip between her teeth. "All right," she said, her voice faint. She took the jug and stared down at the open mouth, then raised it to her lips and took a long drink. Abbie watched in amazement as Maura swallowed once, twice, three times. When she lowered the jug, her face was flushed, her eyes bright. Cooky grinned at her. She grinned back.

"Goes down smooth, don't it?" As if to demonstrate, he took a drink himself. Then he handed the jug to Abbie. "I figured a fine gentleman like Mr. Worth'nton wouldn't want no ordinary corn liquor on his chuckwagon, so I borrowed some o' that aged whiskey from a cut-glass decanter he keeps in his study." He pushed up his sleeves and opened the medicine kit. "Now, lets see what we gots here."

Abbie set the jug aside and watched as he unwrapped a packet of needles and another of silk thread. The needle looked tiny in his thick fingers, the thread very white against his dark skin. "All right now, Miss Maura, you hold on to Miss Abbie here. And no matter what, you gots to stay still. I'd hate to see your pretty little face with a big old ugly scar."

Abbie put her arm around Maura and held tightly to one hand. She felt dizzy as she watched the needle sink into her friend's skin. Maura sucked in her breath, and Abbie had to look away. But though Maura squeezed Abbie's hand until it ached, the maid never flinched.

"You know I sewed up your daddy once, Miss Abbie." Cooky made a neat knot in the first stitch and clipped the thread with a pair of scissors from the medical kit.

"You did?" Abbie tried to remember a time when her father had had stitches, but could not.

"You was a little bitty thing then. He used to strap you on behind his horse, and you'd ride with him all morning. After dinner, you'd bed down in the chuck wagon for a nap."

She had vague memories of snuggling down amid a pile of bedrolls, lulled to sleep by the familiar aromas of wool blankets, harness leather and boiling coffee. "Why did you have to sew him up?" she asked.

"Oh, he got crossways with a calf he was cuttin'. Knife slipped and gashed his arm." He chuckled. "Didn't have no silk, so I stitched him up with red thread from a flour sack. Looked pretty funny, he did, with that fancy stitchin' up his arm, but nobody woulda dared say anything about it."

Abbie nodded. Her father was not the kind of man others dared laugh at.

"Your daddy was jus' about the proudest man I ever knew." Cooky tied off a second stitch and clipped the thread. "He always did things his way, and nobody could tell him different. Especially where you was concerned."

Abbie glanced at him, but he was intent on making the next stitch. Between them, Maura sat as still as a rabbit trying to blend into the scenery. Abbie might have thought she wasn't affected at all, except for the stark whiteness of her face. "What do you mean?" she asked. "What did people try to tell Daddy about me?"

"Some folks thought it was wrong raisin' a little child that way, with jus' a bunch of rough cowboys for comp'ny. Some said he ought to send you off to school to get a proper education."

"And what did he say?"

"He tole 'em he'd teach you everythin' you needed to know. You was gonna run his ranch one day." He glanced at her. "Guess he was right about that."

She looked away, blinking back sudden tears. Her father had been dead three years now, and yet at times her memories of him were so strong, her grief still fresh. She could almost see him, sitting tall and proud in the saddle, staring down the critics who would take his daughter from him. "Do you think he was wrong, Cooky, to raise me the way he did?"

He shook his head. "What's done is done, Miss Abbie. You gots to live with it. I can't see you done all that bad."

"But do you think he was wrong not to teach me 'women things'?" She ran one hand down her riding skirt. "Do you think I'm too *different* from other women?"

"Aww, child, don't matter what your daddy taught you; you're still female through and through. Some men don't look close enough to see it, but some do. Mr. Worth'nton do."

Yes, Reg acknowledged that she was a woman, but what good did that do her? Reg was going away before long; he'd made that clear. He was going home to England, to fine ladies with fancy manners and fancier dresses. Once there, he'd forget all about Abbie.

If only Alan could be made to see her through Reg's eyes. If she were married to Alan, she wouldn't miss Reg so much when he left.

"There, that ought to do it." Cooky snipped the last thread and stood back to survey his work.

Maura sagged against Abbie's shoulder. "Thank you," she whispered.

"Better have another drink." He offered her the jug.

She gave him a weak smile, but accepted the jug and took a sip of its contents. Abbie relaxed as a little color returned to her friend's cheeks. "You'd better take it easy the rest of the day," she said.

"Hop down off the table, though." Cooky took the jug, then helped her to the ground. He lifted the edge of the table, folded the legs under it, and folded it up so that it formed the front of the chuck box. "We gots to get movin'. When the men catch up with the herd, they don't want to have to ride all the way back here for chuck."

Abbie helped put out the fire and strike camp. Maura insisted on doing her part, though they did persuade her to ride on the chuck wagon with Cooky when they set out to find a new campsite.

Abbie rode a horse from the herd, a half-wild mustang that pitched her off once before she brought him in line. "I can't find Toby," she complained to Cooky as she rode alongside him. "It's not like him to run off."

"Maybe the lightning spooked him. Or maybe one of the other men borrowed him."

"They should have asked first," she grumbled. "You don't just help yourself to someone's horse."

"Maybe you weren't around to ask and they were in a hurry." Cooky yawned. "He'll come back. Horses are like bad luck—they always come back around."

The ground was cold and damp against Reg's cheek and smelled of turned earth and manure. A rock dug into his temple, but he ignored the pain. The very fact that he could feel meant he was alive.

In those terrifying moments when he had fallen from the horse into the path of the stampeding herd, his only thought had been that death would be his ultimate failure. A long line of Worthington men before him had expired on the battlefield, or in duels, or even comfortably in their beds after long, successful lives. Only he, Reg, would meet his end trampled in the mud on this godforsaken prairie.

Apparently he had been spared that indignity, at least. He rolled over on his back and stared up at the sky. Already the gray clouds were receding, like cotton wrapping pulled back from a plate of china blue. He strained his ears, but no sound of running cattle or galloping horses reached him. He was alone. Either no one had seen him fall, or he'd been left for dead.

With a few choice curses, he raised himself into a sitting position. "We can safely rule out paralysis," he said to no one in particular. "I'm certain I can feel every damn bone in my body." Every nerve, every muscle, every fiber reported in with a complaint. He looked down at his legs and winced. The fabric of his trousers hung in ribbons, and the red imprint of hooves showed clearly on his thighs. Further examination found his back to be in similar condition, his skin sticky with dried blood. As he moved to stand, a sharp pain pierced his side. He sucked in his breath and rose slowly, one hand pressed against what he surmised was a cracked rib.

Once upright, he surveyed the country around him. The path of the stampede was clearly marked in the churned mud, a hundred-yard swath stretching to the horizon. Apparently, the bulk of the herd had avoided him, though his hat had not fared so well. It was crushed flat in the dirt, mere inches from where his head had lain. The saddle, or what had been the saddle, rested a few feet from the hat—a smashed heap of wood and leather ground into the dirt. He kicked it free of the mud, then bent to examine the cinch strap. But too little was left of the leather strip to tell much. Perhaps it was only his bad luck that he had been riding it when it broke.

It might have been Abbie. His stomach clenched at the thought. If she had reached her horse before he had, she would be the one limping home right now. Or she might be crushed in the dirt, along with her saddle.

He shuddered and pushed the thought from his mind. He wasn't a prayerful man, but he paused to send up a word of thanks that Abbie had been spared.

He looked around for the horse, not really expecting to find it. The frightened animal was probably miles from here by now. Gritting his teeth against the pain, he began following the trail the herd had taken. Eventually it would lead him to the rest of the roundup crew. All he had to do was stay upright and keep walking.

He concentrated on putting one foot in front of the other. Mud stuck to his boots, weighting his steps. He knew he should move to the side, to firmer ground, but in his weariness and pain, even that seemed too much of an effort to make. Twice he passed dead calves, trampled by larger animals. He thought about looking to see if they bore his brand. But he didn't stop. Most likely the dead calves *were* his. That was just the kind of luck he expected to have these days.

The earl would fly into a rage when he saw the losses on the monthly reports. Never mind if natural forces beyond his control had conspired against him—Reg would take the blame.

He kicked at a dirt clod and sent it flying. Maybe he should quit while he was ahead. Move and start over. Forget his family. Forget trying to prove himself. He could go to Australia, or maybe back to sea.

He looked up, at the empty expanse of prairie. Pale green grass undulated across its surface, stirred by a breeze from the west. He thought again how much it was like the sea, vast and empty, with the capacity to make things and people appear small.

It wasn't a good place to be alone, to try to live one's life alone. He had never minded being alone before, but now the thought of having only himself for company pained him. What had happened since coming here to change him? Why this sudden longing for a place to call home?

The cowboys began to trickle into camp in late afternoon, tired and dirty, but triumphant. They had succeeded in turning the herd, which rested peacefully nearby. The storm had passed, promising a quiet night.

Abbie made a bed for Maura inside the chuck wagon, away from prying eyes. Between the whiskey and tension of the afternoon, the poor maid was exhausted. She barely protested when Abbie insisted she lie down. Then Abbie went to help Cooky serve coffee to the returning men.

"Well, Miss Abbie, I don't reckon I've ever seen you in an apron before." Donnie Best grinned at her as she filled his cup. "I'd say it suits you."

She flushed and looked away. She felt anything but suited to the task. She'd always been on the other side of this serving line before.

"Fill 'er up, darlin'," Tim O'Rourke drawled, and had the audacity to wink at her.

She resisted the urge to toss the hot coffee in his face. The men never spoke to her this way when she was riding as one of them. Why was it, the minute she picked up a coffeepot and tied on an apron, she became less in their eyes?

Maura didn't seem to mind the men's teasing, but then, she'd never known anything different. Abbie knew what it was like to carry on a conversation with men as an equal, and the sudden demotion to servant and ornament chafed.

Alan held out his cup to be filled, and she studied his expression. Did he see her differently now, too?

He met her scrutiny with his usual pleasant smile. "Have you seen Reg around?" he asked.

With a start, she realized she *hadn't* seen the Englishman in quite some time. "I thought he was with you," she said.

Alan shook his head. "I haven't seen him all afternoon. His horse came in a little while ago, still saddled and dragging its stake rope."

"My horse, Toby, is missing, too."

Alan frowned into his cup. "I saw your horse a little while ago. He wasn't wearing a saddle. I thought you'd turned him out to graze."

She swallowed, trying to control the tempo of her heart, which insisted on racing like a panicked mustang. "Maybe Reg's horse ran away and he borrowed mine," she said. She thought she'd seen Reg near Toby right before Maura distracted her with her scream. "But where is he now?"

"Could it be, Miss Abbie, that you're sweet on that Brit?" Best grinned and nudged O'Rourke.

Her face burned, and she looked away. "What makes you say that?" she snapped.

"Well ... I noticed you two spendin' a lot of time together. And you seem awful concerned about him now."

"Mr. Worthington and I are neighbors. Of course I'm concerned about him. He could be lost, or hurt." Her voice caught as she said the words. Reg wasn't used to Toby—if he had been with Toby at all. What if he'd been thrown and was lying out there somewhere, injured?

She turned to Alan. "Maybe we should go look for him."

He nodded and drained his cup. "I'll get some men together for a search party."

He was turning to go when Banjo began barking. The little dog pricked his ears and wagged his tail, then shot out across the prairie.

Abbie stared at the man staggering toward them. He was dressed in dirty rags and moved with a lurching gait. He walked with his head down, as if concentrating on every step. As he neared, Abbie's heart skipped a beat. She set the coffeepot aside and took off running toward the man. "Reg!" she screamed, just before he collapsed in the dirt.

By the time she reached his side, he was already struggling to his feet again. She put her shoulder under his arm and helped support him. "What happened?" she asked. She stared at his dirt-streaked face. He'd lost his hat, and his always neatly combed hair was tousled. A trickle of blood had dried on the side of his face. She couldn't keep herself from touching his cheek, reassuring herself he was, in fact, all right.

He closed his eyes a moment, leaning into the palm of her hand. The rough stubble of his beard grazed her skin. She was aware of his body pressed against her, the hard muscles of his arm lying along her shoulder, the planes of his chest flattening the curve of one breast, the length of his thigh aligned with her own. The heat of him seeped into her, the warmth settling in her breasts and her stomach and the crux of her thighs. She stared at his mouth, the lips full and moist beneath the soft moustache. She wished he would open his eyes and kiss her. She had never wanted anything more.

"Lawdy, suh, what's happened to you?" Reg's eyes snapped open, and he drew away from Abbie as Cooky ran up to them, followed closely by Alan.

"The cinch on my saddle broke." He glanced at Abbie, a frown creasing his brow. "Or rather, it was Abbie's saddle."

"How could that have happened?" she protested. "It wasn't an old saddle."

Reg shrugged and wrapped one arm around his chest. "I can't imagine why it happened, but it happened nonetheless."

"What's the matter?" Alan nodded toward Reg's chest. "You crack a rib?"

Reg winced. "I think so."

"Let's get you over to the wagon and take a better look." Alan stepped in front of Abbie and took her place at Reg's side, while Cooky supported him on the other side. The three men walked slowly to the chuck wagon, Abbie and half the camp in their wake.

Abbie started to follow them around the side of the wagon, but Cooky paused and waved her away. "You get on outta here, Miss Abbie. This ain't no concern of yours."

No concern of hers? Reg was her friend. Her neighbor. Not to mention he'd been injured riding *her* horse. She put her hands on her hips, ready to fire off an angry retort. Cooky winked at her. "Now, don't you get all riled with me," he said. "I'm gonna have to strip him down to examine him proper, and that ain't for you to see."

Her face grew hot, and she whirled around, heart racing. Though whether it beat faster from embarrassment, or from the thought of Reg without his clothes, she wasn't prepared to answer.

Chapter Twelve

Reg allowed himself to be stripped to his drawers and subjected to a thorough examination of his wounds. Cooky fussed and fretted under his breath as he wiped away mud and clotted blood. "All I kin say is the angels mus' be watchin' out for you, boss," he said. "You is sure 'nuff lucky you ain't a dead man."

Reg winced as the cook began swabbing the worst of the cuts and scrapes with a strong-smelling black ointment. "I fail to see the luck in having ended up in this condition in the first place," he said through clenched teeth.

"You say the cinch broke?" Alan leaned against the chuck wagon, watching them.

"I felt it give way as I went down."

Alan frowned. "It's not like Abbie to let her tack get worn. She's particular that way, just like her pa."

"She apparently overlooked this." Reg grunted as Cooky rubbed a tender spot on his back. *Or someone tampered with Abbie's saddle.* The thought came to him like another kick in the gut, but he didn't say anything to Alan. His friend was intelligent enough to draw his own conclusions. Besides, who could have wanted to harm Abbie?

"What happened to you?"

He jerked his head up and saw Tuff Jackson sauntering toward them. The foreman looked Reg up and down and let out a low whistle. "I could have told you, chief. You can't stop a stampede by throwin' yourself in front of the herd that way." He chuckled at his own joke.

Anger churned Reg's stomach like a tea kettle brought to boil. The picture flashed clear in his mind of Jackson bent over Abbie's saddle just before the stampede. He had been prepared to live with the man's insolence, to keep his suspicions of hair branding and theft silent. But he would not stomach a threat to Abbie's safety.

He wrenched out of Cooky's grasp and took a step toward Jackson. "Get out!"

The foreman glared at him. "What did you say?"

"I said get out. You're fired."

"Now, Reg—"

He shoved away Alan's restraining hand and took another step toward Jackson. "Collect your belongings and leave."

Jackson's eyes narrowed. "Make me."

Reg's first punch almost lifted the foreman off the ground. A second blow broke his nose in a spurt of blood. As Jackson struggled to land a solid punch of his own, Reg continued to pound. *Take that! for all your insolence. And that! is what I think of your reputation as a top hand.*

He had almost died because of this man. *Abbie* could have almost died—the thought flooded his senses with fear and adrenaline, made him keep hitting long after it was reasonable or just.

At last Alan and Cooky and Donnie Best dragged him off Jackson and shoved him up against the wagon. "What are you trying to do, kill him?" Alan squeezed Reg's arm in a painful grip. The rancher's voice was angry, but his eyes held a look of confusion and more than a little fear.

Reg turned away from his friend and watched as two other cowboys helped Jackson to his feet. The foreman's face was a mass of blood and bruises. His lip was smashed, one eye was swollen shut and the other would soon follow. He shot Reg a last hate-filled look, then turned and limped away.

"Lawdy, where'd you learn to hit like that?" Cooky kept a firm hold on Reg's right arm, as if he feared he might decide to follow Jackson.

"Club . . . boxing champion." Reg swallowed and tasted blood from his own cut lip. He struggled to control his ragged breathing. He was keenly aware of the circle of men gathered around him. Some gaped at him in amazement. Others considered him with looks of admiration, while still others scowled in deep suspicion. How would they treat him now that he had attacked one of their own?

After a moment, he managed to stand straight. "I'm all right," he said to his captors. "You can release me now."

He snatched up his trousers and pulled them on, then shrugged into his shirt. The rough cotton dragged across his bruised back, but he willed himself not to flinch, not to show any weakness. The circle of cowboys split to let him pass. "All right, y'all get back to work," he heard Alan call out behind him.

He made his way toward his horse, ignoring the pain in his legs, the dull ache behind his eyes. He wanted a cup of hot, strong tea, heavily laced with Irish whiskey; he settled for lukewarm water from his canteen.

"Reg?"

He raised his head at the sound of Abbie's voice. He realized he had been waiting for her, hoping she would seek him out. Drawing in a deep breath, he turned and saw her walking toward him. "Are you all right?" She stopped a few feet from him, her eyes filled with caution.

He wished she would come closer—close enough that he could put his arms around her and hold her until this shakiness inside him subsided. "I'm fine," he lied. He carefully replaced the lid on the canteen, avoiding looking at her.

"What happened back there—with Tuff?"

He sighed. "It'll be better this way, with him gone."

She took a step closer. "Donnie Best said you almost killed him."

"Then, he exaggerates." He hung the canteen on his saddle horn.

She worried her lower lip between her teeth. He remembered how soft her mouth had felt against his own. "What are you going to do now, without a foreman?"

"I'll find someone else. I have the roundup to finish first."

She looked down; he could no longer see her face and try to guess from her expression what she was thinking. "Tuff wasn't always a nice person, but he was a good cowboy. Some people will think you're making a mistake, getting rid of him."

"What do you think?" He held his breath, waiting for her answer.

She raised her head and looked him in the eye with an almost masculine directness he had admired from the first. "I think you're not the kind of man who acts without a reason. I wish you trusted me enough to tell me what that reason was."

He curled his hands into fists at his sides, when what he really wanted was to pull her to him. She had watched him nearly beat a man to death, yet she could still give him this vote of confidence. He spoke past the tightness in his chest, bound by emotions he couldn't even name. "Maybe

I'd had enough of his insolence. Maybe I believed he couldn't be trusted. A man like that isn't a help to me."

She nodded and took the last step toward him, closing the gap between them. Before he could speak, she put her hand up and touched the corner of his lip. "You're bleeding," she whispered.

The contact breached his thin veneer of control. He turned his head, capturing the tips of her fingers in his mouth.

Her eyes widened, and her lips parted to emit a shallow gasp. He ran his tongue across her fingertips, tasting his own blood from the cut she had touched, and the saltiness of her skin. She did not resist, but instead leaned toward him. He smelled the lavender that permeated her clothes, overlaid with the lingering scent of the cook fires. Her eyes remained locked to his, dark with a desire that answered his own longing.

Yet even as he filled his senses with the smell, feel and taste of her, he knew he indulged in a dangerous game. Abbie was too naive to see the danger; it was up to him to put an end to it. Gently, he reached up and took hold of her arm and pushed her away from him. "We'd better go. There's work to do."

Confusion flickered across her face; then she pulled in a deep breath and nodded. "I . . . I'll see you later, then."

He didn't answer, but swung up into the saddle. She tipped her head back to look up at him, and he stared at the graceful column of her neck rising up out of her rough cowboy clothes. She was a woman full of contradictions, not the least of which was why she should kindle these feelings in him. She wanted—and deserved—a husband and children and a house with roses growing by the door. Reg had none of those things to offer her. In another few months, he would be returning to England; his dreams were not Abbie's dreams.

* * *

All afternoon, Abbie could feel her fingers tingling where Reg had swept his tongue across them. Her whole body had trembled at the contact, like a lightning-struck tree; now only the humming in the nerves of her fingers remained.

She borrowed a saddle and selected a horse from her string and rode hard all afternoon, determined to put the incident aside. She and Reg had both been overwrought, their nerves still raw in the aftermath of his fight with Tuff.

She still could hardly believe what she'd seen with her own eyes. She'd heard shouting and had run around the corner of the wagon. By the time she'd elbowed her way through the gathered cowboys, Reg was straddling Tuff, pounding him with his fists. His face was set in an expression of rage, a hardness she'd sensed in him but never seen. Then she'd realized he was naked except for a pair of close-fitting woolen drawers. The muscular lines of his body gleamed with a thin film of sweat. Even battered and bruised, he was strong and powerful enough to take her breath away. This was the untamed man she'd glimpsed at the branding fire, the side of Reg usually hidden by his polished manners and tailored suits.

She stripped off her gloves and stared at the fingers he'd kissed. If she wasn't careful, she'd make a fool of herself over Reg. She'd destroy her chance for happiness with Alan, for a man who couldn't possibly care for a cowgirl like her.

Reg belonged to another world—a world of lords and ladies and drawing room teas. She had no interest in that kind of life.

Men! She was growing heartily sick of all of them. Thank God for Maura. At least Abbie could talk to her without feeling all muddled inside.

She found the maid peeling a small mountain of potatoes. Maura had combed her hair forward to cover most of the line of stitching, though the ends of silk thread were visible in a couple of places. "How are you feeling?" Abbie asked, taking a seat on a crate nearby.

"Better. Me head is hurting some, but that may be more from the whiskey than the sewing." She cut a neat curl of peeling from a potato. "It seems while I rested me eyes I missed all the excitement."

Before Abbie could answer, Alan came around from behind the wagon, carrying a kettle of water. "Where do you want this?" he asked.

"Here beside me, I think." Maura smiled and indicated a spot at her feet. "It was right kind of you to fetch it fer me, Mr. Mitchell."

"Call me Alan." He grinned and set the kettle beside her. "Evenin', Abbie." He nodded toward her, then hunkered down between the two women. "I was just telling Maura about the dance we're hosting to celebrate the end of roundup," he said. "You'll both come, won't you?"

Abbie smiled. Could it be Alan actually looked forward to seeing her at the dance? "I'll look forward to it," she said.

Alan turned to Maura. "Promise me you'll dance at least one dance with me."

She blushed. "I don't know as how it'd be proper fer me to attend your party—"

"Oh, Maura, of *course* you'll come," Abbie said. "I *insist.*"

Maura smiled. "Well, then, I'd be honored to dance with you ... Alan." She raised her foot and daintily pointed her toe. "I've always fancied meself as quick on me feet. It's been a good long while since I've had the chance to take a turn on a dance floor with a handsome gent."

Alan grinned at her, unanswering. Then he apparently remembered his manners and turned to Abbie. "I'd ask you to dance, too, but I know you don't generally indulge. Though Reg did persuade you out on the floor at our last barbecue, didn't he?"

Abbie flushed. As long as she lived, she would never forget the sound of the crowd's laughter as she stumbled over Reg's feet. She'd never forget how graceful Alan had looked, twirling around the floor with Hattie Simms.

"How is Reg doing?" Alan's question broke through the unpleasant memories.

She shifted on her seat. Why did Alan assume *she'd* know all about Reg? "I haven't seen him all afternoon."

"Mr. Mitchell—" Maura nodded at him, and her smile brightened. "I mean Alan was telling me about the fearful bust-up Mr. Worthington had with Mr. Jackson."

"Any idea what that was about?" Alan asked Abbie.

"What makes you think *I'd* know?" She scowled at him.

He shrugged. "I don't know. Seems like Reg is friendlier with you than he is anybody else around here."

"Reg is as much your friend as he is mine," Abbie said. "If you want to know anything, why don't you ask *him*?"

"Maybe I'll do that." He rose to stand over them. "Good evening, ladies."

Abbie watched him walk away, her frustration growing. "I didn't mean to run him off," she said.

Maura began cubing the potato in her hand and tossing it into the kettle of water. "Beggin' pardon, miss, but you mustn't be cross with Alan. No doubt he was only meaning to flatter you, saying Mr. Worthington was partial to your company." She winked. "I was thinking he might even be a little sweet on you."

"That's ridiculous. Reg is one of the most arrogant, pompous, stubborn—"

"He's also kind, handsome, and a right fine gentleman," Maura interrupted.

"I'm not interested in any gentleman," Abbie countered.

"Then, who would you be interested in, miss? Beggin' pardon, but most of these cowboys don't seem suitable for a young lady like yourself."

Abbie sighed. "I'm not a young 'lady,' Maura."

"Still, you're a woman of property. You can't mean to tell me you'd settle for one of these cowboys, without two pennies to rub together and the manners of a pig in the sty." Maura looked indignant.

Abbie smiled at the maid's outrage on her behalf. "No, you're right. Most of these cowboys wouldn't be good husbands for any woman. I imagine that suits them fine."

"Then, tell me, miss. What sort of man have you set your cap for?"

Abbie flushed. "I . . . I don't know," she stammered. "Another rancher, I suppose. A man who knows the land and cattle and can understand why I love it." She paused. "But someone who won't want me to give up my independence. A man who'll let me share the responsibilities of a ranch with him."

"Sure, and a man like that will be hard to come by," Maura said. "For giving up your independence is exactly what you'll be doing once you put a ring on your finger. 'Tis a man's nature to be the boss of things."

"I want to be my husband's partner, not his servant," Abbie said.

"Aye, well, there be ways of *servin'* without bein' a man's *slave.*" Maura cut the last of the potatoes into the pot and flashed Abbie a grin. "The trick, me granny used to say, is to make a man think he is in charge. But a wise woman always rules her own home, and her own heart." She stood and picked up the kettle. "Now, if you'll be excusing me, miss, I'd better be putting these on to boil before Cooky comes crying for me head on a platter.''

Abbie left Maura to her cooking and wandered over to where a group of cowboys had gathered to wait for dinner. Even from a distance, she could tell they were discussing Reg's fight with Tuff. Donnie Best stood in the middle of the group, punching at the air, his face twisted in a mock scowl. "I tell you, if we hadn't pulled him off, he woulda killed Tuff for sure," Donnie said.

"That proves how crazy these Limeys are. Why attack a man for no good reason?" Fred Lazlo said.

"Who says Worthington didn't have a reason?" Tim O'Rourke countered. "Tuff's been ridin' him hard all week. Maybe he finally got a belly full."

"I still say he's a fool to fire a top hand like Jackson," Moses Wilson said. "It'd be different if he knew his hind end from his head when it comes to ranchin', but he don't."

Donnie looked up and caught sight of Abbie on the edge of the group. He elbowed Moses hard in the side and nodded to her. "Afternoon, Miss Abbie," he said, tugging on the brim of his hat.

Abbie flushed. Since when did the men address her as Miss Abbie? For as long as she could remember, she'd been Abbie plain and simple. Just another waddie who worked alongside them. She looked down at her gathered riding skirts. She'd never tried to dress any differently from them before, never tried to act like a lady and not a cowboy.

"Sure was nice to see that storm pass over, wasn't it, ma'am?" Tim O'Rourke said.

She winced, suddenly uncomfortable around men she'd known for years—some of them all her life. "Yes, uh, I'm glad it passed over." She turned to Fred Lazlo. "I don't think we lost many calves during the stampede, do you?"

"Uh, no, ma'am." He scuffed the toe of his boot in the dirt. "Not too many."

She struggled to think of something to fill the long silence that followed. She'd never had any trouble talking with these men before. "It's a good thing Maura wasn't standing any closer to the tree than she was," she said at last. "But she's feeling much better now."

"That's good," Fred mumbled.

"Miss Maura sure is a sweet little thing, and pretty, too." Donnie Best grinned. "It was right nice of you to bring her with you, Miss Abbie."

If he called her "Miss" one more time, she thought she'd scream. Instead, she pasted a smile on her face and nodded. "Well, I'd better be going," she said. "Goodbye."

They mumbled their own farewells, and she moved out of their circle. She could almost hear their sighs of relief at her departure.

Reg was the only man she could have a decent conversation with lately. She fought the urge to seek him out. What had Maura said—that she thought Reg was sweet on her? She didn't intend to do anything to encourage that kind of thinking.

After all, Alan was the man she wanted. *He* was the man she'd described to Maura, the rancher who would respect her independence and allow her to be a partner in their marriage. She smiled. If the other men were beginning to see her as a woman, then Alan must have noticed the changes in her as well. Why, he'd even mentioned wanting to dance with her, hadn't he? Well—almost.

If she knew how to dance, Alan would probably dance with her. He'd hold her in his arms, and they'd whirl around the dance floor. He'd look deep into her eyes and see all the love she had for him, and he'd forget about anyone else.

She had to learn to dance; that was all there was to it.

She'd ask Maura to teach her. The maid had already said she was light on her feet. They could practice in Abbie's kitchen, and no one would be the wiser.

She hurried to where Maura was stirring a pot of beans and made her request.

"Teach you to dance, miss?" The maid frowned. "I don't rightly see as how I could be doing that."

"Why not? You said you were a good dancer."

"Aye. But when a lady dances, she follows the lead of the gentleman."

"What does that have to do with your teaching me to dance?"

Maura raised her eyebrows. "Beggin' pardon, miss, but I'll not be knowing how to lead." She smiled. "The young ladies at me last situation had a dancing master come in to teach them, a handsome young man."

"I don't think we have any dancing masters in Fairweather, Texas," Abbie said. "And we don't have time to hire one. The dance is next week."

"I'm sure Mr. Worthington knows how to dance, miss. Why don't you be asking him?" She hefted the kettle and moved toward the serving line of hungry cowboys.

Abbie stared after her. Ask Reg to teach her to dance? She'd already proven to him what a poor pupil she was, that day at Alan's barbecue. Hadn't she vowed to put some distance between herself and Reg?

The men began to move into line to eat. Reg took his place, among them, but not of them. His ramrod straight posture, his regal bearing, even the cut of his clothes set him apart from the other men. He understood what it was like to be different, to not belong.

He was the only one who knew of her secret love for Alan. Reg had promised to help her, to teach her. Surely that help included dancing lessons.

She'd consider it part of the bargain they'd made. Strictly a business agreement. Nothing more.

After she filled her plate, she sought him out. He sat alone, back against his saddle. Bruises from the stampede and from his fight with Tuff made dark patches on his face. She wondered if he was in much pain, and fought the urge to ask.

He glanced at her when she lowered herself to the ground beside him. "I'm not in the mood for conversation at the moment."

"I came to talk business," she said.

"Mine or yours?"

"Ours."

He raised one eyebrow in question. "Yes?"

She stabbed at the meat on her plate, avoiding his penetrating gaze. This close to him, her fingers had begun to tingle again. "I want you to teach me to dance."

"As I recall, I already attempted that."

"That was different. There were other people around, watching us."

He set his plate aside. "Why are you so interested in learning to dance now?"

"The Mitchells are hosting a dance next week, to celebrate the end of roundup." She flushed. "Alan said he'd dance with me, if I only knew how."

She looked up and was surprised to see Reg scowling at her. "He said that, did he?"

"Well, in so many words." She leaned toward him. "You promised to teach me to be a lady. A lady should know how to dance, shouldn't she?"

"What would you teach me in return?"

She hesitated, thinking. Of course Reg would expect something from her in return. "I'd show you what you should do at the livestock auction next month," she said at last. "You're going to want to buy some new breeding stock."

"You'll help me choose the stock?"

"I'll make notes for you to take with you, teach you what to look for."

He looked at the ground, seemingly lost in the contemplation of tufts of grass and patches of scraped earth. She stared at his shoulder, remembering the feel of the hard muscles beneath her fingers. Maybe dancing with Reg was a bad idea. Something about him brought out this wanton side of her. . . .

"All right," he said. "I'll teach you to dance. On one condition."

"What is that?"

He raised his head to look at her again. His eyes held a challenge. "You'll come with me to the livestock auction. Help me *personally* select the stock I need."

"Reg, the auction is in Amarillo. It's a two-day trip. I can't possibly—"

"Maura will come with us, of course." He gave her a mocking look. "I thought you weren't concerned about propriety and what people think."

Her own thoughts concerned her far more than those of others, thoughts of Reg holding her, kissing her, his tongue grazing her fingertips. She took a deep breath, trying to clear her head, but she inhaled the leather and musk scent of Reg. Her heart pounded. "I . . . I care what Alan thinks," she stammered.

"Everything will be perfectly aboveboard," Reg said. "You'll be traveling to the auction with a chaperon, for the purpose of purchasing stock of your own. There's no reason we should not be traveling on the same train."

"It will be a business trip," she said.

"Of course."

She nodded. "All right. I'll do it. And you'll teach me to dance?"

His mouth slowly curved into a smile. "It will be my pleasure."

Chapter Thirteen

Roundup ended on a Saturday. Abbie and her *vaqueros* cut her cattle from the herd and trailed them home to the Rocking W. The last she saw of Reg, he was working alongside his new foreman, Donnie Best, to gather the Ace of Clubs stock. Cooky trailed after them, driving the chuck wagon toward his new home; he'd somehow persuaded Reg to allow him to stay on to shoe horses and mend wagons and perform other odd jobs. Abbie wondered what Mrs. Bridges would have to say about that.

"So tell me, miss, what should we be wearing to the dance next week?" Maura rode up beside Abbie as they neared the ranch house. "I want to look nice for me first American ball."

Abbie turned to look at her maid. Her cheeks were flushed pink with excitement, and red tendrils framed her face. She sat erect in the saddle, her riding habit accentuating her generous curves. "Oh, Maura, you couldn't look anything *but* nice," she said. "The cowboys will be waiting in line to dance with you.'' She turned her attention back to the trailing cattle. ''Besides, it's not really a ball. Not like you're thinking. It's more of a square dance. A bunch of folks getting together to celebrate.''

''Sure, and there'll be music, won't there?'' Maura asked. ''And ladies in their best frocks and the lads all spit-shined to boot.''

Abbie smiled. The cowboys with their newly shorn faces and slicked-back hair would, indeed, look ''spit-shined.'' ''Yes, there'll be that. But don't worry about what to wear. I'm sure any of your dresses will do fine. No one will care.''

''Beggin' pardon, miss, but that's proof if I ever needed it that you're not as educated in such matters as you should be. I'd wager a half crown that every lady there will be wearing a new gown. Sure, and they'll be noticing if you or I show ourselves in an old one.'' She nodded decisively. ''There's nothing for it but for me to get to work right away on new frocks for us both, though of course, ma'am, I'll sew yours first. I'll make it suitably fine for a woman of your station.''

Abbie started to protest. But then she remembered the only other dress she owned—the russet-colored gown she'd worn to Alan's barbecue. She still blushed at the memory. Of course she needed something more fashionable if she was going to impress Alan. ''Um, what exactly did you have in mind?'' she asked hesitantly.

Maura tilted her head and studied her. ''Something in a deep blue silk taffeta, I think. With a draped bodice. I saw a gown in a magazine trimmed with little bows, with a ruffled underskirt, that would look ever so nice.''

''I don't know. All those ruffles and frills sound a little fancy for me. Maybe something plainer—''

''Nonsense, miss.'' Maura looked offended. ''I won't be accused of dressin' me mistress like a charwoman.'' A smile teased at the corner of her mouth. ''And the fact of the matter is, the fancier your dress, the fancier me own can be without fear of people thinking I'm oversteppin' me place.''

"This is America, Maura. People won't think that."

Maura shook her head. "Beggin' pardon, miss, but I'm not so certain of that. I've me own standards to live up to, after all. You can't be taking a lifetime of teaching out of a girl after a few months in America. I couldn't conscience dressing fancy while you went plain. So there's nothing for it but for you to put up with a few ruffles and frills.''

Abbie chuckled softly. For all her pretense at humility, Maura had a way of always getting exactly what she wanted. Maybe Abbie herself could learn a few lessons from her.

"As long as I'm sewing, miss, I think we'd better go ahead and make you up a few new dresses," Maura said.

"Why?" Abbie asked. "The divided skirts you made are fine for ranch work.''

"For work, yes, but you can't expect to wear them to town, now can you?''

That's exactly what Abbie expected, but she didn't dare confess this to Maura. And what about her upcoming trip to Amarillo? Perhaps it would be best to dress like a lady for her trip to the city. She nodded meekly.

"We'll measure you up tonight, and I'll ride into town Monday to purchase material." Maura waved, then urged her horse into a canter, riding out ahead of the trailing cattle.

Abbie stared after her, the fluttery feeling in her stomach growing. Ordinarily, she would have looked forward to a trip into Amarillo. She liked the challenge of the auction ring, sizing up the cattle and outbidding the other ranchers. She had a reputation as having a sharp eye for good stock, something she'd inherited from her father. Other ranchers had come to respect her judgment.

But traveling on a train with Reg and spending the auction at his side was unfamiliar territory for her. No doubt, he'd be dressed in his handsomely tailored suit, with his manners as polished as his accent. He'd expect her to play the part of a lady. The thought made her shaky with nervousness.

Other thoughts plagued her, too, thoughts she didn't want to examine too closely. What would happen when she and Reg were away from the familiar territory of their ranches, alone together? Twice now they'd almost succumbed to the attraction—the desire—that hovered between them like quicksand below a crust of firm earth. No matter how much she fought to resist it, she couldn't deny those feelings existed. Maybe it was because Reg was so different from the other men she knew, or maybe it was because he was the first man to acknowledge the feminine side of her. Whatever the reason, Reg had awakened this wild longing in her.

If only women weren't restrained by those unwritten rules of propriety, she thought. *If only we could behave like men, satisfying our curiosity and desires without suffering consequences.* No doubt Reg could teach her things she'd find useful to know when she became Alan's wife. . . .

She shoved the thought from her mind and took off after a heifer that was trying to make a break from the herd. But she couldn't shake the feeling trouble was waiting for her, somewhere in Amarillo.

Abbie refused to accompany Maura to town to shop for dress material on Monday. The thought of standing in Pickens' Mercantile sifting through bolts of fabric and stacks of pattern books made her feel panicky. She couldn't tell a dimity from a damask, and she didn't care to show off her ignorance in public. No doubt the usual collection of old-timers would be gathered around the cracker barrel, ready to gawk and comment on her choices.

Instead, she told Maura to use her own judgment and sent her to town alone, then decided to devote her afternoon to cleaning out the horse stalls. It was a job that occupied the body without taxing the mind. As she shoveled manure and straw, she thought about what she should say to Alan when he came to discuss this horse she was supposedly planning to purchase. She had to find a way to turn the conversation, and Alan's thoughts, to more personal matters.

"Don't you have cowboys to do this sort of menial labor for you?"

The familiar smooth accent startled her out of her musing. She took a firmer hold on the shovel and turned to see Reg standing at the end of the stall, mouth twisted in a grimace. "Miguel and Jorge are my employees, not my servants." She leaned the shovel up against the stall and stripped off her gloves. "My father taught me a man works better if he knows you won't ask him to tackle anything you wouldn't, or couldn't, take on yourself."

"Wise advice, I'm sure. But impossible to follow if one is inept at the job." He stared out across the corral, his expression blank.

"I'd hardly call your performance during roundup inept." She walked past him, out of the barn.

He followed her. "Did you know I lost eight calves during the stampede?"

She opened the gate and stepped through. "Losses like that are a part of ranching."

"My father is unlikely to see it that way." He shut the gate behind him and turned to face her once more. "He'll place the blame squarely on my head."

From the way he spoke, Abbie could tell Reg agreed with his father's assessment. She shook her head. "So don't tell him about the calves. They're not important—not compared to the eight *thousand* other cattle you have."

"I'm required to make a monthly report to the syndicate's stockholders," he said stiffly.

She shrugged. "It's a long way to England. What are they going to do if you miss a report or two? Tell them you were too busy doing your job to mess with a bunch of papers."

He scowled. "Those papers are a part of my job. My father expects me to keep him informed."

"Why? If he trusted you, he'd let you run the ranch without interference."

"Exactly." He walked past her, up onto the porch.

Abbie stared at his back. He held his shoulders as if braced to ward off a blow. What had she said to put him in this mood? Or had he brought it with him, wearing his ill humor like a hair shirt?

"I did not come here to discuss my personal affairs," he said, turning to face her once more.

"Then, what are you doing here?" she snapped.

"I came to give you your dancing lesson."

"Now?" She brushed straw from her shirtfront, suddenly aware of how awful she must look. She was wearing patched trousers that were too tight for riding and a man's shirt with the sleeves rolled up. She'd plaited her hair into two pigtails and tied the ends with strips of torn sheeting. She was dusty and perspiring and probably reeked of manure. Of all times for Reg to see her. . . .

"The dance is less than a week away. You'll need plenty of practice to master the steps between now and then. That is, if you still want to learn . . ."

"Of course I want to learn. But you can't possibly teach me like this. I need to change clothes and bathe and—"

"On the contrary, you look quite fetching." His gaze

swept over her. Her skin tingled, and she felt feverish, as if he'd actually touched her.

"I . . . I have to change." She hurried past him, into the house. He followed. "Wait here. I'll only be a minute," she told him, then rushed into the bedroom and shut the door behind her.

Of all the times for Maura to decide to go to town! she thought as she stripped off shirt and trousers and filled her wash-bowl with water from the pitcher. She lathered a washrag and began sponging her arms and shoulders. But really, what did it matter if she and Reg were alone? It had never bothered her before.

Before he'd kissed her in the cave. Before she'd felt her body tremble at his touch. . . . *Stop it!* She dropped the washrag and plunged both hands into the water, as if she could wash away the disturbing thoughts that crowded her mind. Reg and she were friends, nothing more. Alan was the man she intended to love.

When she emerged from her room, in fresh shirtwaist and riding skirt, her hair neatly combed and tied behind with a ribbon, she found Reg seated at the kitchen table, staring blankly out the window.

"What's wrong?" she asked, walking up behind him.

"What?" He started. "Nothing's wrong." He stood and kicked a rag rug—one of Maura's many improvements—out from in front of the door, then moved a rocking chair and a foot stool back against the wall. "There, that should give us enough room. Now for music."

Abbie looked around the room. "We haven't any. Even if I could play an instrument, I couldn't very well do it and dance at the same time."

"Never mind. We'll improvise." He held his hands out to her. "Come. Let's begin."

Feeling awkward, she put her hands in his and let him lead her to the center of the cleared-off space. His grasp was warm, and the warmth seemed to flow from her fingers, down through the rest of her body to pool between her thighs. She wanted to stand closer to him, to feel the strength and heat of him pressed against the length of her, but she fought that urge, forcing herself to stand as far from him as possible.

"You'll have to move closer than that," he said, pulling her nearer. "You act as if you're afraid to touch me."

Only afraid of what I'll do if I touch you.

He put one hand on her waist, and her stomach trembled. "Your hand goes on my shoulder," he instructed.

She rested her fingers lightly against the soft fabric of his coat. He shifted his arm, and she felt the muscles move beneath her fingertips. She'd never been so aware of another person's body before, or so alive in her own.

"I think we'll begin with a waltz." He cleared his throat, then began to hum a simple, lilting tune. He took a step to the side, pulling her along. "Follow me," he sang, and she did her best.

"One, two, three. One, two, three. Left, step, step. Right, step, step. Nice and easy. Not too fast." Somehow Reg managed to sing his instructions.

Abbie listened, and followed his lead, but she felt as stiff as a branding iron and awkward as a new calf. "I'm so sorry," she moaned when she trod on Reg's foot yet again. She looked down, to watch her feet, but Reg nudged her chin up with their clasped hands. "Close your eyes," he sang.

"What? I'll fall."

"No you won't. Close your eyes and follow me."

She shut her eyes, and her steps faltered. But Reg relentlessly pulled her along. "Relax," he crooned. "I'll never let you fall."

She inhaled deeply, filling her head with the masculine aromas of starched linen and sandalwood soap. With a sigh, she surrendered herself to the coaxing of Reg's hands, the gentle urgency of the music. He pulled her closer, his hand moving from her waist to the small of her back. She felt her skirt brushing his thigh with each step.

He began to sing. "O, Genevieve, Sweet Genevieve, I see thy face in every dream. My waking thoughts are full of thee; Thy glance is in the starry beam."

She smiled, letting the words wash over her. His voice was clear and deep, the notes of the song seeming to float around them. She leaned back and abandoned herself to the music, and the words, and the joy of moving in the rhythm of the dance.

Reg stared down at the pulse that throbbed in the smooth ivory column of Abbie's neck. She had bent her head back, eyes still closed and smiling, lost in some private enjoyment of the music and the moment. Once she had relaxed, she had followed him quite well, their bodies moving in perfect rhythm.

He swallowed hard, and clenched his teeth against the urge to cover that beating pulse with his lips. He wanted to feel that heartbeat rhythm against his mouth, as he imagined another rhythm they might find together, another kind of dance they might enjoy.

The thought of making love to Abbie no longer shocked him as it once might have. He could no longer deny the physical attraction he felt, though he readily acknowledged the impossibility of ever acting on his feelings. Abbie was an unschooled virgin, intent on marrying the one man Reg counted as a friend in this foreign land. She would spend the rest of her life on this ranch she had been groomed since birth to rule, while Reg was destined to return to England, to find some place in his father's small kingdom.

But logic could not keep him from growing hard whenever he was near Abbie, and reason did not stop the thoughts he had of making her his own. He flexed his fingers against her waist, its soft curve unhampered by boned corsets. With his eyes, he traced a path from the indentation of her waist to the swell of her breasts. He ached to stroke the rounded flesh, to feel the weight of her breasts resting in his palms.

"Genevieve, my early love, The years but make thee dearer far! My heart shall never, never rove: Thou art my only guiding star." He forced his eyes upward. She was still smiling, eyes closed, head tilted back as if inviting his kiss. One kiss. He could allow that. The briefest brush of his lips against hers, and when she opened her eyes, she would wonder if it had been a dream. Still humming softly, he bent his head. One kiss would be enough . . . for now.

"Beggin' your pardon, me lord. I had no idea you was here."

Reg jerked his head up and saw Maura standing in the open doorway, her arms full of packages. Abbie gasped and wrenched out of his grasp.

"I'd quite forgotten Miss Abbie telling me you was to come by soon to school her in dancing." Maura bustled past him and dumped her purchases on the kitchen table. She brushed off her hands. "Oh, miss, wait until you see the lovely things I found."

"Where do you want this lot?" Alan stepped into the room, his arms also full of wrapped parcels.

"Put them on the table with the rest," Maura instructed.

"Alan, what are you doing here?" Abbie's cheeks flushed bright red, and she edged farther away from Reg.

"I ran into Maura in town, and she needed help with her packages." He removed his Stetson and hung it on a peg by the door. "I figured now was as good a time as any to stop by and talk to you about that horse you wanted to buy."

Abbie looked from Alan, to Reg, and back again. He

could almost read her thoughts. After all, he had coached her that the aim of asking Alan's advice was to spend time alone with him. "I was just leaving," he said, heading for the door.

"Oh, no, Mr. Worthington, don't go." Maura intercepted him. "I was just brewing a nice pot of tea. Stay and have a cuppa."

"No thank you. I really must be going."

"Please stay, me lord. I'm sure you're thirsty after all your dancing."

Reg glanced back at Abbie. She was staring at her feet, smoothing her skirt over and over with her hands. If he left now, Maura would no doubt dominate the conversation. Abbie wouldn't have a chance to say the things she wanted to say to Alan.

Not that the rancher deserved a prize like Abbie, anyway. If he hadn't recognized her worth by now, what would a few minutes' conversation do? Reg shook off the thought and turned back to Maura. "Actually, I was wondering if I could induce you to come riding with me for the afternoon."

It was Maura's turn to blush. Reg wondered if he had made a mistake, pretending an interest in the maid; but it was the only thing he could think of to provide Abbie and Alan a moment alone. "Oh, sir, how nice of you to offer, but I really must—"

"Maura, did I hear you say something about tea? I'm so thirsty I could drain the well dry." Alan crossed the room and stood beside the maid. He frowned at Reg.

Reg turned to give Abbie a look of apology, and found her scowling at him as well. So much for his attempt at helping her. "I'll be going, then," he said, and turned to retrieve his hat.

Maura intercepted him once more. She glanced at Abbie, then back to him. "Please stay," she said. "Me feelings will be sorely hurt if you won't stay and taste me scones and cream. Remind you of home, they will."

"Let him go, Maura," Abbie said. "I'm sure Reg has enjoyed all of my company he can stand today."

"Yes, I'm sure Reg is busy," Alan said.

Reg glanced from one to the other. Alan watched Maura, Maura looked at Abbie, while Abbie studied the floor. The afternoon was already shaping up to be a romantic failure, whether he stayed or departed. He replaced his hat on the peg. "On second thought, tea and scones sounds wonderful."

Maura put a kettle on to boil, then set about clearing the table. Abbie led the men over to the sofa. Reg sat in the only chair, leaving Alan to take the place beside Abbie. "So tell me about this horse," Alan said.

"The horse. Oh, yes." Abbie smoothed her skirt across her knees. "Well, I was thinking of buying another cutting horse."

"You're not thinking of selling Toby, are you?"

"Of course not. I thought it would be nice to have another animal in my string."

Alan nodded. "I hear Abner Folsum has a cutting horse for sale. You might try him."

"I didn't know that. Um, maybe you'd like to ride over there with me sometime." Abbie cast a hopeful glance toward Alan, but the rancher had turned his head to watch Maura move about the kitchen.

Reg wished he was seated close enough to give Alan a not-too-gentle nudge with his boot. "Abbie says you have a good eye for horseflesh," he said.

"Yeah, well, Abbie doesn't need me or anyone else to help her pick out a horse." Alan smiled back at her. "I don't know why she wanted my advice."

"I just thought . . . I'd enjoy your company." This bold admission shook Reg. It was the closest Abbie had ever come to confessing her longing for Alan's attention to anyone but Reg himself. He clenched his fists at his sides. So help him, if Alan hurt her—

"Tea is served." Maura came to usher them to the table. Reg blinked at the feast laid before them. As promised, Maura had produced scones and cream, jam and assorted finger sandwiches, as well as a steaming pot of fragrant tea.

"Now, isn't this something," Alan said as they gathered around the table. "Maura, you're a miracle worker," he said.

He took a bite of scone. "Mmmmm. Delicious."

"Abbie and I were discussing the dance you're hosting Friday," Reg said, searching for a new topic of conversation.

"Yeah." Alan grinned. "Maura already told me she's going to whip up new dresses for her and Abbie." He looked at Abbie. "Won't that be something? She says she plans to turn you into a regular lady."

Reg winced as a pink blush swept up Abbie's cheeks. Why did Alan find the notion of Abbie as a lady so impossible? "I've no doubt Abbie and Maura will be the belles of the ball," he said.

Alan smiled at Maura. "The cowboys will be waitin' in line for dances. That's one reason I've already put in my request."

"Reg has been teaching me to dance." Abbie added sugar to her tea and stirred vigorously.

"Well, how about that?" Alan said.

Ask her to dance! Reg stared daggers at the rancher across the table, but Alan's attention was focused on Maura.

"Did you bake these cookies yourself?" he asked, helping himself to another. "They're delicious." He continued to rain compliments on the pretty Irish maid throughout the meal. Reg's attempts to turn the conversation back to

Abbie met with little success. Abbie grew quieter and quieter, and Reg noticed she hardly touched any of the admittedly delicious food.

"Now, about this horse." Alan drained his cup and turned to Abbie.

She sat up straighter. "Yes, I'd like you to ride over to Abner Folsum's with me to look at it," she said.

Reg smiled. *That's the spirit,* he thought. *Don't give up yet.*

"I was fixing to say, I don't think you want one of Abner's horses," Alan said. He wiped his mouth and dropped the napkin on his plate. "He's got a reputation for shady dealings with livestock—I'd steer clear of him if I were you. But I'll keep my ears open if I hear of anything else."

"Oh." Abbie slumped in her chair. "Well, thank you."

"I'd best be headed home now." Alan turned to Maura. "Thank you for the fine meal," he said. "I'll look forward to seeing you again at the dance."

She blushed and batted her eyes prettily. Reg could almost feel his friend melting from the feminine attention. Alan was clearly smitten; what chance did Abbie have now?

"Maybe you should check out the auction in Amarillo next month," Alan said as he and Abbie and Reg walked to the door.

"I *was* thinking of attending the auction," Abbie said.

"Might be a good idea." Alan settled his hat on his head and pulled open the door. "It's always good to check out of town for a change. Could be you'll find what you're looking for at auction."

Reg felt a shiver run down his spine as he shut the door and caught Abbie's glance. He thought again of the moment when he had held her and almost kissed her. Would he find what he was looking for at auction? Or what he most wanted to avoid?

Chapter Fourteen

"If you think I'm letting you truss me up in that thing, you've got another think coming." Abbie glared at the corset Maura held in her hand and shook her head. "A woman can hardly breathe in one of those things, much less move around or be comfortable."

"But, miss, you'll look ever so lovely in it." Maura held the undergarment in front of her. "It'll pinch your waist in real small and lift your bosoms up nice and high."

"I don't want to be pinched or lifted, thank you." Abbie folded her arms across her chest and looked at the dress laid out on her bed. The royal blue satin shimmered in the lamplight, the fabric gathered in strategic places with satin bows, the skirt trailing ruffles. "I'm not even sure I want to wear all this fluff and folderol. Maybe I could wear a shirtwaist and riding skirt—"

"Oh, no, miss." Maura looked horrified. She dropped the corset on the bed and rushed to Abbie's side. "You can't be showing up at the ball wearing everyday clothes. What will people think?"

"That I'm a woman with sense enough not to deck myself out like some china doll?" She sank down onto the bed. "Oh, Maura, I don't think I'm cut out for this business of being a 'lady.' I'm more comfortable riding a horse and wearing trousers."

"Beggin' your pardon, miss, but nobody ever said being a lady had anything to do with being comfortable. Now stand up and let me help you into your dress. You'll feel better once you see yourself in all your finery."

Reluctantly, Abbie stood and allowed Maura to settle the new gown over her head. "Oh, this color is perfect for you, miss," Maura said as she fastened the row of buttons up the back of the dress. "And that draping makes your waist look small even without the corset." She moved around Abbie, smoothing folds and straightening ruffles. "Oh, miss, you'll be a smashing success, 'tis sure," she said, stepping back at last.

"It's not a ball," Abbie said. "It's just a little get-together."

"If there's to be dancing, then I don't see as it can be improper to be calling it a ball." Maura took Abbie's arm and led her to a chair. "Now come sit down and let me do your hair."

Abbie carefully lowered herself into the chair, afraid of crushing her skirts. The voluminous satin and layers of starched petticoats added an unfamiliar weight. No wonder most women walked so slowly, with all these pounds of fabric dragging them down. "Ouch!" She flinched as Maura dragged a comb through her hair.

"Sorry, miss, but you must try to sit still."

So Abbie clenched her jaw and held firm against Maura's onslaught on her head. The maid attacked Abbie's tresses like a surgeon, with curling iron and crimper, brushes and barrettes. When she was finished, Abbie had a headache, and her neck and shoulders felt awkwardly bare of any covering of fabric or trailing curls.

"There now. We'll add a *touch* of powder." Maura applied the powder puff. "And we'll pinch your cheeks for color."

"Yeooww!" Abbie jumped back from the maid's fierce hold of her cheeks.

Maura grinned. "Come, miss, and see how lovely you look." She shooed Abbie toward the mirror.

Abbie stared at the woman who looked back at her from the beveled glass. The cowgirl she knew had been replaced by this elegant-looking woman. Her skin glowed white as cream against the deep blue of the dress, and the low-cut neckline displayed an embarrassing hint of cleavage, even without the "lift" of a corset. Her neck and shoulders were smooth and bare, her hair piled in ringlets atop her head and crowned with a circlet of blue ribbon. "I can hardly believe it's me," she whispered.

"Believe it, miss." Maura replaced the lid on the dusting powder and gathered the hair from the brush and stuffed it in the celluloid hair receiver. "The woman what taught me at me last post said dressing a lady is like putting together a flower arrangement. The blossoms look lovely in the garden, but once you cut them and fuss with them and place them just so, then they're fit to grace a royal banquet."

Abbie glanced at the vision in the mirror once more. Who would have guessed she could ever be so fine and "fit to grace a royal banquet"?

Reg saw it, she thought. *He never doubted he could turn me into a lady. What will he think of me tonight?*

She turned and saw Maura struggling to pull her own gown over her head. "Here, let me help you." She rushed forward and tugged the dress down over the maid's shoulders, then began to do up the buttons in back.

"Thank you, miss. I practiced fastening it meself, but it was a bit of a stretch." Maura smoothed out the full skirts of the dress and straightened the fitted bodice. The confection of sea foam green was not as ornamented as Abbie's dress, but the simple design set off the maid's generous figure and red hair to perfection.

"You're the one who will be the belle of the ball," Abbie said, feeling a twinge of envy. No matter how pretty her new finery made her look, she could not deny that Maura was beautiful enough to take a man's breath away. Her gold-flecked eyes shone like topaz, and her cheeks wore a natural blush needless of painful pinching. Abbie picked up the brush and began to stroke Maura's hair.

"Oh, miss, I can get it meself." Maura took the brush and began sweeping it through her curls with swift strokes. "It's ever so nice of you to offer, though." She sat down on the edge of the bed and began pinning curls atop her head. "Do you think there'll be lots of dancing, then, miss?"

Abbie sat back down in the chair and nodded. "You might as well rest now. Once the cowboys see you, they won't let you sit out a single song."

Maura smiled. "I'll love to dance with them all, but there's one in particular I hope will be asking me to dance. He's not a cowboy, though."

"Oh, who is he?"

Maura's cheeks grew pinker. "Can't you guess? I was fearful I'd been mooning over him something awful."

Abbie shook her head. "I can't guess. Tell me."

"It's Alan Mitchell."

Abbie caught her breath. She'd been aware of Alan going out of his way to be helpful to Maura, but she'd assumed he was acting out of his usual concern for a neighbor. Now she wondered if his interest in Maura was something more. She supposed she ought to be jealous of her maid. After all, Alan was the man Abbie intended to marry.

"Miss?" Maura leaned toward Abbie. "You don't think me too forward, do you, for hoping for his affections?"

Abbie looked into Maura's wide eyes and felt only concern for the other woman's feelings. "Of course you're not being too forward," she said, putting a hand on the maid's arm. "You've never behaved improperly that I've seen."

Maura worried her lower lip between her teeth. "Then, you don't think I'm touched to hope a man of property like Mr. Mitchell might look with favor upon a serving girl like me?"

Silently, Abbie thought the whole thing sounded like a plot for a romantic novel. "This is America," she said gently. "Things like that don't matter here." She hesitated, then added, "Has Alan indicated that he's, um, interested in you?"

"It's hard to say, miss." Maura went back to arranging her hair. "He comes around often enough, but maybe it's you he's coming to see instead of me."

That news should have thrilled her, but try as she might, all Abbie felt was—nothing. Alan was Alan. He was her friend and neighbor, someone she'd known forever. She still admired him and liked him, but she wasn't so sure anymore that what she felt for him was love. Her heart never beat faster when Alan was near; she never felt a rush of warmth through her body, or the longing to press her lips to his. She didn't *desire* Alan, and shouldn't a woman desire the man who was going to be her husband?

She hadn't thought the physical side of marriage was very important before. Oh, of course it was necessary in order to have children, but she'd assumed she and Alan would work things out once they'd said their vows.

But that was before she'd realized how wonderful a kiss could make her feel, and what a thrilling thing desire could be. Unfortunately, the only man she'd desired so far was Reg. Surely that was because she'd spent more time with him than other men lately.

Maybe her desire for Alan could grow and be nurtured. Probably she hadn't really thought about him in the right way—as a handsome, desirable man, instead of a familiar friend and neighbor.

No, she couldn't give up on Alan yet. Time was running out, and she had to marry if she was ever going to have the family she wanted. If she didn't marry Alan, who else could she find to be her husband?

Reg? She blinked, startled by the thought. Marry that arrogant English nobleman? They had nothing in common. Besides, he was headed back to England at the first opportunity.

Marry Reg? Ridiculous!

She'd have to marry Alan; that's all there was to it. Maura would understand. A beautiful woman like her would find someone else soon enough. Abbie didn't have another choice.

Abbie could hear the fiddles tuning as she steered the buggy into line among the others waiting beside the Mitchells' well-lit house. Lamplight glowed in every window, spilling in yellow pools onto the ground. Men stood in groups along the broad front porch, or gathered around a keg of beer set under the lone tree beside the front gate.

"Oh, do hurry, miss. I'm not wanting to be late for me first Texas ball." Maura gathered her shawl about her and stood, ready to leap from the wagon box before the wheels had even stopped rolling.

"Ma'am, allow me to help you down." A cowboy in a

red-and-white-striped shirt rushed up to offer Maura his hand, while a second man assisted Abbie.

"Sure is nice to see two such pretty ladies," Abbie's escort said. "I'd be pleased if you'd reserve a dance for me."

Abbie studied the moustached man with the slicked-back hair. He reeked of pomade. "Tim O'Rourke, is that you?" she asked.

He blinked in confusion, then squinted at her. "Abbie Waters, is that you?" He laughed, braying like a donkey. "Didn't recognize you all dolled up." He stepped back and looked her up and down. "You clean up real nice."

"I could say the same for you," she said, feeling the heat of a blush sweep across her cheeks.

"Don't forget you owe me a dance," he called after her as she and Maura made their way toward the house.

Alan and Brice Mitchell stood at the door, welcoming their guests. "Abbie. Maura. You both look lovely," Alan said. Was it Abbie's imagination, or did his gaze linger on Maura? "So glad you could come."

Abbie moved past her hosts, into a room warm with lamplight. The air was heavy with the scents of lamp oil, leather and the pomade cowboys used to slick back their hair. A dozen or more men, and a few women, were already gathered in the large room that spanned the front of the house. The furniture, except for a line of straight-back chairs, had been removed to make room for dancing. A band, consisting of a fiddle and two guitars, was tuning up in front of the fireplace.

At the sight of the instruments, her stomach fluttered. Would she remember the steps Reg had taught her? Or would she once again make a fool of herself in front of Alan and her neighbors?

"We've got enough women here now to make a set,"

Brice said, coming up behind her. "I'll tell the fiddler to get started."

"What would they do if we hadn't come?" Maura asked Abbie as they made their way to the back bedroom that had been set aside for ladies' shawls. "Would they hold the dancing until more women arrived?"

"No. Some of the men would tie bandannas around their arms and take their turn dancing the women's part." She smiled. "Nothing would keep a cowboy from a chance to cut loose and dance."

Alan and Brice claimed the privilege of starting the dancing and led Abbie and Maura into the first set. Abbie watched Alan's face as he swung Maura into the first steps of "Virginia's Reel." The rancher was grinning from ear to ear—from the fun of the dance, or pleasure in his dancing partner?

She had little time to contemplate the question, as Brice pulled her smartly along. Despite a few false steps, she finally got the hang of dancing without getting tangled in her skirts and petticoats and lost herself in the delight of the movement. She liked the fast songs best, but she danced every one, fast or slow. Even if she'd wanted, the cowboys wouldn't have let her or Maura sit down.

Several men expressed surprise at seeing her dressed up, but all were quick to compliment her transformation. They brought her punch and cookies and entertained her with funny stories and generally went out of their way to see that she was well looked after.

Maybe there's more to this being a lady than meets the eye, Abbie thought as she sipped her second cup of punch, which Tim had eagerly fetched for her. Dancing was thirsty work. The punch was heavily laced with whiskey. Most of the women pretended they couldn't taste it or refused to drink it altogether, but Abbie enjoyed the smooth way it slid down her throat and the warm feeling it kindled inside her. When she smiled, the men around her smiled back. For once instead of having to fight for a place among a group of men, she found herself at their center. She felt light-headed and happy enough to float right out of the room.

She couldn't help but notice, however, that Reg was not part of her string of admirers. She searched the room and spotted him. He was handing a cup of punch to Hattie Simms. The pretty banker's daughter smiled up at Reg, perfect dimples forming on either side of her mouth. Reg returned the smile and leaned forward to say something. Abbie felt a sharp pain in the stomach. *Perhaps the punch doesn't agree with me,* she thought, and dragged her gaze away from Reg.

Obviously, he wasn't aware she was here, or he would have stopped by to at least say hello. She looked back toward him, hoping to catch his eye. She was anxious to hear what he thought of her dress. Everybody had said it was "first-rate," but what did a bunch of cowboys know about fashion? Reg was the only one in the room who would know if she was suitably outfitted for a lady.

The fiddler sawed out the opening bars of a waltz, and Reg bowed low before Hattie Simms. The banker's daughter simpered again, and allowed Reg to lead her onto the dance floor. Now, what was he dancing with *her* for?

Abbie whirled around and almost collided with Alan. "I was coming to ask you to dance," Alan said. He nodded toward the dance floor. "Care to give it a whirl?"

She turned her best smile on him. So what if she didn't have dimples? "I'd love to, Alan." She slipped her hand into his, and they walked out onto the floor and began the waltz.

Abbie's heart pounded as she moved into Alan's arms. She reminded herself of her vow to think of Alan as a potential lover and not just a neighbor she'd grown up with. She admired the solid feel of his shoulder beneath her hand, and his admirable height, which made it necessary for her to tilt her head back to look up at him. "It's a lovely party," she said, to get the conversation started.

"Yeah, it turned out right nice." He guided her easily among the other dancers. Abbie didn't have any trouble following his lead, but something was missing. She didn't feel any tingles on her skin, or rush of warmth through her body. Maybe it was the way he was holding her. He rested his hand lightly on her waist, keeping her a dignified arm's length away. She was sure she and Reg had danced closer together.

"Um, you can hold me closer, Alan," she said.

"But then I might tromp all over your skirts." He shook his head. "Hate to ruin a pretty dress like that. Where'd you get it?"

"Maura made it."

"She did?" His smile broadened. "Is there anything that gal *can't* do? I never met anyone like her before."

"No. Neither have I."

"I reckon she made the dress she's wearing, too," he said. He raised his head and searched the room until he spotted Maura, who was dancing with a cowboy from the Ace of Clubs. "She looks as pretty as a picture in it."

Abbie's heart sank. Alan had finally asked her to dance, and all he could talk about was *Maura*. She was grateful when the song finally ended and he returned her to a spot by the front window. "I think I'll go say hello to Maura," he said, and departed.

Abbie twisted one of the bows on her skirt until it was a wonder it didn't fall off. Where was Reg when she needed him? Maybe he'd have some ideas about what she could do to catch Alan's eye. The new dress and dancing lessons hadn't helped a bit.

She spotted his lordship over by the buffet table and

decided to head him off before he delivered a plate of goodies to Hattie Simms or some other hapless female. She had business to attend to. The ladies could fetch their own food.

"We need to talk," she announced, stepping up beside him.

He glanced at her, then quickly looked away. "Hello, Abbie. You're looking lovely tonight."

She flushed. "Hello, Reg. Uh, thank you." She smoothed her suddenly damp palms down her skirts. "I need to talk to you," she tried again.

He selected a tea cake and added it to his plate. "I'm listening."

"Not here. In private." She put her hand on his arm. "Come outside with me."

He frowned, but set aside his plate and allowed her to lead him out the door. They walked to the end of the porch. Lanterns hanging from the eaves cast a soft light over the area, and the lilting notes of the fiddle serenaded them. The group of cowboys around the beer keg had grown more raucous; from time to time they burst into loud laughter. Another group of men stood in a far corner of the yard, the glowing embers of their cigarettes marking their places. But in their corner of the porch, Abbie and Reg enjoyed a measure of privacy.

"What is so important you felt it necessary to interrupt me?" Reg leaned against the railing and folded his arms across his chest.

"I didn't notice you doing anything so awful important," she said. She straightened the bow at her waist. "Why haven't you said a word to me all evening?"

"I've been . . . distracted."

"Yes, I noticed. Do you think Miss Simms' voice is that high naturally, or is it something she worked at?" She stuck one finger at the corner of her mouth. "Oh, Lord

Worthington, I'd be *delighted* to dance with you," she simpered.

Reg stared at her. "What the devil are you carrying on about?"

She dropped her arms to her sides. "I thought you were my friend, Reg. I've been on pins and needles all week about this dance. The least you could have done was stop by to say hello, and tell me if my dress was all right."

His gaze wandered over her. Her skin began to tingle as if he'd made a more physical examination. "The dress is very nice," he said softly. He paused, then added. "Beautiful." He looked away. "Forgive me, Abbie. I did not intend to bruise your feelings. I truly am distracted by some disturbing news."

"What is it?" She moved closer to study his worried face. Small lines creased the corners of his eyes, and his mouth was set in a thin line. "What's wrong?"

He hesitated, as if reluctant to reveal his woes.

"You can tell me," she said softly.

He looked away, toward the corral where the horses stood. "I received a letter in the mail today from my father. To put it mildly, he is not exceedingly pleased with my progress so far."

"What did he say?"

He unfolded his arms and gave a heavy sigh. "The usual. He reminded me I have never had a head for business, and reiterated my past failures. He even berated himself for sending me here in the first place."

"That's awful. How could he say those things about his own son?"

"He's said those things before, and worse. That was not the part of the letter that most concerned me."

"What else did he say?"

He scowled into the darkness. "He railed at me for the loss of the cattle during the blizzard and the stampede.

Said at the rate I was going I'd have him bankrupt before fall.''

"But that's unfair! You can't control the weather. You couldn't have done anything to prevent that stampede either. Everyone experiences losses like that. It's a part of ranching.''

"The earl doesn't see it that way. To him, every one of those cattle represents a sum of money. In his opinion, I am flagrantly wasting his and his investors' pounds and pence.''

"There isn't a rancher here who hasn't had losses like that, and we've all managed to stay in business just fine, and make a profit to boot.'' She raised her chin. "I'd tell your father so myself if I could.''

He glanced at her, then began to chuckle. "I imagine you would at that. I wonder what the earl would think of you, 'A. B. Waters'?''

Was it his smile or the whiskey-laced punch she'd drunk that made the blood sing in her veins? Whatever the cause, she was suddenly anxious to feel his arms about her, to experience again the sensation of floating in time to the music.

"Dance with me, Reg,'' she said, taking him by the arm and pulling him toward the door.

"A lady never asks a gentleman to dance,'' he said. But nevertheless, he let her lead him onto the floor.

His arms went around her as naturally as if they'd been dancing all their lives. She rested her head on his shoulder and gave a contented sigh. "I don't know if I'll ever get the hang of this 'lady' stuff,'' she said. "Why can't I just be me?''

"Would you have worn a silk gown and danced every dance a few months ago?'' He spoke low in her ear. "I think whether you like it or not, you're becoming more of a lady.''

She raised her head and looked into his eyes. They were dark, glinting with amusement and a hint of desire that sent a shiver up her spine. His breath stirred her hair, and she realized she was not the only one who had sampled the spiked punch. He pulled her closer, and she thought he might kiss her, without thought to who was watching.

But the music ended and he released her. She moved out of his arms slowly, reluctantly. "I may never be a real lady," she said, her hand lingering in his. "But you've taught me what it means to be a woman." She squeezed his fingers, then released them and turned and walked away. But she could feel his gaze on her all the way across the room.

Reg stared after Abbie. The lavender scent of her perfume lingered in the air around him, and the warmth of her body still clung to him. Where other women were rigid from the boning of their corsets, Abbie was soft and yielding. His fingers had shaped themselves to the curve of her waist, caressing her. He could still feel the lush fullness of her breasts pressed against his chest.

He had spotted her the moment she entered the room, as if her very presence stirred his senses to some heightened awareness. He had looked up and seen her framed in the doorway, and his breath had caught in his throat.

She had piled her hair up high on her head, and the wide neckline of her gown exposed alabaster shoulders and a regal neck. His mouth watered at the thought of kissing her there, tracing her delicate collarbone with his lips, blazing a trail to the breasts that swelled against the plunging neckline of the gown.

Rough-and-tumble Abbie in bows and silk; a month ago he might have laughed at the idea. Today he could only look on in admiration. The erect carriage of her body, the way she held her head up and met the gaze of every man head-on, revealed the confidence she had gained in making her way in a man's world. This woman who could rope a wild steer or chase down a fleeing calf had an alluring strength more polished women sadly lacked.

He had watched her until she disappeared into the women's cloak room, then turned away and spent the rest of the evening avoiding her. The memory of that moment in her kitchen, when he had almost kissed her, lingered fresh in his mind. No good could possibly come of any involvement with Abbie.

But when she had sought him out, actually taken his hand and led him outside, he had possessed no strength to resist. Being with Abbie, talking with her and admiring her, was a welcome distraction from his other worries.

He still couldn't believe he had told her about the letter from the earl. He had picked it up this afternoon, and the minute Pickens put the crested envelope in his hand, an ill feeling had washed over him, like a wave swamping a ship. This missive was thicker than his father's usual communications; more words could only mean trouble.

He had stopped to read the letter a little ways out of town, then cursed all the way home. Mouse's ears had twitched at his rider's fury; as far as Reg was concerned, his horse was the only one who would ever know of his frustration.

He had told Abbie everything. Sharing the news with her somehow made the picture seem not so bleak. Of course the losses were not his fault. Of course others had suffered similar setbacks and lived to triumph.

He imagined Abbie delivering this message to the old man. The earl would be stunned. No woman ever contradicted him to his face; few people of either sex ever bothered to argue with him. The earl had the arrogance of centuries of power and wealth on his side. None of those things mattered to Abbie. She would tell the earl exactly what she thought, and if she did not charm the old man, she would at least intrigue him.

Reg had no way of intriguing or charming his father. He knew well enough what the old man was up to—the earl wanted him to quit, to admit defeat and come crawling home. He straightened his shoulders. He wasn't about to give his father satisfaction. He would see this through and return home victorious. For once he would have the last word.

"Reg, there you are. I've been looking for you." He turned and saw Alan Mitchell walking toward him. "Saw you dancing with Abbie," Alan said. "You two looked good together."

Reg shrugged off the compliment. "Thank you for inviting me. I shall have to return the favor some day soon."

"Aww, don't worry about that." Alan clapped his arm on Reg's shoulder. "So how's Donnie Best working out as your new foreman?"

"He's doing quite well." Reg nodded. "I like him. He's not afraid to speak up, but he asks for my input and listens."

"Good. That's good." Alan shoved his hands in his pockets. "I hear Tuff Jackson is still hanging around town, running his cattle on school land and predicting your downfall every chance he gets."

He should meet my father, Reg thought. "Tuff doesn't worry me," he said.

Alan frowned. "Maybe he should. It doesn't take much for some men to step over the line from good to bad. Maybe Tuff's one of them who doesn't have to walk too far."

"Thanks for the advice." Reg meant the words. He liked Alan—liked him enough to feel guilty about his own attraction to Abbie. After all, he had promised Abbie he would help her win this man for a husband. What did it say about his character when he spent half the time lusting after her himself?

Brice hailed Alan from across the room, and the rancher went to answer his father's summons. Reg watched him walk away. Strange, Abbie hadn't said a word about Alan tonight, though he had seen them dancing together. She had come to Reg right after that dance, and asked *him* to accompany her on the floor. He couldn't deny the pleasure he had felt, holding her close in his arms.

What had she meant at the last there—about him teaching her what it meant to be a woman? The words were almost like a challenge to him. He could teach her so much more about being a woman—if he only dared. The thought sharpened his desire to a keen edge.

He pushed the thought away. Better to keep his distance from such dangerous territory. He needed to concentrate on the ranch. Leave Abbie to someone more her kind— someone like Alan. Reg would turn a profit in the fall, then sail home to England and find some proper British miss to start his nursery.

The sound of familiar laughter caught his attention. He turned to see Abbie and Maura laughing with Alan. Would a proper British miss ever be as contrary and stubborn as Abbie was? Would she try his patience as Abbie did time and again? Would she make his heart race the way it did when Abbie was near? Would the thought of lying with her ever arouse him the way the thought of bedding Abbie could? How could he bear to sail away from here with those questions unanswered?

Chapter Fifteen

Standing on the platform at the Fairweather station a week later, Abbie pulled her father's watch from the pocket of her skirt and flipped open the polished metal lid. Ten after. Of all days for the train to be late. She snapped the lid shut and shoved the watch back into her pocket. Maybe the train wasn't coming today. Maybe it had broken down up the tracks somewhere, or there'd been a wreck. If it didn't arrive, then she didn't have to get on it. She and Maura could ride back to the house and get out of these fancy traveling duds and go on working like any other day.

She walked to the edge of the platform and leaned forward as far as she dared, searching for some sign of the wayward locomotive. Instead, she saw a sight that made her want to run and hide. Reg, dressed in the most elegant suit she had ever seen, strolled out onto the opposite end of the platform. To make matters worse, Alan was with him.

"Look, miss, there's Mr. Mitchell come to see us off."
Maura raised her hand to wave, but Abbie pulled her back.

"Please don't draw their attention," Abbie said. "Just . . .
just pretend you don't see them."

"But why ever would we want to be doing that, miss?"
Maura turned a puzzled frown on her mistress.

Abbie flushed. "I . . . I don't want anyone to think that
Mr. Worthington and I are traveling together." She especially didn't want *Alan* to think that.

"But it's all very right and proper, now, miss, with me
along to chaperon." Maura straightened her shoulders.
"And weren't you telling me yourself, this is all for business,
buying cattle and such?"

Abbie nodded. "That's right. It *is* a business trip."
Except that ever since she'd agreed to accompany Reg
to the auction in Amarillo, she'd been having some very
*un*businesslike thoughts about spending so much time with
him over the course of several days. Those few moments
in his arms at the dance the other night had only served
to fuel her fears over what might happen if she and Reg
were left alone. Something about the man brought out a
wild side of herself she had never known existed before.

"Well, I'm sure Alan would never be spreading gossip
about you and Lord Worthington," Maura said. "He's too
much of a gentleman." Her lips curved in a fond smile.

Oh, dear, Abbie thought. In her worry over Reg, she'd
let Maura's infatuation with Alan slip her mind. How was
she going to go about capturing Alan's attention for herself, without hurting the maid's feelings? As soon as they
returned from Amarillo, she'd have to set about finding a
suitable cowboy to distract Maura. Maybe Reg's new foreman, Donnie Best?

"Oh, I'm almost forgetting, miss. I've something to give
you afore we set out." Maura searched through the small

reticule that hung from her wrist. "I know I'll be finding it somewhere in here."

"What is it, Maura?" Abbie glanced down the track once more. Thankfully, Reg and Alan had turned to walk in the opposite direction.

"Ah. Here it is, miss." Maura held up a small cloth bag, suspended from a narrow satin ribbon. She pressed the object into Abbie's gloved hand. "It'll please me to no end if you'll be wearing this, miss."

Abbie stared at the curious bag. It was sewn of plain muslin, gathered with white cotton thread. "What is it?"

"It's me special good luck charm. There's comfrey and mint, and a shamrock all the way from home." She nodded, her face serious. "I've been noticing you don't carry so much as a rabbit's foot with you, so I fixed this up special."

Abbie smiled. "I see. And do you have one, too?"

"Oh, indeed I do, miss. Plus me St. Christopher's—for travelers, you know, and me rosary, me rabbit's foot, a caul from a seventh son . . ."

Abbie stepped back, half afraid Maura would pull this arsenal of good luck from her bag. She opened her mouth to speak, but a whistle blast from the approaching train drowned out her comment. "Thank God," she breathed, and grabbed up her carpetbag. The sooner she was on the train and out of sight of the prying eyes of the town, the better.

She and Maura found their seats in the forward car and had just settled in when a conductor approached. "Miss Waters?" he inquired, tipping his hat.

"Yes, I'm Abbie Waters."

"If you and your companion will follow me, ma'am, I'll show you to your car."

"Excuse me. Have we taken someone else's seats?" Abbie looked around, confused. She checked the ticket in her hand.

"It's all right, miss. If you'll follow me, please."

Reluctantly, Abbie gathered her belongings, and she and Maura followed the conductor through the cars until they came to a private Pullman at the rear of the train. Abbie balked at the door. "There must be some mistake," she said.

The conductor shook his head and opened the carved wooden door. "No mistake, miss. Mr. Worthington gave strict instructions that you were to share his car."

Abbie would have protested; but the train lurched forward, and she was thrown off balance, into the Pullman, and into Reg's arms.

"Hello there, Abbie," he said, smiling down on her, a roguish gleam in his eye. "How nice to see you."

She was uncomfortably aware of her breasts pressed against his chest, his strong arms enfolding her. The starched linen and polished leather scent of him filled her senses even as she struggled to push away from him. A moment too long in Reg's arms and she might forget herself altogether. "Let me go," she said through clenched teeth.

"I was merely standing here when you launched yourself at me." He set her upright and stepped back. "Would you care for some refreshment?" He reached toward an embroidered bellpull.

"What I want is to go back to my seat," she said. "What did you mean, telling the conductor we're sharing the same quarters?"

"I merely took the liberty of arranging more comfortable accommodations for you." He motioned toward a velvet-upholstered Chesterfield sofa. "Please, sit down."

He was so infuriatingly *calm*. So frustratingly *regal*. "You had no right to do that," she said.

He raised one eyebrow, obviously skeptical. "Do you mean to tell me you would prefer to sit up all night in the second-class coach, having cinders blown on your dress and the sounds of crying babies and coughing strangers to lull you to sleep?"

"I thought we agreed it would be best if people did not know we were traveling together."

"Precisely my reason for hiring a private car. No one can see in—" He gestured to the velvet-draped windows. "No one can pass through—" He nodded toward the closed door. "And with every convenience, you'll have no need to venture outside these private walls. No one will even know you are on this train, much less traveling with me."

"Perhaps he's right, miss," Maura said from behind her. "And it's ever so lovely."

Abbie looked around the well-appointed car. Gilt-framed oil paintings adorned walnut-paneled walls, and many-crystalled chandeliers hung from a ceiling trimmed in gold medallions. Two sofas and half a dozen chairs were arranged around the room, all upholstered in royal blue velvet, the cushions thick and heavily tufted. Plush carpeting muffled the sound of footsteps on the floor. There was even a walnut writing desk, should the urge strike one to compose a letter. She couldn't imagine a more comfortable way to travel. But where would she sleep? The thought of reclining on the sofa in Reg's presence made her feel flushed.

As if reading her thoughts, Reg walked to a set of folding doors and pulled them back to reveal a four-poster bed and trundle, washstand and clothes press. "You and Maura can sleep here. I'll make myself comfortable on one of the sofas."

She hated to admit Reg was right, but she could find no fault with his argument. Reluctantly, she nodded. "All right. I guess we'll have to stay."

"I'll see to our things, miss. You and Mr. Worthington

will be wanting to discuss business, I know." Maura picked up their bags and bustled into the bedroom.

Abbie sank into a chair, and Reg settled himself across from her on the sofa. "That's another advantage in traveling this way," he said. "You can instruct me on everything I need to know about the auction."

As the train rolled farther and farther away from Fairweather, Abbie began to feel farther and farther removed from her "normal" life. She sat in that ornate parlor, dressed in one of the new traveling dresses Maura had made, and discussed cattle prices and breeding lines with Reg as if she'd merely stopped by his ranch for afternoon tea. Toward evening, in fact, Reg did order tea, which a red-coated porter delivered and Maura poured. Abbie nibbled sandwiches with the crusts cut off and diminutive fruit pastries and began to feel as if she'd slipped into another life, another body even. She balanced a delicate china cup on one knee and ate a whole meal with her gloves on as if she'd been doing it all her life.

"I discovered the advantages of the private railcar after a particularly harrowing trip across India," Reg said, stirring milk into his second cup of tea.

"Oh, m'lord. When was you in India?" Maura stared at him, wide-eyed. "Was it very awful there, with all them heathens and what not?"

"Actually, I rather enjoyed it there." He sipped the tea. "I found the country beautiful, and the people were most interesting, and very peaceful. I enjoyed getting to know them."

"What did you do in India?" Abbie asked.

"I managed a tea plantation."

"And if you liked it so much, why did you leave?" she asked.

His hands, holding his teacup, were as steady as ever, but Abbie could have sworn she saw him flinch. His eyes took on a shuttered look. "The plantation I managed went bankrupt."

An uncomfortable silence followed. Abbie stared into her teacup and thought of Reg riding through fields of dark green plants. She had never seen India, but she imagined it to be a tropical, verdant place, very different from the stark Texas plains. What had led to the failure of his plantation? Had weather conspired against him, or had his own poor judgment brought about his defeat?

"Before that, I was a sailor for a time," he said abruptly. He leaned forward and set his cup on the low table between them. "My father thought it might make a suitable career for me."

"That's a romantic life, traveling from port to port," Maura said, a dreamy look in her eye.

"I enjoyed the travel."

"But in the end, you decided against a naval career?" Abbie tried to affect the right tone of idle curiosity, when in reality she was anxious to hear what had led Reg to once again fail to meet his father's expectations.

"The navy decided against *me*," he said. "I had the unfortunate habit of questioning the judgment of my superior officers."

"Anyone could see, m'lord, that you should be one as who gives orders, not takes them," Maura said. She plucked a peach tart from a tray on the table. "What would be the most exciting place you ever visited?" she asked.

Abbie set aside her cup and leaned back against the chair cushions, lulled by a combination of rich food, warm tea and the gentle sway of the train. She watched Reg as he related an entertaining story of derring-do in foreign ports to a starry-eyed Maura. He was full of such stories this evening, but had said precious little about England, his home and family. Had he spent so little time there in recent years he'd ceased to think of it as home? Or had the friction she sensed between him and his father tainted his feelings for his country as well?

She let her gaze wander around the Pullman. Every possible thought had been given to a traveler's comfort. A nickel-plated parlor stove could provide heat in winter weather, while transoms could be opened above the windows to improve circulation in the summer. The bellpull would summon a porter to fetch water or food or answer any other request. Reg seemed perfectly at home in the luxurious suite of rooms, and even Maura perched in her chair and poured tea and made conversation as if she'd been born to a life of ease.

Abbie looked on in wonder. Despite her success so far, she could never be comfortable for long in such close quarters. The velvet drapes and paneled walls squeezed the breath out of her as tightly as any corset.

While Reg and Maura reminisced about sea voyages, Abbie stood and made her way to the door at the rear of the car. She stepped out onto the platform and leaned on the railing, the rumble of the wheels on the tracks filling her ears.

All around her was black; she had the feeling of being suspended in space. But as her eyes adjusted, she could make out the shadows of bushes and trees, or the single, winking light of a homestead in the distance. She closed her eyes and inhaled deeply of the cinder-scented breeze. She swayed with the rhythm of the train, feeling the vibration in her feet, traveling up through her body. She absorbed the motion and the sound, taking its rhythm for her own.

"You prefer the out-of-doors."

The words were spoken so close to her ear she could feel Reg's warm breath. Her eyes snapped open, and her body gave a jolt of surprise.

He reached out to steady her, wrapping his hands

around her upper arms and pulling her toward him. "I didn't mean to startle you," he said. "I thought you heard me come out."

She shook her head. "I was listening to the train," she said, realizing how foolish that sounded as soon as the words were out of her mouth.

Reg didn't laugh at her. He moved his hands as if to release her, but instead turned her so that her back rested against his chest, his chin brushing the top of her head. It was an intimate gesture, a scandalous one even, but in the concealing darkness, with the rumble of the train shutting out the sounds of the world around them, Abbie welcomed the closeness.

"You're like a wild bird," he said. "Unhappy in a cage, no matter how gilded."

"I appreciate your hospitality," she said. "But I'll admit I feel hemmed in when I spend too much time inside. I've spent all my life working the land, not even setting foot in a house for weeks at a time."

"You've only been away from your ranch a few hours and already you sound homesick."

She hugged her arms across her chest. "I suppose I am."

"I've spent most of my life wandering. I've never known that feeling of being rooted to one specific place." He sounded wistful.

"It's not too late, you know."

"Too late for what?"

She pulled away and turned to face him. She could barely make out his features in the darkness, but she could feel his warmth, sense his gaze upon her. "It's never too late to put down roots," she said. "To find a place and make it your own."

"Brand it?" He sounded amused. "Like a maverick calf?"

"In a way, yes."

He turned his head, staring out at the landscape rushing by them. "Maybe it's the other way around," he said. "Maybe the right place makes its mark on you, and then you know you belong." He turned to her again. "Or maybe the right person in that place touches something inside you and ties you to one place."

Would she tie Reg to her if she could? She closed her eyes against the thought—she might as well try to turn a racehorse into a ranch pony. A smile curved her lips. That didn't mean she couldn't enjoy that fine racehorse, even if he'd never be hers to keep.

The solid sound of a closing door made her open her eyes. Reg was gone, leaving her alone in the darkness once more.

"No, don't take that one. See how she's all matted around the eyes. Could mean she's sick. Now *that* one. Number sixteen. Yes, bid on her. See how broad she is through the shoulders?" The auctioneer called for bids on sixteen, and Reg raised his hand for the opening offer. A red-haired man across the ring made a challenge, but quickly lost interest. No one raised the price, and the animal was led off for Reg to claim at the end of the day.

"That's good," Abbie whispered, leaning on his arm. "Now let's see if we can spot something with a feisty personality."

Reg studied the steady parade of young heifers through the auction ring, but his mind was only partially on the scene before him. The rest of his attention was fixed on the young woman on his arm. His head was full of the lavender scent of her, and every nerve of his body was attuned to her slightest movement. She stood so close he could feel the tensing of the muscles of her thighs when she shifted her weight. When she leaned forward to get a closer look at the ear markings of a particular heifer, her breast brushed his arm, sending a shiver of sensation through his already strained nerves.

"There. I like number thirty-two. See how she shakes her head and almost swaggers when she walks? She has a good spirit." Her breath was moist in his ear, and a wayward curl peeking beneath her straw bonnet tickled his neck. He shifted to accommodate the uncomfortable stiffness in his crotch. Standing like this for hours on end was sheer torture; torture he was reluctant to see end.

He forced his mind back to the job at hand. "What about eighty-six? The one with the star-shaped blaze on her forehead." He nodded toward the heifer in question.

"Yes. She's such a lovely deep red color."

He looked at her in surprise. "And here I thought all your selections were made purely on the basis of business and scientific principles."

She flushed. "Well, she has good shape to her, too. But there's nothing wrong with choosing an animal that *looks* nice, is there?"

He smiled and shook his head. Just when he had deluded himself into thinking he could predict her behavior, she would confound him with a new response. Like a many-sided children's puppet, she constantly presented a new facet of her personality for him to wonder at. She could go from hard-riding cowgirl to kittenish flirt while his back was turned, from Puritan-practical rancher to a woman who would choose her stock as much for their color as for their conformation.

Since they had left the ranch to come to Amarillo, he had enjoyed more glimpses of the lady inside the rancher. Away from the day-to-day drudgery of ranch work, minus the rough work clothes, Abbie revealed a softer side. She smiled more, and took more care with her appearance.

But it would be a mistake to underestimate her. More

than one man in this auction ring had flinched at a piercing look from her emerald eyes. She refused to be outbid on an animal she wanted; the roughest man in boots and spurs could not force her to back down.

Reg admired that kind of confidence even more than he admired her beauty. Abbie might not realize it, but she was teaching him in more ways than one.

"That's an even dozen," he said now, looking at the card where he had been keeping track of his purchases. "That's enough for me, don't you think?"

She glanced at her own card. "Yes. For me, too. It looks as if the rest of the sale is steers and odd lots." She slipped her hand out of his arm. "You did very well for yourself today."

"Except for the two I lost to you." He winked at her.

She blushed. "I couldn't let you take everything good." She looked around the auction barn. Reg followed her gaze across the rows of wooden bleachers surrounding the dirt ring, and the raised booth where the auctioneer surveyed the steady flow of livestock. The air was redolent with the odors of manure and tobacco smoke. "Spending the day here with you today makes me think of my father," she said.

He winced. He wasn't *that* much older than Abbie. "So I remind you of your father, do I?"

"Not you. This place." She swept her hand out to take in the arena. "I can't help but think of him when I walk in here. He brought me with him from the time I could walk. He'd hold me in his arms so I could see the animals, and talk to me about the ones he was bidding on."

"He was training you even then."

"I suppose so."

They began to walk toward the exit. Reg tried to imagine Abbie as a little girl, carried in the arms of a tall man in a Stetson, who even then treated her less like a child and more like the business partner she would one day be. "You're very fortunate that your father trained you to take over his business," he said as he and Abbie stepped out into the yard in front of the auction barn.

She nodded, her expression pensive. "He wanted me to be able to look after the ranch, and myself, even when he wasn't around to help me any longer."

"My father spent time with my brother, Charles, grooming him to follow in his footsteps. Naturally, as the eldest, he will inherit the title and the duties that come with it." He shook his head. "There were never any specific duties for a middle son, no prescribed training one can give." He tried to keep his voice light, but he feared she would sense the bitterness he could never quite block out. God, here he was, thirty-four years old, and he was still picking at that old wound like a schoolboy.

Abbie looked at him as if she wanted to ask a question, but after a moment she looked away. "So much of what Daddy taught me wasn't really specific to ranching," she said. "Most of all, he taught me to think for myself—to make my own decisions and stand by them. He taught me to live independently, to be responsible for myself."

"Unconventional training for a woman."

She raised her chin. "Is that so bad, then?"

"It's stood you in good stead, made you successful."

"And left me alone." She hugged her arms across her chest. "I wonder sometimes if my failure to marry has been more because I am a woman who insists on standing on my own, than because of any lack of femininity on my part." She stopped and turned to face him. "I can go through the motions of being a lady all right, Reg, but I can't change what I am inside."

He stared into her eyes, green as meadow grass, dark with concern. "Do you want to change?"

She bowed her head. "I don't see why taking a man's name should mean I take his direction also."

Reg reached out and lifted her chin and stroked his thumb along her velvet cheek. Hard and soft. Independent and longing for union. Such a lovely contradiction. "You'll find the right partner one day. Maybe not Alan—but a man who'll see your value. A man who's looking for a partner as well as a wife."

She gazed back at him, clear-eyed and unwavering. "What do you want, Reg?"

He sensed her probing him for answers he wasn't prepared to give. "I want to take you to dinner this evening," he said lightly. "To celebrate a successful day at the auction."

If she was disappointed in his answer, she did not show it. She looked away, and nodded. "All right. Give me a chance to clean up and change."

"Six o'clock, then? I'll meet you and Maura in the lobby of our hotel."

"That sounds fine. I want to speak to the stock agent first, arrange for shipping."

"I can do that," he said.

"No, I'll do it. You'd better see to your heifers, though. Don't forget to pay the cashier."

He bit back a smile as he listened to her list of instructions. Lesser men might, indeed, be daunted by such competence. Ah, but Abbie didn't deserve a lesser man. Only a man as strong as herself would satisfy her. Even now, Reg felt a stab of envy for that unknown man who would one day win such a fair prize.

Chapter Sixteen

Abbie frowned at the figure huddled under the quilts in her hotel room. "But you can't be ill," she said. "You were right as rain less than an hour ago."

"It come on me sudden like, miss." Maura gave a weak cough and pulled the covers closer around her chin. "I'm ever so sorry to inconvenience you this way."

"You've nothing to apologize for." Abbie felt the maid's forehead. It was cool to the touch. "Maybe we should call a doctor . . ."

"Oh, no, miss." Maura's eyes went wide, and she shook her head. "I'm sure all I'm needin' is a good night's rest to set me right again. You go on and enjoy your dinner with Mr. Worthington."

The thought of dinner alone with Reg sent a tremor through Abbie's stomach. She'd already spent more time with him today than was wise; the constant contact left her edgy and impatient, longing for something she could not name. "If you're ill, you shouldn't be left alone," she said to Maura. "I'll send a note to Reg and stay with you."

"Oh, no, miss." Maura struggled to a sitting position. "You needn't be putting yourself out like that for me." She clutched the quilts around her. "It's not so much ill I am as overtired." She nodded. "The excitement of traveling and seeing a new city has taxed me nerves. A good night's sleep and I'll be back to me old self."

Abbie gave her a doubtful look. Other than a slight flush to her cheeks, Maura looked healthy as ever. Having seen her work, Abbie was convinced the maid had an iron constitution. "This doesn't have anything to do with your believing it's not your place to eat with Reg and me, is it?" she asked. "I've told you before, those class distinctions don't hold in Texas."

"Yes, miss, and I'm beginning to see the truth in what you're saying, and I'd be most honored to be going with you and Mr. Worthington. But I'm plumb tuckered, I am." As if to confirm this, she slid back beneath the covers.

So much for the idea that the maid would be a suitable chaperon, Abbie thought. She'd begged off accompanying them to the auction this morning, and now she was opting out of dinner. Abbie sighed. Nothing to do but get the meal over with, she supposed. She picked up the ridiculously small bag that held her room key and handkerchief, then paused to check her appearance in the mirror by the door. "Do you really think this dress is all right?" she asked. The shimmering purple silk gown left much of her shoulders bare and clung tightly to the curves of her waist and hips.

"You look divine, miss," Maura said, raising herself to a sitting position. "Mr. Worthington will love it."

"I feel half naked."

"Oh, no, miss. It's quite modest—no more revealing than those trousers you're fond of wearing."

She nodded. Of course Maura was right. Time to quit stalling and go downstairs and meet Reg. After all, what could happen with a dining room full of other people watching them?

She left the room, walked down two floors, then descended the curved staircase into the hotel's main lobby. She walked slowly, partly on account of the cursed high heels she could never quite get used to, and partly because her stomach was doing somersaults with every step closer to her rendezvous with Reg.

Stop it! she silently ordered her nerves, but they behaved no better than an untamed mustang. How was it her mind had turned something as simple as a dinner into a dangerous ordeal? She had eaten dinner with Reg before, she reminded herself.

But never alone. Never away from her familiar territory of the ranch. And never dressed in a clinging, low-cut gown that made her look, and feel, every inch a woman. She smoothed her hand down the shimmering skirt. Would Reg like the dress? Would he like her in it?

Oh, confound it! What difference did it make what Reg thought? They would never be—*could* never be—anything more than friends.

She spotted him in the crowd below, standing with his back to her. Her breath caught as her gaze swept over his shining black hair and the broad shoulders outlined against his perfectly tailored suit. She had never met a man who was so handsome, so elegant. She ought to feel all awkward and ignorant beside him, but he never made her feel that way.

As if sensing her eyes on him, he turned, and caught sight of her on the stairs. His gaze swept over her, and a hint of a smile curved his lips. He nodded, as if in approval, and moved toward her. "Abbie, you look splendid," he said. He reached for her hand, but instead of taking it to lead her the rest of the way down the stairs, he bent and kissed it.

She felt the warmth of his breath through her glove, and remembered the day they'd met, when he'd kissed her that way. Even then, the touch of his lips had made her tremble. He raised his eyes to meet hers; his dark, sultry gaze shook her as much as the kiss. "Every man in the room is watching us now, and wishing he were in my shoes," he said.

"Every woman here wishes she were in mine," she replied, sliding her hand from his grasp. "And to tell you the truth, I'd gladly trade these heels with them for a pair of comfortable boots."

He laughed out loud and offered her his arm. "Then, I'd best take you in to dinner before someone comes up and makes you a better offer," he said.

She put her hand on his arm and smiled up at him. "Maura says she's sorry she can't come with us, but she isn't feeling well."

"Nothing serious, I hope."

She shook her head. "It doesn't seem to be."

"Perhaps I shouldn't say so, but I'm pleased to be able to entertain you alone, *without* a chaperon."

A pleasant shiver ran up her spine at the words. He squeezed her hand and led the way toward the dining room. She concentrated on walking demurely by his side to their table, when what she really wanted was to stop and crane her head to take in all the sights. Even keeping her eyes straight ahead, she saw enough to amaze her. What looked like an acre of tables stretched out in front of them, each one topped with a dazzling white cloth and laden with silver polished to a mirror finish and half a dozen glasses and goblets that winked in the glow of the candles that flickered at each table.

In case the candles didn't provide enough light, gas

chandeliers as wide across as a Conestoga wheel hung
overhead, dripping with glass crystals like icicles on a January day. Gentlemen in elegant black suits and ladies dressed
in all colors of the rainbow, most of them decked out with
all manner of sparkling necklaces, earrings, bracelets and
brooches, sat at the tables and dined on steaks and fish
and what looked like whole little chickens and a lot of
other things Abbie couldn't even identify.

"Here we are." Reg held out a chair for her at a table
near the back wall. She lowered herself slowly into the
upholstered seat, careful not to crush her skirt. Reg helped
scoot in her chair, then took the seat across from her. "I
believe we'll begin with champagne," he said to the waiter.

While Reg and the waiter conferred on the choice of
wine, Abbie tilted her head back and looked up at the
ceiling. Her eyes widened as she gazed at a trio of winged
babies cavorting among the clouds. Except for a few strategically placed wisps of clouds, the babies were naked.

"The cherubs are a bit much, don't you think?"

Reg's voice made her remember herself and look down
once more. "Is that what they're called—cherubs?"

He nodded. "The decor here is rather overdone, but
the food is supposed to be excellent." He opened the gold-tasseled menu. "What would you like?"

Abbie opened her menu and stared at the long list of
choices, many of which were written in a foreign language,
and it wasn't Spanish. "You choose," she said, closing the
folder. "But I'd just as soon have beef instead of one of
those scrawny chickens."

He tried to fight back a grin, but failed. "Those are
squab. You're right. They do look, um, 'scrawny.' Why
don't we try the beef tenderloin?"

The waiter delivered the champagne, while another
appeared to take their order. Abbie sipped the bubbly
liquid and tried to suppress the similarly bubbly feeling

inside of her. Never in her wildest fantasies would she have dreamed she'd ever be seated in such an elegant restaurant, dressed in fancy clothes and seated across from a handsome man who, if not exactly British royalty, was certainly kin to some.

"Why are you smiling?" Reg asked as he filled his glass.

"Was I smiling?" She sipped more champagne and grinned.

"You were."

"Then, I must try to be more serious." She attempted a frown, but failed. How could she frown when she felt so happy?

"Don't. You're even more beautiful when you smile."

"Oh, Reg, go on." She could feel a blush working its way up her throat.

"Why do you deny it?" He leaned toward her. "I thought you were beautiful the first day I saw you, in pigtails and men's trousers."

"You'd never seen a woman in pants before."

"And you'd never seen—what was it you said? Such a 'poor excuse for a cowboy.' "

Her blush deepened at the memory. "I hoped you'd forgotten about that."

He sat back in his chair, smiling. "I will never forget that day. If not for that fortuitous meeting, I might never have decided to apprentice myself to you, as it were. I might find myself considerably worse off than I currently am."

"You haven't needed that much help. You've done very well for yourself. Why, at the auction today, you were spotting almost as many good buys as I was."

"That part of the cattle business interests me," he said. "Building up stock and trying to breed better blood lines. Instead of leaving so much to chance, it seems to me a rancher would do better to line breed to reinforce the best characteristics, as is done with race horses and hunting hounds.''

"Exactly. Reg, you have already realized something that some of the old men who've been doing this fifty years still haven't hit upon. To them a cow is merely a cow, and the only way to make money is to ship them out in quantity. There's some of us who see the money to be made in producing better quality cattle.''

"It would take several years to build up a good breeding program, but in the end, it would pay off." Reg leaned forward, his eyes alight with excitement. "We could breed cattle with more stamina for harsh conditions and the ability to hold their weight to market.''

"Maybe you should consider putting that kind of program into place on the Ace of Clubs," she said.

He sank back against his chair, his enthusiasm vanished. "I'm due back in England at the end of a year. My father will be expecting results by then and no later.''

A sinking feeling entered Abbie's stomach at the thought of Reg's leaving. "What will you do back in England?" she asked.

He stared into the dregs of his champagne, idly turning the long-stemmed glass in his hand. "I don't know. Whatever is expected, I suppose.''

Expected by whom? She wanted to ask, but the arrival of their dinner silenced her. Despite Reg's attempts at entertaining conversation, she was unable to regain the joy she'd felt at the beginning of their meal. Reg had reminded her that this evening was nothing more than fantasy; he would soon return to his old life, just as she would return to hers. He'd go back to being Lord Worthington, son of an earl, and she'd likely end up an old maid wearing men's trousers, her pretty silk dresses packed away in a trunk, along with her dreams of love and marriage.

Reg noticed Abbie's sudden silence; he blamed himself

for spoiling the evening with talk of his own dreary future. Why should Abbie care what became of him after he left Texas? In years to come, she'd no doubt remember him only as that stuffy Britisher who had intruded upon her life one year.

After dessert and coffee, he paid the tab and they rose to leave. Suddenly, the thought of going back up to his room alone was too much to bear. "I'm not ready to go upstairs yet," he said. "Come walk with me."

"All right."

They walked out of the hotel and into a street that was lit almost as brightly as day. Light and music and people poured forth from the hotels and restaurants and theaters in the area. Except for a preponderance of cowboy boots and Stetsons among the men, they might have been on the street of any cosmopolitan city in the world. He looked down at Abbie. The streetlights glinted off the gold strands of her hair. "When you came here with your father, what did you do in the evenings, after the auction?" he asked.

"Oh, well, we would usually go to a store for supplies and have supper at a diner. Sometimes he'd buy me an ice cream." She shrugged. "Then we'd walk back to the boardinghouse where we usually stayed, and I'd go to bed." She looked down the street, a wistful expression on her face. "I never even knew any of this existed."

A breeze stirred the tendrils of hair around her face and molded her dress to her body. Reg felt a tension in his loins at the sight of her feminine curves.

She shivered and hugged her arms across her breasts. "Here, take this," he said. He slipped out of his jacket and draped it around her shoulders, letting his hands linger on her arms. She looked fragile, vulnerable in the oversized coat. His sense of protectiveness toward her surprised him. "Perhaps we should go back," he said.

"No, let's walk a little farther." She leaned close to him,

so that it seemed the most natural thing in the world for him to put his arm around her. They walked in comfortable silence down the lighted streets.

She tilted her head up, looking past him, to the sky. "You can't even see the stars from here," she said.

"It's because of the bright lights."

She shook her head. "It's as if they don't exist. As if the plains and my ranch and all don't even exist."

Reg looked at the lighted storefronts around them. "I suppose for some people, those things don't exist." He smiled back at her. "It's as if we each have our own world into which we fit best." *Which world is the one where I fit?* he wondered.

The winds gusted higher, bringing the smell of rain. "We'd best turn around," he said, regretting that this moment of quiet companionship should end so soon.

She nodded and clutched the jacket more tightly to her throat. They turned back into the wind, hurrying now as thunder rumbled in the distance.

They were half a block from the hotel when rain began to fall, a driving curtain of water, lashing at them and quickly soaking their clothes. They bent their heads and tried to run, but Abbie stumbled. "Damnation!" she cried, and he caught her. She wrenched from his grasp and bent to remove her high-heeled shoes. She came up with the shoes in her hand. "It may not be ladylike, but I can't stand these one minute longer."

Her hair trailed in a wet stream down one cheek, and her silk gown clung to her like a second skin. Reg thought he had never seen anyone more beautiful, more desirable, in his life.

He knew his feelings showed on his face, but he could not take his eyes from her. She blushed and looked down at the rain running down her body in little rivers. "I can't go back into that hotel lobby looking like this," she moaned.

"There's bound to be a back way in." He took her arm once more. "Come on."

They ran faster now, feet slapping in puddles on the sidewalk, his coat flapping behind Abbie like the wings of a crow. They darted into the alley beside the hotel, and he swept her up in his arms.

"What are you doing?" she protested.

"There might be broken glass," he said. "They throw the garbage out here."

She started to argue, then heard the telltale crunch of glass beneath his shoes. He kept close to the overhanging eave of the building until they came to a back door and, inside it, a flight of stairs leading up.

"You can put me down now," she said.

"No, it's all right." He enjoyed holding her too much to relinquish her yet. He began to climb. One, two, three flights. A single gas lamp marked the door at each landing. They emerged into a carpeted corridor. He checked the number on the nearest room. "Ours must be at the opposite end," he said.

He started to put her down, but the sound of voices approaching startled him.

"Oh, my God, Reg. Someone's coming!"

Abbie's hair was fully undone now, and her sodden dress left little to the imagination, though she tried her best to hold his jacket around her with one hand while she carried her shoes with the other. Her stockinged feet peeked provocatively from the trailing hem of her skirt. His shirt was plastered to his back, his shoes were full of water, and he was balancing a woman in his arms. Strangers coming upon them would no doubt suspect the sort of behavior that was not condoned by fine hotels. They would be fortunate to escape arrest and ejection from the hotel; they would most certainly not escape humiliation.

The voices grew louder, nearer. He scanned the corridor; a blank wall at one end provided no avenue for escape. The path to their rooms lay in the direction of the approaching voices. His only choice was retreat. He opened the door to the stairs and darted behind it once more.

"Thank God no one saw us," Abbie breathed. He lowered her legs until she was standing, though she continued to lean against him.

"We'll wait here a moment, give them time to leave," he said softly. He rested his chin on her head and waited for the loud thudding of his heart to slow.

She smelled of damp lavender, like a cottage garden on a rainy afternoon. He inhaled deeply, wanting to memorize the aroma. Here, in the lamp-lit silence, he wanted to suspend time. As they clung together, he could feel her warmth seeping into him, kindling an answering heat inside him.

She shifted in his arms; they were so close she could not mistake the effect she was having on him. His erection pressed firmly into her belly; he made no move to hide it.

"Reg." She whispered his name, her breath warming his cheek.

He opened his eyes. In the soft glow of the light on the landing, her skin was like alabaster, her eyes dark pools. He met her gaze, and felt his heart hammer in his chest.

He saw desire in Abbie's eyes—not merely the raw lust a man might feel when he's lonely and alone and a beautiful woman makes herself available to him. What he saw in Abbie's eyes was a deeper emotion than that, a more pointed longing. Abbie didn't just want a man—she wanted *him*. The realization grabbed him by the throat and threatened to squeeze the very breath from him.

He closed his eyes, trying to shut out the sight, to ignore the revelation there. But in the darkness, her body drew him. His lips sought hers; a sigh escaped him when they touched. He rubbed his mouth across hers, allowing himself little tastes of her, as if more would be too much.

But he couldn't be content with such meager fare for long. He pressed his mouth to hers more firmly, coaxing her to part her lips, to allow his tongue to sweep inside and savor her sweetness.

God, she was sweet. Warm and yielding. His heart stumbled in its rhythm as her tongue began to move in concert with his. Thrust and parry, then entangled like lovers.

With a moan, he pulled away, trailing kisses along her cheek, her chin, down the satin column of her neck. He nibbled at the tender flesh at the base of her throat and was rewarded with a low laugh. The vibrations of her laughter passed through him, a ticklish sensation.

She shifted against him, pressing her body closer. Her breasts were crushed against his chest. He brought one hand up to stroke the rounded flesh. Her nipple hardened at his touch, and he fondled it with his thumb, feeling the response in his groin with each sharp intake of her breath.

He kissed the tops of her breasts where they curved at the neckline of her gown. He could see her nipples now, hard points against the fabric. Slowly—so slowly—he eased the dress down, pushing aside the camisole and revealing rose and cream perfection.

When he surrounded one taut peak with his mouth, she threw back her head and sighed. He teased her with his tongue, lavishing attention on first one side, then the other. She squirmed beneath him, her short, breathy cries urging him on. The way she pressed her pelvis against his leg left no doubt she was aching for him.

She grasped the front of his shirt, and he thought at first she was trying to push him away. But when he raised his head and tried to take a step back, she pulled him toward her again and began fumbling with the buttons of his shirt. "I want to feel you," she whispered.

Before he could answer, she tugged at the cloth, popping the buttons. As he watched, she parted the fabric and laid her head against his naked chest.

Her cheek was cool against his feverish skin, her hair brushing against him like softest down. He rested one hand atop her head and closed his eyes again, savoring the moment.

She turned her head, rubbing her face against his chest hair. His heart pounded, and every nerve hummed with desire. He felt heat and dampness and realized she was trailing kisses across his chest. She found his nipple and slid her mouth over it, licking and suckling, driving him half-mad. He bit down on his fist to stifle the groan.

The most accomplished courtesan could not have aroused him more. Her innate passion guided her; her lack of inhibition freed her to follow her feelings.

A burst of laughter right outside the door startled them. Abbie let out a small cry and jumped back. "Shhh." He laid a gentling hand on her shoulder. She looked toward the door and calmed. She must have realized, as he had, that the laughter came from the same group of revelers who had driven them into hiding in the first place.

Gently, he pulled her back to him. They clung together, waiting for the revelers to pass. Reg felt her heart pound and savored the sensation of her naked breasts against his chest.

"You . . . you don't think they heard anything, do you?" she whispered.

He looked down. Her eyes were wide in the dim light. She looked very young, and very innocent. He had been prepared to take advantage of that innocence, despite the hurt he might bring her later. "No, I don't think they heard." Gently—reluctantly—he pushed her away from him and wrapped his coat about her naked beauty. He turned his back and began to button up his shirt. "You'd best see to your dress."

"Reg." He clenched his teeth as she laid a hand on his shoulder. "Reg, we don't have to stop. I mean . . . I could come back to your room . . ." The words ended in a question. It took every ounce of will not to turn to face her once more. But if he looked at her, he might surrender to the desire that clawed at him like a wild animal. He shook his head. "No. I will take you back to your room."

She took her hand away. "But—"

"Abbie, get dressed."

Even to him, the words sounded harsh. But he couldn't summon the composure to soften them. If he so much as looked at her again, he feared he would forget all propriety and morals and duty. They would become empty words in the face of his longing for her.

He listened to the sounds of her getting dressed—the rustle of silk, the slide of wet fabric against wet skin. Closing his eyes, he inhaled her damp lavender perfume, torturing himself with the aroma.

"All right, I'm ready." Her voice was steady, angry even. He breathed more easily—better angry than wounded. But then he might have known Abbie would never succumb to hysterics.

Avoiding her gaze, he opened the door and looked out. The hallway was empty, silent. He held the door wide and allowed her to pass, then followed her down the passage to their rooms, which were side by side at the end.

"Thank you for dinner," she said, her gaze fixed on the gilt numbers on her door. "And for your coat." She slipped the garment from her shoulders and handed it to him, only the flush of her cheeks betraying any emotion.

"Good night," he said as she put her hand on the knob.

He leaned on the doorjamb, his shadow looming over her. He wanted her still; he would not stop wanting her for a long time. "Abbie."

Her eyes met his, wary.

"Lock your door. The adjoining one, too."

She flushed bright red then, but nodded, and slipped inside. Reg pushed himself upright and went in search of the hotel bar.

Chapter Seventeen

Abbie left her ruined dress in a heap by the door and slipped under the covers without turning up the lamp. Maura snored softly from her own bed across the room. Abbie buried her head under the quilts and let loose the sobs that choked her. *Fool!* she silently berated herself. How could she have thrown herself at Reg that way?

He had not even been able to look at her while they dressed. *He must be disgusted,* she thought. She was disgusted with herself, that she had let her emotions overcome her common sense.

She sniffed and dried her eyes on a corner of the sheet. The first part of the evening had gone so well; they had been having fun, even. She'd enjoyed looking at the lights, seeing a part of Amarillo she'd never known existed. Reg had been so dashing, offering his coat against the evening chill. And the rain—even that had been fun in its own way, running through the streets barefoot, being swept up into his arms and carried into the alley.

She'd felt so safe in his arms, so . . . *cared for*. She closed her eyes against a cascade of fresh tears. Then those other feelings had started—she'd become aware of his broad chest and felt the muscles of his shoulders shift beneath her cheek. He smelled of starched linen and shaving lotion, and another subtle scent she could only think of as male.

She could have stayed in his arms forever, luxuriating in the feel of his body close to hers. When they'd fled the prying eyes of those people in the hall, she'd enjoyed the conspiracy of hiding out with him. And then she had looked into his eyes and seen the same desire she felt for him. Kissing him seemed the most natural, most *wonderful* thing in the world. And kissing had led to touching, and a whole host of new and exciting sensations.

Reg had wanted her as much as she had wanted him. Surely he had. Even when they'd parted just now, she'd glimpsed regret and longing in his eyes. So why had he refused her?

They were both adults, free to make their own decisions. If they both wanted each other, why was it so wrong for them to satisfy their desires?

Yet, something had happened to make Reg change his mind. Something she'd done, or said . . . or something else altogether?

She admitted she was ignorant in the ways of men and women. Oh, she knew the basics of breeding—one didn't grow up on a ranch without figuring that out at an early age. She'd heard a few bawdy stories around the campfire, too, when the men thought she wasn't listening. But she didn't really *know* what a man and a woman were supposed to act like when they were in love.

She sat up in bed and opened her eyes wide in the dark. Was she in love with Reg? They were obviously physically attracted to each other, but surely it wasn't anything more than that. After all, they were so unsuited for each other.

He was arrogant. But didn't she have her pride, too? He was totally ignorant about ranching. But he was learning. He was accustomed to fine manners and fine living. Surely he hadn't seen much of that as a sailor. And what about his time in India?

She hugged her arms across her chest. Maybe she and Reg weren't so different after all. They were both outsiders of a sort—he because he was a foreigner, she because she was a woman. They were both stubborn, but willing to learn. They thought alike on a lot of things—cattle breeding, for instance.

Maybe she was in love with Reg. But that didn't mean he was in love with her. For whatever reason, he'd turned away from her tonight, and he still intended to return to England at the end of the year. The only chance she had been given in her life for love and he was leaving. She flopped back down on the bed and pounded the pillow. It was so unfair!

So what was she going to do about it? Hadn't her father taught her to look for a solution to every problem? "You have to learn to fix things yourself, girl. You can't count on other folks always doing it for you," he'd said. He'd been showing her how to mend a fence at the time, but surely that advice could work for her relationship with Reg as well. There had to be a way to "fix" things between them. She couldn't let him leave without at least making the effort.

Reg arrived at Abbie's door the next morning after a sleepless night, determined to make a proper apology for his behavior the night before. He had been wrong to let things progress as far as they had. The last thing he had meant to do was hurt her, which was exactly why he had stopped when he had. As soon as he explained that to her, he was sure, being the practical, sensible woman that she was, she would understand. Things could return to normal between them, except that he wasn't certain what "normal" was for him and Abbie. She had been throwing him off balance since the day they had met. He feared he was beginning to enjoy that precarious state of affairs entirely too much.

A stern-faced Maura answered his knock. "I'd like to speak to Abbie," he said.

"She isn't in."

He frowned. She was out very early. "Where is she?"

Maura studied the toes of her shoes. "I'm not certain she'll be wanting to speak with you this mornin', m'lord."

Reg stiffened. "And why is that?"

"It's you who should be tellin' me, m'lord." She cut her eyes up to him. "Maybe it's not me place to say, but I coulda sworn the young miss looked as if she'd spent the night crying. And then I find her new dress in a sodden heap on the floor, and not one word she has to say about her evening, does she. It seems to me if a young lady has a fine dinner with a gentleman, she'd be in a mood to talk about it. But Miss Abbie was up and out of here without so much as a fare-thee-well this morning."

Reg's stomach clenched at the thought of Abbie crying because of him. "Did she say where she was going?"

The look Maura gave him now was an outright glare. "It's hoping I am that you haven't done anything to hurt the young lady."

"We had a . . . a misunderstanding." He swallowed hard. "Maura . . . please. Tell me where she went and I promise I will apologize at once."

She hesitated, then gave a curt nod. "She went to the stables, to rent a horse."

The clerk at the hotel desk informed him that the closest stables was J&B livery. Reg walked the three blocks to this establishment at a rapid clip, rehearsing in his mind what he would say to Abbie when he saw her again. He only hoped he could locate her before he lost his nerve.

After determining that Abbie had, indeed, procured a riding horse from the livery, Reg paid double for the fastest mount in the place and rode out toward the edge of town. He had a feeling Abbie would head for open prairie and the kind of terrain that looked like home.

He found her on a creek bank south of town, drumming her heels against a piebald mare's flanks and cursing under her breath. The animal paid her little heed, but continued to move along at a slow walk. "Good morning," Reg called when he was still a little ways from her. He still recalled the gun she had pulled on him during their first encounter. Depending on how angry she was over last night, she might try more of the same.

She looked up and her frown deepened, but she made no move toward a weapon of any kind. "What are you doing here?" she asked.

"We need to talk," he said, reining in beside her.

She nodded, and turned her attention back to her horse. "I thought a ride would clear my head, but then the only horse they'd rent me was grandma here." The horse rolled its eyes back toward them and continued chomping grass. "And they made me use this dad-blamed sidesaddle."

Reg bit back a smile at her tone of disdain. Abbie looked quite the lady, perched on the western sidesaddle, but it obviously did not suit her.

"I notice they gave you a decent horse," she said.

"I paid double."

"So would I have, but the man said this was the only horse suitable for a 'lady.'" She scowled. "I tried to tell him I'd been riding since I could walk, but he wouldn't hear of it. He said a woman riding astride would be indecent."

"Perhaps you should have tried another stable."

"I was so anxious to get out of town for a while I couldn't wait." She leaned forward and stroked the mare's neck. "Reg, about last night—"

"I handled the situation poorly," he said. "I want to apologize."

"You didn't do anything wrong."

He stared at the ground. "I never should have kissed you. I should have controlled my passions—"

"I *wanted* you to kiss me."

He swallowed hard. "Nevertheless, I shouldn't have taken advantage of your innocence."

"I'm not as innocent as you'd like to think, Reg. I didn't want to stop."

She looked at him, her eyes dark with desire. His heart began to pound. "Surely you realize we could not have continued."

"Why not?" She leaned toward him, until her face was only inches from his. Her lavender scent washed over him, intoxicating. "We're both adults. Why did we have to stop something we both enjoy?"

He could feel beads of perspiration forming on the back of his neck. He gripped the reins until the leather bit into his gloved hands. "Abbie, as much as I am . . . *attracted* to you, you must realize a relationship between us is impossible. You have been clear about your intentions to marry Alan Mitchell, who is also a friend of mine. I could never betray his friendship. And you know I have an obligation to return to England when my year here is over. I am patently unsuited for life as a rancher, while you are the consummate cattle woman."

She nodded, cool and calm as ever. "Those are all sensible reasons why we cannot *marry*," she said. "But I don't see why that should keep us from becoming lovers in the time you have remaining here." She smiled. "After all, you promised to teach me."

The breath went out of him, as if he had been struck. "I promised to teach you the things a *lady* needs to know."

"And a wife—doesn't a wife need to know those things, too?"

He could feel the heat of his face burning red. "It is a husband's privilege to teach his wife such things," he said stiffly.

Her smile broadened. She appeared to enjoy his discomfort. "And where do husbands learn what they teach?"

"That is beside the point."

"No, it's not." She thumped one foot against her saddle. "The idea that men can do anything they want before marriage while a woman can't have *any* fun is as ridiculous as that livery stable owner making me ride sidesaddle."

He frowned. "But you might become pregnant." There was an argument she couldn't counter.

She looked him in the eye. "You've traveled all over the world, Reg. Surely you've learned a thing or two in that time to prevent that."

He gasped. Was the woman completely without inhibition? "Well, yes . . . there are ways," he admitted.

"Then, I don't see what your problem is."

"Sex is not a game," he snapped. "Despite what men, and yes, I include myself, have sometimes made it."

"Then, what is it?" Her expression grew solemn. "Is it only for breeding, like with animals?"

"No. It is . . ." He struggled for words. He had never thought about it much before last night. He had had long, sleepless hours to consider why he had pulled away from Abbie there on the stairs. He had had affairs before, even a mistress in India. But none of those women had touched him the way Abbie had. She was more to him than a casual fling. Some part of him realized he could not join himself

to her without committing part of his soul to her care—
a part of himself he could not afford to surrender, only
to leave it behind when the time came for him to go.
"When a man and a woman come together, it can be the
deepest commitment they can make," he said solemnly.
He looked away from her pleading eyes. "I can't make
that commitment right now, Abbie."

"Not to me."

The words were a statement, not a question. Sadness
weighted him down at the words. "I haven't done a very
good job of apologizing," he said. "This has nothing to
do with you."

"I wish I could believe that."

"Believe it."

"We won't talk about it anymore." She turned her horse
onto the road back to town. "Come on. I think we have
a train to catch."

The trip home was more solemn than the journey to
Amarillo, though no less civil. Abbie and Reg managed to
act as if nothing unusual had passed between them while
they were away. If Maura was puzzled by their behavior,
she made no comment, though Abbie caught the maid studying her with a curious expression on her face.

Abbie sat on the Chesterfield sofa and stared out the
window at the darkened countryside rolling past. She felt
as if her life was moving by just as swiftly; she had as much
chance of slowing it down as she would stopping the train.

Her conversation with Reg this morning hadn't ended
the way she'd hoped; he was no closer to admitting any
feelings for her, and he steadfastly refused to deepen their
relationship, even temporarily. He'd said his decision had
nothing to do with her, but how could she believe otherwise?

She wouldn't try to deny the truth, no matter how much it hurt. Reg didn't love her. All his talk of protecting her virtue and respecting his friendship with Alan was just another way of saying that.

She swallowed tears and jerked the curtain shut. Fine. If that was the way he felt, she wouldn't beg for his attention. She'd go on as she always had, running her ranch, looking after herself. She didn't need a man's help or a man's company. She didn't need Reg.

The train arrived in Fairweather early the next morning. Abbie felt her spirits lift as she stepped onto the platform. She inhaled deeply of the sage-tinged air and smiled. Home. It was as if she left part of herself behind every time she went away from this place. Coming back was like putting all the pieces together again.

"I'll see about your trunk," Reg said, stepping off beside her.

"I can get it. I have to check on those two bulls I bought anyway."

His expression clouded, and he gave a curt nod. "As you wish."

Confound it, she thought. Now he was going to take offense. Were all men this impossible?

"Reg. I say, Reg Worthington!" A man in an ink black frock coat and striped trousers hailed them from the station.

"What the devil—?"

Abbie glanced at Reg and saw that he'd blanched white as a ghost. His mouth was set in a grim line.

"What is it, Reg? What's wrong?" she asked.

The stranger strolled up to them. He was a strikingly handsome man, with golden hair, brilliant blue eyes and a dazzling smile full of good humor. He slapped Reg on the back. "Don't know when I've been so glad to see anyone," he said.

"What are you doing here?" Reg growled. His face was flushed red now, and Abbie could see the pulse throbbing at his temple.

"Just got in last night," the man said. "The overseer at your place told me you'd gone traveling." He took a step back and grinned. "I must say, this ranching business agrees with you. You're looking jolly well."

"What are you doing here?" Reg asked again.

"It's a long story, really. Bit of a dust-up back home, you know. I needed to get away for a while, and, well, I've never been to Texas. We can talk about it later, but say, aren't you going to introduce me to your lovely traveling companion?" He beamed at Abbie.

She turned to Reg. "Yes, please introduce us."

His scowl darkened. "Abbie, may I present my brother, Camden Michael Worthington. *Reverend* Worthington, that is. Cam, this is Miss Abigail Waters."

Reg scowled as Cam bent low over Abbie's hand. "Delighted to meet you, Miss Waters," Cam said. "And here I thought all the tales I'd heard about the beauty of Texas women were mere fantasy."

Abbie smiled and blushed prettily. "How nice to meet you, Reverend Worthington."

"And who is this lovely lass?" Cam turned to Maura, who actually *giggled* at the onslaught of Cam's infamous smile.

"This is my maid, Maura O'Donnell," Abbie said.

"Pleased to make your acquaintance, sir." Maura executed a curtsey worthy of an audience with the queen.

"The pleasure is all mine, ladies."

Reg stifled a groan. Women were always falling all over themselves around Cam. His combination of impeccable manners and flawless good looks had proved deadly to more than one unfortunate young woman's heart.

"I believe Miss Waters was just leaving," Reg said abruptly. He put a hand on his brother's arm. "We wouldn't want to keep her."

Abbie frowned at him. "Yes, I suppose I shouldn't keep the stock agent waiting." She smiled at Cam. "Perhaps I'll see you again soon, Reverend Worthington. Are you planning to stay in Texas long?"

"Oh, yes, indeed. I intend to have a nice long visit with my good brother, here."

They watched the two women walk away, then Reg turned on his heels and headed toward the baggage cars. He had cabled ahead that he was arriving with the dozen cattle he had purchased in Amarillo and was pleased to see Donnie Best already at work unloading the new stock.

"Mornin', Reg. Mornin', Rev." Donnie tipped his hat to them. "I see you two found each other."

"I take it you've already met my brother?" Reg asked.

"Yes, sir. Rev rode up to the ranch last night. Had supper with me and the boys."

Reg rolled his eyes. Like their older brother Charles, Cam had the knack of making friends with anyone and everyone. Men liked him and women swooned over him.

"Your man Best here was telling me about the new cattle you bought at auction." Cam propped his foot on the bottom rail of the loading chute and surveyed the livestock rushing past. "Splendid looking bunch, Reg."

Reg waited until Best was out of earshot before he turned to face his brother. "Cam, why don't we dispense with this fiction that you are merely here on a friendly holiday and admit what we both know—the earl sent you here to spy on me."

Cam raised his eyebrows. "Spy, Reg? Don't you think that's a bit harsh?"

"You don't deny it, then?"

"I won't deny Father was a tad concerned when he failed to receive reports from you for two months in a row. For all we knew, you might have been shot by some desperado, or scalped by red Indians."

"I seriously doubt my scalp was Father's chief concern."

"You underestimate the old man, Reg, you do. Now, about these cattle—"

Reg sighed. "Really, Cam. The only thing you know about cattle is how it tastes cooked medium rare and served up on a plate with béarnaise."

Cam smiled, as if delighted with a good joke. "Ah, but I've no doubt you can teach me, dear brother."

Reg gave no answer, but walked purposefully toward the wagon yard. Cam kept pace beside him. "Where are you going now?" his brother asked.

"Home."

"Ahh. Then, we'll ride together. I took the liberty of selecting a mount from among your stable, though I must say, these Texas horses would hardly pass muster with the Hunt Club."

"Horses here are bred for work, not beauty." Reg spotted Mouse among the saddled mounts along the hitching rail and suppressed a smile. Like Cam, he had been unimpressed with Texas horses when he first came to the ranch. Interesting, how his opinion had changed in so short a time.

"I never thought I'd see the day when you'd be riding such a singularly ugly beast." Cam swung up onto the back of a black stallion that had been groomed until it shone like obsidian. Reg would lay odds Cam had not been the one to do the grooming.

"Mouse serves me well," Reg said. He leaned over and patted the gelding's neck. Mouse twitched his ears and stamped his feet.

"Mouse?" Cam laughed. "Reg, Reg—what have these Texans done to you?"

They've made me think differently about a lot of things. But he didn't share this with his brother. "Come along," he said. "I've got work to do."

They had not ridden far when Cam spoke again. "So, are you going to tell me about the young lady, or do I have to pry it out of the servants?"

"They're not servants, Cam, and you won't win friends by addressing them as such."

"Come now—who is she? Some neighboring rancher's daughter?"

Reg laughed, and was rewarded by a look of confusion from Cam. "Abbie Waters *owns* the neighboring ranch," he said. "She can outride, outrope and no doubt outshoot most men in the area."

Cam raised one elegant eyebrow. "Oh? You sound proud of her—as if she were your protégée."

"Well, I . . . I think Abbie can speak for herself." He had started to tell Cam about the bargain he and Abbie had struck, but it was none of his brother's concern. Besides, he didn't trust Cam not to relay every word he said directly to the earl.

"I'm sure she can." Cam grinned. "In fact, I'll have to pay a call on your beautiful neighbor at the first opportunity. You did say she is unmarried, did you not?"

Reg shot Cam a warning look. "Abbie is not the sort of woman to be interested in you."

"And why not?" Cam straightened his collar. "Many women find a clerical collar gives a man an added appeal. Though that in itself can present certain, shall we say, problems, if it's the wrong woman."

Something in Cam's voice told Reg the truth. "I take it the wrong woman found you attractive?"

Cam looked sheepish. "My patron's sister. Put my living

quite in danger, I tell you. Lord Eversole obviously had
his sights on better prospects than a clergyman and a third
son for his sibling.''

He glanced at Reg again, as if gauging his reaction to
this announcement. "So you see, there's good reason for
me to be taking a sabbatical, as it were, in the States, and
it has nothing to do with you.''

Reg eyed his younger brother warily. Cam had a talent
for presenting only the most advantageous side to any
story. "And the earl made no mention of your checking
up on me, did he?''

Cam's fair skin flushed. "I wouldn't say that, exactly.
After all, I had to do something to persuade him to pay
my passage . . .''

"I knew it.'' Anger tightened his throat. "Leave me
alone,'' he lashed out. "I didn't ask for your interference,
and I won't stand for it.'' He dug his heels into Mouse's
flanks and shot forward, not waiting for his brother's reply.

Chapter Eighteen

"Hyahh! Get along there." Abbie edged Toby up alongside a heifer that was determined to break away from the herd. Given half a chance, the cow would dash back into the dry brush along the draw. Toby skillfully cut off the heifer's path and forced her back into line. Up ahead, Miguel swung open the gate and began driving the herd into the adjoining pasture.

Abbie reined in her horse and watched the herd amble past. Using the tail of the bandanna knotted at her neck, she wiped the dust from her face. July heat had scorched the land to little more than rocks and dirt. With minimal replenishment from scant spring rains, the water holes and creeks were rapidly drying up. She and her *vaqueros* were forced to move the herds often in search of water and grass.

"All through, *mijita.*" Miguel rode up, calling her by the name he'd used since she was a child. "You think we should move the steers next?"

"Let's wait a few more days on them," she said. "The creek over there still has some deep holes with water."

"Not much grass, though," he said.

"We can always burn pear." She hoped it wouldn't come to that. Burning the spines off prickly pear with kerosene torches was hot, dangerous work. Yet if it came down to it, the fleshy cactus leaves could save the lives of cattle when there was nothing else to eat. "All right, Miguel. I'll ride over to Spanish Creek and check on the yearlings. You see to the heifers over in the canyon."

She was turning away when she heard a voice calling her name. "Miss Waters! Miss Waters!" Abbie looked up to see a man riding toward them at a gallop. As he drew closer, her eyes widened as she recognized Cam Worthington.

"I say, so glad I managed to find you." He reined in beside her and doffed the new Stetson he wore.

"Reverend Worthington, what can I do for you?" She suppressed a smile. The formal title seemed absurd for one so full of youthful exuberance. Reverends should be old and solemn and rather plain, not young and handsome and decked out in the gaudiest western "dude" clothes available. She swept her gaze from the top of the coal black Stetson to the pointed, shiny toes of his boots. In between, he wore tan ducking trousers and striped shirt, with a red bandanna tied jauntily at his neck.

"I wanted to personally respond to your kind invitation to dine with you tomorrow evening," he said.

"I hope this means you and Reg will be coming."

His face took on a somber expression. "I'm afraid my brother sends his regrets."

Abbie tried not to let her disappointment show. She had not seen Reg at all in the two weeks since they'd returned from Amarillo. She'd decided to use his brother's visit as an excuse to invite him for dinner. And now he wasn't coming. Did he have such a low opinion of her that he'd decided not to associate with her again? "Well, perhaps some other time—" she began.

"I, however, would be delighted to accept your hospitality," Cam interrupted. "I'm looking forward to getting to know you better."

Abbie felt herself blushing, even as she looked away. She didn't quite trust Reg's charming brother. He was almost *too* nice. Reg might be arrogant and overbearing at times, but at least he didn't hide his opinions behind polished manners. "I'll look forward to seeing you tomorrow evening, then," she said.

"Do you mind if I ride with you for a bit?" He turned his horse in line with hers. He was riding a gleaming black stallion. Along with the black hat, it gave him a particularly dashing look. Abbie was certain he had chosen the horse and the hat exactly for that effect. Cam Worthington struck her as a man who always set himself to the best advantage.

She shrugged. "Suit yourself."

She headed out across the pasture, Cam at her side. "I say, when your maid told me you'd be wearing men's trousers and hat, I couldn't quite picture it. But you do look smashing."

"A dress would hardly be practical for herding cattle and mending fence."

"So you really do a cowboy's job, right alongside your, uh, 'hands'?"

"It takes every person doing his or her share of the work to run a ranch, Reverend Worthington."

"Please, call me Cam. Or if you insist, Rev. It's what the cowboys call me."

"Have you been enjoying your visit to Texas, uh, Cam?"

"Immensely. The people here are delightfully friendly."

Abbie smiled and leaned down to open the pasture gate. "Maybe it's because you're so friendly yourself." She'd already heard talk in town of "Rev's" largess in the local saloons, and his compliments to every lady he met. He was a ready audience for any story, and a willing donor to any cause. "I hear you're becoming just about one of the most popular people in town." She motioned for him to ride through, then followed.

He gave a deprecating smile and shook his head. "I doubt my brother would agree with you. Reg would certainly cheer my return to England."

Abbie had noticed that there seemed to be no love lost between Reg and his younger brother. "Why do you say that?" she asked.

"He is convinced our father sent me here to spy on him and interfere in the management of the ranch."

"And *is* that why you're here?"

He shook his head. "I needed to get out of England for a while for, um, *personal* reasons. My father suggested I stop in and see Reg as long as I was here. But it was never my intention to interfere."

His voice held a tinge of regret. Abbie glanced at him and saw that his smile had faded. "I've always had a great admiration for my brother," he added. "While I have remained home and led a life of staid decorum, he has gone adventuring throughout the world."

"Have you told him that?" she asked.

"He would never believe me." He sighed. "As it is, he is hardly speaking to me these days. He's absorbed in his work."

"Reg is very determined to be a successful rancher," she said.

"He says he has things to prove to our father, but I think rather he has things to prove to himself."

Abbie looked at him in surprise. "And I think, Cam, that you aren't as frivolous as some people might believe."

He straightened his shoulders. "You think so, eh? Well,

this 'shallow' personality has seen me through more than a few scrapes in my day. If Reg was destined to play the martyr in our family, then surely I must be the one to play the fool.''

''I'd hardly call you foolish.''

''And I'll thank you for that.'' He tipped his hat. ''I'll take my leave of you, dear lady. Until tomorrow.''

''Until tomorrow.'' She watched him turn the horse and race across the pasture. Cam was turning out to be as big an enigma as his brother. Were all men so contrary? Or had the Worthingtons really cornered the market?

Reg clenched his jaw and stared at the thin parchment envelope in his hands. His father's missives were shorter these days, and increasingly demanding. Send a report on the status of the ranch or suffer the consequences.

Come, Father, why be so subtle? We both know the 'consequences' you allude to. There's nothing you'd like better than to see me fail and be forced to come home with my head hanging. It would once again prove your assessment of my character. He tucked the letter into his pocket unread and stepped out onto the sidewalk in front of Pickens' Mercantile.

''Hey! Better watch where you're headed.'' He felt a hard shove against his shoulder and looked up into the angry, bloodshot eyes of Tuff Jackson. ''Folks around here don't clear a path for you British lords,'' Jackson drawled.

Reg bit back a groan. As if he didn't have enough problems to deal with. ''Excuse me, Jackson, I have business to attend to.''

He started to step around the cowboy, but Jackson blocked his path. ''Think you're too fine to waste time with me, do you?'' Jackson jutted his chin in the air. ''Well, you and me are equal now, *Lord* Worthington.

I'm done workin' for other folks. I'm a rancher now, same as you."

Reg's gaze flickered over his former foreman. Jackson had added a black suitcoat to his wardrobe, a coat very similar to Reg's own. Were anyone else involved, Reg might have been flattered by this bit of imitation. But Jackson's malevolent stare negated any possible feelings of good will. "I'm sure we'll be seeing each other again, then. Now, if you'll excuse me—"

Tuff grabbed his arm and held him in a crushing grip. "Where are your manners? Didn't your mama teach you if you meet a neighbor on the street, you should stop and pass the time of day?"

Reg took a deep breath and let it out slowly. For whatever reason, Jackson wasn't willing to let him pass. His gaze flickered to the hip-level bulge beneath Jackson's coat. Word around town was that Jackson had taken to carrying two loaded revolvers. Some suspected he had crossed the line from cowboy to criminal.

A few minutes' stilted conversation was preferable to a bullet in the back. "Is there something particular you wished to discuss with me?"

"I hear you've got Donnie Best doing my old job."

"Yes. Mr. Best is my new foreman."

Jackson snorted. "Can't send a boy to do a man's job. But then, I suppose the likes of you can't do any better."

"The 'likes of you'?" Reg slipped easily into an attitude of royal disdain. "What a curious expression. Some local colloquialism, no doubt."

Confusion flickered across Jackson's eyes, then his expression darkened once more. "Go ahead. Make fun of me now. But you won't be laughin' when this drought starts killing off your stock. Them foreign stockholders you represent are gonna be left with nothin' but a bunch of dead cows. That's what they get for trusting an upper-class ignoramus to look after their investment, instead of someone like me who knows which end of a cow the chips come out of."

Reg's stomach clenched. How often had he had that very thought? Though he detested Jackson, he couldn't deny the fact that the man knew a hundred times more about the cattle business than Reg could even begin to absorb in the short time he had been allotted to turn the ranch around. The drought only complicated matters more.

His face betrayed none of these thoughts, however. He tipped his hat to Jackson and gave a regal nod. "Thank you for that totally unsolicited opinion. Now, if you'll excuse me, I really must be going." He shoved past Jackson this time, refusing to be held back any longer. As he strode down the sidewalk, he could feel Jackson's eyes boring into his back, and he steeled himself for the slamming impact of a bullet.

"Reg, how are you?" He started at the sensation of a gentle hand on his arm and looked up to see Abbie beside him. She peered into his face. "Is something wrong? You look upset."

He shook his head. "No. I'm quite all right." The lie felt awkward on his tongue; Abbie of all people deserved the truth from him.

"I haven't seen you in a while." She took her hand away and shoved it into her pocket. "I guess you've been busy."

He nodded, trying not to stare. God, he had missed her. Just seeing her again gave his spirits a badly needed lift. His eyes traced the gentle arch of her neck. How could he have forgotten how delicate her features were—how incredibly graceful she looked even in her mannish clothes? The curves beneath those clothes—how many times in memory had he traced them again?

Don't go there, Reg, he told himself. *Nothing good will come of such thoughts.*

"Reg, are you sure you're all right?" She was staring at him, a frown creasing her brow.

"I am perfectly fine. Why do you keep asking?"

"I've been talking to you for a full minute, and you look as if you don't understand a word I've said."

He reached up and rubbed his eyes. "I apologize, Abbie. I have a lot on my mind right now."

"Is there anything I can help with?"

"Thank you, but no."

Her frown deepened. "I thought we had a bargain," she said. "Are you backing out already?"

He sighed. "I think we've both gained all we can from our previous arrangement," he said stiffly.

She put her hands on her hips and glared up at him. "So you think you know all there is to know about ranching already?"

He glanced around, suddenly aware they were attracting an audience. Taking her arm, he pulled her aside. "I would not deign to consider myself an expert," he said. "But you are hardly in need of my tutelage anymore."

She held her left hand in front of his face. "Do you see a ring on this finger?" She waggled her ring finger at him.

He frowned. "I hardly think—"

"You agreed to help me win Alan for a husband," she said. "I haven't had a proposal yet, and your year here isn't up, so I'd say our arrangement is hardly at an end."

Reluctantly, he took his hand from her arm. Touching her was too keen a reminder of how much more contact he craved with her. "Abbie, you don't need my help to attract Alan or any other man," he said. "You're a beautiful, intelligent young woman whom any man would be proud to call his wife."

She raised her chin, her eyes sending him a challenge.

"A bargain is a bargain," she said. "Or is an Englishman's word not as good as a Texan's?"

He stiffened. "How dare you question the sincerity of my word? I am merely pointing out that you no longer need my assistance—"

"That doesn't mean you don't need mine."

"Donnie Best is helping me."

"And you think Donnie Best is a better rancher than I am? I've been herding cows since before Donnie Best was born."

"Really, Abbie, this argument is pointless. I would help you if I could, but I see no point—"

"Then, come to dinner tomorrow night."

He sighed. He might have known Abbie would not be put off easily. "I appreciate the invitation, but I really don't have time. I have a lot of paperwork to do."

"Alan is coming. You can give me pointers on how to handle him."

"Has it ever occurred to you, Abbie, that Alan might not be the right man for you? I agree, he is a fine man, but I am beginning to have grave doubts about his potential as a suitor. He seems to have missed seeing what is right beneath his nose for far too many years."

"Fine." She crossed her arms over her chest and glared at him. "Your brother, Cam, is coming. Maybe *he'll* help me."

"Cam is coming?" Reg choked out the words. "I didn't realize he was even invited."

"Well, of course he's invited. I'm giving the dinner as a way of welcoming him to Texas."

"He's already been here over two weeks."

"I needed time to get ready," she sniffed.

"He never said anything about it when he told me about the invitation."

"He probably didn't want to interrupt your precious

paperwork." She started to turn away. "Don't worry. Cam and Alan and I will have a wonderful time without you. Do you think Cam would like the blue taffeta dress better, or the purple silk?"

"I thought the purple silk was ruined." He spoke through clenched teeth, a sudden image of purple silk being peeled back from lush breasts clouding his vision and making it difficult to breathe.

"Oh, Maura was able to salvage it after all. Do you think Cam would enjoy it?"

Cam didn't deserve the purple silk. He certainly didn't deserve Abbie. "What time should I be there?" he snapped.

An altogether too self-satisfied smile spread across her lips. "Seven o'clock will be fine," she said. "I'll look forward to seeing you."

She turned and strolled on down the sidewalk. Reg stared after her. He had the distinct feeling he had just lost an important battle before he could even fire the first shot. For a woman who had so little experience with courtship, Abbie certainly seemed to know how to handle men—him in particular.

The next evening, Reg emerged from the Ace of Clubs ranch house to find Cam already waiting with their horses. "Hurry, big brother. We wouldn't want to be late at a dinner where I'm to be the guest of honor." Cam grinned and flipped Mouse's reins toward Reg.

Reg caught the reins and swung up on the gray's back. He scowled at Cam, who was more dapper than ever, in a blue-striped silk waistcoat and midnight blue suit. His eyes came to rest on a paper-wrapped bundle draped across the saddle in front of his brother. "What's that?" He pointed at the bundle.

Cam grinned and folded back the paper to reveal brilliant yellow blossoms. "Flowers. For our hostess."

"Abbie doesn't need your flowers," he growled.

"Ah, but she does." Cam smiled. "A beautiful woman always needs flowers. Abbie *is* beautiful, wouldn't you agree?"

"She's beautiful, and too smart to fall for your tricks and flattery." Reg turned his horse toward the Rocking W ranch.

"Maybe. But I'll have such a splendid time furthering my acquaintance."

"I won't allow you to play fast and loose with Abbie's affections." Reg glared at him.

Cam's grin grew. "And what will you do to stop me, brother dear?" He laughed and spurred his horse forward, leaving Reg choking in a cloud of dust, cursing the day Cam had stepped off the train in Fairweather.

Reg reached Abbie's house in time to see Cam presenting his bouquet to her with a sweeping bow. Reg noted, with some relief, that she was dressed in a plain white shirtwaist and tailored skirt. But even in these simple clothes, she was beautiful. He couldn't deny she made his heartbeat quicken whenever he was in her presence.

She blushed and took the flowers from Cam. "Well, how kind of you, Reverend Worthington."

"Ah, ah, ah." He shook his finger at her playfully. "You must call me Cam."

"Why not discard convention altogether and address him by his childhood nickname?" Reg walked across the porch to them. He gave Cam a challenging look. "Hello, Stinky."

Cam's cheeks flushed a satisfying scarlet, but he recovered quickly. "Pay my brother no mind," he said, turning to Abbie. "His slavish devotion to business of late has left him addled and ill-tempered."

Abbie gave Reg a curious look. "Perhaps we should all go inside." She held open the door.

"After you, dear lady." Cam put his hand on the door and motioned her ahead of him. Reg started to fall in behind Abbie, but Cam stepped neatly in front of him. "You'll get the door, won't you, Reg?" he said as he followed Abbie into the house.

Maura and Alan were already inside. Alan was carrying a platter of sliced beef from the kitchen; Maura followed with a bowl of potatoes. "Hello, Reg, Cam," Alan said. He set the platter on the table and came forward to shake hands. "Good to see you both."

"Um, why don't we all sit down, since the food's all ready." Abbie motioned toward the laden table.

"Allow me." Reg and Cam spoke simultaneously and rushed to pull Abbie's chair away from the table. Alan grinned and held Maura's chair for her, while the two brothers awkwardly pushed Abbie's chair in behind her.

She sat at the head of the table, with Alan at the other end, Cam and Reg on either side of her, and Maura to Alan's left. "Oh, dear," she said, surveying the seating arrangement. "I suppose to be proper, I should have invited another woman. I wasn't thinking."

"Think nothing of it." Cam unrolled his napkin with a flourish. "I'm sure your company is worth two of any other woman."

Reg chewed the inside of his cheek to keep from groaning. Cam was laying it on a bit thick, wasn't he? Surely he didn't think a sensible woman like Abbie would fall for that kind of act?

He turned to Abbie for confirmation of his opinion, but found her watching Cam with a look of interest. "You must be quite popular with the ladies back home in England, Cam," she said, passing him the plate of beef.

He smiled and nodded and started to speak, but Reg

beat him to the punch. "Yes, a bit too popular at times. His flirtatious ways have gotten him into trouble more than once."

Cam's smile hardly wavered, but his eyes were telegraphing evil messages across the table to Reg, who struggled not to laugh at his brother's discomfort. "I'm sure whatever tales my brother has heard have been wildly exaggerated. In any case, I'm delighted to be in Texas."

"Sounds as if you've been enjoying yourself," Alan said. "Seems like everybody in town knows you now."

"Yes, well, I do like to mingle with the natives, so to speak, wherever I go. You Texans certainly know how to make a man feel welcome. Everyone here, with one or two exceptions, has been most accommodating." He sliced into the beef on his plate. "Which reminds me, I encountered one man who positively *detests* you, Reg."

Reg stabbed at a potato with his fork. "I imagine that was Tuff Jackson. He's upset because I fired him."

"He's upset because you whipped his a—um, because you beat him up." Alan sent an apologetic look to Maura, who smiled in return.

"You mean you actually *fought* this Jackson character?" Cam leaned forward. "Whatever for?"

"It's a long story." Reg concentrated on his plate.

"Strange." Cam chewed thoughtfully, then added, "I got the impression this Jackson person was rather *envious* of you."

Reg looked up in surprise. "Tuff, envious of me? On the contrary—he spent most of his time belaboring my ignorance and shortcomings."

"I don't know, Reg. Your brother may have a point." Alan waved his fork in the air to emphasize his words. "John Grady pretty much let Tuff run things when he had the ranch. It made Tuff mighty sore when the bank sold the ranch to your syndicate, instead of Tuff himself."

"If Tuff wanted a ranch of his own, it seems there would be others he could buy," Reg said.

"On the other hand, perhaps Mr. Jackson envies more than your ranch," Cam observed. "Perhaps he resents your intelligence and poise, your *style*, as it were."

Reg shook his head. But the thought intrigued him. Could Tuff—the consummate cowboy—really be jealous of a "greenhorn" like him?

"Tuff Jackson is just looking for trouble," Abbie said. "The best thing to do is ignore him. Most people do."

Reg glanced at her. "Do they?"

She shrugged. "I do. Alan does. Anyone with any sense does."

She smiled, a look that melted into him. If only he could tell her how much her encouragement meant to him. He took a firmer grip on his knife and fork, resisting the urge to touch her.

"The main topic of conversation in town seems to be this drought you folks are wrestling." Cam took a sip from his water glass. "I must admit, I thought things were dry here most of the time."

"Not this dry." Abbie pushed peas back and forth on her plate with her fork. "We hardly had any rain this winter and spring—not enough to do any good. What do you think is going to happen, Alan?"

"What? Huh?" The rancher shook his head and tore his gaze away from Maura. "I'm sorry, Abbie, I was, um, distracted."

"Yes, I see." She frowned. "I was asking what you thought would happen with the drought."

Reg scowled at Alan, but the rancher didn't seem to notice. The man was hopeless—he would choose a simple girl like Maura over a talented, intelligent woman like Abbie.

"The places with the best water will come out ahead,

though we may end up buying feed for the stock," Alan said. "I'll probably sell off some stock—steers maybe—and keep the breeding stock."

"You won't get any kind of price for them in this market," Abbie said.

He shrugged. "Better some price than no price."

She traced the path of water droplets down the side of her glass with the tip of her index finger. "I'm considering drilling a well and putting up a windmill," she said.

Alan shook his head. "That's a lot of money to sink into a hole in the ground, and there's no guarantee you'll hit good water. Plus the windmills take a lot of maintenance."

"But if you do find water, you don't have to depend so much on tanks and creeks."

"An expensive gamble, if you ask me," Alan said. "I'm surprised you'd consider it. It's not the kind of thing your father would have done."

Reg saw a melancholy look flicker in her eyes, and he watched her straighten her spine, as if shouldering a burden. He glanced around the table, but no one else appeared to have noticed the shift in Abbie's mood. "Daddy didn't think much of newfangled gadgets, that's true," she said. "But he taught me to be independent from anyone else. Finding my own water and having a windmill to bring it up to the cattle sounds like a good way to preserve that independence."

"Suit yourself," Alan said. "Guess I'm too old-fashioned."

"I say, speaking of old-fashioned, I met one of the area's first settlers this afternoon." Cam inserted himself into the conversation once more. "He told the most fascinating stories . . ." For the rest of the meal, Cam entertained them with his rendition of the Texan's tales.

Leave it to Cam to lighten the mood once more, Reg thought. No wonder his brother was so popular. He never seemed burdened with the kind of problems that plagued Reg. No doubt Cam would have had Abbie married off to Alan in no time at all, while cowboys and ranch hands gathered around to do his bidding concerning the ranch. If anyone had "style" to be envied, it was Cam, not Reg.

After the meal ended, the men gathered on the porch while the women cleared the table. "I've never seen such gorgeous sunsets before," Cam said, nodding toward the horizon, where a half circle of salmon-colored sun sat on a landscape bathed in orange and gold.

"People in cities never get to see a sunset like that," Alan said. "There's too many buildings in the way."

"That's it exactly. The land is so open here." Cam turned to Alan. "No wonder you Yanks talk so much about freedom. A man comes to learn the meaning of the word in a country like this."

Reg studied his brother out of the corner of his eye. What had triggered Cam's sudden interest in freedom?

Abbie and Maura stepped out onto the porch, bringing the scents of soap and lavender sachet. Reg was drawn to Abbie's side, despite the vows he had made to keep his distance. She smiled up at him, her cheeks flushed—from washing dishes, perhaps, or did nearness to him produce that lovely blush? He shook his head. Abbie had professed a physical attraction to him, but it was no doubt a fascination born of inexperience. If another, more suitable man had caught her eye, she wouldn't have given Reg a second look. Abbie needed a cowboy, not a British dilettante.

"I say, I've been thinking of purchasing a horse." Cam turned to Abbie. "Would you be interested in selling one of yours?"

Why would Cam need a horse? He was free to use any of the Ace of Clubs mounts during his time here. Reg started to say as much when Abbie spoke up. "As a matter of fact, I do have a horse I've been thinking of selling. I bought him with the idea of training him for ranch work, but it hasn't worked out. He's a fine saddle horse, though."

"Would you mind showing him to me?"

"Now?" She glanced at her guests.

"The others won't mind if we step out to the barn for a moment, will they?" Cam smiled at the others on the porch.

Reg glared at his brother. "As a matter of fact—"

"Oh, go on, miss," Maura said. "We'll entertain ourselves while you're away."

"Don't mind us, Abbie," Alan added.

"All right, then. He's just over here." She set off across the yard, Cam beside her. Reg watched them disappear around the side of the house, supper resting like a rock in his stomach. Leave it to Cam to find a way to get Abbie off to himself. No telling what he would try, given the opportunity.

He glanced at Maura and Alan. They had taken a seat in the porch swing and were deep in conversation about who knew what. As a matter of fact, most of their communication consisted of long looks into each other's eyes.

Reg looked away. It was hopeless. Abbie had about as much chance of attracting Alan's notice as Reg did of winning "cowboy of the year."

Did that mean, then, that Abbie was condemned to live a spinster's life? Surely there was some man among these Texans who could see not only her outer loveliness, but her inner beauty as well—her strength of will, her compassion, her uninhibited passion. . . .

What *was* Cam up to out at that barn? They had been gone quite some time, hadn't they? Surely they should be back by now? He walked to the end of the porch and leaned out to look toward the barn. The sun had all but set now, bathing the land in a gray twilight. But even in the dimness, it was clear the corral was empty. Maybe they had walked around back.

Or maybe they were inside. Cam must have persuaded her to step inside the building on some pretext. The man was infamous for the way he twisted women around his little finger. It was a wonder he hadn't been shot for his many seductions, but his infallible charm saved his neck every time. Even women he had loved and left were willing to forgive him, as if he were no more than a misguided boy.

Cam wasn't a boy. And Abbie was no innocent girl, despite her inexperience. The right words from Cam and she might very well be persuaded to kiss him. One of Abbie's kisses would only leave Cam wanting more. . . .

"I'm going to check on them," he announced, and took the steps into the yard two at a time.

He heard voices as he approached the barn. Low murmurs—the sounds one would make speaking words to a lover. Choking with anger, he hurled open the barn door. "Cam, come out of there at once," he demanded.

Cam and Abbie turned toward him. Abbie's eyes were wide with surprise. With one hand, she held the halter of a chestnut horse in the stall behind her. Cam smiled— really, the look was more of a smirk. "Is something wrong, brother?" he asked. "You seem upset."

Reg swallowed hard. "I, um, I feared something had happened to you, you were away so long."

"We got to talking about riding," Abbie said. "I never realized there were so many differences in the English style and the way we do things here in Texas."

"Ah, well, I see." Reg looked away from her, feeling his face redden.

"I think my brother suspected I lured you here for immoral purposes." Cam laughed and walked toward him. "I wonder where he'd get ideas like that." He slapped Reg on the back. "If you'll excuse me, I will return to the other guests. I'm sure I can trust you, brother, to see Abbie safely back to the house."

He strolled to the barn door, then turned and gave them a wink before shutting the door firmly behind him. Reg heard him whistle as he walked away. The sound faded, and Reg was aware of the silence around them. He could hear the sputtering of the lamp hanging just inside the barn door, and the sough of his own breath. Something stirred behind him, and without turning around, he knew Abbie had moved closer.

He could feel the heat from her body, smell her lavender scent, mingled with the odors of fresh hay and horse. His heart hammered in his chest. He had only to put out his hand and touch her. Her skin would slide like warm satin beneath his hand. He curled his fingers into fists to stop their trembling.

"Reg." Her voice was a whisper, piercing him like a scream. He wanted to block his ears, to run from the temptation that dragged at him.

A tremor rocked him as her hand sought his. Her grasp was firm, beckoning. "Reg," she whispered again. "Why don't you kiss me?"

Chapter Nineteen

For a split second, Reg stood frozen. Abbie feared he hadn't heard her. Then, in a swift, fierce movement, he crushed her to him and covered her mouth with his own. His lips were hard, almost hurting her. But as she melted against him, the pressure lessened, and she felt his tension ease, replaced by an overwhelming tenderness. He cradled her head in one hand as if it were finest porcelain and stroked her back in a way that both soothed and tantalized.

"Abbie, Abbie." Her name was both endearment and plea. She squirmed against him, longing to be closer, and opened her mouth to taste him more fully.

His moustache was soft against her skin, his tongue satin slick as it danced within her mouth. He sucked and caressed until her lips were tender and swollen, and her whole body ached for more.

Gripping the lapels of his coat with both hands, she urged him toward the bed of hay in a vacant stall. He raised his head and gave her a questioning look, his eyes dark with passion. He opened his mouth as if to speak, but she smothered the words with an urgent kiss and pulled him toward the shadowed stall.

They embraced again, her curves shaping themselves to the hard planes of his torso. Slowly, never breaking contact, they sank to their knees in the sweet-smelling hay. His hands cupped the fullness of her breasts, then slid around to find the buttons on her shirtwaist. With agonizing slowness, he began to unfasten them. Her already erect nipples quivered at the brush of his hand, and she arched her back, aching for something she could not name.

At last, his lips left hers and sought her breasts. A cry of pleasure escaped her as he sucked first one and then the other. Her breath came in gasps, and she pressed against him, supported by his hand at her back.

When it seemed she could stand no more, his hand delved beneath her skirt. He brushed his fingers across the sensitive interior of her thighs and parted the slit in her drawers. She felt a rush of heat and dampness as his finger delved into her. Her whole body trembled at his touch.

"God, I want you," he murmured into her hair. "But we shouldn't—"

"Shhh." She put her hand to his mouth and felt his tongue graze her fingertips. "It's what I want," she gasped, in agony at the thought that he might leave her now. "Dammit, Reg, do I have to beg?"

He moved away, but only enough to look into her eyes. "I am the one who should be begging you, my precious girl." Her cupped her chin in his hand. "And may the devil curse me if I ever hurt you."

She smiled at the flowery language. How like Reg to make a production out of everything. "Then, stop talking and take your clothes off," she said.

He laughed, a joyous, bawdy sound that made her skin

tingle. "Why should I be the one to do all the work?" He stretched his arms wide. "Mam'selle, I am yours."

She caught her breath, awed by the words and all they implied. But the passion burning in his eyes urged her on. With pounding heart, she began to unfasten the buttons of his shirt. Then she pushed aside the fabric and ran her hands beneath his undershirt, along his heated skin. He leaned toward her and kissed alongside her ear. "Don't dawdle, now," he teased, his voice breathless.

Smiling at his eagerness, she kissed a path from his neck down his chest, pausing to suck at each nipple, a new wave of heat flooding her as his body jerked in response. She could feel his hard maleness pressed against her stomach, urging her to hurry.

But when she reached for the waistband of his trousers, he pushed her away. "Not yet," he said, then lowered her gently onto the hay.

He stretched out to lie beside her. "My sweet Abbie," he breathed, and feathered kisses around her eyes, along her jaw. He slipped his hand beneath her skirt once more and found the opening in her drawers. As he lavished attention on her lips, his hand worked beneath her skirt, coaxing sensations she had never dreamed of before. He trailed kisses to her breasts, teasing her nipples with his tongue, scraping them with his teeth. She was in agony; she was in heaven. He slid two fingers inside her, and she gave a cry. He pulled away. "Forgive me if I hurt you," he said.

"No. No." She urged his hand to return to its explorations. "It feels so wonderful."

But instead of lifting her skirt once more, he unfastened his trousers and slid them down. She undid her skirt and slipped out of it, then lay back once more, breathless with anticipation.

Reg was surprised to find his hands trembling as he

worked to free himself from his clothes. He couldn't remember wanting—needing—a woman this much. Not even when he was a green boy interested only in satisfying his physical urges. With Abbie this meant so much more. Her reference to begging had been his undoing. Until now, he had been selfish, thinking only of his own need to avoid entanglements, his precious dignity and honor. He hadn't once considered her feelings and needs. Now he was determined not to disappoint her. He would do his damnedest to see that she never looked back on this moment with regret.

Naked at last, he lay down beside her once more and cradled her body to him. She wrapped one leg around him and arched against him, the contact sending fresh tremors of desire through him. She was ready for him, and he could wait no longer.

He rolled her onto her back, and she smiled up at him, eyes full of trust and longing. Moving quickly, he knelt between her thighs and entered her smoothly, groaning with pleasure at the warm caress of her. He hesitated, fearful of hurting her, but she clasped his buttocks and urged him on. As he eased farther inside of her, he met no resistance.

She blushed, as if realizing the avenue his thoughts had taken. "Sometimes, when a woman rides a lot—"

"Shhh, my darling. I understand." He leaned forward and kissed her, taking his time, until he felt the tension within her reside. "All the better for us now," he whispered, and slid the rest of the way inside her, no barrier to his pleasure.

He heard her gasp, and brought his hand down to stroke the nub of flesh within her nest of curls. At his touch she moaned, and he felt her tighten around his shaft. With a sigh of pleasure, he began to move in and out, long, smooth strokes leading to deeper, faster ones. Abbie writhed and

moaned beneath him, her cries driving him to a fever
pitch. When it seemed he could hold back no longer, she
cried out in delight, her body bucking beneath him. He
plunged deeper, and found his own release, an explosion
of sensation both satisfying and sweet in its intensity.

He collapsed against her, heart pounding, a smile on
his face he felt he might never erase.

"I say, is everything all right in there? You haven't been
kicked by a horse or something, have you?"

The sound of Cam's voice, just outside the barn door,
made them sit bolt upright. Their eyes met, alarmed. As
Reg watched, a deep blush washed over Abbie's face. "It's
all right," he soothed, wanting to draw her close once
more, but knowing he could not. Cursing his brother
soundly, he withdrew and rose to his feet, reaching for his
trousers. "I'll distract him while you dress," He shook his
head, no longer able to meet her eyes. "I don't know what
I was thinking," he said. "A stall, in the hay—"

"It's all right, Reg." She rose and touched his face,
turning his head until their eyes met once more. He swallowed hard, overwhelmed by the depth of emotion in her
eyes. "It was wonderful," she whispered.

Her smile made him want to cast aside his clothing and
pull her to him once more. Only the thought of Cam, and
perhaps Alan and Maura as well, finding them in such a
compromising position, stopped him. "You deserve better," he said.

Still smiling, she looked around her. "I don't know. It
seems appropriate somehow. I've probably spent more
time in my life around horses than people."

He jerked on his shirt and began fastening the buttons.
He wanted to say more—to tell her how beautiful she was
right now, how wonderful she made him feel. But wouldn't
words make things worse? What had happened tonight

didn't change the fact that he was going to have to leave her.

"Take your time coming out," he said as he pulled on his boots. "I'll handle Cam."

He found his brother leaning against the barn door. "I say, I was debating whether I should come in after you," Cam said.

"What are you doing out here?" Reg scowled.

"I started to walk back up to the house, but when you and Abbie didn't follow immediately, I thought perhaps it wouldn't look entirely proper to leave you two alone. So I took a stroll around the grounds, intending to meet up with you and return to the house together. I didn't realize you would be so long. What have you been up to in there, brother dear?" He leaned forward and plucked a piece of hay from Reg's lapel.

Reg was grateful for the darkness to hide the flush of embarrassment that swept over him. He had little doubt Cam, a rake of some renown before taking up the clerical collar, would have no trouble imagining what had taken place inside that dimly lit barn. He grabbed his brother by the shoulder. "One word—one *whisper*—of anything to hurt Abbie or her reputation and I swear you'll pay in blood," he growled.

Cam frowned. "If Abbie ends up hurt, it won't be any fault of mine." He stepped back and straightened his coat. "Could you say the same about yourself?"

"What are you two doing scowling at each other?" Abbie walked briskly up to them. Reg's heart hammered in his chest as his gaze swept over her. Somehow she had managed to put every pin in place. She looked as neat and lovely as she had at the beginning of the evening. As if nothing at all had happened.

"Let's get back to the house," she said, leading the way.

"Maura and Alan must be wondering what's become of us."

Maura and Alan appeared oblivious to the passage of time, or anything else except one another's presence. They sat in the exact same position on the swing as when Reg had left them. But a brightness in Maura's eyes and a heightened flush to Alan's face hinted that perhaps they had used their time alone for more than talk of ranching and town gossip.

Reg glanced at Abbie. Here in the light, her lips looked swollen from his kisses. Her smile seemed brighter than before, forced even. Had she already come to regret the rashness of their actions?

He would have to find an opportunity to talk with her soon—to make sure she understood that though what they had shared was wonderful and special, it did not release him from his obligation to return to England. She would be more than miserable if she tried to come with him. They would have to look on tonight as a special memory, to be treasured forever.

But how was he going to talk to Abbie without spending more time alone with her? He no longer trusted himself to remain a gentleman in her presence. Having once sampled the joy she had to share, he wasn't sure he cared to try. Duty and honor would only take a man so far in the battle against the charms of a determined and uninhibited lover like Abbie.

Somehow, Abbie managed to get through the rest of the evening, though every part of her being was attuned to Reg's presence so close to her, as if in joining their bodies they had united part of their spirits as well. She hadn't expected that, this sense of a spiritual connection, to match the physical bond they'd shared.

Her body was still warm from his touch; she felt almost as if she glowed, as if everyone could see and know what they had done. She wondered if Cam knew. More than once she caught him watching her, a contemplative look on his face. She shrugged off her embarrassment. She wasn't going to be ashamed of what had happened with Reg. No matter what the future brought, she had tonight to treasure forever.

She served coffee to her guests, then stood on the porch and waved as they departed, Reg riding away with his brother. He gave her a last look that might have been mistaken for an apology. Abbie nodded to him, as if to signal she understood. Despite wishing otherwise, she knew tonight had not changed what the future held for them—not really. Reg had set a course for himself, and like a mule that would only drive forward, he wouldn't turn back for anything or anyone.

Maura went in to bed, but Abbie stayed out awhile longer, gazing at the stars and brooding over the hopelessness of her situation with Reg. "Time changes everything," her father had always said. Would time ever take away this ache in her heart when she thought of Reg?

Banjo raised his head, and a low growl rumbled in his chest. The hair on the back of his neck stood on end, and he stared off into the darkness to Abbie's left. She caught her breath and tried to make out whatever it was that had alarmed the dog.

"It's just me, Abbie. Didn't mean to startle you."

All the breath rushed out of her as Alan moved out of the shadows. "I came back to talk to you," he said. "Alone."

She glanced at the house behind her. A single lamp burned by the front window where she'd left it. "Maura's already gone to bed," she said.

"Good." He stepped up onto the porch beside her and stood staring at his boots.

"What is it you wanted to talk to me about?" She kept her voice low, not wanting to wake Maura, and reluctant to disturb the nighttime stillness.

He shoved his hands in his back pockets. "I have a special favor to ask of you." He raised his head and looked at her, but she couldn't read his expression in the dim light. "We've been friends a long time now, but lately, I've started thinking about you a little differently."

"Differently?" A nervous flutter raced through her stomach.

He shook his head. "I don't know what it is, but for some reason I've just now realized how much of a woman you are. Maybe it's the dresses you've started wearing or something else, but I don't think of you as one of the fellows anymore."

The flutter was practically a storm squall now. What was Alan trying to say? Heavens! He wasn't going to propose, was he? "Now, Alan, hold on a minute—"

"Hear me out now, Abbie. I've been working up the courage all evening to talk to you. I sure don't want to have to go through it twice."

She swallowed and nodded. For years, she'd dreamed of this moment, longed for it, and now she waited in dread. It was all Reg's fault, too. He'd set out to teach her how to win Alan's love, and all he'd really done was teach her that she couldn't love anyone but Reg himself.

"Up until now, I've been content to live as a single man," Alan said. He rocked back on his heels. "I always figured I'd marry up when the right woman came along. Then one day, I was standing in your kitchen, and I knew I'd found the woman I've been waiting for."

She took a step back, until she was pressed up against the porch railing. "Alan, are you saying—?"

"I'm saying it's high time I got married. That's why I'm asking you—"

Abbie thought she might faint. Her heart pounded as if she'd just run a footrace with a jackrabbit. "Oh, Alan, I'm flattered, I really am. But I think it's best if you and I remain friends—"

He frowned, puzzled. "Of course we'll stay friends. That's why I thought of you in the first place. I couldn't ask just anybody, and it had to be a woman."

Her panic began to ebb, calmed by a heavy blanket of disappointment. If Alan was going to propose, couldn't he at least throw in a few declarations of love and undying devotion? Being chosen over "just anybody" wasn't likely to warm any woman's heart. "I really don't think—" she began.

He reached out and took her hand, clasping it between both of his own. She closed her eyes, preparing herself for the words she was sure would come next. "Abbie, I want you to plead my case to Maura. Convince her to marry me."

Her eyes flew open. "Maura?" she managed to croak.

He dropped her hand. "I've been crazy in love with her almost from the moment I laid eyes on her. But she's used to fancy English gentlemen. I want you to convince her that I'll be a good husband to her."

She pulled her hand from his grasp and smiled up at him. "Alan, you don't need me to speak for you. I know Maura's quite fond of you."

"She is?" He grinned. "I mean, I thought she might care for me, but I wasn't sure if she thought enough of me to marry."

"I'll tell you what." Abbie tucked her arm in his and walked with him across the porch. "You go home and think about what you want to say. Then tomorrow, you come by and take Maura out riding and pop the question."

He looked over his shoulder at the silent house. "Maybe we should go wake her up now . . ."

"No. You are going to do this right and proper. Polish up that buggy of yours, and dress in your Sunday best. Flowers would be nice, too. Maura deserves a romantic afternoon to remember, don't you think?"

He nodded. "Thanks, Abbie. I guess I just needed a woman's point of view to help me get things straight in my head." He patted her arm, then made his way back across the yard to his waiting horse.

She watched him ride away. She felt relieved, and a little disappointed, too. She couldn't even get a man to propose to her so she could turn him down. And the one man she might say yes to—well, she had little hope of changing Reg's mind.

"Looks like it'll be just you and me again, Banjo." She knelt and put her arms around the dog. If he noticed the tears that fell to dampen his coat, he didn't seem to mind.

Reg awoke the next morning to thoughts of Abbie. The lavender scent of her still filled his head. Closing his eyes, he could almost imagine her here beside him, naked and yielding, her skin like satin warming to his touch. . . . Blast it, what was he doing? He sat up and swung his legs over the side of the bed. He must put all thoughts of Abbie from his mind. Hadn't his father taught him that duty came before pleasure?

He dressed quickly, anxious to immerse himself in the list of tasks he had set himself for the day. Thank God for work to occupy his mind and body.

He was pulling on his boots when a hard knock sounded on his door. He looked up. "Come in."

To his surprise, Donnie Best opened the door. The foreman stood, hat in hand, just inside the door, his expression grim. "What is it?" Reg asked.

Best shook his head. "It's bad," he said. "You'd better come see for yourself."

Twenty minutes later, Reg stared out on a scene that turned his stomach. Dead, bloated cattle sprawled around the watering hole. The air buzzed with the whine of flies. He pulled his bandanna over his nose to block out the stench of rotting flesh, but the odor seemed to have permeated his clothing, hanging thick in the air around him. He forced himself to walk the horse closer, to memorize the pitiable scene, as if memory might prevent it from happening again.

This particular watering hole, or "tank" as the Texans called it, had once covered half an acre, but now it had shrunk to less than twenty feet across. The earth around it was scored with cracks, dried clay curling up like peeling plaster. What water that was left had turned a putrid green.

"Don't let your horse drink that water, sir," Best said.

"You think the tank was poisoned?" The same thought had occurred to him.

"Looks that way." He pointed across the water. "There's a dead coyote over there. Looks like whatever killed the cattle killed it, too."

"Then, let's get the rest of the cattle out of here as quickly as possible."

"Yes, sir." Best rode off to do his bidding.

"I say, do you suppose this is Tuff Jackson's doing?"

Reg looked around and saw Cam's stallion picking its way among the carcasses. "This doesn't strike me as an act of idle vandalism," Reg said. "I'd say Jackson is my first suspect."

"So what do you intend to do?" Cam reined in beside him and joined him in staring into the putrid water.

Reg sighed. "I've already ordered the men to move the

remaining cattle out of this pasture. This afternoon, we'll set about dragging the dead cattle into the tank and filling in the whole thing. I'll also send a sample of the water to the state agricultural agency. Depending on what's in the water, it may be years before we can graze this pasture again."

"No. I meant what are you going to do about Jackson?"

Reg shrugged. "Seeking revenge on Jackson won't bring my cattle back or give me water when I need it. I'll leave him to the sheriff."

"What if he goes after you again?"

"He may have gotten what he wants with this." Reg swept his hand across the scene in front of them. "He knows I can't sustain this kind of loss indefinitely. Worse than the cattle, this is one of the last watering holes left to me. Without water, there won't be a ranch."

"You mean you'd have to sell?"

He nodded. "I can almost hear the earl now, chiding me for yet another failure. He'll add it to the list which he delights in reviewing whenever I'm in his presence."

"You've got him wrong, you know."

Reg glanced at his brother. "What do you mean?"

Cam gave Reg a searching look. "You think he hates you, when actually, you're his favorite."

"Ha!" The idea was absurd. "What have you been drinking, to put that idea into your head?"

"I speak the truth. Of all of us, you're the son who resembles him the most—in looks *and* temperament. You're a perfectionist, like him, even if you won't admit it. The both of you are as immovable as rock when you've made up your minds on an issue."

"Perhaps I represent only those things he detests in himself. Why else does he demand the impossible from me?"

"Open your eyes. He demands the impossible from all of us."

Reg snorted. "I never noticed you suffering."

"That's because you were too caught up in your own battles." Cam folded his hands atop his saddle horn and stared out toward the horizon. "I had my own crosses to bear—my expectations to meet, and my failures as well."

Cam, failing? The spoiled youngest son—the vicar? "Name one."

"The reason I came here—it wasn't only to do with my patron's sister. There was a dust-up with a group of miners at the Eversole mines. I took the wrong side of an argument they had with Eversole." He turned hurt-filled eyes on Reg. "You don't think I *wanted* to leave home, do you? I was *forced* to leave, under threat of being defrocked."

Reg nodded slowly. "What are you going to do?"

He let out a heavy sigh. "I don't know. I enjoyed my brief time as a missionary in Canada. Perhaps I'll call on the Episcopal Bishop in Houston and see if there's a circuit available."

"You're wedded to the cleric's life, then?" He still had a difficult time seeing his lighthearted brother in the role of spiritual guide.

"I've grown up these past few years while you were away." Cam forced a smile. "Who better to minister to the fallen than one who came so close to falling himself?"

"Then, you really didn't come here to spy on me?"

"Father asked me to look in on you. He worries about you."

"He has a fine way of showing it."

Cam shook his head. "He has a soft spot for you and fears revealing himself. But I can see it in his eyes whenever he speaks of you. Why do you think he keeps calling you home—from the navy, from India? It's because he misses you."

A shiver ran up Reg's spine at the words. Could Cam be right? Did the earl wish for his failure only as a means of keeping him close to home? He shook his head. He would like to believe such a thing was true, but how could he?

"Mail call!" A familiar voice sang out to them. He looked up and saw Cooky riding toward them. "You has sho' nuff got a mess on your hands here," Cooky said, wrinkling his nose as he reined in beside them.

"Find Donnie Best and he'll put you to work helping to clean up," Reg said.

Cooky nodded. "Just come from town. Got a couple letters here for you, boss." He fished in his vest and came up with two envelopes. The first was a buff-colored paper addressed in a firm hand.

"Charles," Reg said, tearing into the envelope from his oldest brother.

"And this one's yours, too." Cooky handed him a familiar blue envelope, crest at the corner. Reg stuffed the letter in his vest. He would stack it with the others, unopened, in the box on his desk.

Cooky rode off in search of Donnie Best, and Reg scanned the scrawled lines of Charles's letter. "He says the earl's health is much improved, to the point where he's terrorizing everyone within earshot."

"I suppose a weak body was no match for his strong spirit," Cam said. "Does this mean Charles will be returning to Texas soon?"

"I'm looking for news of his plans." He read further, skimming over news of crop yields and the latest neighborhood gossip. He came at last to a sentence that made his spirits sink, at the same time his heart was warmed.

"What is it?" Cam leaned toward him, eyes filled with concern.

Reg cleared his throat. "Cecily is expecting her first child."

"Jolly good news!" Cam slapped him on the back. "Charles must be busting his buttons over the news."

Reg nodded. "He does sound rather pleased."

"But you don't." Cam leaned back and studied him a moment. "You were counting on him to be here to help you out, weren't you?"

Reg nodded. "Selfish of me, I know. I can't very well expect that Cecily will be wanting to leave her mother and home at a time like this."

"What does the other letter say? The one from Father."

"It doesn't matter." He pulled the pale blue envelope from his waistcoat and stared at it, curiosity warring with dread.

"Aren't you going to read it?" Cam asked.

"Why? I know what it will say. Every letter the earl sends is a variation on a theme."

"Well, I'll read it, then." Cam grabbed the letter and neatly tore off one end. He shook a sheet of paper and a large square of pasteboard into his hand. Unfolding the paper, he began to read.

Reg watched as his brother's face paled. "What is it?" he asked, alarmed. "Is he all right? Has he taken ill or something?"

Cam shook his head. "Nothing like that." He looked up, his expression grim. "He's ordering you home. At once."

A chill swept over Reg at the words. "He can't be serious. My year isn't up yet. I still have time—"

"He's serious all right." He held up the pasteboard square. "He sent your ticket."

Chapter Twenty

Reg snatched the ticket from Cam's hand and stared at it. The earl had booked first-class passage from Galveston, with a departure date less than two weeks away.

"What are you going to do?" Cam's voice broke through his daze.

"I'll have to put him off." He looked up at his brother. "I can't possibly leave yet. Not when everything's in such a state."

Cam stared out at the dead cattle and the poisoned tank. "You'll only make him angry if you delay."

Reg's stomach clenched. He was no stranger to his father's anger. But this time he had sworn things would be different. This time he had expected to sail home in triumph. "Then, I'll have to work quickly to turn things around before I depart."

Cam jerked his head around to stare at him. "You can't be serious."

"What other choice do I have?" He raised his head, his jaw set in a stubborn line.

"You can't bring these cattle back from the dead. And didn't you just tell me, without water the ranch is doomed? Or do you think you can conjure a sudden flood?"

"I'll drill a well."

"And gamble away what little capital you have left?"

"Abbie says it can be done."

"Alan advised against it, didn't he?"

"If I drill a well, the ranch will have the water it needs. With the new stock I bought in Amarillo, we'll have a chance for profit in the fall."

"What if you drill and don't find water?"

He looked back at the ticket in his hand. Better to hold his head up in defiance than come meekly crawling home. "Father expects me to fail—well, then, I'll fail on a grand scale."

Cam shook his head, then started to chuckle.

"What's so funny?" Reg asked.

"Us. Grown men, still letting the old man rule our lives."

"The Texas thirst for independence has infected you, hasn't it?" Reg took the envelope from his brother's hand and slid the ticket inside. "We're bred to obedience and duty, Cam. Our ancestors have sworn fealty to king and country, and lesser lords, for centuries." He tucked the envelope inside his coat. "It will take more than a few months on the plains to purge that impulse from our veins."

Cam sighed. "I suppose you're right." He watched Reg gather his reins. "Where are you going now?"

"If I'm going to drill a well, I'd better get started."

Cam's eyes sparked with interest. "You're going to see Abbie, aren't you?"

Reg looked away from his brother's searching gaze. If he could think of any way to avoid it, he wouldn't see

Abbie again. Last night had proved he could no longer
trust himself with her. No matter that his reason told him
a liaison with her was wrong—in her presence emotion
overruled all logic.

"You and she certainly spent a great deal of time in the
barn together last night," Cam said. "I'm beginning to
wonder if perhaps there isn't something between you and
our lovely neighbor."

"You are the one who insists on wooing every woman
you meet, not I." Reg gave his brother a cool look. In
this case, Cam's own interest in Abbie might prove useful.
"Perhaps you'd like to come with me to the Rocking W?
I want to ask Abbie what I need to do in order to drill a
well."

To his surprise, Cam declined. "No, I think you'd better
handle this on your own. All that talk about business would
only bore me."

"Any other time, you'd be chomping at the bit to come
along."

Cam smiled. "Only because I sensed you didn't want
me." He gathered his reins. "Haven't you learned by now?
It's in my nature to be contrary. Now, if you'll excuse me,
I have some errands in town." He tipped his hat, then
rode away.

Reg glared at Cam's retreating back. He was genuinely
fond of his brother, but at times Cam was the most frustrat-
ing person on earth to deal with, outside of the earl himself.
He frowned. If it was true that Reg had inherited their
father's stubborn desire for perfection, then the earl had
passed along his obstinance to his youngest son.

He began walking his horse slowly away from the poisoned tank. He had to see Abbie, but not alone. If Cam
wouldn't come with him, who could he ask?

Only one man came to mind. He kicked the horse into
a trot and headed for the A7.

He found Alan Mitchell in the barn, polishing a buggy. It seemed an odd occupation for a man who traveled everywhere by horse. "Hello, Reg," Alan said, looking up from the task.

Reg came to stand beside the buggy. The black painted-wood sides shone so that he could see his reflection in the surface. "I came to see if you'd like to ride over to Abbie's with me."

Alan stopped polishing the buggy's already gleaming exterior. "What are you going to do at Abbie's?"

"I need to talk to her about drilling a well."

He waited for Alan to ask why he needed to know about well drilling, but the rancher merely resumed polishing the buggy. "I can't go with you right now, Reg. Gotta get this buggy polished. Sorry."

"Might I ask, why are you polishing this vehicle? I've never seen you use it."

To his amazement, his friend actually blushed. "Well, uh, it's kind of personal," he said. "But I've got to get it done this afternoon."

"Then, suppose I wait until you're finished? We can ride over to Abbie's then." He crossed his arms and leaned against an empty stall, prepared to wait all afternoon rather than risk facing Abbie alone.

Alan frowned and continued to burnish the buggy's surface. "Well, I suppose that'd be all right," he said after a while. "But we'll have to go in the buggy."

Amused at his normally easygoing friend's insistence on this odd condition, Reg nodded. "All right. We'll go in the buggy."

Approximately two hours later, Alan emerged from his house. "I'm ready now."

Reg looked up from his seat on the edge of the porch.

His eyes widened as he stared at his friend's transformation. In place of the drab cotton shirt and leather vest he had been wearing, Alan had donned a well-tailored black suit. He wore a crisp white shirt, a paisley four-in-hand tie, and a low-crowned black hat. Black boots, polished to a mirror shine, completed the outfit.

"Whatever you are about this afternoon, I would say it is serious business," Reg said.

"It is."

Smiling, Reg followed his friend to the buggy. He climbed in, Alan took up the reins, and they were off.

As they drove, he tried to compose himself for his meeting with Abbie. He wanted to prepare a list of questions, things he would need to know in order to drill a well as quickly as possible. But his wayward thoughts insisted on ruminating on the woman herself.

He had met many women in his years of travel, but none had affected him as Abbie had. He had been drawn to her from their first meeting, intrigued by her combination of strength and tenderness, touched by her longing for home and family. He thought often of late of putting aside his wanderlust and settling down. But what woman would he choose as his bride? After last night, how could he ever accept any woman other than Abbie by his side? Taking Abbie to England was out of the question. He might as well try to transplant a Texas bluebonnet to the chill English moors.

What if she were pregnant? The thought brought a cold sweat to his forehead. Of course he would marry her then. But how could he bear to watch her wither and fade away from her beloved Texas plains? Perhaps he could find a way, in a few years, to return here. . . . He shook his head. He couldn't risk his own and Abbie's future on idle dreams. Better to pray that their joining last night did not result in a child.

Banjo's barking pulled him from his thoughts. He looked up to see Abbie's ranch house in front of them. The dog raced around them, barking and wagging his tail. Alan braked the buggy beneath a tree and reached behind the seat. He pulled out a paper-wrapped bundle of yellow roses. Reg raised one eyebrow in surprise. Well, well. It appeared the "personal" business to which Alan referred might be of a romantic nature.

By the time the two men had crossed the front porch, Maura stood in the door. "Good afternoon, Alan, Mr. Worthington," she said, smiling.

"Good afternoon, Maura." Alan held out the roses. "These are for you."

Her eyes twinkled with delight. She took the flowers and inhaled deeply of their perfume. "Oh, Alan, they're ever so nice." She and Alan gazed adoringly at each other for a full minute, until Reg cleared his throat.

"Oh!" Maura started, and blushed a becoming pink. "What can I do for you gentlemen this afternoon?"

"I'm here to see Abbie," Reg said. He glanced at the roses in Maura's arms. "On business."

"Oh, yes, m'lord." She stepped to one side. "She's in the parlor."

"I'm right here." Abbie appeared behind Maura. "Come on in, Reg." Even as she spoke, she didn't look at him.

Maura stepped aside to allow Reg to pass, but made no move to follow him inside. Reg hesitated. He would prefer Alan and Maura come with him. "Reg, come *in*," Abbie said again.

Reluctantly, he went inside. Abbie shut the door behind him, then crossed the room and sat on the sofa. "Now, what did you need to see me about?" She busied herself plumping a sofa pillow. Was it his imagination, or were her cheeks more flushed than usual?

He told himself he shouldn't look at her, but he could not keep his eyes from her. She was dressed as he had first seen her—in men's trousers and faded flannel shirt, her hair in braids. The trousers clung to her thighs and hugged her hips. The shirt lay soft against the swell of her breasts, the top button undone, showing a triangle of creamy skin. He felt the immediate physical response in his groin, and turned away from her, hoping to disguise his arousal.

"Please, sit down." She moved over to make room beside her.

He sat in the chair across from her instead, holding his hat in his lap. "I won't take up too much of your time."

She sighed, a regret-filled sound that tugged at his emotions. "Don't hurry on my account. Besides, I imagine Alan and Maura will be gone a little while."

"Gone?"

She nodded toward the window behind him. He turned to look, and his heart stopped beating for a moment as he saw Alan drive the buggy away, Maura at his side. "Where are they going?" he exclaimed, rising from his chair.

"Just for a ride. They'll be back in a bit." She settled back against the sofa, looking, Reg thought, entirely too pleased with herself. "We have all the time you need."

He sank down in the chair and took a deep, steadying breath. The scent of lavender assailed his nostrils. Abbie shifted on the sofa, and the sound seemed amplified, so that he could identify the scrape of the fabric of her trousers against the upholstery. The room suddenly felt too small to contain the both of them safely.

Business, Reg, he reminded himself. *Concentrate on business.* "I've decided to drill a well," he said.

She raised her eyebrows in surprise. "A well? What made you decide that?"

"I've given a lot of thought to what you had to say

last night, and it seems like a sensible precaution against drought."

She studied him a moment. "There's something else you're not telling me."

She knew him too well. He nodded. "Someone appears to have poisoned the tank over in the north pasture—the one they call Red Rock. We lost at least a dozen cows before one of my men saw the vultures and rode out to investigate."

"Oh, Reg!" Her voice carried all the anguish he felt. "Who would have done such an awful thing?"

"I have my suspicions, but no proof."

"You don't think Tuff would do something so terrible, do you?"

He shook his head. "I don't know. That doesn't particularly concern me at the moment. Right now I need to find a new source of water for my stock, before the few tanks I have left go completely dry."

"You heard what Alan said last night. Digging a well is a gamble."

"One I feel compelled to take." He leaned forward. "I want to act as quickly as possible. I was hoping you could tell me who to contact to arrange for the drilling, and everything else I'll need."

"I can give you some names." She worried her lower lip between her teeth. "But I don't know . . . you could be throwing your money away."

"I thought you'd decided to drill a well yourself."

"I said I was *thinking* about it. But Alan has a good point. He was right about it not being something my dad would have done."

"But it's your ranch now—your decision."

She nodded. "Yes, but I've always followed my dad's teachings in running the ranch. He never steered me wrong."

Reg caught her gaze and held it. He felt the warmth of her fire even as he cautioned himself not to move close enough to get burned. "I didn't know your father, but I know you," he said. "You've been my best teacher in all my time here, and I don't think you would ever have considered drilling a well if there were not some merit in the idea."

"Some merit, yes, but I don't know if it's worth the risk. Why not wait a little longer? It might rain, or you might find another solution."

He shifted in his chair. "I don't have time to wait. I must have the well in place in less than two weeks."

"Two weeks? Why so soon?"

He looked away, a feeling of dread weighting him in his chair. "My father has ordered me home. He sent my ticket today." Telling Abbie made the words seem so much more real. He had thought he would have more time to get used to the idea of saying goodbye; but here it was upon them, and he was far from ready.

He heard her gasp. "But why?"

He shook his head. "The earl keeps his own counsel."

"And you must obey."

He nodded. "It's my duty to do so." He cleared his throat. "You will, of course, let me know if there are, uh, consequences from last night."

"You mean if I'm pregnant?" She raised her chin defiantly. "I'll be fine by myself. I wouldn't want to trouble you."

He frowned. "I suppose I can't blame you for being angry. I never should have—"

"Don't say it. I'll never be sorry for what happened last night. What we shared was . . . special. To me, anyway." She lowered her head, but not before he saw the brightness in her eyes of unshed tears.

The thought that he had made her cry was like a stabbing

pain to his heart. In two long strides, he crossed the room and knelt beside her, taking her hand in his. "Last night was special to me, too," he said. "But that doesn't change the obligations we each have. You must stay here and run this ranch. I must return to England."

"Because of duty? Well, I say damn your duty."

He flinched. How could he explain to her his reasons for leaving her behind? He stroked her work-roughened hands, fighting the urge to pull her close, to hold her and kiss her until they had both forgotten about anything but their need for each other. "Tell me, Abbie," he said softly. "Your father spent his life teaching you to run the ranch, did he not?"

She nodded.

"Would you ever have considered going against his wishes and doing something else, something besides ranching?"

"No. Of course not."

He sighed. "My father instilled in all his sons a desire to please him, to do his will—a sense of duty to the family name, he called it. It's something we can't quite shake."

"So if your father wants you to return to England, you will?"

"I'll have no peace unless I do. Not that it will improve his opinion of me, but he will never be able to say that I have not done my duty." Silence stretched like a chasm between them. He wanted to tell her how sorry he was to be leaving, how he wished there was a way he could see her again. But he knew, once he was back in England, his father would have other plans for him. He doubted he would ever return to Texas. He wanted to tell her these things and more, but what good were words in the face of the sorrow he was feeling?

She drew a deep breath, as if gathering her strength, then slipped her hand from his grasp. "You're right. You

have to go. I have to stay here. That's all there is to it."
She stood and walked to the window, her back to him.
"Tell me what it is you need from me in order to drill
your well."

For the next half hour, they discussed possible locations
for a new well, pump sizes and windmill designs. Abbie
gave him the name of a driller to contact. For the right
price, Reg hoped he could persuade the man to begin
work right away.

Often as they talked, he felt Abbie's gaze on him, searching. When he glanced her way, he saw the hurt he had
never meant to inflict upon her. Why had he ever let things
go as far as they had? If only he had controlled himself.
If he had never laid a hand on her, she wouldn't feel the
way she did now.

"I hope it works out for you," she said. Reg wasn't sure
if she was speaking of the well or his return to England.
Though her words were encouraging, her voice was heavy
with regret.

Banjo's barking interrupted them, and they turned to
watch Alan's buggy roll up the drive. Was it Reg's imagination, or was Maura sitting closer to Alan than she had been
when they had departed?

Abbie hurried onto the porch, Reg close behind her.
Alan set the brake on the buggy and grinned at them.
"She said yes," he announced, and put his arm around
Maura.

Abbie squealed and ran to hug them both. Reg stood
on the porch, watching the scene, understanding beginning to dawn. Alan left the women and came to stand
beside him. "You can congratulate me, Reg. Maura has
agreed to be my wife."

He clapped Alan on the back. "Congratulations,
indeed." He shook hands, smiling all the while, though

behind the smile he felt the pinch of envy. If only he were free to make such decisions.

His gaze drifted to Abbie, locked in a joyful embrace with Maura. It hurt to look at her, knowing she could never be his. He was afraid the pain he was feeling now was only a prelude to the misery he would endure when he did finally leave this place. If regret was any measure of depth of feeling, he had lost his heart to Abbie, in spite of his every effort to resist her.

Chapter Twenty-one

Abbie agreed to help Maura plan her wedding, though it might as well have been a funeral, for all the sadness weighing her down. She was happy for her friend, but she couldn't escape the feeling that Alan's wedding Maura, coupled with Reg's looming departure, spelled the end of all her dreams for a husband and children of her own. Alan, the most suitable match for her, loved someone else, and Reg, the man she loved, was determined to leave her.

"I call it a real shame that Mr. Worthington will be leaving us afore the wedding," Maura observed one morning almost two weeks after she and Alan had declared their intention to marry. She and Abbie sat sewing linens for her trousseau.

"Ouch!" Abbie stabbed at the sheet she was attempting to hem and pricked herself instead. She sucked on the bleeding finger and frowned at the uneven row of stitches before her. Despite Maura's lessons, her sewing ability hadn't improved.

"When is it he plans on leaving, miss?"

Abbie smoothed the sheet over her lap in an attempt to hide her shaking hands. "Today."

"So soon!" Maura sounded alarmed. "Couldn't you persuade him to stay, miss?"

Abbie shook her head. "I haven't seen him since the day Alan proposed to you." She'd started to ride to him more than once, but she wasn't about to stoop to begging. Her father was right—independence was best. She didn't need anyone else.

"Well, I imagine he's been busy, what with the well going in and all." She knotted her thread and neatly clipped it. "Still, if anyone could convince him to stay, I'm thinking it's you, miss."

Abbie's frown changed to a scowl. "No one can change Reg's mind. He's the most obstinate man I've ever met."

"Now, miss, Mr. Worthington has been ever so kind to the both of us." She studied Abbie through lowered lashes. "It's been me opinion that he's positively sweet on you."

"Hah!" Abbie tossed aside the sheet and stood. "Reg Worthington is the *last* man I want to have anything to do with." She began to pace. "I've never known anyone so arrogant in my life. And I could write books about what he doesn't know about ranching."

"Could you now, miss?" Maura rethreaded her needle. "And what'd be wrong with a man having a little pride?"

"Nothing. Unless he lets his pride get in the way of good sense."

"Oh, you think Mr. Worthington's pride is getting in the way of his good sense, do you, now?"

"I don't know if Reg ever had any good sense. If he did, he sure enough wouldn't be high-tailing it back to England just because his father said so."

"Well, maybe you're right, miss." Maura smiled at the pillowcase she was stitching. "You wouldn't be wanting for common sense yourself. I imagine you and your father disagreed many a time, may the good Lord rest his soul."

Abbie stopped in her third pass across the room. "No. Daddy and I seldom argued."

"Oh. So you agreed on everything?"

"I learned everything I know from my father. He knew all there was to know about ranching. I respected his judgment. Why shouldn't I agree with him?"

"Well, then, maybe Mr. Worthington is feeling the same way about his father. Like he ought to follow his advice and come back home."

"That has nothing to do with it." She resumed her pacing. "Reg told me himself he was only going home because he thought it was his duty to do so."

"Oh." Maura made a row of neat stitches along the edge of the pillowslip. "If that be the case, then perhaps you can find a way to persuade him to stay—for the sake of me wedding, of course. What would your dear departed father have done?"

Abbie frowned. What *would* her father have done if he had been in her shoes? "Daddy was one for letting people make up their own minds," she said after a moment. "He believed in always standing on your own feet—looking after yourself. That way you never needed to ask anyone for help." *He taught me to be the same way*, she thought. *I never needed anyone for anything—until now.*

"Begging pardon, miss, but I can't very well walk meself down the aisle. I was counting on Mr. Worthington for that."

I was counting on Reg to stay here and love me. The thought came suddenly, like a sharp pain in her chest.

Maura laid aside her sewing and came and put a hand on Abbie's shoulder. "I know you Texans set a great store by independence," she said softly. "But there's times when it's good to let people know you're needing them. It's a far sight better than ending up alone.''

Abbie looked at her maid, wondering at the wisdom behind the words. Had Maura seen all along what Abbie had been afraid to acknowledge—that she loved Reg, *needed* him?

Maura gave her an encouraging smile. "I'd best be checking on the muslin I set to bleach,'' she said, and walked away, leaving Abbie with a pile of unhemmed sheets, and her own unraveling thoughts.

Reg stood on a small rise overlooking the pasture the cowboys had dubbed "Dugout Draw." Half a mile downhill sat the sod-roofed cabin that served as landmark and namesake for the area. A horse-powered cable drilling rig had been set up beside the cabin. Reg had paid double to persuade the owner of this rig to postpone other projects and come at once to the Ace of Clubs. For the past two days, men and horses had labored, sinking a shaft in search of water.

He watched as the team of horses pulled the drill from the shaft. The driller, Pete Emerson, knocked hard clay from around the drill bit. Even from this distance, Reg could tell the soil was dry as dust.

He sighed and looked away, at his shadow stretched out in front of him. The outline of a broad-shouldered, Stetson-crowned man was sharp against the sandy earth. Anyone seeing the shadow might have supposed the man to be the equal of any cowboy in Texas.

But any cowboy would not have been standing here now, watching his last hope for redemption slipping farther away with each dry foot of shaft sunk into the ground before him. Any cowboy would not have made the mistakes that led Reg to this place.

Even the poisoned water hole had been his fault, in a way. If he had only checked his temper, bit back his anger against Tuff Jackson, he might have avoided the man's hatred, and the subsequent ruin of the water hole.

"Do you think if you stare at it long enough, you'll conjure water out of that hole?"

He whirled and saw Cam striding toward him, a tin pail in his hand. The black stallion stood nearby, tethered to a scrub oak beside Mouse. "Here, Cooky sent this." Cam handed him the pail.

"What is it?" Reg held up what looked to be an old lard bucket.

" 'Grub,' he called it. Food." Cam squinted toward the sod cabin. "I don't know why you don't come back to the house where you can eat a decent meal and sleep in your own bed."

Since the arrival of the drilling crew, Reg had been staying in the cabin. "I want to be here when they find water," he said.

"*If* they find water." Cam looked back at him. "You don't fool me, you know. You're staying out here because you hope it will discourage vandalism."

He didn't answer. There were other reasons he had retreated to the isolation of the sod house. Out here he was that much farther from Abbie, as if by separating himself from her physically, he could somehow come to accept the knowledge that they must always remain apart. These past two nights he had lain on a narrow cot in the primitive shack, like a monk in his cell, contemplating his sins. He knew his decision to leave Abbie to her life here in Texas was the right one—but would he ever overcome the pain it caused him?

He set the pail beside him and looked back toward the well. "They're down to one hundred twenty-five feet now."

"What are you going to do if they don't find water?"

"They'll find it. Emerson says it's there."

"And you believe that hocus-pocus of his with the forked stick?"

Reg sighed. "It's called 'witching.' Local people speak very highly of Emerson's ability to find water."

Cam gave a snort of distaste. "I'm surprised at you, Reg. Resorting to such nonsense."

He crossed his arms over his chest. "I need this well. If a Comanche medicine man told me performing a certain dance by the light of a full moon while chanting ancient rhymes would produce water, I'd do it."

"Where's your pride, man?"

"This is all about pride." He raised his head. "I want to go home with this victory to show Father. I want him to see I can succeed on my own terms."

"The only terms Father recognizes are his own."

Reg shook his head. He couldn't dispute Cam's words. But neither could he give up the conviction that someday he would prove himself equal to his father's ideal of perfection.

"When does the train for Galveston leave Fairweather?" Cam asked.

"At two o'clock."

Cam looked alarmed. "That doesn't give you much time."

"No, it doesn't."

They were silent for a while, watching the horses strain against the harness as they turned the drilling machinery and listening to the pop of chain tightening. The shadows shrank as the sun climbed higher in the sky. *It's after noon,* Reg thought. *Less than two hours before I have to leave. Less than two hours to find water, and proof that everything I've done here hasn't been wrong. Less than two hours, and I'll never see Abbie again.* He tried to swallow against the sudden tightness in his throat.

"Who's that over there?" Cam pointed, and Reg saw a figure on horseback, moving toward them from the west. The man wore a black suit coat and a tan Stetson and rode a gray horse very much like Mouse.

"It's Tuff Jackson," Reg said after a moment, as the man rode closer.

"Hello, Worthington. Or maybe I should say 'Worthingtons.' " Tuff reined his horse in a short distance from them and gave a curt nod.

"What do you want, Jackson?" Reg asked.

Tuff looked over his shoulder at the drilling rig. "I came to see the show." He looked back at Reg and flashed a mocking smile. "I wanted to watch you fail again."

"I say, old chap, what do you know about a water hole that was poisoned near here?" Cam asked.

Tuff kept his eyes on the drilling rig. "I heard about it." He shrugged. "Things like that happen sometimes. A good rancher has to be prepared for anything."

"And you're a good rancher, are you?"

Tuff straightened in the saddle and looked down at his questioner. "I'm one of the best cow men in these parts. You can ask anybody."

"Oh, I have made some inquiries." Cam studied his well-manicured nails. Reg wondered what his brother was up to. "One thing I've discovered is that you don't appear to be doing much work with cows these days. It seems you sold off the cattle you had, and I understand that when the man who bought them offered you a position working for him, you turned him down." He looked Tuff in the eye. "In fact, talk is you've turned down several attractive job offers since leaving the Ace of Clubs."

Tuff scowled. "I ain't interested in working for anybody else these days. I'm looking to buy a place of my own."

"A place like this one, perhaps?"

Tuff shrugged. "It's no secret you'll have to sell if your water dries up. Ain't that right, *Lord* Reginald?"

Reg ignored the goad. "Is that a new horse, Jackson?" he asked. "I don't believe I've see you on him before."

"Yeah, it's new."

Reg narrowed his eyes. "And the hat—didn't you have a black one before?"

Tuff looked nervous. "It was about time I got a new one. What about it?"

The coat was a cheaper imitation of Reg's own. The trousers were like his, too. It was as if the rough cowboy he had known was gradually transforming into a man like himself. The Texas accent and the tooled-leather boots were the only remnants of the old Tuff. He shook his head in amazement.

"You ain't gonna find water. You might as well quit now. I'll give you a decent price for the place—not any more than what it's worth, though."

I should be angry, Reg thought. But the only emotion he could muster was pity. There was a time when he would have given his right hand for the skills, and the respect, that Tuff had possessed. Now the man was losing the respect, and throwing away any chance of using his skills, all for a dream of being what he could not.

How different are we, really? A shiver ran up Reg's spine at the thought. Tuff wasn't the only one who had set his sights on an unobtainable goal. How many years had Reg spent trying to be his father's ideal of the ever-successful son? How much had he thrown away, reaching for that elusive brass ring—those words of approval from a man he both loved and hated?

"Reg, it's quarter past one." Cam snapped shut the lid of his watch and tucked it back into his vest pocket.

He nodded and raised his hat, a signal to Pete Emerson.

Emerson stopped the lead horse and hauled up the measuring chain. He looked back at Reg and shook his head.

Reg's shoulders slumped.

"Still dry?" Cam asked.

He nodded. "I've paid Emerson to stay the rest of the day. If he hasn't found anything by then, you may release him." He walked to the tree where Mouse was tethered and mounted up. "I had Best take my trunk to the depot this morning. I'll leave my horse at the livery for someone to pick up later."

Cam walked over to him. "Why are you doing this?" he asked.

Reg frowned. "Why am I doing what?"

"Why are you leaving when you want to stay?"

He looked over his brother's head, at the horses powering the machinery that was drilling a dry well. "The earl will want an explanation for this. I won't run away, as if I'm afraid to face him."

"Sometimes there's bravery in retreat, too, in marshaling your forces to fight more important battles."

He shook his head. "All battles are important to the earl."

Cam put a hand on his arm. "You've never been a coward, Reg. I hate to think you'd be a fool now."

Reg shrugged him off. "I don't know what you're talking about."

Cam shook his head. "Go, then! Catch your bloody train." He turned his back and stalked away.

Reg glared after his brother. This wasn't the parting he had had in mind. These last few weeks he'd begun to feel closer to Cam than he ever had before. He had counted on his brother to be the one person who could understand why it was so important for him to obey the earl's summons to return home. Apparently, he had judged him wrong.

Suddenly impatient to be free of this place and all the

conflicting emotions it aroused in him, he turned Mouse toward town and spurred him on. As it was, he would have to hurry to make the train.

Reg was turning the horse over to the stable man when a whistle blast announced the arrival of the train in the station. The engine would stop long enough to take on wood and water before continuing on its journey east. Reg pulled his valise from behind the saddle, then paused to rub Mouse's nose. He had spent a lot of hours with this animal these past few months; he had come to see past the rough exterior and appreciate the gelding's good qualities.

The train sounded a second blast. Reg pulled a silver dollar from his pocket and pressed it into the stable man's hand. "Take good care of him," he said, then turned and strode toward the depot.

The area around the platform smelled of cinders and sawdust. Reg remembered the last time he had stood here—the day he had returned from Amarillo with Abbie. He had a sudden memory of her smiling as he had introduced her to Cam. Even now, that memory had the power to make his pulse race and his heart pound.

He forced himself to go on, to climb the steps into the first-class car. He found a seat next to a window and stared out at the front of Pickens' Mercantile. Old Hiram Pickens would certainly be sad to see him go.

He thought of Abbie and the tears that had glistened in her eyes when he had seen her last. He had never even stopped to say goodbye to her. What was it Cam had said, about him not being a coward? *Oh, but I am a coward*, he thought. *I didn't even have the courage to face her again.*

He had called it bravery, to rush home to face his father's wrath. But in truth, the earl could not care less whether Reg's well struck water or found only more dry dirt. The ranch was just a parcel of foreign real estate to him, another business venture to dabble in for a short time. He would rail at Reg because it was his habit to do so, but nothing Reg said or did would change the way things were between them.

He remembered what Cam had said—that he was their father's favorite son. If that were true, then he didn't have to work for his father's love. He already had it.

If Cam was wrong, then would anything Reg did at this point change his father's feelings for him? Surely their roles were set in marble now.

Cam had called him a fool. A fool to leave Texas? He looked past the general store, to the gently rolling prairie that stretched to the horizon. The country was like his horse—the very things he had disliked about Texas when he had first arrived had grown to be the things he loved the most: the vastness of the land, the wildness that tested him at every turn, the rewards to be had in meeting each new challenge.

This stretch of prairie had come to mean so much more to him. On these stark plains, beneath this achingly blue sky, he had felt more at home than he had felt anywhere in his life. He had tested his mettle and found new friends, things worth taking risks for.

And he had found Abbie. Of all the treasures Texas had yielded to him, she was the one to be prized the most. He was more than a fool to ever think of leaving her.

Abbie leaned forward along Toby's neck and urged him on. "Faster, boy. We've got to catch him. You can do it." The horse's hooves pounded over the dried-out land, raising clouds of dust. She pulled her bandanna up over her nose and scanned the trail in front of her, watching for any approaching rider. The east-bound train left the station at two; Reg might already be on his way to catch it.

"Oh, Lord, please help me find him," she prayed. He couldn't leave before she had a chance to talk to him—a chance to tell him all that was in her heart.

She'd wrestled with herself all morning, her father's teachings of independence warring with the fear that she was passing up the one chance in her life for happiness. Maura's words had made her realize how much pride—her own and Reg's—had stood in the way of their feelings for each other.

What were those feelings, really? In all their time together, they'd never said they loved each other. What if all the love was on her side only? Was she making a fool of herself, coming to bare her soul to Reg this way?

Or would she be too late?

She crested Dugout Draw and saw a horse tied to a scrub oak. Her spirits sank when she recognized Cam's black stallion. She spotted Cam himself with another man in front of the dugout and rode down the hill to them.

Cam looked up at her approach. "Hello—Abbie, is that you?"

She jerked the bandanna off her face. "Where's Reg?" She was out of breath, her heart racing.

He glanced at the other man. "Excuse us a moment, Mr. Emerson." He motioned for Abbie to follow him around the corner of the dugout.

"I'm too late, aren't I?" she asked, twisting the reins in her hand.

He pushed his hat back on his head and looked up at her. "The train stops at Magdalene, just up the track. If you hurry, you can catch him."

Magdalene was little more than a siding. She had a picture of herself flagging down the train like a bandit, demanding Reg surrender to her or else.

Cam must have sensed her hesitation. "My brother is a stubborn fool," he said. "It may very well take being accosted at the station to bring him to his senses." He smiled. "Or perhaps the sight of you will be enough to make him realize what he's giving up by leaving."

She returned his smile. "All right. I'll do it." She started to turn her horse, then heard a shout behind them. She jerked her head up and saw a horse galloping down the hill toward them.

"It's Reg!" Cam said.

But Abbie's body had already recognized the rider, her heart racing even before her brain registered that this was indeed Reg, coming back to her.

He pulled up sharply in front of the dugout, his clothes covered with dust, his hat askew. Abbie dropped her reins and leapt from the saddle as Reg slid from his. They both spoke almost at once.

"I was on my way to see you, as soon as I talked to Cam," he said.

"Reg, I came to tell you I can't let you leave—not until you know how I feel."

He shook his head. "I'm not leaving. I'm staying right here." He reached into his coat and pulled out his ticket. "Here." He handed it to Cam. "I won't be needing this now."

Then he took Abbie's arm and led her away from the dugout. "We have a lot to talk about."

"Reg, what happened?" She studied his face for some clue to his emotions, but his solemn expression revealed nothing. Was he staying because of her—or because of something else? "What about your father?"

"My father can get along fine without me." He stopped and turned to her, his eyes alight with a feverish passion. "Sitting on that train, waiting for it to leave the station, I realized I've been struggling all this time to win my father's respect—but what I was really looking for was something to respect within myself." He put his hands on her shoulders. "I want to stay and make something of this ranch."

She looked down at the dirt between their feet. Right now she felt as if her heart were somewhere down in that dirt, crushed. "So you came back for the ranch."

He gripped her so tightly she almost cried out. "No, I came back for you!" He put his face close to hers, so that when he spoke, his breath was hot in her ear. "The ranch doesn't mean a thing if I don't have you to share it with."

All the breath went out of her at his words. She raised her head and stared at him.

"I'm trying to say I love you," he said. "But maybe I'm going about it all wrong." He pulled her close, wrapping his arms around her and covering her mouth with his own. The heat of that kiss seared her, melting away any lingering suspicion or resistance, thawing the cool shell she'd tried to wrap herself in these past weeks as protection against his leaving. His lips coaxed life back into her limbs—her skin began to tingle, every nerve awake and aware. When at last he raised his head, she felt a new exhilaration, like someone waking from a stupor.

He smiled and stroked the hair back from her forehead. "I want to marry you, Abbie. If you'll have me."

"I was going to ride to Magdalene and flag down the train," she said. "To tell you I love you and I couldn't let you leave. I didn't dare hope you'd really stay—I only knew I had to tell you how I felt."

His expression grew serious once more. "Answer me one question." He nodded toward the drilling rig. "If that well comes in or not—if I pull the ranch through or have to sell out—will you still love me?''

She tightened her arms around him. "I'd love you if you were a dirt-poor sodbuster and all we had was a shack like this one." She grinned. "Or I'd love you if you were the king of England himself. I love *you*, Reg, not what you've done or what you have.''

"I may never be much of a rancher." He frowned at the creaking machinery.

"And I'll never be a proper lady. But that doesn't matter, does it—as long as we love each other?''

"That's all I need to hear." He grinned back at her and bent his head to kiss her once more. She pressed herself against him, savoring the feel of her body against his. She thought the sound she heard was the pounding of her heart and the roar of her own blood in her ears. Then she felt a cool dampness on her head and a spray of droplets on her skin. She opened her eyes and squealed. "The well, Reg. The well! You've found water!''

A silvery flood poured from the shaft, fountaining up and raining down upon them and everything around. "We got a good one, Mr. Worthington!" the driller shouted. "Tapped into an artesian pocket. Your water worries are over!''

Reg swept Abbie into his arms, then whirled her around in the refreshing shower until they were both dizzy and breathless from laughing. "Oh, Reg, let me go," she gasped.

"I'll never let you go." He began to hum a waltz, and to dance with her in the gathering mud.

"Reg, you've gone crazy!''

"I was lost the day I first looked into those emerald eyes of yours," he said. He stopped and smiled down at her. "I ended up in the mud that day, and look where I am again.''

"As long as we're together, Reg—that's all that matters."

"That's all that matters," he agreed and kissed her once more, water falling in a silver shower over and around them.

Epilogue

"A toast to the bride and groom. Or, I should say, the brides and grooms." Cam stood and held his glass of champagne aloft. He smiled at the couples flanking him at the table. If he did say so himself, his brother looked quite dashing in his morning suit, and Abbie shone in her confection of satin and lace. Maura, dressed in white silk and pearls, only added her beauty to the day. Alan Mitchell looked a little stiff in his formal suit, but there was no mistaking his happiness as he smiled at his bride. "May Abbie and Reg, and Maura and Alan, find eternal happiness."

Glasses clinked around the table, and the guests echoed their own congratulations. Cam returned to his seat at the head of the table and addressed the lavish wedding breakfast Cooky had prepared. One thing was certain; Reg wouldn't go hungry any time soon. Cooky had agreed to take over kitchen duties at the Ace Clubs, now that Maura was moving on to the A7 and Mrs. Bridges was returning to the Double Crown.

"I have an announcement of my own to make." Reg pushed back his chair and stood. He smiled at his guests. Cam had never thought of his brother as a smiling man, but Texas had changed a lot of things about Reg. As far as he could determine, it was all for the better.

"Abbie and I are entering a partnership together." Reg grinned at his bride. "Both a personal and a business partnership. We plan to start a breeding program with stock from both ranches."

"From the looks you two are giving each other, I'd say you'll be breeding more than cows," Joe Dillon boomed. Abbie flushed red, but joined in the laughter along with everyone else. Reg sat down and took her hand.

"It looks as if the Ace of Clubs will do all right this year, since Reg drilled that well." Abbie smiled proudly at her husband. "A lot of other ranchers in the area are following his example. In fact, Pete Emerson's scheduled to come out to my place—I mean *our* place—next week."

"And you've never had any more trouble from whoever poisoned that water hole, have you?" Alan asked.

Reg shook his head. "No. Tuff Jackson seems to have disappeared. No one's seen him since the day the well came in."

Cam helped himself to another serving of coddled eggs. "Oh, I imagine our boy Tuff is wandering London High Street as we speak," he said archly.

"What?" Abbie gasped.

Reg narrowed his eyes. "Why do you say that?"

"When I realized you weren't going to be needing your ticket, I gave it to him."

"Whatever for?" Reg asked.

He shrugged. "I could see the man wanted to emulate you. I thought I would give him the chance."

Cooky appeared in the doorway, his considerable bulk swathed in a white apron. "Sorry to interrupt, folks, but this here special delivery jus' come from town."

"Special delivery? Let me see." Cam held out his hand.

Cooky gave him a withering look. "It's addressed to Mr. Reg." He walked past Cam and handed the envelope to Reg.

Everyone waited in silence as Reg slit open the envelope with his table knife and shook the contents into his hand. He stared at the single sheet of paper for a long time.

Abbie reached up and touched his arm. "Reg, what does it say?"

"It's from the earl." He handed her the letter.

Cam stiffened. After the day at the well, Reg had cabled their father, announcing that he wouldn't be returning home and why. It didn't take much imagination to picture the earl's reaction to such uncharacteristic disobedience. It was a wonder they hadn't heard the explosion across the Atlantic.

"He says 'despite your deliberate disobedience' he's nevertheless impressed." Abbie looked up in wonder. "He says the gamble you took with the well reminds him of something he might have done in his younger years."

Reg nodded, his jaw tight. Cam suddenly realized that instead of being angry, his brother was simply too moved to speak.

Abbie glanced at the letter again. " 'From what I understand, your quick thinking has saved the ranch,' " she read. " 'As for your decision not to return to England, I cannot say I am pleased with the prospect of not seeing you again. I know you think I have been harsh with you, but it was only my intention to equip you to realize your full potential.

" 'Congratulations on your marriage. This lady rancher you've wed sounds like a remarkable woman—all the more so because she has chosen you. I hope you both will honor me with a visit soon.' " Abbie looked up, eyes shining. "He sounds like someone I'd like to meet. Not nearly as . . . as fierce as I thought."

Reg shook his head. "It's not exactly the reaction I expected from him."

"Perhaps the old boy's mellowing in his old age." Cam raised his glass again. "To the Earl of Devonshire," he said. "And to the lessons he has taught us."

"To the earl," came the echo.

Reg and Abbie gazed at each other, eyes filled with devotion. Cam watched them over the rim of his glass, until the tightness in his chest forced him to look away. Would he ever know a love like that? The prospect seemed as remote as the North Pole.

And yet, if roaming Reg could settle down to happily-ever-after and make a success of a failing ranch, who was to say Cam couldn't turn his life around also and find his place in the world, and the right woman to fill the emptiness in his heart?

If you liked LAST CHANCE RANCH, be sure to look for Cynthia Sterling's next release in the Titled Texans series, RUNAWAY RANCH, available wherever books are sold in January 2001.

Outspoken and unconventional, Cam Worthington, the youngest son of the Earl of Devonshire, has come to Texas as a new member of the clergy in the hopes of changing people's lives for the better. He gets the chance right away when a sudden thunderstorm finds him standed in a barn, facing a farmer with a shotgun, a nervous young woman named Caroline Allen, and a preacher ready to perform a hasty marriage ceremony—with Cam as the elected groom. . . .

Dear Reader,

I fell in love with Reg the first time he walked through my imagination, and when I "met" Abbie, I knew I'd found the perfect match for this hero.

Reg isn't the last of the lovable Worthington brothers, however. Look for the youngest son Cam's story, RUNAWAY RANCH, in January 2001. A former rake turned parish vicar, Cam can't leave his wild ways behind and ends up banished to Texas, where a troubled young woman with a shady past teaches him about love, honor, and trusting the leading of one's heart.

I love to hear from fans. Write to me on the web at CynthiaSterling@aol.com or P.O. Box 816, Pine, CO 80470.

Cynthia Sterling